1968

1968

DREAMS OF REVOLUTION

Wilber W. Caldwell

Algora Publishing
New York

Library of Congress Cataloging-in-Publication Data —

Caldwell, Wilber W.
  1968: Dreams of Revolution / Wilber W. Caldwell.
    p. cm.
  Includes bibliographical references.
  ISBN 978-0-87586-678-9 (pbk.: alk. paper) — ISBN 978-0-87586-679-6 (alk. paper)
— ISBN 978-0-87586-680-2 (e-book) 1. Nineteen sixty-eight, A.D.—Fiction. 2. United
States—History—1961-1969—Fiction. I. Title. II. Title: Nineteen sixty-eight.

  PS3603.A4385A614 2009
  813'.6—dc22

                    2008048532

Front Cover:
Above: Columbia University counter-demonstrators on the grounds outside the
Low Memorial Library as the campus insurrection enters its seventh day. The counter-
demonstrators have vowed to cut off the food supply to those inside the library. Image: ©
Bettmann/CORBIS. Date Photographed: April 29, 1968
Below: May 1968 Riots in Paris. Riot police in the streets during the May 15
demonstration. © Alain Dejean/Sygma/Corbis

Printed in the United States

Acknowledgement

I'd like to extend my heartfelt thanks to Natalia Parra for her timely support and encouragement. While a graduate student at the University of Maryland, Natalia read the manuscript for 1968. Her firm embrace of this novel, its characters, and its message rekindled my then sagging zeal for the project and fueled my future determination to realize the book's publication.

Also, and once again, I wish to express my loving gratitude to Mary Fitzhugh Parra for devotion, tea, sympathy, and for her enduring patience in the face of my endless ponderings.

Author's Note on Historicity

This is a work of fiction within a larger work of nonfiction. In tandem, these narratives combine to chronicle the widespread student revolts that took place in the spring of 1968, including the student occupation of Columbia University, the simultaneous West German student revolt at the University of Frankfurt, and the widespread and violent upheaval of the so-called "Paris May." I have made every effort to present the historical characters, Mark Rudd, Ted Gold, Tom Hayden, Rudi Dutschke, Karl Wolff, Daniel Cohn-Bendit, Theodor Adorno, Herbert Marcuse, and others in strict conformity with published accounts. I have also endeavored to present everything in a way that is fully consistent with the historical record and to structure dialogue that is faithful to the historical characters' published accounts, ideas, and convictions. Nonetheless, this is a work of fiction, and in some instances historical characters have been fictionalized, especially in the case of their interaction with the novel's fictional characters that are drawn to represent the students of the era.

Wilber W. Caldwell

TABLE OF CONTENTS

Table of Contents

PROLOGUE: FRANKFURT

Unreal City,
Under the brown fog of a winter dawn,
A crowd flowed over London Bridge, so many,
I had not thought that death had undone so many.
— T. S. Eliot, "The Wasteland"

A specter is haunting Europe.
— Karl Marx and Friedrich Engels, "Manifesto of the Communist Party"

FRIDAY, APRIL 12, 1968

A dark river of young men flowed down the Hamburger Allee and turned west onto the Mainzer Landstrasse. On the surface, their mood appeared festive. There were banners, shouts and torches, jokes, laughter, and chants of "Rudi, Rudi, Rudi," like the familiar rhythms of a sporting event. However, not far beneath the surface, lurked a pervasive tension born of anger, frustration, contempt, and fear, a fear so intense that it soon melted away the veneer of raucous theatrics and exposed a transparently false bravado.

In the center of the crowd, Steffi Siegel was still clutching the single-page mimeographed handout that had been stuffed into her hand when they left the university. On it was a list of recent inflammatory Springer Press tabloid headlines: "Stop the Terror and the Young Reds Now," "Do Away with Them," "Don't Leave the Dirty Work to the Police."[1] She could feel the tension bearing down upon her. "Springer, Nazi!" the crowd began to chant in an effort to muster some new kind of blind courage. Here and there along the way, students with bloodstained shirts sat on the curb, tended and comforted by their girlfriends and fellows.

---

1 Kai Kracht, "The Revolution of 1968," 2001, http://www.kaikracht.de/68er/english/index.htm.

The chanting grew louder as they approached the *Allgemeine Zeitung* Building where the Springer newspaper was printed.[1] In the last few blocks before the printing plant, the streetlights were out. They grew quiet and walked resolutely on in darkness. They could hear shouting just ahead. Steffi felt a chill and adjusted her scarf. She wore dark jeans, a leather jacket, and a man's short-billed cap with all of her hair tucked up beneath it. Ahead the street was dimly lit by the dull red-brown glow of temporary lighting set up by the police to illuminate the area in front of the printing plant that they were defending. Steffi could see a large crowd of students in the median where the streetcars ran in the center of the wide boulevard. Across the two eastbound lanes on the shadowy sidewalk in front of the plant, she could make out three neat lines of black-uniformed police in full riot gear. Farther along more police were attempting to clear the makeshift barricade that the students had thrown up to block the exit used by the Springer delivery trucks. They were dragging away park benches, sections of metal fences, and all manner of junk that the students had piled there. Off to one side, a small Springer delivery van lay burning on its side. The scene appeared at once surreal and psychedelic — surreal because the red-brown light was dead, depthless, shadowless, and psychedelic because there was a strobe-like quality to the illumination. Flat zombie-like figures seemed to jerk about in slow motion.

As Steffi's group approached, the students in the median seemed to gather new energy from their arrival. A police ambulance tried to negotiate the space between the police line and the protestors. A few students blocked its path while others rocked the vehicle in an effort to turn it over. The police suddenly charged. There was a loud shout, and the students rushed to meet the assault. Many of the students in Steffi's group picked up the shout and began to run toward the mêlée.

Steffi froze, suddenly overpowered by a strong odor she had never encountered before. It was something unfamiliar, and yet inexplicably she knew exactly what it was. She somehow clearly identified the odious aroma of pure adrenalin and fresh blood, laced with a potentially lethal overdose of testosterone.

Steffi had participated in countless protests and demonstrations before, but she had never experienced anything like this. "This is the mind of the mob," she thought to herself. "They have surrendered their free will; they have no autonomy, no personal freedom. They have become that which they attack."

She turned sadly and began to walk slowly back toward the university.

---

1 *The New York Times*, April 13, 1968, 8.

PART ONE, APRIL 1968

April is the cruelest month, breeding
Lilacs out of the dead land, mixing
Memory and desire, stirring
Dull roots with spring rain.
— T. S. Eliot, "The Wasteland"

All fixed, fast-frozen relations, with their train of ancient and venerable prejudices
are swept away, all new-formed ones become antiquated before they can ossify. All
that is solid melts into air.
— Karl Marx and Friedrich Engels, "Manifesto of the Communist Party"

CHAPTER ONE: NEW YORK

Eyes I dare not meet in dreams
— T. S. Eliot, "The Hollow Men"

Finally, in times when class struggle nears the decisive hour...a small section of
the ruling class sets itself adrift and joins the revolutionary class...in particular, a
portion of the bourgeois ideologists, who have raised themselves to the level of
comprehending theoretically the historical movement as a whole.
— Karl Marx and Friedrich Engels, "Manifesto of the Communist Party"

MONDAY, APRIL 15, 1968

"He's talking to Karl Marx again."

"What?"

Two lanky students had mounted the dormitory stairwell, disposing of six flights
of steps in a youthful, two-at-a-time gate. As they pushed open the heavy door and
stepped into the dimly lit hallway, the taller youth had been about to speak when his
friend silenced him, raising one hand before his chest, palm out, fingers spread.

"Listen."

They froze, squinting into the semi-darkness. From half way down the long
empty corridor came the soft sound of muffled speech, like a distant poetry reading
or some kind of ancient chanting.

"Really, he's talking to Karl Marx. He does it all the time."

"Jesus! Who is it?"

"Kurt, that German kid."

They spoke in half whispers.

"I didn't know he was German. He speaks perfect English."

"Well, he's probably speaking German now, 'cause, I'm telling you, he's talking to
Karl Marx. I've heard him do it in English, too."

"I thought maybe he was Canadian or something."

"No, he's German."

"I heard he's a leader in the SDS — some kind of radical thinker. Where'd he come from, anyway?"

"Born in Washington. Grew up in Paris. His father's some kind of bigwig diplomat, a West German special envoy to France or something like that. He came here to Columbia from the Free University in Berlin. I mean, the guy speaks ten damn languages or something like that."

"And he talks to Karl Marx — in English?"

There was a pause. "I didn't know Marx spoke English," said the shorter student, attempting to make a joke out of the idea that the dead had need of language beyond the grave.

"Sure he did," came the straight-faced reply. "He did most of his work in the reading room of the British Museum in London."

"Oh, yeah, I guess I knew that."

"Anyway, I don't think Karl Marx speaks to anyone these days — in any language. Come on."

They crept softly down the hallway and posted themselves just outside the young German's room. Although muffled by the heavy door, most of the words were intelligible, and they were indeed English.

"You'd find it so depressing, Karl," they heard him say.

There was weary sadness in his voice and heart-felt sincerity, ardor, even love, like a man swearing an oath to a family member or confessing a tragic secret to a priest.

"Doctor Marcuse sent it to me. You remember, Karl, Herr Professor Herbert Marcuse. I told you how Rudi introduced me to him last year after we attended his lectures in Berlin."

The two eavesdroppers outside the door looked at each other wide-eyed. "Herbert Marcuse," the tall young man mouthed the name with genuine awe. Then, exaggerating the formation of his silent words so his friend could read his lips, he incredulously mouthed the question, "Does this guy really know Herbert Marcuse?"

"Shhh."

In 1968, virtually every student in America knew who Herbert Marcuse was. As the 1960s unfolded, this mild-mannered German-America intellectual had become more widely discussed than any living philosopher, especially among the young. Marcuse's criticism of advanced industrial society and his defense of revolutionary politics supplied authority and cohesive voice to an idealistic new generation of young people outraged by war, offended by racial injustice, and disillusioned by the continued existence of poverty in the shadow of the fabulous wealth of consumer society. Although few of his youthful followers fully understood his complex analysis, Herbert Marcuse nonetheless and in countless ways spoke for an angry and often inarticulate generation that was, often unwittingly, rejecting the conformity of middle-class life. He spoke for a brash new kind of student population that denounced the affluent society as "a sell out," feared becoming faceless members of an impersonal technological machine, and desperately struggled to radically alter its vision of the world.[1]

---

1 Douglas Kellner, *Herbert Marcuse and the Crisis of Marxism* (Berkley and Los Angeles: University of California Press, 1984), 1-2; Ronald Aronson, "Herbert Marcuse: A Heritage to Build On" in *Moving On*, Fall 1968, 10.

The taller youth held his finger to his lips, fearing his fellow listener was about to speak out loud and blow their cover.

The young German was talking again. "Rudi recommended this book, too. I got a letter from him last week. Now he has been shot. Tragic."

Again, the two eavesdroppers looked at one another in disbelief. Was this kid talking about the attempted assassination of the notorious Red Rudi, in Berlin? The story was all over the news and was the talk of the campus.[1]

Behind the thick door, the eerie "chanting" continued. "It seems Doctor Marcuse gave a copy to Rudi too. He's very generous and very interested in student activism. We've corresponded. He's going to be a good friend, I think. You know, Karl, Doctor Marcuse told me that he taught here at Columbia when he first came to America from Germany in the 30s. Now he's becoming quite famous, or so it seems. 'The Father of the New Left,' everyone is calling him. He defends confrontation politics and revolutionary violence. This puts him at odds with all of those who favor more moderate models of social change."[2]

There was another pause.

"In many ways, Herr Doctor Marcuse is still one of yours, Karl. They all are, all of them at the *Institut für Sozialforschung*."

The young men listening outside the door exchanged uncomprehending looks. Although they knew a little about Herbert Marcuse, they had never heard of the prestigious "Institute for Social Research" in Frankfurt, where beginning in 1923, the intellectual foundations upon which the lofty ideals of the New Left had been carefully laid. Although the youthful eavesdroppers claimed to be members of the rising American counterculture and proponents of the New Left, the fact was that, like so many of their contemporaries, they had more or less blindly embraced a knee-jerk radicalism that flailed impotently at American society while remaining largely unaware of the complex theory that supported their own activism.

"Of course, Herr Doctor Marcuse and the others at the Institute have never called themselves Marxists or even Communists," the unseen young German continued. "Those terms have become so tarnished, a sad state of affairs. In one sense, they reject your ideas, Karl. In his Berlin lectures, Professor Marcuse predicted the possibility of a completely new era[3] — an abrupt shift to a new human epic. He was very hard on you, Karl. He's lost faith in the proletariat as the revolutionary agent, and he is in search of a new revolutionary subject — one that comes from the outside of the established order, from minorities, from students, from intellectuals.[4] Very radical, Karl. So very radical. Still, in many ways he's yours. They are all yours, even though they strongly oppose the Russian communists and the communism of Eastern Europe. In a more pure fashion, they remain faithful, especially this one, Herr Professor Adorno, the author of this book that Herr Doctor Marcuse gave me. I met him, too."

Again, the two freshmen exchanged wide-eyed glances. They didn't know much about Theodor Adorno, but they had certainly heard the name — the hotshot, intellectual, left-wing heavyweight the graduate students were always discussing.

"Yes, the famous Doctor Theodor Adorno, his book is brilliant, but, well, you'd find it so depressing, Karl. So much more resistance than you imagined, so many more

---

1 *The New York Times*, April 13, 1968, 1.

2 Kellner, *Herbert Marcuse and the Crisis of Marxism*, 280.

3 Herbert Marcuse, "The End of Utopia" in *Five Lectures: Psychoanalysis, Politics, and Utopia*, trans. Jeremy J. Shapiro and Shierry M. Weber (Boston, Beacon Press, 1970).

4 Kellner, *Herbert Marcuse and the Crisis of Marxism*, 280.

obstacles, so many more lies — insidious lies, callous manipulations, colossally complex deceptions. It's very depressing."

There was a long silence. The eavesdroppers stood frozen, fearing discovery, hoping for more.

The German finally began again. "Of course, they're all Hegel's too, and Kant's, just like you. *The Dialectic of Enlightenment*;[1] there's a title for you. Herr Doctor Adorno wrote it twenty-four years ago, back in 1944, and it's still brilliant today. He understands that in your day, Karl, bourgeois society appeared to be condemning the proletariat to a life of eternal bondage, that class conflict appeared inevitable, that capitalism appeared to contain the seeds of its own destruction. But now, Herr Professor Adorno contends that capitalism has sedated the workers, assimilating the forces that would bring about its collapse. Modern technological society has provided the workingman with a middle class existence, with security, a modicum of luxury, and a minimum of work.[2] He suspects that your precious proletariat no longer exists, Karl. With all its seductive material and cultural interests, the old proletariat has been appropriated and integrated into the heart of capitalism, into the very process of production itself.[3] The masses now cling to and defend the very thing that enslaves them."

There was another period of silence.

"Where do we find our revolutionaries now, Karl? If Doctor Adorno is right, Enlightenment has perpetuated an insidious mass deception, and the power of capitalism is now absolute. I fear for the revolution, Karl. Even Herr Doctor Adorno, whose theories go to the very heart of our cause, does not fully support us. Who will fight with us now that the revolutionary moment has passed?"

Again, there was silence. Outside the door, the young men, simultaneously and quite independently, had the same strange feeling: that just beyond the door the great Karl Marx was delivering his reply. Somehow, they both half-believed that Marx himself was imparting some great new penetrating insight to this mysterious German graduate student. It should have seemed crazy, but it all seemed so real — so completely sincere and believable.

As they silently stood there in the dim Columbia University dormitory corridor on that fine April evening in 1968, John Kennedy was only five years martyred, and the sudden spark of the assassin's bullet that had slain Martin Luther King only ten days ago had now ignited deadly urban violence and lingering unrest in nearby Harlem and in black ghettos across America, while a young student leader named Rudi Dutschke lay fighting for his life in a West Berlin hospital, and tens of thousands of protesting students raged unchecked in the streets of the great cities of Europe. For these reasons and many others, the question seemed ripe with immediacy: if the workers were no longer game, who would fight in the revolution the students so often discussed? The Black Panthers? The Third World? The SDS? The hippies in the park? Who?

* * *

---

1 Max Horkheimer and Theodor Adorno, *The Dialectic of Enlightenment*, 1944, trans. John Cumming (New York: Continuum, 1973).

2 Adorno, "The Culture Industry: Enlightenment as Mass Deception," in Horkheimer and Adorno, *The Dialectic of Enlightenment*, 120-67.

3 Erik Von Keunnelt-Leddihn, *Leftism: from de Sade and Marx to Hitler and Marcuse* (Arlington House, 1974), 372-380.

After what seemed a very long silence, the young men slipped quietly back down the corridor and disappeared into the nearby dorm room that had been their original destination.

"Weird, isn't it?" said the shorter student when the heavy door had swung to and latched.

The tall lanky youth, whose name was Martin Beam, stood quietly at the window. Outside, the farthest edge of twilight was slowly gathering into darkness. "He may be weird," he said finally, "but he's right."

The taller student smiled. "You mean Marx was wrong?" he mocked, intending irony, delivering only hollow sarcasm.

Martin was not amused. "Maybe," he replied thoughtfully. "Maybe." After a few minutes, he drew the blinds and said, "I've got to ask Eliot about this. He knows that guy Kurt."

TUESDAY, APRIL 16, 1968

After hours of searching, Martin finally found Eliot purely by chance. At about six that evening he had been crossing 114th Street near the enormous Butler Library Building when he spotted his big sister's boyfriend, a young man with the unlikely name of Thomas Stearns Eliot Kincaid, on the sidewalk in front of the neoclassical monolith with Ted Gold, a former vice chairman of the Columbia chapter of the SDS. Martin jogged up and fell into step with the two older students.

"What's up, Eliot?" he chirped.

"Not much," replied Eliot dismissively. After an awkward moment, Eliot reluctantly gave in to protocol. "Ted, this is Melissa's little brother, Martin. Martin, do you know Ted Gold?"

"No. I'm really glad to meet you. I was at the IDA demonstration in Low a few weeks ago. I heard you speak. Great stuff."

Eliot winced at the lanky freshman's transparent hero worship, even though last month he too had admired Ted's audacious style when Gold and the current SDS chairman, Mark Rudd, had led about 100 students into Low Library, Columbia University's central architectural landmark, in direct disobedience of the university's standing policy prohibiting indoor demonstrations.[1] On that day, Gold and Rudd and their followers targeted the university's institutional ties to the Pentagon's Institute for Defense Analyses (IDA), a weapons research think-tank pursuing, among other war related projects, chemical defoliation, tactical nuclear weapons, and the technical feasibility of building an electronic "fence" along the border between North and South Vietnam. During the demonstration the protestors had tried to present the University with a petition containing 1800 signatures opposing the University's support of the IDA, and following this incident, the university administration had placed Gold, Rudd, and four other student leaders on disciplinary probation for violating the institution's recent ban prohibiting indoor demonstrations. Since that time, the university's seemingly arbitrary singling out of Gold and the five other protest leaders had become a rallying point for the extreme Left, and many students agreed that the forthcoming disciplinary action against the so-called "IDA Six" reeked of uneven justice and demonstrated the repressive nature of university bureaucracy. This gathering storm of student discontent precipitated by Ted Gold's bold act was now

---

1 Lawrence Bond, "Morningside Heights: The Causes and the Protest of 1968," student paper, http://ww2.Lafayette.edu/-histclub/lawrencebond.html.

regarded as a major political victory for the SDS with its programs aimed at the radicalization of the university.[1]

Ted nodded and smiled, accepting Martin's compliment modestly. "Thanks," he said, doubtfully eyeing Martin's long hair and flowered shirt.

The freshman went on excitedly, "You were great, really great."

Martin had admired Ted and a few other notable campus activists long before coming to Columbia. He had often heard Eliot and his older sister Melissa, discuss Ted "Acapulco" Gold and the other Columbia radical leaders they knew, like David Gilbert, Bob Feldman, and Teddy Kaptchuk. For Martin and a small group of the senior boys at the exclusive Hill School last year, the youthful cadre of the New Left had represented real heroes. As perspective fledgling members of the rising counterculture, many prep school boys idolized the emerging leftist leaders. Beginning with the riots at Berkeley, the civil rights marches, and the growing antiwar movement, increasing media coverage in the mid-60s had turned some student leaders into national celebrities. For Martin this may not have been exactly like meeting Mickey Mantle; but it was a little like meeting, say, Joe Pepitone.

The bitter irony of his hero worship would not become clear to Martin for years to come. On this fading April afternoon he had no way of knowing that Ted Gold would later join the ultra-radical Weather Underground and that in 1970 his hero would detonate a homemade bomb he planned to use at an Army dance in New Jersey, accidently blowing himself and several confederates to smithereens in a Greenwich Village apartment.[2] By then Martin would consider himself a man of peace first and a radical second. He would dismiss the terrorist tactics of Ted Gold and the other so-called Weathermen as morally unconscionable. However, in April of 1968, the coming rift between the hippies and the radical factions of the New Left was invisible to the idealistic young student, and he stood in boyish awe of his unlikely hero.

Martin brushed his shoulder-length hair from his eyes. "By the way, I almost forgot. I've been looking for you all day. Do you know this guy Kurt Siegel?"

"Sure," said Eliot. "I met him while I was studying in Germany last year. He's a member of the German SDS, *Sozialistischer Deutscher Studentenbund*, German Socialist Student Federation. It's not affiliated with our U.S. organization, but it's similar. Kurt has been a big help to us. He's very well versed ideologically, and he has considerable experience organizing demonstrations and protests."

"Well, I heard him talking to Karl Marx on the third floor of Hartley Hall last night!"

Both Eliot and Ted began to laugh.

"What's so funny? It was weird," said Martin defensively.

"It's just his way — kind of like thinking out loud," said Eliot. "He's quite sane — brilliant really. Did you actually hear any of what Kurt said to Comrade Marx?"

"Yeah, he was wondering who would fight the revolution if the workers become part of the establishment."

"Right!" Ted laughed again, and then continued as with the instruction of a new pupil. "That's the definition of the New Left. We are no longer bound to the old working class as the sole revolutionary agent. At least, here in America, we aren't. In Europe, they're not so sure. Many left-wing movements there still hope to align themselves with the workers. In America today, the New Left is made up of intellectuals, civil rights groups, youth groups, all with a deep mistrust of the Old Left, its ideology,

1 Wikipedia, http://en.wikipedia.org/wiki/Ted_Gold, last modified February 5, 2006.
2 Wikipedia, http://en.wikipedia.org/wiki/Ted_Gold, last modified February 5, 2006.

and its totalitarian bureaucratic offspring including the unions. That is to say, we are Neo-Marxist, if we are Marxists at all. It's kind of a dilemma for Kurt. He still clings to the idea of class struggle, but he's working through it. What was Kurt doing in a freshman dorm, anyway?"

"I asked around and found out that my friend, 'Suitcase' McNabb, lets him crash in his room so he doesn't have to study in the library or go all the way to midtown to his own place to catch a nap. McNabb is almost never there. He's always off somewhere. He stays downtown with his girlfriend."

They turned the corner and headed north on Broadway.

"Does he really know Herbert Marcuse?" Martin asked.

"He does." Eliot said. "I think they're actually pretty good friends. Kurt introduced me to Doctor Marcuse after his lectures at the Free University in Berlin last year."

"Wow!" said Martin, genuinely impressed. "And Adorno?"

"Yes. We both met Doctor Adorno at the Institute for Social Research in Frankfurt. Kurt's sister, Steffi, is one of Adorno's research assistants there. You know, it's all connected with the University of Frankfurt, that is, the Johann Wolfgang Goethe University, where I studied last year. I attended many of Doctor Adorno's lectures. So did Kurt and Rudi. Kurt and Rudi were pretty tight. And now Rudi's been shot."[1]

"Good Lord," said Martin, "You don't mean Red Rudi, the guy who got shot in Berlin last week? Rudi Dutschke? You know him?"

Eliot nodded sadly.

"Good God, Eliot, have you seen the papers, listened to the news? Germany is in chaos, rioting everywhere, Berlin, Munich, Frankfurt, Bonn. There are barricades, police lines, hundreds injured, thousands arrested! It's spreading all over Europe."[2]

"Easy, Martin, we know. We're on our way to a meeting now to discuss the need to demonstrate some kind of solidarity with the German students after the shooting of their leader."

They had reached the subway entrance at the corner of Broadway and 116th Street. "Catch you later, Martin," said Eliot as they descended the steps. "Nice to meet you," shouted Ted as they disappeared into the half-lit stairwell.

"Likewise," but they were out of earshot. Martin Beam's head was spinning. He stood there for a minute and then headed back to Hartley. Passing through the huge iron gates into College Walk, he headed for the "sundial," the famous rallying place for so many demonstrations in the past year. There he turned and began to cross the South Lawn.

The great urban university loomed all around him. "Rudi Dutschke! Jesus!" he said aloud to no one in particular.

---

1 *The New York Times*, April 13, 1968, 1.
2 *The New York Times*, April 13, 1968, 8.

CHAPTER TWO: FRANKFURT

Between the idea
And the reality
Between the motion
And the act
Falls the Shadow.
— T. S. Eliot, "The Hollow Men"

The philosophers have only interpreted the world in various ways; the point,
however, is to change it.
— Karl Marx, *Theses on Feuerbach*

TUESDAY, APRIL 16, 1968

"You have spoken with Frau Dutschke?"

"Yes, Herr Professor, and with Karl Wolff, the new SDS leader, and with my
brother Kurt in New York. They all send their best to you."

"Give me a little moment, Fräulein, and we will speak of this. Please, take a seat,
my dear." The little round man gallantly gestured toward the chair beside his desk. In
front of him lay several neat piles of books and papers. He was working on what he
hoped would be his masterpiece, *Aesthetic Theory*, and as always his research had led
him back to his old friend Walter Benjamin, whose writings continued to inspire his
formidable intellect. In these troubled times, thoughts of his departed friend seemed
always with him — dear Walter, who had died such an untimely and mysterious
death in the tiny Spanish Catalonian village of Portbou in the Pyrenees while fleeing
the Nazis in 1940.[1]

---

1 Lisa Fittko, "The Story of Old Benjamin," in Walter Benjamin, *The Arcades Project*, Howard
Eiland, trans. (Cambridge, MA: Harvard University Press, 1999), 929-54.

13

Over the years, Theodor Adorno had often pondered the death of his old friend and colleague. Although generally considered a suicide, a self-administered overdose of morphine, Benjamin's death had remained the subject of considerable controversy. He and Max Horkheimer, his colleague and collaborator at the Institute for Social Research, had arranged for Walter's American visa, and their successful efforts in obtaining that document had occasioned a desperate Benjamin to attempt to escape Nazi-occupied France to Portugal, beginning with a hazardous crossing of the Pyrenees on foot.[1] No one really knew the exact circumstances of the great Jewish intellectual's death, but few understood the depths of Walter Benjamin's depression the way Adorno and Horkheimer did, and therefore few appreciated the logic behind their easy acceptance of the story that their friend's death had come at his own hand despite the many circulating theories regarding Nazi or Russian or Spanish Fascist assassins bent on repressing Walter Benjamin's radical social and political theories. Dismissing these memories of his long-lost friend, Doctor Adorno looked up at his beautiful young research assistant, Steffi Siegel, and smiled.

Frail and good-looking in youth, now bald and slightly rotund, Theodor Ludwig Wiessengrund Adorno had become a pleasant-looking little old man. At age 65, the widely acclaimed "genius" of modern Critical Theory looked out on the world with large sad eyes that peered through thick horn-rimmed glasses. While Steffi sat patiently, the celebrated author, professor of sociology at the Johann von Goethe University in Frankfurt (the University of Frankfurt), and director of the *Institut für Sozialforschung* (Institute for Social Research) continued to ponder a page of handwritten notes. After a few minutes, he scribbled something in the margin and looked up at Steffi.

"Good," he said. "I hope the news of Herr Dutschke is hopeful." He eyed the young woman seated before him. Steffi Siegel was a very bright and a very beautiful girl, and Doctor Adorno enjoyed having her around for both of these reasons. Indeed, there were times when the great scholar thought his young assistant's beauty to be almost overwhelming. Slender and yet perfectly proportioned with wide hips and a full bosom, the young blonde glided through his occasional daydreams with the face of a fashion model, high cheekbones, perfect lips, and riveting blue eyes. However, there was a great deal more to his attraction to his former student than an old man's harmless fantasies. He had watched this young woman's intellect blossom under his tutelage, and there was little doubt in his mind that she was a brilliant, self-confident, highly motivated, and naturally intuitive scholar of the Modern Condition. In addition, he was fascinated by her ongoing inner battle between the power of her emotional attachment to the radical student Left and her equally compelling intellectual awareness that the time was not ripe for violent action. For Adorno, Steffi Siegel was the perfect model for the ongoing dialogue between praxis and theory. He understood, in ways that only men of his intellectual insight could understand, that Steffi was repelled by the mindlessness of the crowd, fully aware of its present hopeless impotence, and yet at the same time drawn to the surge of student activism in ways that seemed to her idealistically irresistible. Like all of the radical students, Steffi saw radical action as an imperative, and yet at the same time she understood that, given the current situation, such action was futile. She understood that society was far too engrossed in the false needs created by an all-engrossing material consumer prosperity to be able to see the growing menace of individual powerlessness and loss

---

1 Stefan Müller-Doohm, *Adorno: A Biography*, trans. Rodney Livingstone (Cambridge: Polity Press, 2005), 262.

of identity imposed by a ruthless and self-perpetuating military-industrial system. Hers was the dilemma of the New Left, and Adorno, in his own fatherly way, loved her for both her radical zeal and for her rational restraint, a zeal that he knew to be born of the times and a restraint that he knew to be born of a powerful intellect not given to many.

"I spoke with Gretchen Dutschke yesterday, Herr Professor," said Steffi after a moment. "As you already know, they have operated to remove the bullet, but Rudi has suffered considerable brain damage, and his doctors are very guarded regarding his condition. However, Gretchen said that Rudi did speak to a nurse yesterday morning, which is a very good sign, indeed.[1] All he said was, 'Hello, Sister,' so it's difficult to assess from this the extent of his memory loss. The doctors all say that memory loss, sometimes severe memory loss, is to be expected in brain trauma of this magnitude, but they also say that memory often returns over time or can be reconstructed with hard work and therapy. Gretchen suspects that most of the medical experts now think that Rudi will survive, although they're not officially saying so at this time. They remain very guarded. As for the long-term effects of his injury, should he survive...well, it seems to be a matter of 'wait-and-see.' Gretchen seems to be holding up well under the circumstances. This has all been very difficult for her. She is pregnant, you know, and with Rudi's work with the SDS and all of the threats on his life over the past few months, she has had a hard time. But Rudi has many friends, and they're now coming to her aid."[2]

Steffi paused and looked up at the little man she had come to admire in so many ways. He was more than just a former teacher, more than a mentor, and more than the world-famous contemporary thinker for whom she now worked. He was the object of rare kind of passion given only to persons whose lives are touched by men of genius, a pure passion of aesthetics and intellect, a passion that evoked intense loyalty. Over the years, as Steffi had begun to grasp Doctor Adorno's complex ideas, she had become devoted to this strange man. For the bright, young German academic, Doctor Adorno was the living source of the most profound visions — penetrating visions of an increasingly dysfunctional Western society. At the feet of Theodor Adorno, Steffi Siegel had come to understand that modern society is today locked in a deadly struggle with the very elements that make it modern. In her quick and fertile mind, Theodor Adorno clearly stood as the inheritor of the wisdom of the most profound German thinkers of the previous age, the heir to Freud, Marx, Nietzsche, and Weber, the new bearer of the torch of *Aufclärung*, Enlightenment, itself.

"Is she vexed by the violence, as am I?" he asked, after a brief silence.

"She says that Rudi would have handled it just the way the new leadership under Karl Wolff is handling it. Rudi, as you know, was dedicated to a course of radical action. He was, I mean is, a brilliant theorist, as you also know, Herr Professor, but he is also devotedly political. I need not open the dialogue between theory and practice for you, of all people, Herr Doctor."

Steffi knew well where he stood on this issue. As a graduate student, she had studied his work carefully. In Doctor Adorno's view, praxis inevitably degraded thought to the level of mere pragmatism, demanding of thought immediate solutions to immediate problems and closing off the power of thought to contemplate the totality of social relations that lie beyond the horizon of any given situation. He saw

---

1 *The New York Times*, April 13, 1968, 1.

2 Gretchen Dutschke, *Wir Hatten ein Barbarisches, Schones Leben: Rudi Dutschke: Ein Boographie* (Cologne: Kiepenhauer U Witsch, 1996).

activism as a dangerous retreat from the labor of thinking into collective narcissism and self-congratulatory moral superiority.[1] If the separation between practice and theory were to be lost, then practice would emerge victorious by resorting to totalitarian means and identity thinking. Without theory, without critique, the individual would always be forced to yield to the collective will.[2] Steffi had to admit that, on a purely philosophical level, this made sense. She had seen that mindless mechanism at work in front of the Springer plant last Saturday night, and yet she still found it hard to divorce herself completely from the students' efforts to further their cause.

"Still we must remember," she continued, "for Karl Wolff and the others, this is not a time for dialogue. Nor would it have been for Rudi if he were leading the students today. Gretchen knows this."

"What do you think, Fräulein?" Doctor Adorno asked, as if he had been reading her mind. "You say you have spoken with the current SDS leader, Herr Wolff?"

"Yes. He is a good friend here in Frankfurt. Karl has studied in the United States, and he was very impressed with the freedom in the universities there. He was arrested during the demonstration on *Mainzer Landstrasse* Saturday night and freed on Monday.[3] I think, for the most part, Karl is doing a good job managing the SDS response to Rudi's shooting. That is, to the extent that a thing like this can be managed. We must remember that there is an incredible amount of spontaneity in this, and it cannot be fully handled, managed, or controlled in any conventional sense. At best, the SDS leaders, who have so far planned over 500 demonstrations all across Germany, can only guide it a little here and there. Karl told me that he has consulted with our friend Daniel Cohn-Bendit at the University of Nanterre in Paris. Danny is from Frankfurt and he is a close friend of Karl and my brother Kurt. He has extensive experience in organizing protests of this sort. I hear he was at the Springer protest Saturday night, but I did not see him there."[4]

"Yes," said Doctor Adorno, "I know Danny's father. He was a friend of Walter's in Paris before the war. He was briefly interred in a Nazi detention camp with Walter."

His attractive young assistant nodded. "Karl Wolff told me that if things do not die down by Thursday, the day after tomorrow, he plans to officially call for an end to the demonstrations and protests.[5] Whether or not that will have any effect is anybody's guess. Karl and the other leaders have continually warned protestors to refrain from violent acts that might, in the end, hinder our cause, but clearly his warnings have had little effect. I agree with him that a call for an end to protests now would probably be futile. However, after two more days, perhaps the students will have burned themselves out a bit. By then they will have been at this for a week. I hope so because Danny has asked Karl, me, and some others from the Berlin SDS to speak to the students in Paris at Nanterre this weekend."

---

1 Tyson Lewis, "From Aesthetics to Pedagogy and Back: Rethinking the Works of Theodor Adorno," *InterActions: UCLA Journal of Education and Information Studies*, Vol. 2, Issue 1, Article 5, http://repositories.cdlib.rog/geseis/interactions/vol2/iss1/art5; Theodor Adorno, "Marginalia of Theory and Practice," Theodor Adorno, *Critical Models: Interventions and Catchwords* (New York: Columbia University Press, 1998), 268-760.

2 Müller-Doohm, *Adorno*, 462.

3 *The New York Times*, April 13, 1968, 8.

4 Daniel Cohn-Bendit, in Frankfurt "for personal reasons," did participate in demonstrations there in early April 1968. Ronald Fraser, et al., *1968: A Student Generation in Revolt* (London: Chatto and Windus, 1988), 168.

5 *The New York Times*, April 17, 1968, 1.

Again, the young woman paused. Doctor Adorno nodded and smiled a weary, slightly painful smile. Steffi knew that the great man could never endorse the students' violent methods; still, she felt compelled to try to explain their motives, so she pressed on. "At this moment, the students truly believe that they have the power to change history. The SDS leadership, I think, rightly believes that both the violence itself and the police reaction to the violence are catalysts for the rapid radicalization of the present student population here in Germany and indeed around the world. As you know, there is a considerable show of solidarity with our cause all over Europe. In Rome, Paris, London, and elsewhere thousands of students have stormed West German embassies.[1] My brother in New York told me they're planning a show of solidarity there as well. Already we see student demands radically escalating. First, they protested Rudi's shooting and Springer's campaign of hate. Now their rage is broadening to include opposition to the pending *Notstandsgesetze*, Emergency Legislation, and finally to the general autocratic nature of Western government as a whole. In Rome, the students shouted 'bourgeois power has killed Dutschke.'[2] Karl Wolff and the other SDS leaders are trying to make the most of what they're calling a "revolutionary opportunity," while at the same time trying to prevent something that will, in the end, do damage to our cause — or so it seems to me."

Doctor Adorno frowned. "As you know, I think that viewing this as a 'revolutionary opportunity' is a terrible mistake, a hopelessly myopic view of the students' actual position."

"Yes, Herr Professor, I understand your position very well on that matter, and I am more inclined to agree with you than you may know." Steffi looked at the old man lovingly. "Still, perhaps it is a symbol. As you are well aware, symbols have great power."

Doctor Adorno shrugged. After moment he said, "My friend Herbert Marcuse might agree with you, Fräulein. In a way, he supports the students. He believes that the student revolt has nothing to do with the classic revolutionary force, but rather represents an opposition 'concentrated among outsiders within the established order,' an educated opposition 'whose consciousness and instincts break through or escape social control.'[3] Walter believed in this kind of transcendence of false consciousness, but I, myself, am not so sure. Whatever the case, it is clear to me that the students themselves do not see themselves as separate from the classic revolutionary force, and their actions place the university and any attempt at free theoretical scholarship in an unacceptable position."

The beautiful young woman nodded. She agreed, but found it difficult to affirm her position. Anyway, she was not about to discuss Marxist theory with perhaps the most brilliant modern Marxist scholar alive, and after a moment she changed the subject. "If I may say so, Herr Professor, given your position, you too have handled this well — at least that is my opinion. I know you are trapped between, on one hand, wanting to support the students on many issues, and not wanting to endorse their methods, on the other. I also understand that you are accused by some students of betraying their cause by your silence, while at the same time you are attacked by the establishment for betraying them because you created so much of the intellectual theory upon which the entire student protest is built in the first place. You have worked so hard, and now you seem to be damned no matter what you do."

1 Fraser, et al., *1968: A Student Generation in Revolt*, 168.

2 *The New York Times*, April 13, 1968, 8.

3 Herbert Marcuse, "The Problem of Violence and the Radical Opposition" in *Five Lectures*.

"We cannot get around the fact that these students have been influenced by us,"[1] said Doctor Adorno formally, as if he were addressing a group of his peers. Then he was silent.

After a few thoughtful moments, he continued in a more personal tone. "I appreciate your kind words and your understanding, Fräulein Siegel. I find all of this very difficult. The students are becoming more and more disrespectful, and I can't help but take their insolence personally."

"I know it is not my place to ask, Herr Doctor, but what will you do?"

"I have signed an open appeal," the old man said wearily, "calling for an inquiry into the social reasons underlying the attempted assassination of Herr Dutschke and in particular into the manipulation of public opinion by Springer Press. Beyond that, I will not — I cannot — endorse the anti-authoritarian student movement, for it would politicize and thereby taint the very essence of academic scholarship itself. In this regard, I will no longer allow my lectures to be a forum for discussions of revolt or even for discussions of how to block the emergency laws, no matter how abhorrent I find these laws to be."[2]

Steffi nodded her understanding.

Professor Adorno thought for a moment and then added, "That is my public stance at this time. Privately, I will tell you that I fear that the students' across-the-board attack on all authority is extremely ill conceived. Despite its flaws, West Germany today is not a fascist state. It has laws, and they protect all of us who know what it means when the doorbell rings at 6 a.m. and you do not know whether it is the Gestapo or the baker."[3]

Steffi tried to picture Doctor Adorno as a young Jew fleeing the Nazis in the early '30s. His flight to America, along with that of Max Horkheimer and Herbert Marcuse, was legendary, as were their vain efforts to facilitate the escape of their friend, Walter Benjamin. As his assistant, Steffi knew how powerful a force Benjamin's work had been in molding Adorno's ideas. He had once told her that he considered Walter Benjamin to be the greatest mind of the first half of the twentieth century. She had been surprised at the time that he had not named Martin Heidegger, with whom she was more familiar. After that, she had tried to read Benjamin herself, but found his work disjointed, arcane, and strangely unfocused — an odd collection of powerful mystical imagery, Marxism, seemingly unrelated historical insights, surrealistic fragments, and trivia. Still, Doctor Adorno returned to it over and over.

"Oh, Herr Professor, I almost forgot. Here are the books and documents you wanted." She dug into the bag she carried and produced two small volumes containing some of Walter Benjamin's early essays and a file folder containing loose copies of some of the great man's letters, all from the Institute's famous archive of Benjamin's papers and work.

"Thank you, Fräulein, and thank you for your words of support. I feel the need of them now more than ever." He held up a copy of *Merkur*, a magazine of contemporary scholarly German thought. Steffi knew that it contained slanderous charges made in an article by the well-known German-American intellectual, Hannah Arendt. In her article, his old friend charged that in 1955 Doctor Adorno had been misleadingly

---

1 Theodor Adorno, letter to Herbert Marcuse, April 5, 1969.

2 Müller-Doohm, *Adorno*, 459.

3 Theodor Adorno, in a conversation with Peter Szondi, quoted in Wolfgang Krausharr, *Frankfurter Schule und Studentenbewegung: Von der Flashenpost zum Molotovcocktail*, 3 vols. (Hamburg, 1996), 2:237, quoted in Müller-Doohm, *Adorno*, 456.

selective in his editorial choices regarding the material included in *Schriften*, a collection of writings by his late friend Walter Benjamin, and again in a book of Benjamin's *Letters*, which Doctor Adorno had edited in 1966. The article had stirred considerable controversy, casting a dark shadow upon Doctor Adorno's personal and scholastic integrity.[1]

"Don't worry about that, Herr Professor," said Steffi, rising to leave. "I think everyone now knows what a good friend you were to Mr. Benjamin, and absolutely no one suspects your motives to have been anything other than honest and scholarly in compiling his work."

"Perhaps. I hope so. However, I fear that my refusal to involve myself with the students in the current political controversy has made some people question my motives and my integrity."

"Don't be silly, Herr Professor. You mustn't take it personally."

"Perhaps you are right, Fräulein. Thank you, and good day."

"Good day, Herr Professor."

Theodor Adorno watched her leave the room. "Lovely," he thought, "so many lovely women, and so much heartache — and me an old man."

He thought of his lover in Munich, the young actress, his "beautiful child," as he called her. He knew he was losing her, and his heart ached. His heart ached for his wife too, the once lovely Gretel Karlus, his intellectual equal, whom he had married in England in 1937 after their fourteen-year international courtship. Gretel had known Walter in Paris, and she had helped him edit both *Schriften* and Benjamin's *Letters*. Over the years, he had scarcely tried to hide his many love affairs from her, but through it all Gretel had remained unwaveringly loyal. Now, there was Hannah Arendt, the former lover of Martin Heidegger, also once beautiful, also brilliant, and also one of Walter's inner circle in Paris during the '30s. He remembered well the lovely Hannah Arendt of those pre-war years. At the time, her connections to Walter Benjamin had been strong. She and Walter were distant cousins, and her husband, Heinrich Blücher, who was also a Jewish-German exile during his Paris years in the late '30s, was one of Walter's close friends. In a way, Theodor Adorno had unconsciously considered Walter Benjamin's work to be his own private property. After all, he had earned the right, archiving, translating, and publishing reams of his late friend's documents, letters and manuscripts. In this regard he now found it ironic and deeply troubling that it was Hannah who had brought him Walter Benjamin's last completed work, the brilliant "Thesis on the Philosophy of History," which Hannah had miraculously managed to find, preserve, and smuggle out of Europe in 1940.

Perhaps more clearly than anyone else, Theodor Adorno knew how impossibly problematic his late friend's work actually was. Walter was secretive and indirect. His approach was profoundly original and often wildly experimental. Perhaps most confounding, the central reality, or lack of central reality, in his writings always seemed to emanate from a kind of radical incompleteness. Walter Benjamin saw history as something necessarily discontinuous, incomplete, something not yet really begun except as the kind of lies that civilization employs to mask the stain of its own continuing barbarism.[2] For Benjamin, set rational programs, established logical

---

1 Müller-Doohm, *Adorno*, 457.

2 Walter Benjamin, "Thesis on the Philosophy of History," in *Illuminations, Walter Benjamin, Essays and Reflections*, ed. Hannah Arendt, trans. Harry Zohn (New York, Schocken, 1969), 256.

systems, or consistent methodologies all constituted detours.[1] The way was not to be found through logic or reason, for the path to truth was illogically labyrinthine, hopelessly complex, impossibly fragmented, erratic, even random. Yet connections could be found. Threads of opposition could be unearthed in the examination of the trivial, the mundane, the obscure. The telltale negative fragments of historical truth could be re-created in a whirling assemblage or montage that generally confined itself to the invisible margins of history, well outside the highly visible central narratives. This was the essence of Benjamin's legendary *Passagenwerk*, or *Arcades Project*, the unfinished work of the last thirteen years of his life, the manuscript lost to the world somewhere high in the Pyrenees, an irreplaceable masterpiece lost forever just before or after Walter Benjamin killed himself.[2] Theodor Adorno mourned the loss of this work almost as much as the loss of his friend.

Other manuscripts had also been thought lost in Walter's hasty flight from Hitler's Europe. Among them was his "Thesis on the Philosophy of History," but Hannah Arendt had courageously managed to get that manuscript out, bring it to New York, and place it in Adorno's hands in 1941.[3]

"A remarkable woman," he mused aloud. "What have I now done to deserve such treachery from her pen?" the sad little genius asked his now empty office. Over the years since his death, Walter's work had grown in importance, and speculation swirled around the missing wartime manuscripts. Some insisted that, during his ill-fated attempt to escape across the Pyrenees, Benjamin had carried with him the finished *Arcades Project* manuscript. Others speculated that he carried something completely new. They had no way of knowing that, when Walter left Paris in 1940, he had left a copy of his Arcade notes with the writer Georges Bataille, who had promised to hide it in the bowels of the Bibliothèque Nationale and that the library's archivists would excavate it from among Bataille's papers after his death in 1979.[4]

"What have I now done to deserve such treachery?" he again said aloud.

Doctor Adorno felt as though he were losing his exclusive hold on his old friend's intellectual legacy. Somehow, it all seemed to lead back to the students and their ill-fated revolt. For years, Walter Benjamin's work had seemed to him like a private treasure. It had existed only in obscure German-language publications, and he himself had controlled all of the unpublished documents in the Walter Benjamin Archive inside the Institute in Frankfurt. However, recently a few essays had appeared in English and students everywhere were beginning to embrace Benjamin's radical views of the world. Especially compelling to the New Left was his uniquely humanistic interpretation of Marxism. It was only natural that the students would be drawn to Walter for, as obscure and difficult as his work was, it contained that strangely transcendent quality so often associated with the use of drugs, a subject upon which Walter had been very well-versed. Although Walter's view of Marxism contained Marx's notion of history moving through the necessary epochs, the primacy of materialistic desire, and the vision of the proletariat as motive force toward the next epoch, Walter had added something of his own. Walter Benjamin, unlike Marx, believed that the individual within the proletariat could come to full awareness of his

---

1 Lloyd Spencer, "Walter Benjamin: Some Biographical Fragments," The Walter Benjamin Research Syndicate, www.wbenjamin.org.wbbiog.htm.

2 Benjamin, *Arcades Project*, 1999.

3 Müller-Doohm, *Adorno*, 269.

4 Marshall Berman, "Lost in the Arcades," in *Metropolis Magazine*, http://www.metropolismag.com/content_0200/review.html.

part in the demise of the bourgeoisie, that capitalism's false consciousness could be penetrated through art, literature, observation, and through "transcendent" experience. By "transcendent," Walter meant drugs. His extensive experiments with hashish were well known. Walter had even published accounts of his "trips" in his journals entitled "On Hashish," which appeared in German in *Protocols to the Experiments on Hashish, Opium and Mescaline, 1927–34*. How could the students resist Walter's softer enlightened form of Marxism, combined as it was with the compelling notion that the modern world was on the edge of a radical break with the past, something completely new, something unheard of in the labyrinths of history, something gleaned and previewed in visions precipitated by the use of mind-altering chemicals. Walter Benjamin was, to say the least, ahead of his times.

The little man sighed, leaned back in his chair and regarded the ceiling. "Walter's understanding of Marx was flawed," he thought. "That is why I edited out some of his material. It was not to suppress Walter's turning to Marxism, but to avoid the publication of some of Walter's ideas that, in my opinion, had not been fully thought through.[1] Perhaps that did represent an unacceptable editorial bias."

The thought pained him despite the fact that much of the academic community was now coming down on his side. At the bottom of it all, there was more to his pain than just doubts about his editorial criteria. The foundations of his entire intellectual career seemed to be crumbling. He knew that Hannah was about to publish a collection of English translations of Walter's work including his remarkable "The Thesis of the Philosophy of History" and his even more extraordinary "The Work of Art in the Age of Mechanical Reproduction." These were the works that had so influenced his past work and which lay at the heart of his current work on aesthetics theory.[2]

"Perhaps she only wishes to create a little publicity for her new book," he mused, but the explanation carried little solace.

With the students' embrace of Walter Benjamin and with Hannah's new English translation of Walter's most important essays, Theodor Adorno somehow felt that the secret source of his lifelong inspiration and intellectual strength was about to be exposed. "Like pearls before swine," he thought arrogantly. It was as if some kind of cerebral Delilah was preparing to cut his intellectual hair. He felt betrayed by those closest to him: by Hannah, who had slandered him and was about to publish Walter's masterpieces; by the students, who were embracing Walter's work for all of the wrong reasons; by his friend Herbert Marcuse, who lent his support to the ill-conceived student revolt; by his lover in Munich, who was about to leave him; even by Walter, who had killed himself almost thirty years ago.

---

1 Müller-Doohm, *Adorno*, 458.
2 Benjamin, *Illuminations*, 1969.

Chapter Three: New York

No! I am not Prince Hamlet, nor was meant to be
An attendant Lord, one that will do
To swell a progress, start a scene or two....
— T. S. Eliot, "The Love Song of J. Alfred Prufrock"

The writer may very well serve a movement of history...but he cannot...create it."
— Karl Marx, "Moralizing Criticism and Critical Morality"

Tuesday, April 16, 1968

Ted Gold and Eliot Kincaid stood on the subway platform beneath 116th Street and Broadway waiting for the downtown train. The rioting in Germany was all over the news and the talk of the Columbia campus, and Europe suddenly no longer seemed far away and irrelevant. Both young men felt a certain excitement, sensing that world events were now presenting them with opportunities that demanded local action, and the "emergency" meeting of the SDS leadership to which they were bound was unusual enough to spark anticipation and speculation. Surely the impromptu gathering had something to do with the Dutschke shooting. Could the actions of the European students add fuel to the SDS's plans for a large organized protest at Columbia?

"What do you suppose the wild man is up to now?" Eliot asked, referring to the new SDS chairman, Mark Rudd, who had been elected only a few weeks before.

"He probably has a directive from the regional office regarding the revolts in Europe. I don't know what we should do in this situation, what with our own big protest only a week away," said Ted.

A contentious debate still smoldered within the organization. Last year, under the leadership of the organization's former chairman, Teddy Kaptchuk, the SDS at Columbia had emphasized a non-alienating, consciousness-raising program, which sought to expose the university administration's policies, as opposed to militant action. This educational program had been considered the best way to develop the organization's campus base.

In many ways, Gold still favored this intellectual, although slightly pedantic, approach. He considered activists like Rudd and his so-called "action faction" unrealistic dreamers, vulgar Marxists, anarchistic hippies, or worst of all, young men with no politics at all. Gold's more intellectually centered, so-called "praxis axis" thought Rudd's activist plans overestimated the level of radicalization at the university and badly misread the willingness of the student Left to participate in civil disobedience or violent protest.

At the same time, Gold himself was becoming increasingly radical. He knew that world events had begun to turn the tide in favor of student action. By early 1968, the mood at Columbia and other colleges and universities across the country was quickly shifting from left-wing ideological rhetoric to overt radical protest. In February, student strikes, protests, and riots had broken out all across Europe, where student radicalism appeared to be even more prevalent and considerably more extreme. On February 7, angry students had occupied the University of Bonn; on February 14, there were enormous strikes in Madrid, Barcelona, and Salamanca, Spain; on February 15, radical students erected barricades in Nantes, France; on February 18, thousands demonstrated in Berlin; and on February 19, there were large student demonstrations in Rome. To Ted Gold and many others, there seemed to be a rising tide of revolt brewing, and violence and protest seemed to be thriving, reinforcing itself with the force of its own audacity.

In the wake of these upheavals, Mark Rudd had urged student radicals to stop verbalizing what ought to be done and start doing what they really felt like doing, which was to make their feelings about the Vietnam War dramatically known to the establishment and to the public.[1] On this platform Rudd, a junior, was elected chairman of the Columbia chapter of the SDS in March of 1968, and he immediately pressed forward a plan for a large demonstration on campus to be held in late April.[2] On April 12, the 25 members of the SDS Steering Committee had endorsed plans for Rudd's demonstration on April 23 in order to focus attention on racism on campus and to protest the ongoing construction of a new gymnasium in Morningside Park, adjacent to the university, which had been begun without consulting community leaders in neighboring Harlem. The demonstration was also aimed at the university's participation in the work of the IDA and at the administration's uneven enforcement of its ban on indoor demonstrations and the singling out for sanction of six students who had led a demonstration inside Low Library back in March. As Ted stood waiting for the subway, he knew that the next day, April 17, the 100 or so members of the Columbia University chapter of the SDS would attend a general membership meeting and approve Rudd's plans.[3]

"Do you think the big demonstration on the 23rd is a good idea?" Eliot asked. He suspected Gold and many of the "praxis axis" members remained unconvinced or were at least skeptical of Rudd's new activist policies. He could see that their reluctance to follow the path of radical activism was, at least in part, a product of experience.

The express train came roaring through, and they were silent until it passed.

---

1 "Mark Rudd" in Wikipedia, http://en.wikipedia.org/wiki/Mark_Rudd, last modified March 6, 2006.
2 Bond, "Morningside Heights."
3 *The New York Times*, May 19, 1968, 1.

"Well, if you had asked me back in November right after that totally screwed-up demonstration at the Hilton, I would have said no."

Eliot remembered it all too well. In November of 1967, Rudd, Gold, and a number of Columbia SDS members had participated in a demonstration outside New York's Hilton Hotel where Secretary of State Dean Rusk was attending a Foreign Press Association gathering.[1] Their efforts to block traffic, and specifically to block the limousines of dignitaries, proved impotent and virtually invisible in the face of heavy police security. Ted, who, along with Mark Rudd, had been arrested outside the Hilton for inciting a riot, later labeled the entire episode "a fiasco."

"But now, I'm not so sure," Ted continued. "You know, last October I went to Washington to the big March on the Pentagon. I mean, it was wild; 70,000 protestors, man. What a scene! The Pentagon March exposed the brutal nature of the government's opposition to the Left, and the nationwide fallout now suggests that radical action can generate both high visibility and public sympathy, as well as further radicalize the participants. I mean, look at the recent demonstration that Mark and I led inside Low, you know, the IDA protest. It has helped to radicalize a lot of students who were formerly on the fence, and I have to admit that Mark has used the disciplinary action leveled against us by the university administration to good advantage."

Eliot had to agree. There was a growing hostility among many students who believed that the university had been wrong in its support of the Pentagon and its affiliation with the Institute for Defense Analysis (IDA), selective in its enforcement of the ban on indoor protests, as well as unfair and autocratic in its singling out demonstrating student leaders for sanction.

"Whatever the case," said Gold, "students everywhere are taking to the streets, and it has become abundantly clear to almost everyone in the movement how powerful a radicalizing force overt violent action can be."

Again, Eliot reluctantly had to agree. As the spring of 1968 had progressed, it was clear that a growing faith in the radicalizing power of violent action was propelling young men like Ted Gold and Mark Rudd to ride a rising tide of outrageous political behavior. Eliot was of a divided mind. The escalating penchant for violence seemed both promising and troubling. By the end of that year both his hopes and his fears would be justified; not only would progress be made, but also, by then, both Mark Rudd and Ted Gold would be members of the ultra-radical Weather Underground, a clandestine leftist organization split off from the SDS and dedicated to the violent overthrow of the United States government. A year later, Gold would die in the horrific accident precipitated by his own violent intent, and Rudd would be among America's most wanted fugitives, remaining at large until 1977 when he would finally turn himself in to the FBI.[2]

"I mean, I read that in France at the beginning of this year the radical Left numbered only about 2000 students," Ted continued. "But by the time the French students took over the University of Paris at Nanterre a few weeks ago, French activists represented a major national political force. Statistics like that are impossible to ignore. Despite his reckless, 'wild-in-the-streets' reputation, it may well be that Mark Rudd has been right all along."

Eliot wondered.

The "local" eased to a stop. The doors opened, and they entered the train.

---

1 *The New York Times*, May 19, 1968, 1.

2 *Time*, September 26, 1977; Wikipedia, "Mark Rudd," http://en.wikipedia.org/wiki/Mark_Rudd, last modified March 6, 2006.

* * *

Eliot and Ted were the last to arrive. The tiny apartment was filled with the lanky bodies of young men, about fifteen in all, sprawling everywhere, sitting awkwardly on the low couch, slumping in armchairs, perching precariously on the windowsills, and leaning against doorways. Strewn among the human clutter were dense heaps of paper. Books where piled on tables, chaotically spread across low shelves, stacked in boxes, and papers lay strewn about on the floor. Despite the disorder, the overall effect was surprisingly Spartan. The furnishings were simple and colorless, and there was no decoration of any sort save a large poster of Che Guevara taped to the wall opposite the front door. The room smelled faintly of marijuana.

Mark Rudd, the newly elected chairman, was anxious to get started. "Great," he said, "We're all here. We can begin."

Ted took the chair that had been reserved for him beside the speaker, and Eliot found a place on the floor in front of the couch next to Robert Weaver, a friend of his in the sociology graduate program. As he leaned his back against the arm of the sofa, he spotted Kurt Siegel across the room, and the vision of young Martin trying to come to terms with Kurt's conversation with Karl Marx made him smile. More than any American he knew, Kurt understood Marxist theory and Modern Critical Theory inside and out, and if this bright young German chose to occasionally speak with the great man himself, then who was he to argue?

Mark Rudd was a tall, thin, nice-looking young man with a long face. His engaging, deep-set gray eyes peered out seriously from beneath heavy brows. He addressed the group in a comfortable, offhand manner. He had considerable personal charm, and when he spoke, his eyes betrayed the faintest hint of a mischievous smile. Eliot always got the feeling that Mark was about to deliver some ingeniously ironic joke and was unable to keep a very straight face in anticipation of the humor that only he knew was about to come.

"The fat's in the fire," Mark began dramatically. "As you all know, this special meeting was called to discuss our need to deliver some kind of visible symbol of solidarity with the students in West Germany, who are right now on the barricades in 27 cities all across that country. They're protesting after the attempted assassination of their leader, Rudi Dutschke, last week in Berlin. The protests are focused on the offices and plants of the Axel Springer Press, a large reactionary newspaper syndicate in that country. I think you all know Eliot Kincaid and Kurt Siegel. I have asked them to join us tonight to give us some background on the West German student movement and to update us on the current situation in Germany. As many of you know, Eliot studied at the University of Frankfurt last year, and Kurt is a West German national who has studied at the Free University in West Berlin and has unofficial connections with his country's Department of State. Both Eliot and Kurt have worked with Rudi Dutschke and count him among their friends."

He looked around the room and then went on. "Before we hear from Eliot and Kurt, I must tell you that I have received word from the New York Regional SDS office urging us to support a protest to be held tomorrow afternoon at Rockefeller Center where the Springer Group has its New York offices.[1] I propose we spread the word tonight in order to muster as much support for this demonstration as possible in the short time left. OK? Any discussion?" Mark paused and looked around the room. "Good! Meet at the sundial at 11:30 a.m. tomorrow. You can take the subway

---

1 *The New York Times*, April 18, 1968, 14.

to Roc Center. I won't be going, as I want to prepare for the General Membership Meeting tomorrow night. Robert Weaver has agreed to lead our group. How many of you will participate?"

About half of the group raised their hand. "Fine, but I must also tell you this." The little smile ran away from Mark's face. "While I strongly feel we must act now to demonstrate our support for the West German students, I feel even more strongly that we must not let our response to this in any way siphon energy away from the firm commitment voiced last week by the steering committee concerning the protest planned here at Columbia for April 23. The entire local SDS organization will meet tomorrow to endorse plans for the April 23 demonstration. Tomorrow we have an opportunity to give a boost to the upcoming protest, but we must proceed with care. We must stay focused on our own issues and structure our response to the West German revolt in such a way as to use it to further radicalize our own members and invigorate our own programs, not to distract from them. As Kurt and Eliot will tell you, the issues involved the West German student revolt are, with only a few exceptions, quite different from our own."

Mark Rudd paused to let his words sink in. Ted Gold was scowling. He felt quite certain that Rudd had not mentioned the Rockefeller Plaza protest before this meeting, withholding the information until the last minute in order to ensure minimal participation and thus keep the organization focused on his precious protest planned for the 23rd. After an awkward moment Rudd went on. "Now let's hear from Kurt Siegel, who can give us an update as to what is going on in West Germany and place the recent events in Europe in a political and ideological context."

Kurt rose to his feet and set the stack of newspapers he had been holding on a small table beside him. He was a good-looking young man of average height with fine "dirty-blond" hair and startlingly light gray eyes. Despite his slight build, he looked quite fit, even athletic, an effect that was curiously contradicted by his thick wire-rimmed glasses. Eliot could see *Le Monde* on top of the stack of papers at Kurt's side. *Pravda* lay beside it along with what appeared to be a raft of German-language papers. Several large photos were clear, including one of police using water cannon to disperse a student mob and a close-up of a grim-looking young man with blood running down his face.

"I trust all of you have read the papers," Kurt began in perfect English with no discernable accent. He held up *The New York Times*. "Street Fighting Breaks Out Again in West Germany," the headline announced. "I have read papers from all across Europe, and thanks to my friend at the West German consulate here in New York, I managed to obtain the use of a diplomatic overseas line to call my sister, who has participated in some of the demonstrations in Frankfurt. Steffi is very well connected. She is a graduate assistant to Herr Professor Theodor Adorno at the *Institut für Sozialforschung* in Frankfurt. She knows Karl Wolff, the new West German SDS leader there, and Steffi and I are old friends of Danny Cohn-Bendit, the student leader at the University of Nanterre in Paris, who is also from Frankfurt."

With the thought of his sister and his boyhood friend, Danny, Kurt suddenly felt homesick. Visions of the past flooded his brain — his sister Steffi, their childhood in Paris, his adolescence in Frankfurt where he had first met the expatriate German Jew named Daniel Cohn-Bendit. He remembered the first time he met Danny, whose parents had fled Frankfurt 1933 ahead of Hitler's purges. Danny had been born in

France in 1945, and he had returned to Frankfurt with his family in 1958 at just about the same time Kurt and Steffi arrived from Paris. Danny and Kurt thus had much in common. Later they had both attended the Odenwaldschule in Heppenheim near Frankfurt, where they had become fast friends. Being officially stateless at birth, when Danny reached the age of 18 he had been entitled to select either German or French citizenship. Although he had at that time thought of himself as French, he had renounced French citizenship in order to avoid conscription in the country of his birth; but he had nonetheless matriculated to the University of Paris as soon as he finished high school.[1] The gray-eyed German youth had paused for only an instant in his address to the gathered SDS leaders at the mention of his sister and his boyhood friend. As the lightning flash memory receded, he quickly refocused his thoughts to the present and continued on seamlessly.

"Steffi has a good feel for the situation in Europe, and after speaking with her I'm confident that the accounts of the actual events of the past five days as reported by the *Times* and the rest of the mainstream world press are generally accurate and fair. Buildings are being occupied, stones are being thrown, cars are being overturned and set ablaze, and the police are responding with their usual authoritarian brutality. In Munich, some 50,000 students are still confronting approximately 21,000 police, some of them mounted. They have been fighting for four days now, stones and bottles against truncheons and water cannon.[2]

"However, what is not being fully conveyed here," he held the *Times* high and shook it a little, "is the motivation behind the violence from the students' point of view. Without an unbiased account of their motives and demands, all of this appears to the public as little more than unprovoked anarchy. This is what the establishment wants, and this is what I would like to discuss with you tonight."

The young German paused and then went on. "Student unrest has been sharply on the rise in West Germany since June, 1967, when a student, Benno Ohnesorg, was killed during a demonstration in Berlin. He was shot in the back by police."[3]

Kurt's thoughts flashed back to Berlin and to the student occupation of the great Free University in the wake of the Benno Ohnesorg shooting. In June of 1967, the shah of Iran had paid an official state visit to Berlin. It was widely believed by most students that the Iranian government under the shah was dictatorial and was suppressing and torturing its political opponents, and on June 2, during a demonstration outside the state opera house, where the shah was attending a performance, police and demonstrators had clashed. In the turmoil, Benno Ohnesorg had been shot in the head from behind. The following days saw nationwide demonstrations protesting police brutality. Kurt drew up images of police lines, bloody young faces, barricades, water cannon, and great barrages of cobblestones.

Again, he recalled himself to the task at hand. "At the most fundamental level," he continued, "the current German student movement shares with the student movement here in America a keen sense of what the New Left stands for. It is radical, anti-authoritarian, and anti-capitalist. The German students oppose both the bureaucratic oppression in present Eastern Bloc communist regimes as well as the systematic social and political oppression perpetrated by late capitalism in the West. Like us, they refuse to accept the rules of the democratic establishment when these rules be-

---

1 Wikipedia "Daniel Cohn-Bendit," http://en.wikipedia.org/wiki/Dainiel_Cohn-Bendit, last modified February 5, 2006.
2 Müller-Doohm, *Adorno*, 459.
3 *The New York Times Sunday Magazine*, April 28, 1968, 26.

---

come the instruments of the preservation of the system. They share our support for emerging revolutionary factions in the Third World. And also like us, the German student movement has focused an increasingly large part of their protest on the war in Vietnam, not only as a humanitarian horror and an imperialistic injustice but also as the most visible and the most easily assailable symbol of international capitalist tyranny. Of course, with the German students, this is largely an emotional, moral, and intellectual issue, whereas here, in the shadow of the draft, it also becomes quite personal indeed."

Kurt looked around the room. Everyone was focused, intent. It was clear that for all of these young men there was great drama in this moment, a sense of witnessing unfolding history and a general feeling of being part of something larger than themselves. These were the faithful, the true believers of the New Left. For them, the sound of the words "capitalist tyranny" had the chilling ring of truth, and it was clear to all that this young German was an astute and unusually articulate spokesman for their cause.

Kurt went on. "Beyond this, the specific issues addressed currently by West German student radicals are quite different from our own. Unlike America, Germany is a very old and very inflexible society. Perhaps, nowhere is German conservatism more clear than in the universities. The educational system in West Germany is stiff, formal, hopelessly tied to protocol and tradition, and stiflingly autocratic. It is in desperate need of modernization and reform. To a slightly lesser degree, this is also the case with German society as a whole, with both the East and the West German parliament, and with German domestic family life. At the bottom of it all, the West German students, like us, seek to make the university not the preserver of society but the reformer of it."

Kurt considered the shared dream for a liberal university as a patch of common ground occupied by both the American and the German student movements. However, he understood that the German students faced a much steeper uphill struggle. He clearly conceived modern German conservatism to be rooted in, and sustained by, a national refusal to come to terms with the nation's recent past.

"Repression and guilt are pervasive in all of Germany today," he told the young radicals who were now hanging on his every word. "Ex-Nazis occupy positions of authority in the governments of both the East and the West and in virtually all of the universities. In West Germany, our parents hide behind *Der Wirtschaftswunder*, the economic miracle. Pretending the Nazi nightmare never happened, they allow themselves to be diverted and seduced by commerce and consumerism. In East Germany, they hide behind leftist ideology believing that, if they're communists, then by definition they cannot possibly be fascists. For the younger generation — our generation — who wants to know how Hitler happened — how all this it *could* have been allowed to happen — this kind of denial is maddening."

Like most educated German youth of the his era, Kurt Siegel suffered from a kind of schizophrenia born of guilt, frustration, denial, and the fear that the fascist epic would happen again if the German nation, or nations, continued to ignore it. He also understood that the problem was made even more complex by the daunting proximity of communism, its failures, its promises, its alluring ideology, and its deeply entwined influence on the question of future German unification. "In Germany today," he concluded, "we face a highly complex social and political dynamic. The students want to clear the table, face the facts, set the record straight, modernize society, end the oppressive epic of national silence and denial that haunts them, and move on."

He paused to allow his words to sink in. "Knowing all of this, then," he continued after a moment, "it is not surprising that the object of the present West German student protest is the ultra-conservative Springer Press, a Berlin-based, worldwide newspaper and publishing concern that controls over 80% of the newspapers in West Berlin and over 35% in West Germany nationwide. Not only do the German students see Axel Springer and its reactionary media network as the establishment's willing tool for political and social oppression in my country, they also believe that Springer with its hate-mongering tabloid press is directly responsible for the attack on Rudi last week in Berlin."[1]

The young German paused and ruffled through the stack of newspapers on the table at his side. Finding the one he wanted, he held it up for all to see. It was a copy of the Berlin tabloid *Bild-Zeitung* with the bold headline, "*Halt Dutschke Nun.*" "This is from earlier this month," said Kurt. "For those of you who don't read German, the headline reads, 'Stop Dutschke Now.' Most of the protests that we are seeing this week are, in actual fact, efforts to block the delivery of Springer papers," Kurt continued. "As we have seen, while the underlying issues are myriad and less transparent, this is the only visible objective of the current revolt."

Kurt stopped to assess his audience, and again the room was still. All eyes were intently fixed on him, waiting for more. "Let me close by saying a few words about Rudi," he continued in a softer, more personal tone. "Rudi Dutschke is my friend. He is a former graduate student at the Free University in Berlin. He was born in East Germany and escaped to West Berlin the day before the Berlin Wall went up in 1961. Thus Rudi, like many other Germans of his generation, has been twice disillusioned, first by the communists and later by anti-communists. Like many young people on the left, he seeks a new ideology. Unlike most leftists, he is a Christian, and he believes that Christ was, or should I say is, the greatest revolutionary of all. Despite his spiritual side, Rudi is thoughtful, analytical, and idealistic. He joined the German SDS in 1965, and through the force of his dedication and charisma he has propelled that organization to its present position at the center of the West German student movement."

Kurt's tone had again become instructive, and he stopped as if to gain control of his abstract political side which had overpowered his softer, more human side. After a moment, he continued, again in an intimate manner. "I first met Rudi at the Vietnam Congress that he organized in Frankfurt in 1966. Professor Herbert Marcuse participated in that conference, and Rudi and Doctor Marcuse became fast friends. Rudi also established a personal intellectual rapport with Herr Professor Max Horkheimer and Herr Professor Theodor Adorno, the undisputed intellectual leaders of the German Left at the *Institut für Sozialforschung*, the Institute for Social Research, in Frankfurt where Eliot studied."

"Last week, on April 11, Rudi was shot outside his home in West Berlin by a deranged rightwing fanatic or Neo-Nazi named Josef Bachman. Bachman was taken into police custody after attempting to end his own life. Rudi suffered a serious head wound. As I mentioned, I have spoken with my sister Steffi in Frankfurt. She told me that a few days ago she spoke with Rudi's wife, Gretchen, who, by the way, is

---

1 Kai Kracht, "The Revolution of 1968," 2001, http://www.kaikracht.de/68er/english/index.htm.

an American. Gretchen said that Rudi was conscious but seriously disoriented. The prognosis is guarded at best."[1]

The handsome German graduate student paused and there was again total silence. Again, he shuffled through the newspapers at his side and held one aloft. Again, the headline was in German, but this time Kurt did not translate. He remained silent. Everyone focused on the photograph. It was a picture of a man's shoe, just an extreme close up of a simple black leather lace-up shoe lying in a city street. Far in the background were storefronts and some men milling around.[2] The impact was curiously powerful, such intense drama emanating from the black and white image of a simple everyday object. The inescapable poignancy came from what was not in the photograph, the man who, one had to assume, had been wearing the shoe not long before the photo was taken. It was an image of pathos, loss, and loneliness to be sure, but it was also an image of horrible violence — Rudi Dutschke had, quite literally, been blown right out of his shoes.

No one spoke. Kurt sat down, and Eliot looked at Mark Rudd, who gestured with his hand and a nod of his head that Eliot should proceed. It was clear that introducing Eliot, whom everyone already knew, would only break the dramatic tension which Mark hoped Eliot could sustain.

Eliot stood up. "I too am privileged to know Rudi Dutschke," he began. "On the excellent foundation just laid for us by Kurt, I would like try to give you an idea of what Rudi and the West German student movement stands for. Kurt has discussed their goals; now I would like to discuss their ideology. I would also like to touch on the question of the present violence."

Eliot looked around the room. He knew that after his friend's dramatic closing, the powerful mood could not last. But the tension had only been partially broken. As he scanned the room, all eyes were intently fixed on him. This was rare. Usually when he was called in to discuss leftist ideology with this group, which he often was, he encountered distant blank stares, especially from the so-called "action faction." Despite the more conservative efforts of Ted Gold and others, and despite everyone's high-minded Ivy League intellectual credentials, in early 1968 this group was not much interested in talk. They were frustrated, and they wanted action. In this regard, Eliot was thankful that Kurt had so skillfully set the stage for what could have otherwise been another obligatory dogmatic ordeal for these young American radicals.

Eliot Kincaid might have been described as an average-looking young man had it not been for the odd aura of intensity that always seemed to surround him. He was of average height and build, with unruly dark brown hair and a pale Celtic complexion. Still, something set him apart. There was about him an unmistakable sense of concentration, rigor, and precision, a sense of focus and awareness so powerful as to alter his physical appearance. So it was that Eliot Kincaid appeared unique, for the intensity of his passion, keen wit, and intellect were written clearly on his face and manifest in his every gesture. With a disarmingly penetrating gaze, he looked out on the world with a carefully reasoned passion to change it. Not surprisingly, intellectual abstraction had always come easily for this intense young man, and he had often joked that with a name like Thomas Stearns Eliot Kincaid, he was a natural born critic, just like has namesake T. S. Eliot, whose dark poetic assessments of the Modern Condition Eliot often recited from memory. After his studies in West Germany under

---

1 *The New York Times*, April 13, 1968, 1.

2 "Topfoto," http://www.topfoto.co.uk/gallery/Germany1963_1988/default.html.

the tutelage Theodor Adorno, one of the world's best-known Neo-Marxist minds, he was well prepared to teach Marxist theory.

He hastened to continue while the mood was right. "The ideology of the current students demonstrating today in West Germany has two sources: first, the early writings of Karl Marx, which we have discussed in some detail in earlier meetings, and second, what is now called 'Critical Theory,' a product of the so-called 'Frankfurt School' at the *Institut für Sozialforschung*, where I studied last year. At its very heart, Critical Theory has a simple goal, the emancipation of mankind. Its starting point is that Enlightenment, even Reason itself, has been corrupted and used to achieve human domination, both in the Eastern Bloc and in the West. In order to regain our freedom, Critical Theorists like Max Horkheimer, Theodor Adorno, and Herbert Marcuse believe that it is necessary to radically analyze our existing un-free social system. Their work is extremely theoretical; still, student revolutionaries everywhere find their ideas to contain a hidden call to action. At its heart, Critical Theory urges us to 'think liberation.'"[1]

"However, while abstract thinkers like Doctor Adorno are working to redirect enlightenment through such theoretical works as *Negative Dialectics* and *Aesthetic Theory*, the German SDS is out in the streets chanting the slogan 'Enlightenment through Action.'[2] This places Doctor Adorno and the entire Frankfurt School in between a rock and a hard place. They're aware that their theories form the intellectual platform for revolt, but they're skeptical of the current revolutionary strategy of breaking the rules, violence, and civil disobedience. Many people in Germany today see in student violence a reflection of 1933, an image of fascism, albeit from the Left. Really! Think about it. It is easy to interpret the student revolts as constituting a radical kind of censorship. After all, they're trying to stop the presses at newspaper plants all across West Germany. No matter how reactionary the newspaper, this is a problem.

"Although Doctor Adorno defends the students against the charge of fascism, he knows that the SDS must be very careful in this regard. He has said that the students are making the mistake of 'attacking what is democracy, however much in need of improvement, rather than attacking the enemy,' which, he says is, 'already starting to stir ominously.'[3] The enemy Herr Professor Adorno is referring to is the repressive tendency of the Right, which today is seen in political pressure to pass the *Notstandsgesetze*, so-called Emergency Legislation, aimed at limiting West German civil rights in times of emergency. Thus, in Germany today, the Right, the establishment, accuses the rioting Left of fascism, while the Left continues to protest what it sees as fascism on the Right."

Eliot paused to assess his audience. They were still hanging on every word, but he knew he could hold them too much longer, so he began to wrap up. "Doctor Adorno and others have signed an appeal calling for an inquiry into the social reasons underlying Rudi's attempted assassination and in particular into the manipulation of public opinion by Springer Press. However, he opposes any broad anti-authoritarian movement, which might attempt to politicize academic scholarship. Doctor Adorno described his situation beautifully when he said, 'I established a theoretical model for

---

1 Noah Isenberg, "Critical Theory at the Barricades," Lingua Franca, http://linguafranca.mirror. theinfo.org/9811/inside.html

2 Isenberg, "Critical Theory at the Barricades."

3 Theodor Adorno, in a conversation with Peter Szondi, quoted in Krausharr, *Frankfurter Schule und Studentenbewegung),* 2:237, quoted in Müller-Doohm, *Adorno,* 456.

thought. How could I have suspected that people would want to implement it with Molotov cocktails?"[1] It is a decision we all have to face."

Mark Rudd frowned darkly and a few of the radical "action faction" stirred in place and cleared their throats. Ted Gold and others in the conservative "praxis axis" nodded gravely. Eliot pressed ahead quickly. "Another member of the Frankfurt School is Doctor Herbert Marcuse, who as many of you may know is the stepfather of Mike Neumann, a member of our SDS chapter right here at Columbia." Eliot smiled at Mark Rudd. Everyone knew that Mark and Marcuse's stepson were close friends, and that Mike had first introduced Mark to the organization and to its most influential members.[2]

"Kurt also knows Doctor Marcuse well," Eliot continued. "Unlike Doctor Adorno, Doctor Marcuse, who is now an American citizen, is supportive of the current student revolts. He believes that, if legal means of protest become inadequate, illegal means are justified.[3] However, like Doctor Adorno, he warns us to be guarded. Kurt and I heard Doctor Marcuse speak in Berlin in July of last year. One of his talks was entitled "The Problem of Violence and the Radical Opposition." This lecture is particularly apropos to this meeting, for in it Doctor Marcuse urges 'setting up connections between student oppositions of various countries,' calling this our 'most important strategic necessity.' Nevertheless, Doctor Marcuse reminds us that when we resort to violence, we precipitate a clash between public violence (wielded legally by civil authority, i.e., the police) and private violence (our own illegal civil disobedience). He tells us that 'private violence will always be defeated by public violence until it can confront the existing public power as a new general interest.' The choice between theory and practice is a choice we all have to make. If we are overly aggressive in our actions, we risk damaging the political base that we have been working so hard to build. If we fail to act, we risk missing the revolutionary moment and reducing all of our theory to little more than dust in the wind."

Eliot looked around the room, trying to make eye contact with everyone. "That is the question," he concluded. "We are all — each one of us — Prince Hamlet."

---

1 Theodor Adorno, quoted in Martin Jay, *The Dialectical Imagination. A History of the Frankfurt School and the Institute of Social Research* (London, 1973), 279.

2 *The New York Times*, May 19, 1968, 84.

3 Herbert Marcuse, "Repressive Tolerance," in Robert Paul Wolff, Barrington Moore, Jr., and Herbert Marcuse, *A Critique of Pure Tolerance*, 1965, (Boston: Beacon Press, 1969), pp. 95-137 cited in Theresa M. Mackey, "Herbert Marcuse," *Dictionary of Literary Biography*, ed. Paul Hanson (Los Angeles: The Gale Group, 2001), 242:315-329.

CHAPTER FOUR: PARIS

> If the lost word is lost, if the spent word is spent
> If the unheard, unspoken
> Word is unspoken, unheard:
> Still is the unspoken word, the Word unheard,
> The Word without a word, the Word within
> The world and for the world.
> — T. S. Eliot, "Ash Wednesday"

> The bourgeoisie...has left remaining no other nexus between man and man than naked self-interest, than callous cash payment. It has drowned the most heavenly ecstasies of religious fervor, of chivalrous enthusiasm, of philistine sentimentalism, in the icy water of egotistical calculation.
> — Karl Marx and Friedrich Engels, "Manifesto of the Communist Party"

SUNDAY, APRIL 21, 1968

The overnight train from Frankfurt was scheduled to arrive at La Gare de l'Este at 7:15 Sunday morning. After seven and half hours of trying to sleep in a third-class coach seat, Steffi felt stiff and a little grimy. She made her way to the tiny lavatory, where she tried to wash her face, comb her hair, and brush her teeth while steadying herself against the lurching of the car as it noisily clattered over cross tracks and switches on the outskirts of Paris. She had an unsettled feeling in her stomach, and although she did not feel particularly tired, she was not sure exactly how much sleep she had gotten on the train.

When she returned to her seat, she found Karl Wolff and the others retrieving their knapsacks from the overhead racks. They seemed alert and quite animated. Steffi nodded to them as she reclaimed her seat. She did not feel like talking, so she stared blankly out the window. The train shot past gray factories and featureless warehouses, and the clatter of cross tracks grew even louder. After a few minutes, the train began to slow in its approach to one of the world's great railway terminals. She glanced at the others standing in the dim light of the lurching coach. Self-styled clandestine revolutionaries on their way to plan an international libertarian insurrection, they seemed to glow with a keen assurance that they were about to become vital players in the great moving pageant of human history. All Steffi could think about was a cup of coffee.

Inspired by the size, visibility, and duration of the recent German student riots that flared up in the wake of Rudi's shooting, her friend Danny Cohn-Bendit had invited Karl Wolff, the West German SDS president, and two other German SDS leaders to Paris to address the striking students at the sprawling University of Paris X at Nanterre.[1] Danny and his followers were in their fourth week of a boycott at the new university in that Paris suburb, and, for reasons that were not clear to her, Danny had asked Karl to invite Steffi as well. She suspected that he may have had a secret crush on her. Alternatively, perhaps he just wanted to appear evenhanded with regard to the gender of the German delegation. After all, she was the only female activist Danny knew in Frankfurt. Whatever the reason, Steffi found the opportunity too enticing to pass up. This was undoubtedly a historic time, even if the grand sweep of their revolt was not so all embracing as Danny, Karl, and the others wanted to believe. Steffi agreed with Doctor Adorno: this was not the revolutionary moment. Nonetheless, it was something — a sign of things to come, a warning, a chink in the armor of Western capitalist tyranny, the birth of a new revolutionary vanguard. She knew that traditional Marxist theory did not include this kind of upheaval. As for the Neo-Marxists like Doctor Marcuse and Walter Benjamin, Steffi was aware that they had created a theoretical place for the student rebellion and the so-called New Left. It was a place intellectually hammered out of a vague notion of the transcendence of false consciousness, but neither the exact nature nor the precise meaning of this theoretical transcendence was clear to her.

As the train slowed to a stop, she looked at Karl and the two young men from Berlin, Jürgen and Peter. They had been introduced to her last night at the railway station in Frankfurt, but this morning she couldn't remember their last names. They had an odd, intense look in their eyes. It was the aroused look she had seen that night in front of the Springer building in Frankfurt — something primal, something sexual. At this moment, these young men were not interested in theory.

"They're like wild animals that have tasted blood for the first time," she thought. "Is this what the New Left really means when it speaks of radicalization — nothing more than the crossing of the sacred boundary that separates reflective theory from violent action?"

* * *

"Let's get some coffee," said Steffi as they passed from the crude functionality of the great train shed into the towering stone splendor of the grand nineteenth-century terminal building.

---

1 It appears that Karl Wolff visited Danny Cohn-Bendit at Nanterre in Paris twice in April of 1968, first on April 2 as a "representative of the German SDS," Daniel Cohn-Bendit and Gabriel Cohn-Bendit, *Obsolete Communism: The Left Wing Alternative*, trans. Arnold Pomerans (New York: McGraw Hill Book Company, 1968); and again as a "speaker" sometime (probably on April 21) after the shooting of Rudi Dutschke, "Biography," www.cohn-bendit.com.

"There are some small cafés in the passageway leading to the Metro," said Karl, who had made the same trip from Frankfurt to Nanterre only a few weeks before. They found a quiet table and ordered coffee and croissants.

"Karl, why not fill us in on the situation here? All we really know is what we have read in the papers," said Peter.

"Right," said Jürgen, "and we've read the controversial pamphlet created last year by the French students at Strasbourg. Pretty radical. You know, the thing about 'Student Poverty.'"

"Yes," said Karl, "*On the Poverty of Student Life*," an odd bit of anarchist rambling. In many ways, it was influenced by the Situationists International, a vaguely anarchist, quasi-artistic group with a lot of fuzzy notions about the freedom gained through what they call 'the imagination of spontaneous revolt' or something like that. The Situationists believe that the young hold a special place in this kind of revolt, and I think they have had an effect, not so much in what they say, but in the French establishment's reaction to it."

"Yes," said Steffi, finally coming awake. "Guy Debord is the Situationist leader. I read his book, *The Society of the Spectacle*, another radical critique of capitalist consumer society. It's pretty good, actually. Sort of a modern twist on Marx's notion of commodity fetishism. Marx thought that capitalism develops to the point where 'things' control, or at least mask, the human condition, resulting in alienation and a false sense of well-being. Debord goes a step farther. He says that in the society of the spectacle everything is artificial and inhuman. We have reached the point of 'the spectacle,' when our entire culture has been reduced not only to the realm of things, but to the production and consumption of the images of things, copies of copies of images for which there are no originals — when 'to be' is replaced by 'to have' and finally by 'to appear.'"[1]

"Right," said Karl. "The Strasbourg pamphlet was produced in late 1966, and in it the students used this Situationist quasi-intellectual platform to subversive ends. They took a swipe at God, at the government, at the university, and at society as a whole. The university is depicted as a 'sausage machine,' turning out students with no real culture, automatons, trained to fit the needs of the materialist economic system. It was extremely subversive. According to the pamphlet, there is no middle ground. It even discusses theft as a form of rebellion. Needless to say, this made a really big stink with the establishment, even though it was not widely accepted on the left as an accurate portrayal of the role of student minority groups. Still, it had considerable effect here in France. I mean, it built awareness of the issues addressed by the Situationists and increased student radicalism."

"How far left is the mainstream leadership of the French students?" asked Peter.

"I'd say that they're a lot like us," said Karl. "That is, their awareness grew out of sympathy with the free speech movement at Berkeley in '64. Like us, their radicalism has been fueled by their opposition to the Vietnam War and by issues concerning the educational system and living conditions in the universities. They differ from us in that they're perhaps more attuned to spontaneous action than to strategy and theory. Hence, many are attracted to the Situationists and even to anarchist thinking. They also believe that the workers will join their fight. This idea might be folly in Germany; however, here in France we have seen some evidence that this is possible. The young workers especially are a force here. Almost ten percent — 250,000 young people —

---

1 Guy DeBord, *The Society of the Spectacle*, trans. Donald Nicholson-Smith (Brooklyn: Zone Books, 1995).

are now out of work in France. You remember the violence during the workers strike at Caen a few months ago followed almost immediately by violent anti-Vietnam marches by students and workers, and then by nationwide disturbances in the universities demanding free speech.[1] I suspect that there is more serious unrest here than most people are inclined to believe. The government has promised reform, but no one much believes this will happen. "

"And the situation at Nanterre?"

"It's an amazing scene, actually. When I was there three weeks ago, on April 2, the students had already taken over the university administration building, their 'Bastille,' as they called it. They had organized discussions and debates on political issues and administration policy, and they were all sitting in small groups out on the lawn, hundreds, perhaps thousands, of them, discussing politics and social issues, while a virtual army of police surrounded the campus, which had been closed since March 28."

Karl Wolff went on to explain to his colleagues that the French general student population was widely in support of university reform and he reminded them that last fall at Nanterre alone — that is, at the University of Paris X at Nanterre — ten to twelve thousand students boycotted their exams to protest university policies.

"There has been considerable unrest since that time," Karl continued. "The current upheaval is called 'The 22nd of March Movement.' About a month ago on March 22, there was a demonstration to protest the war in Vietnam, and a group of about 150 University of Paris X students decided to occupy the administration building. These students called for debates not just on university reform to establish a free university after the Berlin model, but also on revolutionary strategy and on the nature of what they considered to be an all-encompassing student revolutionary movement. That was the situation at Nanterre when I visited Danny three weeks ago. By that time, the core group had grown from 150 to over 1200, and these radical students enjoyed broad support among the other students at Nanterre, and indeed students nationwide."

Karl told them that by all accounts the French university system was in crisis, that it was being torn apart by the inability of its archaic inflexible organization to meet the needs created by rapidly changing social forces in France and by the demands of an exponentially growing student population. The French system, he explained, had doubled in size between 1958 and 1968. The University of Paris at Nanterre, where they were headed, opened in 1964 with 2,000 students. Attendance had gone from 4,000 to 8,000 in 1966 and then to 15,000.[2]

"The French students have a lot to be angry about," the German SDS leader went on. "Although Easter break interrupted their demonstrations two weeks ago, last week the same students resumed their protests bolstered by our open rebellion in Germany in the wake Rudi's attempted assassination. That's the situation so far, and

---

1 On January 26, 1968, there were violent exchanges between police and demonstrating workers at Caen. On February 7, 1968, an anti-Vietnam demonstration erupted into violent clashes between police and demonstrators in Paris, and February 14, 1968, saw a large demonstration at the university in Nantes followed by demonstrations and confrontations at universities all across France led by students demanding freedom of speech and movement.

2 Alain Touraine, *The May Movement: Revolt and Reform: May 1968 — The Student Rebellion and Workers' Strikes — the Birth of a Social Movement*, trans. Leonard F. X. Mayhew (New York: Random House, 1971), 83-119, 125; Alain Schnapp and Pierre Vidal-Naquet, *The French Student Uprising: November 1967–May 1968: An Analytical Documentary*, trans. Maria Jolas (Boston: Beacon Press, 1969), 30.

that's why we are here," Karl concluded dismissively. "Danny will fill us in with more details when we arrive. Now, let's get going. We have to catch the Metro to Chⵣtelet, and then change for Saint-Germain en Laye."

* * *

Steffi loved Paris. She had loved it as a child when her father had been at the West German Embassy in the French capital. Now he was back in Paris as a special envoy. She and Kurt had spent endless hours exploring the elegant streets and passageways of the Rive Droit. She had loved it as a young woman studying sociology as an undergraduate at the Sorbonne, this time frequenting the twisting passages and alleyways of the Rive Gauche. Danny's invitation had tempted her beyond her interest in the students' cause. She needed little excuse to return to Paris. Her companions would return to Frankfurt on the next night train, while Peter and Jürgen would travel on to Berlin tomorrow, making it a hellishly long trip for a single day in the French capital. She planned to stay overnight, spend some time in the city, and have lunch with her father before returning to Frankfurt the following night. Just the thought of wandering the streets of the great European city filled her heart with anticipation. As they boarded the Metro, she mused that to be in Paris on a Sunday and to remain below ground probably constituted some sort of mortal sin.

* * *

The express train rattled beneath the Paris streets, rocking with a soothing regularity. Steffi closed her eyes. As she pondered the underground route Karl had described, an unfamiliar wave of dreaminess swept over her. She could picture the route in vivid detail: a southbound train beneath the busy Rue de Strasbourg and beneath the old markets at Les Halles to the elegant Rue de Rivoli; then the eastbound express beneath Rue de Rivoli (beneath the Louvre, beneath the gardens of the Tuileries), beneath the broad open expanse of the Place de la Concorde, beneath the wide tree-lined Champs Élysées and the massive Arc de Triumph, then above ground beside the bustling Avenue de la Grande Armée; across the Seine at the Île du Pont, and beside the modern Avenue Perronet that ran near the beautiful Bois de Boulogne on the way to the great suburban University.

As this tangle of Parisian landmarks shot through Steffi's aboveground mind, the train shot through the Paris underground. Passing the station at Les Halles, the last stop before their train change at Châtelet, Steffi looked out onto the platform. Like the waiting passengers outside the passing train, the beautiful young German's vision of modern Paris began to a blur. It was mysteriously replaced by a vision of the Paris that had mesmerized Walter Benjamin, the Paris of the mid-nineteenth century. She could see in her mind the cast iron and glass arches of the old markets of Les Halles that she knew now stood just above the speeding train. She saw the web of passageways and blind alleys, intersecting and doubling back, appearing and disappearing in a tangle of vendors' stalls and shops. Although constructed in the 1850s, Les Halles suggested to Steffi a remnant of *Die Passagenwerk*, the older, long ago demolished, labyrinthine arcades that formed the backdrop for Benjamin's enigmatic lost masterpiece. She thought of the suicide note Walter had sent to Doctor Adorno: "In a situation with no escape, I have no other choice but make an end of it."[1] At the edge of the crowd, she saw the looming ghost of Baudelaire.

---

1 Just before his death, Walter Benjamin purportedly gave a letter to one of his companions, Henny Gurland. One version of the story relates that his instructions were for her to memorize the letter and then destroy it. She was told to later repeat his words from memory in her own letter to Theodor Adorno. After Henny Gurland escaped from Europe, she sent

* * *

Stepping off the train at The University of Paris X at Nanterre, Steffi felt like she had been magically transported from the Old World to the New. In Europe, most of the great metropolitan universities blend almost invisibly into the cityscape. Most consist of a few blocks of elegant classical urban structures that are identical to those of all of the other institutions that surround them. Were it not for the occasional small door sign denoting "School of Architecture" or "College of Fine Arts," one could easily pass right by the École des Beaux Arts in Paris without ever recognizing one of the most famous institutions of higher education in the world.

Nanterre definitely broke the European urban university mold. Completed in 1964, the sprawling campus in the outskirts of Paris was a picture of modern design: rational, open, airy, high-rise, and hopelessly sterile. Everywhere Le Corbusier's principles of sun, space, and greenery prevailed. At Nanterre, it was clear that a purely Modernist architectural mindset had prevailed. Like all good Modernists, its designers had been clearly of the mind that a pure clean style would lead to pure clean virtuous occupants and that good form would lead to good content. However, as had so often been the case, modern rationalism contained fatal congenital naiveties. Despite its idealized plan, Nanterre suffered the fate of a great deal of modern architecture: it failed to communicate with its users.

They found Danny in the administration building, in animated conversation with a small group of students. He greeted them warmly and introduced everyone around. He was small but a strong-looking young man, with red hair, freckles, and bright blue eyes that never seemed to smile, even when he laughed, which he did a lot.[1]

"Come on, I'll show you around. Good news, Herbert Marcuse is coming this afternoon. He's in Paris to address the UNESCO conference next week on 'The Role of Karl Marx in the Development of Contemporary Scientific Thought,' and he has been speaking at bookstores all over Paris and at the Sorbonne and the École des Beaux Arts. Karl will share the podium with the famous Doctor Herbert Marcuse.[2] How about that!"

Steffi was excited. She had always wanted to meet Doctor Marcuse. She knew that Drs. Adorno and Marcuse were good friends and that they corresponded regularly. She also knew that a debate was in progress between the two great intellectuals regarding the student movement. She hoped to relate to Doctor Marcuse her feelings regarding the untenable position the student radicals in Frankfurt were creating for Doctor Adorno.

---

to Adorno her best recollection of Benjamin's words. They were as follows: "In a situation presenting no way out, I have no other choice but to make an end of it. It is in this small village in the Pyrenees, where no one knows me, that my life will come to a close. I ask you to transmit my thoughts to my friend Adorno and to explain to him the situation in which I find myself. There is not enough time remaining for me to write all the letters I would like to write."

1 Jean Durieux, recollections of Daniel Cohn-Bendit in Phillip Labro et al., *This Is Only the Beginning*, trans. Charles Lam Markmann (New York: Funk And Wagnalls, 1969), 47.

2 Marcuse came to Paris sometime ahead of the UNESCO Symposium, "The Role of Karl Marx in the Development of Contemporary Scientific Thought" held on May 8, 9, and 10, 1968. He was in Paris during the height of the disturbances, and during this time, although he did not come to Nanterre, he did hold a number of informal meetings, debates, and spontaneous lectures for students, including appearances at the Sorbonne and the École des Beaux Arts. Barry Katz, *Herbert Marcuse and the Art of Liberation* (London: Verso, 1982), 185.

Danny was still ranting away in high gear in response to Peter's question about The 22nd of March Movement. "It all came together serendipitously, actually," he was saying. "On March 20, there was a demonstration at the American Embassy and a few windows were broken. The next day, six Nanterre students were arrested in their homes. We had long suspected that the university kept a black list of radical students, and these arrests seemed to confirm our suspicions. A general assembly of students was called, and my proposal to occupy the administration building was approved. There was a little fight with campus security, and about 150 of us took the building and proceeded to conduct a search for the black list in the chancellor's office. We didn't find it, but that night we moved to the conference room on the top floor, and over sandwiches and beer around the grand oval table, we formed a sort of coalition.[1] We were all members of different organizations: the UEC (*Union des Étudiants Communists*), the Maoist UJC (*Union des Jeunesses Communistes*), the Trotskyist JCR (*Jeunesses Communistes Révolutionaires*), and so on. Now, all of these organizations did not see eye to eye on all issues, so when 150 students of all different persuasions signed a proposal to create a leaflet explaining the reason for our occupation and calling for an anti-imperialist day to be held the following day, it was something of a phenomenon. Given our differences, we couldn't sign on behalf of our respective organizations, so we all signed as 'Le Movement du 22 Mars.' Without formal leaders, without common theoretical positions, the new movement is able to act as a kind of 'go-between' to facilitate a bond between all the factions of the Left in France.[2] We believe that the only path to real freedom lies in revolution and that the expression of the French student revolution is spontaneous. It does not need revolutionary leaders to express itself; it can do perfectly well without the help of a 'vanguard.'[3] It is a motivation that is felt more than thought. It gives priority to acts of disruption over intellectual criticism or political strategy.[4] Our revolution is based on our spontaneous 'imagination to take power.'"

Steffi frowned. She had heard it all before, and she did not like it. This was not the voice of revolution, nor was it the disciplined social critique urged by Drs. Marcuse and Adorno, a critique that sought new political and theoretical space in the modern Western world. It was not even the voice of sound strategy. It was the strategy of impulse that the Situationists so often used, a voice that urged the creation of radical ruptures in the pattern of everyday life, a strategy that lay somewhere between Dada and anarchy.

"Leaders like Danny only use men like Drs. Adorno and Marcuse," she thought. "They use them to validate their actions, to intellectually explain to them and the world that the whole of Western civilization is a vast conspiracy of powers working to make their freedom illusory. They have no real intellectual underpinning for a broad-based revolt against 'society as a whole' and no real agenda for what will happen after that revolt. They have been reading a lot more Guy Debord than Theodor Adorno."

Steffi was beginning to suspect that Danny, like so many of the student radical leaders, was more of a theatric rebel than a serious revolutionary.

---

1 Touraine, *The May Movement*, 143.

2 Fraser, et al., *1968, A Student Generation in Revolt*, 164.

3 Cohn-Bendit and Cohn-Bendit, *Obsolete Communism*, 58.

4 Touraine, *The May Movement*, 151.

CHAPTER FIVE: NEW YORK

Do I dare
Disturb the Universe?
— T. S. Eliot, "The Love Song of J. Alfred Prufrock"

History is nothing but men in pursuit of their ends.
— Karl Marx and Friedrich Engels, "The Holy Family"

WEDNESDAY, APRIL 17, 1968

The New York offices of the notorious German publisher Axel Springer were on the 50th floor of the Associated Press Building at Rockefeller Plaza. Eliot had met Robert Weaver, Kurt, and fourteen other members of Columbia University's SDS core group at the sundial and walked to the subway at 116th Street. They caught a downtown local, changed to the B Train at Columbus Circle, and arrived at Rockefeller Plaza just before two in the afternoon.

Across from the West 51st Street entrance to Rockefeller Plaza, police had set up barricades defining a small area reserved for demonstrators. The sidewalk already overflowed with a crowd of about 40 protestors. Eliot recognized a few guys he knew from the New York University SDS and a few from the Student Mobilization Committee for Youth Against the War and Fascism. Across the street, families were lined up on the sidewalk waiting for the special Easter Spectacular at Radio City Music Hall. A dozen or so policemen looked relaxed as they mingled with the crowds in the Plaza. It was clear that an invisible line had been drawn at the entrance to the plaza, and that the police did not expect any attempt from this small, disorganized-looking group of protestors to cross it.

As soon as they arrived, Robert Weaver sought out the SDS leader from NYU. The SDS at NYU had become more active since their protest against the Dow Chemical Company's recruiting efforts on their campus had drawn huge crowds back in March. Approximately 500 NYU students had demonstrated against the presence of

the petrochemical giant's recruiters on their campus. Dow was the principal manu-
facturer of the napalm used by the U.S. military in Vietnam, and the NYU demonstration had followed on the heels of demonstrations at Columbia in February which
involved student sit-ins in the Low Library and Dodge Hall, where over 200 students
protested the university administration's sanction of Dow's on-campus recruitment
there.

"The police are telling us to stay on the sidewalk," the NYU leader was saying.
"They say blocking the street is illegal and that the Plaza itself is private property. We
can't go in. It's bull."

The veteran of countless protests and demonstrations, Robert surveyed the situation. He had a lot of experience with this kind of thing, and he knew that the NYU
leader was already beyond his depth. "The hell with that!" he said, after a minute.
"We've got to get into the Plaza to command any real attention. Spread the word to
cross over and enter the Plaza on my signal. If the police stand in the way, tell your
people to insist that they have the right to free assembly in a public place and the
right to demonstrate and to speak out against Springer's oppression. Tell everyone
to put up a struggle if the police try to move them or to arrest them, and to shout
'police brutality' and scream bloody murder if the police grab them or hit them. One
of our goals here is to make the police look like they're violating our right to speak
out; another is to make them appear to overreact." The young man from NYU nodded.
"And if anyone gets through the police line, tell everyone to try to enter the building
and get up to the fiftieth floor, if they can. We'll carry this demonstration right into
Springer's offices."

"We've got a Nazi flag that we plan to burn," said the young man.

"Good! Burn it in the Plaza, not here. It will get a lot more attention over there."

"OK," said the young man. "Give me a minute."

"I'll wait about fifteen minutes to see if any more demonstrators show up. Then
I'll give the sign and lead this group across the street myself. Tell your people not to
hesitate, to follow me quickly, but not to run. Everyone should just move resolutely
into the Plaza as quickly as possible.

"OK." The young man moved away and began to spread the word.

Eliot shot a crooked smile at Robert. "Fifty thousand in Munich yesterday," he
said. "Fifty here today."

"We'll just have to make the best of what we have," said Robert. "Let's spread the
word."

They began circulating among the protestors.

* * *

When Robert Weaver stepped into 51st Street and motioned for the protestors to
follow, the police were caught totally off guard. They had not expected such a small
group of protestors to disobey the "ground rules for demonstrations" that they had so
clearly and emphatically explained to the New York University students before the
arrival of the Columbia SDS group.

Carrying signs emblazoned with great black swastikas and the words "Springer
had a Finger on the Trigger" and "Remember Rudi," they rallied beneath the NYU
group's great red, white, and black Nazi flag and streamed unopposed across the
street, quickly infiltrating the sizeable crowds in the Plaza. A few police tried to
block a group of protestors near the Radio City Music Hall queue. There was a brief
struggle, and moms and dads rushed about leading away crying children. The rest

of the protestors entered the Plaza shouting "Rudi, Rudi, Rudi." There were police whistles and angry shouts from both students and passers-by.[1]

Eliot and Robert dodged a fat patrolman and slipped into the crowd. The confused cop did not give chase but turned away to loudly confront the onrushing mass of protestors behind them. They circled away from the API building and then doubled back, walking right through the revolving door and casually joining the crowd waiting for the elevators. After about two or three minutes it was clear that the elevators had been turned off.

"Stairs," said Robert.

They walked around the corner of the lobby toward the stairs and right into the arms of four waiting policemen. Two of the officers grabbed Eliot and pushed him up against the cold marble wall, roughly cuffing his hands behind his back. Robert began to shout, "Police brutality," and continued to make vocal accusations and assert their rights to free speech as the two were led away.

"You are under arrest for criminal trespassing and resisting arrest," said one of the policemen, as they were marched through the plaza. Some bystanders shouted insults, but there were jeers at the police and words of encouragement mixed in.

As they crossed the great open Plaza, they could see police scuffling with the NYU students who were trying to burn the Nazi flag. One cop was stamping out the flames with his shoe.

"There's a chilling image," said Eliot. "I wish I had a camera."

Elsewhere amidst the crowds in the great art deco public space, some of the protestors were locked in a scuffle with police. Eliot saw one policeman pushed to the ground. Two more came to his aid, batons flailing. Those who had managed to avoid the police were leaving in small groups. Others were just milling about. Here and there, a few were being led away in handcuffs. A few young faces were bloody. A surprisingly large number of "New York's finest" had appeared quite suddenly, seemingly from out of nowhere. They were herding the bulk of the now-docile protestors back across 51st Street. Eliot spotted Kurt in this group. The whole thing had lasted less than half an hour, but it had sparked an ugly militancy that would endure deep in the hearts of both police and demonstrators.

Eliot's handcuffs were much too tight, and he was afraid that they were restricting circulation in his left hand. When he complained to one of the officers, the man told him that he should have thought about that before he crossed the police line. The young patrolman spoke as if their crossing of the imaginary line drawn around Rockefeller Plaza had represented some kind of highly offensive insult to him personally. Two cops placed them in the back of a squad car and headed uptown. On the way to the police processing facility, the cops stopped for coffee, leaving them handcuffed in the back of their patrol car. Later, they made another stop so that one of the cops could use a pay phone to call his girlfriend. By the time they arrived at the booking facility, Eliot's hands were completely numb.

* * *

Eliot had never been arrested before, and he was glad that Robert was with him to explain how the system worked.

"The regional SDS office will be all over this," Robert explained. "They'll see to our release, but first, the police have to book us and set bail. That could take a while — probably about five or six hours. Most likely we'll be out of here by midnight."

---

1 *The New York Times*, April 18, 1968, 14.

Eliot looked at his watch. It was four-thirty in the afternoon.

Eliot and Robert were searched, photographed, fingerprinted, and placed in a small holding cell with about twenty other prisoners. They were the only white men in the cell. The other students who had been arrested at the demonstration were nowhere to be seen. The crowded cell was one of many that looked out onto a large open area filled with rows of chairs and benches. This spacious low-ceilinged central area was empty except for a group of women seated in chairs in the far corner of the room. The great central space was ringed with holding cells like the one they were in, all packed to overflowing with mostly black prisoners.

Eliot looked around the crowded cell. It was about 15 feet square. On one wall there were bunk beds, and along the opposite wall, a few folding chairs. A large stainless steel toilet adorned the back wall and dominated the small room like some kind of high-tech ritual altar. There was no other furniture of any kind. The twenty or so prisoners sat on the bunks, in the folding chairs, and on the floor.

"Welcome, my brothers," said one of the men from the top bunk. "Make yourselves comfortable." He motioned to a place on the floor near the stainless steel toilet. Everything smelled of strong disinfectant.

Robert went over and sat down with his back against the wall. Eliot followed suit, still rubbing his left wrist. Circulation and sensation were slowly returning to his hands.

"Hook you up too tight, did they?" asked the short man next to Eliot.

The graduate student nodded.

"What'd they get y'all for?"

"Criminal trespass and resisting arrest," said Robert.

"You're lucky they didn't beat the livin' daylights out of ya," said another man eyeing their longish hair. "Where'd you two 'criminals' do all do this criminal trespassing?"

"Roc' Plaza," said Robert.

The man whistled, obviously impressed. "What was it about?"

"We were protesting the oppression of the masses by the autocratic forces that control Western society," said Robert sarcastically. He smiled at them very broadly.

There was laughter and a chorus of "right ons" and "I hear thats."

"You must be college boys. I'll bet you're really smart," said another man with obvious irony.

"Yeah, we're real smart, all right," said Eliot. "We're the ones sitting on the floor by the toilet."

There was some more laughter, and after it died down another man said, "Well, we're college boys too. Most of us did our 'ma-tric-u-lating' at Riker's Island University. You know that fine school, I'm sure."

"I know it," said Robert. "An institution of higher learning if ever there was one."

They all nodded.

After about half an hour, the holding cell doors were opened and everyone was allowed to go out into the large open space.

The policeman who opened the door to the holding cell recited the rules in a bored monotone. "There's to be no talking in the common area and no gathering in groups. The pay phones are available to all. Listen for your name to be called, and then report to the Sergeant."

Eliot and Robert sat on some benches outside the entrance to their holding cell. They could see some of the others from the Rockefeller Plaza demonstration sitting across the room in groups of two or three — about 10 or 12 in all. Kurt did not appear to be among them.

After about half an hour, the mood seemed to relax a bit. Everywhere men were quietly talking among themselves. Suddenly everyone was ordered back into the holding cells and locked up again. After another half hour, they were all allowed back out into the common area. This odd ritual of lockup and release went on all evening at about half hour intervals. Around nine o'clock the police began to call out the names of those for whom bail had been set. It was announced that those who could not make bail by three a.m. would be sent upstairs to the regular jail for the night and arraigned in the morning.

When Robert and Eliot's names were called, they reported to the sergeant as instructed and were told that their bail for criminal trespass and resisting arrest was $1,000 each. Robert called to tell the regional SDS office and learned that they were indeed on top of everything. A bondsman had been engaged, and all of them would be free to leave in an hour or two.

They sat back down on the bench.

"I keep thinking about hearing Herbert Marcuse last year in Berlin," said Eliot after a few minutes.

"This is a hell of a time for theory," said Robert.

"No, listen, he gave a lecture about violence and opposition. He had it all exactly right. I mean, he described what happened today down to the last detail. It's amazing, really. Now I see exactly what he was talking about."

"Even the part about the cop stopping on the way to the slammer to call his girlfriend?"

"No, seriously, listen to me. Doctor Marcuse said that with demonstrations like the one you just led, confrontations with state power and with institutionalized violence are inevitable. He said that demonstrations are not confrontations as long as they remain inside the framework of what is legal. However, he also said that the state controls that framework. What is legal one minute can be made illegal the next, thus justifying the state to employ violence."

Robert wrinkled his brow in a pained look.

"Don't you see," said his passionate young friend. "When we got to the Plaza, it was a public place, filled with all kinds of people doing all kinds of things. But quite suddenly, it ceased to be a public place for us. Unlike everyone else, if we ventured into the Plaza, we were breaking the law. They had changed the law, or at least changed their selective enforcement of the law. Can't you see how easily laws against trespass, disturbing the peace, blocking the flow of traffic, and the like are used to turn us into criminals and to make us the object of legal violence?"

"Right. So what's the point?"

"The point is that we are forced into a situation that makes our civil disobedience appear totally unjustified, and then we are suppressed by what appears to be totally justifiable institutional violence. We are politically manipulated, and then we are clobbered. As Doctor Marcuse put it, 'the establishment has a legal monopoly on violence.' All we have is a 'higher moral right' to resist, and no matter how pure our motives may be, our violent protest will always be rendered illegal, and their violence will always be legal, because no social system, no matter how free, will constitutionally legalize violence against itself. Still, Marcuse believes that violence that comes from the rebellion of the oppressed has historically reduced injustice, cruelty, and war, and furthered the progress of civilization, where the legalized violence of the ruling class has resulted in oppression and fascism.[1] In the end, it is our fragile higher moral right against their unassailable institutionalized right."

"So it's right against right," said Robert.

"Yep, they use their legal right to dominate society. We use our moral but illegal right to try to liberate it."

"And they win," said Robert.

"And they win," said Eliot with a broad gesture toward the huge room filled with down-trodden black men, some perhaps desperate and mean-spirited criminals but most obviously just harmless vagrants, down on their luck.

* * *

"Earlier this year, the Tet offensive changed everything," Mark Rudd was saying to the assembled membership of the Columbia University Chapter of the Students for a Democratic Society. "Last month, the King assassination changed everything. This month, the Dutschke shooting changed everything. After years of being told that victory in Vietnam is just around the corner, the U.S. military machine has been humiliated by a Third World peasant army, and the antiwar protest worldwide is rapidly accelerating. In the wake of the King shooting, 167 U.S. cities saw riots and rebellions. On campuses everywhere, black and white students are marching arm in arm. Harlem is still smoldering from the fires that burned there. In the wake of the Dutschke shooting, student violence has rocked Europe. There were 60,000 in the streets of West Germany alone. Right now students occupy the universities at Nanterre in Paris and the Valle Giulia in Rome."

While Eliot and Robert waited to be set free, about 100 Columbia SDS members were listening to Mark Rudd "harangue the troops" in preparation for the demonstration planned for the 23rd. "All of this recent history is in our favor," Mark continued. "Right now, here at Columbia, we are perfectly positioned to act."

"First there's the war. Our recent protest against the IDA and the university's arbitrary singling out of the 'IDA six' for discipline has crystallized a broad-based opposition. Most students see this arbitrary use of the university's disciplinary power as bald-faced political repression. Most students are now demanding that the university cease its inhumane affiliation with research that is killing thousands of Vietnamese. Second, there's racism. Virtually all students are appalled by the King assassination, but the immediate symbol for the university's racist policy is the on-going construction of the new gymnasium in Morningside Heights, a project arrogantly undertaken without consulting the black community, which the university has conspicuously ignored and exploited from its very beginnings. I'll meet with Cicero Wilson of the Student Afro-American Society to enlist their support for our protest against the university's racist attempts to build a white hill of affluence and superiority in Morningside Heights, a hill of privilege that looks down on a sea of poverty and color in Harlem. Finally, there's the protest in Europe. Seven of our own were arrested today for protesting outside the Springer Press offices at Rockefeller Center. Police used violence to break up the protest, and several of our members were brutally beaten."

There was a vocal reaction from the gathered members. Jeers and boos filled the room. Mark Rudd paused, and then continued in loud and resolute voice: "Student opinion is shifting. I believe that on the 23rd we can propel 500 or even 1,000 students to stand against the university and the repression and inhumanity its policies represent." His tone became emotional. "The call to action is no longer scribbled on

---

1 Kellner, *Herbert Marcuse and the Crisis of Marxism*, 284.

ghetto walls, no longer written on the far-away faces of dying boys in Asia." Mark was shouting now. "The call to action is now. Everything points to the undeniable conclusion: the revolutionary moment has arrived. Do I hear a motion to approve the proposed demonstration on April 23?"

"I so move," came the mass reply.

"All in favor?"

There was a resounding "Aye!"

They then split up into committees to begin the work of getting the word out.

* * *

Kurt, Ted Gold, and a few others were assigned the task of composing and designing a leaflet announcing the demonstration for members to post and pass out on campus over the next few days.

"Well, at least he kept things focused on local university issues," said Ted. "Hell, I was afraid he would get up there and lobby for the immediate violent overthrow of the entire United States government."

"He's using university issues to stand for much larger social, economic, and political issues," said Kurt. "The IDA stands for the war in Vietnam and the suppression of Third World revolution, the construction of the gym in Morningside Heights stands for racism and the bourgeois oppression of the proletariat, and police brutality stands for the repressive brutality of the entire capitalist system. He knows what he is doing. This is political. Just watch the issues broaden after this thing gets underway."

"Still, if he's right, and we can get 1,000 people out there," said Ted. "I guess I'll have to hand it to him."

"Yes," said the German, "but I'm afraid he really believes that this is the revolutionary moment. I assure you it is not. This is a protest demonstration, not a revolution. There's a big difference — a dangerous, perhaps even deadly, difference."

CHAPTER SIX: PARIS

> In a minute there is time
> For decisions and revisions which a minute will reverse.
> — T. S. Eliot, "The Love Song of J. Alfred Prufrock"

> The oppressed are allowed once every few years to decide which particular members
> of the oppressing class are to represent and oppress them.
> — Karl Marx, quoted in Vladimir Lenin, *State and Revolution*

SUNDAY, APRIL 21, 1968

At Nanterre, the lecture hall that the university administration had reluctantly designated for the striking students' use was packed to overflowing. Students filled the seats, sat in the aisles, on the floor, on the edge of the lecture platform, and stood about in doorways. This created a slightly disorganized atmosphere, but it was at the same time casual, informal, and relaxed. Since the beginning of the Nanterre revolt almost a month ago on March 22, the students had regularly demanded or usurped more and more space from the university administration to accommodate their swelling numbers.

As they entered the hall, they were discussing the program. In order to avoid the possibility of being upstaged, Karl Wolff was asked to speak before Doctor Marcuse. Karl knew that Herbert Marcuse was the main "draw," so he planned to keep his comments brief. Besides, his French was not good enough for public speaking. Accordingly, it was decided that he would speak to the group in English, which he had mastered during his term of study in the United States.

Steffi, Peter, and Jürgen listened from a small adjoining room that opened onto the lecturer's platform. Karl began with an appeal for international student solidarity. He talked of Rudi, the hate campaign waged by the Springer Press, and of the worldwide student reaction to Rudi's attempted assassination. He then reminded the students that the French government, which controlled the media in France, had given massive coverage to the student revolt in Germany in order to deflect attention away from student dissent here in France. He suggested that this could be a good thing for them if they redoubled their efforts in open rebellion. They might thereby regain the headlines. At the same time, their cause might appear all the more powerful when viewed in tandem with the riots in neighboring Germany. There was considerable applause. Karl then began to describe the German concept of the "Critical University," as Danny had suggested he do. He described the formation of the Free University at Berlin and its attempts to establish a curriculum of "non-establishment education."

"The three main areas of study," Karl was saying, "are subjects with direct relevance to students' political activities, like Third World liberation movements, and the Emergency Power laws in Germany; the conditions and implications of social research, including university reform; and a critique of the theoretical and ideological foundations of established university disciplines by the study of psychoanalysis."[1]

At this point a door opened, and Herbert Marcuse strode into the small room where Steffi and the other German student leaders were seated. They all stood, and Danny quietly introduced everyone so as not to interrupt Karl, who was plodding on with his address in the next room. Doctor Marcuse smiled broadly. He was tall and trim, quite robust for a man of 70, and this, along with his luxurious white hair, created a striking aura. As Steffi shook his hand, she could not help but notice that his demeanor was casual, natural, comfortable. He was so very American, so very unlike the stiff Old World formalism that always attended the personas of his contemporaries, Drs. Adorno and Horkheimer. She wondered why he had stayed in America after the war when they had eventually returned to Germany.

"It is an honor, Herr Professor," she said in German as she was introduced.

"Ah, Fräulein Siegel, Teddy Adorno's assistant. Yes, charmed, my dear. I knew your father in Washington years ago. Did you know that I once worked for the CIA?"

He paused for effect, and then laughed at the wide-eyed faces around him.

"From the end of World War II until late 1949," he explained, "I worked in Washington as an analyst for the Research and Analysis Division of the Office of Strategic Services, the predecessor of the CIA," he laughed again and turned back to the attractive young German. "Yes, dear little Steffi, I remember you as a very small child — and your brother as well."

"Yes, Kurt," said Steffi, "He is in New York now, Herr Professor, a graduate student at Columbia University."

"And your father? He is here in Paris, I understand, the special envoy for Franco-German commerce, I have heard. I plan to visit with him while I am here. He is an old friend. He is well?"

"Yes, Herr Professor, thank you. I know he will be very happy to hear from you."

Throughout this exchange, Doctor Marcuse had warmly held onto her hand. "I must tell you, Herr Professor Marcuse, Herr Doctor Adorno is having a difficult time." Steffi reached out with her free hand, taking his hands between hers. "He is very hurt by the students' personal behavior toward him. He takes everything so personally, and he feels that they're rejecting his work. Certainly he must have written you."

"Yes, my dear, I know of this. Teddy and I have something of a dialogue underway regarding recent events." Doctor Marcuse smiled as if to emphasize a euphemistic use to the words "dialogue" and "events."

---

1 Fraser, et al., *1968: A Student Generation in Revolt*, 139.

"Doctor Adorno feels that if he endorses the students' violence and radical behavior, he will risk politicizing the university."

"Ah, my dear Fräulein, we must open his eyes. The university has already been politicized."

"But perhaps not the Institute," said Steffi.

"Perhaps not," replied Doctor Marcuse thoughtfully. "Listen well to my remarks today, Fräulein, and relay them to Teddy. I think you will find that he and I are not so far apart on this issue as he may think."

Then, realizing that he was ignoring his host, he turned to Danny and said in French, "What a lovely girl; I knew her as a child."

"So did I, Herr Professor, so did I," the redhead laughed his reply in crisp German.

Karl was wrapping up his remarks. "The modern university has two contradictory roles," he was saying. "The first is to turn out graduates to perpetuate bureaucratic capitalism. In this, we see the growing enslavement of the university by the controlling powers of government and industry. The second role is the more traditional vision of the free university as the guardian of culture. To free the university from exploitation by the establishment, our protest must go beyond university reforms. We must fix our aim on radical changes within society as a whole."[1]

There was polite applause, and Danny rushed onto the lecture platform to thank Karl and to introduce Doctor Marcuse. There was more applause as Herbert Marcuse walked to the podium. He held up his hands first to acknowledge the cheers and then to end them. All was quiet. He smiled broadly and shuffled some papers on the lectern before him. Steffi was amazed at his easy manner. He was a tall, erect, forceful man, radiant and yet curiously aloof, like an aristocrat who is also a popular hero, Egmont in the streets of Brussels.[2]

He began in fluent French: "Let me first say a little about the present moment in history. I will then speak to you about responsibility — your personal responsibility for your individual conduct at this moment in history." His German accent was quite distinct. "Until the last few years, the present period seems to have been characterized by a stalemate in the dialectic of negativity. Indeed, until just recently, negativity within the antagonistic whole has been barely demonstrable."[3]

The young blonde scholar was used to this kind of language. She understood that by "dialectic of negativity" Doctor Marcuse meant the potentially revolutionary forces of the "antithesis" that opposed the "thesis" of modern Western capitalism. This was the classic dialectic of Hegel that Marx so brilliantly employed as the engine of history, a system of constant change in which each new "thesis" is opposed by the natural "antithesis" within it, a conflict that results in "synthesis," which in turns become a new thesis.

"This suggests," Professor Marcuse continued, "that negation must develop only outside the tightly integrated, one-dimensional system of needs and satisfactions, and it is the existence of such an opposition, however embattled and disorganized,

---

1 Cohn-Bendit and Cohn-Bendit, *Obsolete Communism*, 41-48.

2 From Marshall Berman's description of Marcuse at Brandis University in 1964; Marshall Berman, *Partisan Review*, XXXI, Fall, 1964, 617, quoted in Kellner, *Herbert Marcuse and the Crisis of Marxism*, 3.

3 Herbert Marcuse, "*Die Analyse eines Exempels*," lecture published in *Neue Kirtik*, 36-37, June–August 1966, 33; and "The Problem of Violence and the Radical Opposition" lecture at the Free University of Berlin, July 1967, in *Five Lectures*, trans. Jeremy J. Shapiro and Shierry M. Weber (Boston, Beacon Press, 1970), 86-7; both cited in Katz, *Herbert Marcuse and the Art of Liberation*, xx.

that now gives hope[1] — hope 'for the sake of the hopeless ones' — to use a phrase that sustained Walter Benjamin during the fascist years."[2]

"He's patronizing them," thought Steffi, "pumping them up, saying that they represent a 'hope' for change from outside the system. He is not attempting the reconciliation that he implied when I mentioned Doctor Adorno. Besides, how can dialectic opposition come from outside the system? I thought the antithesis was supposed to be naturally contained within the thesis."

Doctor Marcuse went on. "Today there is indeed a 'New Left,' and it comprises many tendencies which seem most suspect from the point of view of pure Marxist ideology. It is unorthodox in its composition, its spokesmen, including such 'suspect' figures as poets, writers, and intellectuals." There was some laughter. "It is also unorthodox in its spontaneous and anarchic forms, and in its aesthetic, erotic, and utopian dimensions. Still, it represents the only embodiment of the 'scandal of qualitative difference' without which a vital break with the repressive continuum of needs would be unimaginable."[3]

The beautiful young German suddenly sensed a contradiction. What "break with the repressive continuum of needs" was driving the New Left? Where did these new needs come from in a one-dimensional society? Herbert Marcuse's best-known work was *The One-Dimensional Man*, published in 1964.[4] Steffi had read it, and she knew many German and American students who had read it as well. It had become something of the intellectual Bible for the New Left. In it, Marcuse presented a negative picture of a repressive contemporary Western society wrapped in a veneer of meaningless glitter, an un-free society driven by artificially implanted false needs. According to Marcuse, these needs are exemplified by a range of choices offered by the economy. However, each of these choices reinforces the social norms that now exist. Because each choice has the same result (reinforcement of social norms), there is no real choice, no real freedom, no depth to contemporary life in highly developed industrial Western economies. Steffi wondered if any of the others were questioning this seeming reference to needs from outside, from a new "dimension." Are these new needs a condition of the transformation of society, or do they presuppose it?[5] It appeared to be a fundamental departure from the premise of Doctor Marcuse's own book. Wasn't he saying the needs of the New Left came from another dimension? Only later would Steffi come to know that the French students had not read *The One-Dimensional Man*, nor any of Doctor Marcus's other works. Only later would she come to realize that the most radical French students didn't give a "hoot in hell" for theory.

Doctor Marcuse was summing up the first part of his address. "Way out on the margins of the apparently impregnable 'fortress of corporate capitalism,' subverting

---

1 Marcuse's writings and lectures of the period 1967-68 were filled with references to this kind of hope. Katz, *Herbert Marcuse and the Art of Liberation*, 183.

2 Walter Benjamin (1919-1922), "Goethe's Elective Affinities," in *Selected Writings*, vol. 1, ed. Marcus Bullock and Michael W. Jennings (Cambridge: Harvard University Press, 1996); Katz, *Herbert Marcuse and the Art of Liberation* , 183.

3 Herbert Marcuse, "The End of Utopia" and "The Problem of Violence and the Radical Opposition," in *Five Lectures*; Herbert Marcuse, "Liberation From the Affluent Society," address at the London Roundhouse, July 1967, in David Cooper, ed., *The Dialectics of Liberation* (London: Harmondsworth, 1968); all cited in Katz, *Herbert Marcuse and the Art of Liberation*, 184.

4 Herbert Marcuse, *One-Dimensional Man*, (Boston: Beacon, 1964).

5 Katz, *Herbert Marcuse and the Art of Liberation*, 188.

forces are now at work. They're driven by a new faith in the 'rationality of the imagination,' and by 'vital needs for peace, quiet happiness and beauty.'"[1]

"Aesthetic needs?" thought Steffi. "This might make Herr Doctor Adorno happy after all. It will certainly please the hippies." She smiled at her own joke. Still, something was wrong. It was as if Doctor Marcuse was assigning to the student radicals a new revolutionary role and then fabricating the intellectual rationale for this assignment after the fact. However, who was she to question the great Herbert Marcuse? She wanted to talk to Doctor Adorno.

"Now," said the white-haired man, opening his arms to the students as if to gather them all into a warm fatherly embrace, "I will speak to you of your responsibility. Listen to me carefully."

There was a hushed pause. "You are not to provoke confrontations in situations where the odds are hopeless. You cannot fight a revolution from a jail cell or from a hospital bed. No acts of violence are to be directed against individuals, no matter who they are or what you may perceive them to stand for. Modern revolutions must have morals, and for modern revolutions to succeed, adherence to these morals must be crystal clear to all observers. Lastly, the educational means of the university must be preserved at all costs — although perhaps not in their present form. To cut off the branch upon which the revolutionary intelligentsia is sitting would be suicide.[2] Always be respectful of the faculty. And respect the university as well, if not for what it is today, for what it should be, for what it has been, and for what it will become."

Steffi glanced at Danny. His brows were knitted into a dark scowl, and he was shaking his head vigorously as if to refute some kind of colossal lie. It was clear that in his radical vision of the revolution there was no place for rules; the university, like everything else in capitalist society, had to come tumbling down.

* * *

After a question and answer period with some of the French students, Steffi said her farewells and took the train back to Paris. All day she had been distracted, haunted by her nineteenth-century vision of the labyrinthine iron and glass passageways of Les Halles. She knew that the great mid-nineteenth century urban food market that Zola had once called "the belly of Paris" was soon to be demolished.[3] She wanted to walk, so she got off the train at the Place de la Concorde and began to make her way on foot toward the great market, keeping to the back streets and narrow alleys between Rue de Rivoli and Rue Feuillade. As she walked, Paris intoxicated her, embraced her, seduced her. Each approaching street corner seemed to possess a mysterious and irresistible magnetism.[4] It suddenly occurred to her exactly what Walter Benjamin had been talking about when he wrote "Paris, the Capital of the Nineteenth Century" and his two essays on Baudelaire in 1935. Until this moment, these short pieces had baffled her. Doctor Adorno had explained that they laid out the themes

---

1 Marcuse was working on reconciling these conflicts in 1968. His ideas were later published in his *Essay on Liberation* (Boston: Beacon, 1969); Katz, *Herbert Marcuse and the Art of Liberation*, 184-5, 188.

2 Katz, *Herbert Marcuse and the Art of Liberation*, 186.

3 The iron and glass arcades of Les Halles, the great central food market of Paris, were built in 1852 and demolished in 1971 to make way for a large subway terminal, Chatelet-Les Halles, the intersection of three major Paris Metro lines. The replacement project also included open promenades and a modern underground shopping mall.

4 Isenberg, "On Walter Benjamin's Passages," *Partisan Review*, LXVIII, No. 2, 2002.

that Benjamin would later expand to create his lost masterpiece, *Die Passagenwerk*, or *The Arcades Project*, parts of which he had sent to Doctor Adorno for critique.[1]

Steffi suddenly realized that Walter Benjamin's work was so difficult to understand because he saw all events and objects as discontinuous and free flowing. There was no temporal or logical continuity in Benjamin's world. He saw aimless urban wandering as the most accurate way to view the modern world. His seemingly jumbled quotations and notes from obscure documents detailing excursions through the winding passages of the nineteenth-century Paris arcades were metaphors for the modern world as he understood it. In this fragmented universe, nothing was related in an orderly way. There were no categories, no separate intellectual disciplines. Aesthetics could not be separated from history, nor economics from poetry. Objects appeared at random, books, furniture, photos, gestures; anything and everything could spark a meaningful revelation. It was a world of collage, of incoherence, of impossibly complex interaction, a world without boundaries, independent of time, space, causality, and logical continuity. Walter Benjamin inhabited a world of conscious dreams — dreams that themselves had become commodities.[2]

She gazed into the windows of shop after shop and realized that for Benjamin each one had presented a Marxian world in miniature. Up until this moment, she had missed the point. Benjamin was pointing to "the mass marketing of dreams within a system that prevented their realization."[3] The luxury goods in the shop windows represented mere substitute gratifications, manufactured desires, temporary illusions. Benjamin's spontaneous passages through this blossoming bourgeois carnival served as his critique of the capitalist world, the recognition that our materialist monuments are "already ruins even before they began to crumble."[4]

"So this is what Marx really meant when he said, 'All that is solid melts into air,'"[5] Steffi said aloud. "No wonder Doctor Adorno was so drawn to Walter Benjamin's work."

She was finally approaching the old market. The characteristic cast-iron arches of the ornate nineteenth-century glass-covered arcades beckoned in the vibrant late afternoon light. She knew that this market place had a special meaning to Guy DeBord and the Situationists as well. They had their own concepts of urban wandering. Not unlike Walter Benjamin's crumbling dream city, the Situationist City wished for discontinuous places where the only predictable thing was the unpredictable. However, unlike Benjamin's city, in which the past served as a beacon to reveal the false consciousness and to illustrate the present all-encompassing revolutionary moment, the Situationists sought only to discover tiny centers of disruption in modern everyday urban life, to find places where ambiences were suspended at the junctures of time and culture. Les Halles was surely such a place. It was the Situationsits' aim to interrupt capitalism, to disturb the illusion of normality, to break the mirror of "the spectacle," in a kind of Theater of the Street. They emphasized spontaneity and prized

---

1 Theodore Adorno, letter to Walter Benjamin, August 2, 1935, in Bloch, *et al.*, *Aesthetics and Politics*, 100–41.

2 Buck-Morss, "Walter Benjamin – Revolutionary Writer," *New Left Review*, No. 128, July/August, 1981.

3 Buck-Morss, "Walter Benjamin – Revolutionary Writer," *New Left Review*, No. 128, July/August, 1981.

4 Walter Benjamin, *Gesammelte Schriften*, ed. Rolf Tiedemann and Herman Schweppenhäuser, 7 vols. (Frankfurt: Suhrkamp, 1972-1989), 5: 59.

5 Karl Marx and Frederick Engels, *Manifesto of the Communist Party*, 1848.

the imagination to seize power, and they played on the inevitability of dissatisfaction in the young, who habitually confused their modern avant-garde sideshows with real revolutionary strategy and action. She thought about the "Yippies," the newly formed Youth International Party that her brother Kurt had described in a recent letter. They seemed a shabby substitute for the illuminating intellectual power of Marx and Benjamin.

Turning south, Steffi crossed the Île de la Cité and strolled along the Left Bank. There she continued to indulge her passion for Paris, for random aimless urban wandering, and for her newfound understanding of Walter Benjamin.

* * *

After about half an hour Steffi found herself standing in a narrow street just off Rue Saint-Jacques near the Sorbonne, looking at an aged row of four-story flats. She stood there for a minute or two, then approached the central building, took a ring of keys from her bag, and inserted one into the ancient lock, which turned easily without a sound. Closing the great oak door quietly behind her, she ascended the stairs to the fourth floor and stood motionless on the landing. Overhead, an iron and glass skylight bathed the stairwell in the diffuse yellow glow of fading Parisian twilight. She could hear a Mozart piano concerto from behind the door in front of her. After what seemed a very long time, she gently knocked. The music stopped, there were footsteps, the door swung open, and she looked up into the eyes of a tall, thin, dark-haired man of about forty.

They did not speak. His face showed no surprise, revealed no emotion. The lovely young woman before him held his gaze. He reached out and lightly touched the line of her jaw with the back of his forefinger. His touch lingered and then delicately trailed down her elegant neck. In that instant, a powerful wave of eroticism swept over her. It was more than just pure sexual desire; it was a natural energy alive with the raw power to create, to build, to nurture, to protect. As she stepped forward, he gathered her into his arms and led her to the bedroom where they undressed without shyness and carefully began to make love. Steffi could see the shadowy rooftops of Paris in the last glow of twilight. She somehow felt as though, in embracing this lover, she was also embracing the city, caressing it, adding life to it, increasing its vitality, its virility. After a time, she felt his passion begin to crest, and she responded to encourage his natural impulse, to free him from any inhibition, to free Paris, to give the city spontaneous life, to strengthen and protect it from those who would tear it down block by block until not a single stone was left standing. In this act of passion, she sought to save Paris from the central conflict of civilization — the primal urge to create perpetually locked in moral struggle with the primal urge to destroy.

They lay in the dark breathing deeply. Steffi felt the city breathe with her. She sensed that he was about to speak, and she placed her finger to his lips.

"*Charles, non.*" She whispered. She knew that speech would only lead to reason. Spontaneity would be gone, and with its departure would come his work at the university, her life in Frankfurt, their differing views regarding the revolution, his wife, the difference in their ages, and all the rest. In that moment, she half understood Danny's irrational passion for revolutionary spontaneity, imagination, and improvisation. Danny knew that only the impulsive exercise of unfettered passion constituted real freedom, that any rationally derived, set program would necessarily contain traps.

Chapter Seven: New York

> Between the desire
> And the spasm
> Between the potency
> And the existence
> Between the essence and the descent
> Falls the Shadow.
> — T. S. Eliot, "The Hollow Men"

> Philosophy is to the real world as masturbation is to sex.
> — Karl Marx and Friedrich Engels, *The German Ideology*

Sunday, April 21, 1968

Ted Gold caught up to Kurt and Eliot on College Walk. They were returning from a graduate seminar on Social Data Analysis.

"Mark Rudd has published an open letter to Grayson Kirk,[1] the President of the University. Want to hear what he has to say?" Ted asked excitedly.

"Sure," said Eliot.

"He says, and I quote, 'Up against the wall,...! This is a stickup.'"

"Really?" said Kurt.

"Well, it's direct," said Eliot.

"Yeah, and that's not the half of it. Kurt, you were right, he is clearly using university issues to mask an all-out war on the whole damn Western society. Listen to this."

---

1 Mark Rudd's letter was dated April 22, 1968, the day before the demonstration began, but many sources contend that Rudd wrote his "open letter" several days earlier and that copies were circulating on the Columbia campus as early as April 19.

Ted took a sheet of paper from his pocket, unfolded it, and read, "'Your charge of nihilism is indeed ominous, for if it were true, our nihilism would bring the whole civilized world, from California to Rockefeller Center, crashing down upon all our heads.' Then there is this: 'We will take control of your world, corporation, your university and attempt to mold a world in which we and other people can live as human beings. Your power is directly threatened, since we will have to destroy that power before we can take over.' And later on, he says, 'We the young people whom you so rightly fear, say that society is sick and you and your capitalism are the sickness. You call for order and respect for authority; we call for justice, freedom and socialism.' Then he quotes the LeRoi Jones line, 'Up against the wall,...!' and signs it, 'Yours in freedom, Mark.'"

"Those are indeed LeRoi Jones' 'magic words,'"[1] said Eliot. "Let me see that."

"Who's LeRoi Jones?" said asked Kurt.

"A contemporary radical Afro-American poet," said Ted, handing the sheet of paper to Eliot.

"Well, he most certainly does sound radical," said Kurt.

"Oh, for Mr. LeRoi Jones, this is mild. In the same poem, he advocates the murder of the white man. 'Kill him, my man,' he says. In another poem its worse, 'Rape the white girls, rape their fathers, cut the mothers' throat,' or something like that."

"I'll never understand America," said the gray-eyed German, shaking his head.

"Well, I understand this, all right," said Eliot, still reading the letter carefully.

"It's our Mr. Rudd's reply to President Kirk's statement," said Ted. "You remember, the one he issued two weeks ago about the students' 'inchoate nihilism' whose sole objective is 'destructive.'"[2]

"That's what it appears to be," Eliot narrowed his eyes. "But I think there's more to it. It may not be what you think at all. If it's political, it's very shrewd — very shrewd, indeed,"

"Can you share this shrewd political insight with us?" asked Ted sarcastically.

"Sure. Didn't you tell me that, at the meeting, Mark said that he was going to contact the Student Afro-American Society about SAS members participating in the demonstration the day after tomorrow?"

"Yep, I think he has a meeting with Cicero Wilson tomorrow. He's trying to form some kind of alliance."[3]

"Don't you see? He's trying to get the black students to support the demonstration; trying to build our credibility with them. They've never really been with us. They think we're a bunch of spoiled middleclass white kids playing at revolution and

---

1 Amiri Baraka (as LeRoi Jones), "Black People," in *Black Magic: Sabotage, Target Study, Black Art: Collected Poetry, 1961–67* (Indianapolis, Bobbs Merrill, 1969), 225.
   "...[Y]ou can't steal nothin from a white man. He's already stole it, he owes you anything you want, even his life. All the stores will be open if you say the magic words. The magic words are: Up against the wall, motherfucker, this is a stick up!"

2 On April 12, 1968, Columbia University President Grayson Kirk issued a statement saying in part, "Our young people, in disturbing numbers, appear to reject all forms of authority, from whatever source derived, and they have taken refuge in a turbulent inchoate nihilism whose sole objectives are destructive. I know of no other time in our history when the gap between generations has been wider or more potentially dangerous."

3 On April 22, 1968, the day before the Columbia demonstration, Mark Rudd met with Cicero Wilson, the chairman of the SAS at Columbia, and formed a SDS/SAS alliance. "Columbia Timeline: Spring 1968," http:beatl.barnard.columbia.edu/columbia68/time2.htm.

---

spouting theory. It's not about theory with them. They see themselves as different, and they're right because their cause is widely regarded as immediate and very real."

"Yeah, but only 30 or 40 or so of them are militant enough to join us; it can't matter that much." said Ted.

"In the wake of the King assassination there may now be a lot more than that, especially if it's not just students but also people from the surrounding neighborhoods," Eliot argued. "Besides, can't you see what credibility and power having the Negroes in our ranks would give us? I mean the last thing the university wants is a race riot on their hands, especially not with all of us sitting right here in the middle of Harlem. The university doesn't want any black victims on its campus — white victims, they can live with, but not black.[1] Mark knows that. He knows that the American public generally regards white radical students as just a spoiled bunch of ungrateful middleclass brats."

"So the black students represent the true underclass, with a just cause," Kurt mused as comprehension set in. "You're right! They're a potentially real social and political force. Having them involved strengthens our position enormously. The university is afraid of them."

"Exactly," said Eliot, handing the letter back to Ted. "They represent an extension of the entire black community. No university is willing to take that on."

Ted looked at the single page carefully. "Yeah, it fits. The SAS is suddenly much more vocal. Just like us, they're becoming more radical under the new leadership, you know, Cicero, Bill Sales and Ray Brown[2]; but do you really think Mark has thought this thing through like that?"

"I certainly wouldn't put it past him," said Eliot. "I'm certain he thinks that an alliance with the SAS was never possible under the 'Praxis Axis' — with all the educational programs and theory, we must have appeared pretty silly to them. Now he's banking on the fact that the black students will see his new 'Action Faction' as a serious change in SDS policy, a clear switch to radical activism. This would also account for his recent concern over the building of the new gym in Morningside Heights. Up to now that's been a black issue. We have, of course, supported them in this, but it hasn't been high on our list. Now, suddenly Mark has placed it up there with the IDA and the unfair treatment of the 'IDA Six.' He's obviously trying to enlist black support for the demonstration."

"So, the LeRoi Jones rhetoric is just window dressing to impress the black leadership with how radical our fight against the forces of racism has become?" asked Ted.

"It's more than just that," said Eliot. "It's also Mark's way of burning the bridges behind us. If we weren't really revolutionaries before this letter, we certainly are now. There's no taking back an insult like this. In breaking with civility, he's showing the university just how far we have gone toward breaking with all of their norms. He's smart. If he's accused of being crude, he'll just say he's quoting modern poetry. The SAS should eat this up."

"So it's 'burn, baby, burn' if either the blacks or the university calls Mark's bluff," said Ted uncomfortably.

---

1 Stephen Spender, *The Year of the Young Rebels* (New York: Random House, 1968), 24-32.

2 Like the SDS, the SAS (Student Afro-American Society) had kept a relatively low profile at Columbia. In past years, their goals had mostly involved building black fraternity on campus. However, with the election of a more radical and outspoken leadership in Cicero Wilson, Ray Brown and Bill Sales, the organization began to lean toward activism. Bond, "Morningside Heights."

"I don't think Mark is bluffing," said Kurt.

* * *

Lying on his bed in Hartley that evening, Kurt Siegel was having another of his "little chats" with Karl Marx. He was still troubled by the question as to who would fight the revolution if the proletariat no longer represented the one true revolutionary agent.

"Karl, I've been reading more of Herr Doctor Marcuse. He seems so quick to abandon the workers as having sold out to capitalism. Still, I wonder, is it that he rejects them as the revolutionary subject, or is he just saying that they're not the *only* revolutionary subject? I'm puzzled. It would seem that the revolutionary battlefield of today has become issue driven: the war, the environment, race, women's rights, poverty in the Third World, and so on. These issues cut across all stratums of society and class, and therefore shouldn't the new revolutionary subject do the same? Or is it, forgive me Karl, an outdated idea altogether?" Kurt was silent for a moment, as if waiting for the great man to reply. "Whatever the case," he continued, "in my opinion, Doctor Marcuse is far too quick to champion the radical potential of intellectuals and students. How can we believe in a privileged revolutionary subject when social change seems to be propelled by so many diverse groups? I wonder what Danny would say to all of this."

After a moment, he rose and went to his desk. Clicking on the green shaded desk lamp, he took a gold fountain pen from his shirt pocket and began to write in German in a broad looping hand:

April 21, 1968

Columbia University

Dear Danny,

There is a crude but graphic saying here in America..."

* * *

"At the very moment when we are about to exercise the power we have worked so hard to build, I feel pulled in all kinds of different directions," said Eliot, playing with his salad. "It's unnerving."

Melissa Beam looked up from her spaghetti. She was one of those people who found great comfort in fixed routines and set traditions. She always made spaghetti on Sunday night. Eliot never seemed to mind the monotony.

"I can't explain it exactly," Eliot mused.

"Is this about the alliance with the SAS?" asked Melissa. Eliot had told her about Mark's letter and his "courtship" of the SAS.

Eliot regarded her carefully. She was very tall, over six feet — a full two inches taller than he was. Her blondish hair was cut short, and as usual she wore no makeup. Hers was a thin, sleek, angular look, not that of a classic beauty but a simple, attractive, intelligent look, earthy, healthy, natural. Her riveting blue eyes always fixed him in a way that was engaging, mysterious, and often sexy. Eliot had been both intellectually and physically attracted to her the first time they met, and their romance had been something of a whirlwind. After only two months of dating, they had begun comfortably talking of a life together. He had never experienced anything like this before. From an early age girls had attracted him, and he had even been involved with a few "serious girlfriends." However, he had never before considered a truly committed long-term relationship. For her part, Melissa had made up her mind after the first date. Eliot was the man she wanted, and she had remained totally committed to him ever since.

Eliot returned his attention to his spaghetti while pondering all of the various factions and groups that were suddenly spinning around the notion of a "New Left."

"That's part of it, I guess, but it's really something larger."

"Well, no matter how liberal we may be, as middleclass suburban 'white folks,' few of us can fully understand black America. It's hard for all of us; we are victims of history and privilege and circumstance, no matter how hard we try."

Melissa was quite liberal, and she and Eliot agreed on most issues; but Melissa was not a radical. Unlike Eliot, she sought solutions to what she perceived to be America's chronic maladies in the existing political system, despite the fact that she often had to admit that it was seriously flawed. Eliot, on the other hand, felt an occasional duty to give things a little extra-parliamentary push. Early in their relationship, Eliot and Melissa had come to understand their differences and had learned to live with them in an atmosphere of mutual respect. They had been together for over two years, although part of that time Eliot had spent studying in Germany. They reasoned that if their relationship could withstand such a long separation, then something good must be happening. Although they did not "officially" live together, Eliot spent a lot of time at Melissa's comfortable apartment on the Upper Westside.

"Yes," said Eliot, "we are victims, but that's not what's troubling me. If we are to embrace the Afro-American cause, then with which faction do we align ourselves? The NAACP, the Student Nonviolent Coordinating Committee, the Black Panthers, who? It's the same with all the other movements. Can we simultaneously represent the interests of the women's movement, the hippies, the Yippies, the GI organizers, the Black Panthers, all of other minority groups? Where does the true revolutionary constituency lie, who is the true vanguard — the workers, the black proletariat, the Maoists, the intelligentsia, the youth culture? Is a workable coalition possible? Do any of these groups share our beliefs in a truly democratic revolutionary movement?"

"No," said Melissa, "they all have their own ideals. All you can share with them is a common sense of rage."

The passionate young graduate student had to think about this. He concentrated on his spaghetti, twirling it deftly on his fork.

After a few bites he looked up. "Real rage is manifest only on the radical fringe. At the very radical heart of the times — like it or not — there's no real rage; there's only the youth counter-culture. For them the solution seems to lie in rejecting pretty much everything — everything, that is, except a weird kind of individual integrity — the integrity to 'do your own thing,' to 'drop out' and wash your hands of the whole ugly mess. They make terrible revolutionaries. It's as if they think that, by personally setting a living example of peace and love and community, they can change the world overnight without firing a shot. It's an opium dream, a kind of pacifist anarchy, if there is such a thing."

"Sounds a little like Jesus," said Melissa, her compelling blue eyes shining.

"And it's equally unrealistic," said Eliot. "Do we open our arms to these dreamers? Mark says we do. He sees them as just more bodies on the barricades. He doesn't care what they believe. I'm not so sure."

"Well, I'm not so sure that your assessment of the hippies or the counter-culture or whatever you want to call it is politically on the mark. Anyway, you and I may be a little too old to be a real part of any of that. Why not ask Martin? He's a perfect example, and believe it or not he can actually be both analytical and articulate when he is forced to it. He'll be here in a few minutes. I asked him to drop by to get some stuff that Mom gave me to give to him."

"It's supper time. I'm surprised he's not here already. He never seems to miss a chance to mooch a meal."

"Eliot! What a thing to say. Of course he's welcome; he's my brother."

"Easy. Just kidding. I like Martin. He's been a great help in building freshman support for the demonstration."

They ate in silence for a few minutes.

"When all the chips are counted," Eliot said finally, "politically, organizationally, if we align ourselves with either the forces of black rage or the forces of white counter-culture, we align ourselves with groups that have no ultimate plan, no program. They don't have a clue as to what society ought to look like after the revolution."

There was another silence.

"Then, of course, you have the majority of the students," said Eliot. "Some of them are in sympathy with our cause, but the rank and file will not support civil disobedience. Things are getting polarized. There are not so many people left in the middle any more. Now, it's not just the jocks who oppose us. As we grow, the conservative student opposition is also growing, organizing. They call themselves the Students for a Free Campus, and they'll probably try to stop the demonstration in some way. It could get messy. In the meantime, polarization has forced people to choose, and that means there are more of us now, too. Our ranks are swelling, but with disturbingly diverse groups. There is no longer a single ideological mainstream within the SDS."

"So you're left with nothing but your rage. Better make the best of it, sport; or join the rest of us at the ballot box," said Melissa. "Maybe you're not a revolutionary after all, my darling."

"Maybe not."

He returned to toying with his salad. There was a knock at the door. Melissa got up and returned with her lanky longhaired younger brother in tow.

"Jesus, I'm sorry," said Martin. "I didn't know you were eating. Want me to come back later?"

Eliot shot a smile at Melissa, who almost laughed but regained control and said, "Of course not, silly. Join us. There's plenty, if you don't mind spaghetti."

"Well," stammered Martin, "if you're sure you have enough."

"Have a seat," said Melissa. "I'll get you a plate. We were just talking about you."

"Nothing too nasty, I hope."

"No." said Melissa. "We were talking about the counter-culture, you know, the hippies and all. Eliot was trying to define the movement politically. We thought you might have some ideas."

"Yeah, Martin. What do you think your generation is really about?" said Eliot.

As Martin pondered his contemporaries and their place in the world, Eliot regarded him carefully. Like his sister, he was tall and very thin. If he could express himself the way Melissa had suggested, Eliot thought, he was the perfect subject for this interview. He was young, intelligent, well educated, and although he talked of dropping out, he had so far shown no signs of planning to do so. Nonetheless, he seemed thoroughly immersed in the emerging counter-culture of peace and love. He talked, acted, and dressed the part; he wore his hair long, spoke often of marijuana, dressed in flowing, brightly colored floral patterns, and condemned just about everything that conventional society held dear, albeit in a non-confrontational, totally passive, offhand, even pleasant way. Best of all, Eliot thought, he and his older sister were the products of a thoroughly middleclass, white, protestant, suburban upbringing. Their conversion to the New Left and their evolving left-wing politics was more typical than his own. Theirs was simply a widely understood reaction to the times. His was rooted in a long family intellectual tradition. His father had been a college professor and was blacklisted as a communist in the 50s, only to return to academics and eventually to teach Modern Poetry at Princeton and write several books on Eliot's namesake, T. S. Eliot. Like that great poet he revered, Eliot's father had been a scathing critic of Modern society in the West, and because of this Eliot's liberalism was a great deal more complex and intellectually mature than that of his contemporaries. His politics emanated from a long intellectual tradition, not simply from a generational sense of powerlessness and rage.

After a time, Martin cleared his throat. "Well, at the very bottom of it all, I think it's about television," he said.

"No, seriously," said Eliot.

"Really, TV made us what we are. This might sound a little 'druggy,' but then drugs are a part of it too."

"OK, I can't wait to hear this," said Eliot.

The self-styled young Ivy League hippie gathered himself to the task of explaining his vision.

"Well," he began, "all of us were born right after the Second World War. America is victorious, prospering, the rest of the world is in ruins, and for the first time there's this new technology, television. There's 'Leave It to Beaver' and 'Father Knows Best,' you know, a Norman Rockwell picture of the perfect American life. Life is good, everyone talks of freedom, equality, education, and opportunity and everyone has plenty of stuff. But little did we know that the TV image of a perfect America was setting us baby boomers up for a big fall."

Martin looked at Eliot, who gestured for him to continue.

"Well, first, we had just a few doubts, you know, the bomb, the Cold War. Stuff like that. Then, just as we got a little older, there was the Kennedy assassination, Civil Rights, and Vietnam. It was like everything came unraveled all at once; and suddenly we realized that it was all a great big lie. Television had not given us the truth; it had only tried to turn us into drooling consumers like everyone else. But that wasn't the only way television shaped our lives. There was a bonus. All of those hours of watching TV helped us to see through the hoax, to spot all the trap doors in the magic show."

"So you were able to identify the system's subtle manipulation." Eliot tried to help Martin articulate his TV education.

"Exactly! While the rest of the county bought into the hoax, we, the television generation, saw the strings in the puppet show. America was not a gentle nation of perfect families, it was a prison populated by docile robots masquerading as Ozzie and Harriet."

"So you could say that the artless clumsiness of television's bogus fakery revealed to you the moral poverty hidden within American affluence?" Eliot interpreted.

"Right! You just couldn't kid a kidder."

Martin was really revved up, and Eliot shook his head in disbelief.

"To a certain extent, my generation sees things just like you guys in the SDS are always preaching, you know, all that about 'the seduction of consumerism' and 'the oppression of the masses,' and all that stuff."

"So, you came to realize that the country you had learned to love as children — peaceful, generous, honorable — did not exist, and never has."

"Yeah, but our solutions are different. We're not interested in taking over administration buildings. We're interested in blowing people's minds. We're idealists, but not idealists who rebel. We're idealists who reject and withdraw. And that's what I think the counter-culture is all about, using what TV taught us to reject all of the phony values that TV portrays, all the lies of money, religion, sexual repression, family, education, justice, and on and on."

"Sounds cynical. What about the music and the drugs?" asked Eliot.

"Well, that's part of it, you know, music, drugs, a sense of, well, open community, but at the bottom of it all it's not cynical. Sure, it involves the rejection of our parents' values, but it's also about something new, something free, something spontaneous, a new way of life."

"So what you're really saying is that you think your rebellion is cultural, not political," said Eliot.

"Right! If we were to join your revolution, we would change it forever, change it into a festival of life, like the 'Summer of Love' last year in San Francisco, complete with rock and roll, nude grope-ins for peace, and, I don't know, maybe free food. You know, it's like the Yippies say, 'The Politics of Ecstasy.' It's like we want to create an alternative society. As Abbie Hoffman and the Yippies so eloquently put it, 'Rise Up and Abandon the Creeping Meatball.'"[1]

Martin took his fork and speared a large meatball from the huge pile of spaghetti on his plate, holding it aloft as if it were the Olympic flame.

* * *

Eliot Kincaid was more impressed with the freshman's assessment of the growing youth counterculture than he had expected to be. That night, he lay awake thinking.

"Perhaps Mark Rudd is right," he said as Melissa turned out the light. "Perhaps the hippies can be brought into the fold. They share our refusal to accept a cash-register society, but they're all over the place — a jumble of ideals, visions, and negations. They define themselves more by what they reject — by what they're not — than by what they are. Still, perhaps they can be effectively radicalized. Perhaps once they have cleared the ground of all the old identities, they can begin to establish a new one."

Melissa sighed.

"On the other hand, if the New Left seeks a political alliance with the culture of peace and love, they may be weakened by the association. They're courting the hippies, who are primarily an apolitical bunch. What's more, along the way, quite ironically, their evolving new culture is being embraced by the industrial system that it so vehemently rejects. It's becoming a 'style' and is thus being commodified and absorbed into the system.[2] So, in absorbing the counterculture, the system may also absorb the New Left."

Melissa yawned and snuggled up to him. "Go to sleep, Eliot. Even revolutionaries need to sleep."

"I was just thinking," said Eliot. "Your brother said that the youth movement was not about politics, that it was about culture. I don't think that's exactly right. They believe that if they each change their individual lives, then they can change culture,

---

1 Yippy slogan, summer, 1968. Fraser, et al., *1968: A Student Generation in Revolt*, 158.

2 Levitt, Cyril. *Children of Privilege: Student Revolt in the Sixties: A Study of Student Movements in Canada, the United States and West Germany* (Toronto: University of Toronto Press, 1984), 98-100.

and that politics will then change as a matter of natural course. It's not that they don't believe in politics; it's that they believe that politics is built upon culture. Marx argued that it is the other way around."

There was a short silence. Eliot was hoping Melissa would respond so that he could continue his thinking in the form of a conversation.

"Still, they may be of use," he said finally. "Maybe there is a way to fuse politics and culture. I remember in Frankfurt, Doctor Adorno assigned some reading by a Marxist named Walter Benjamin who wrote back in the '30s. It was pretty deep, but I remember trying to come to grips with the issue of culture. Benjamin felt that because culture has become something to be bought and sold in the bourgeois era, any potentially revolutionary value it may have is latent. That is, it has not been experienced politically. He said a curious thing for a Marxist. He said that 'the purpose of a materialist education was to give the revolutionary class the strength to shake off all the cultural treasures that are piled on humanity's back...so as to get its hands on them.'[1] Benjamin believed that culture could be re-fashioned into a revolutionary tool. Maybe that's what the hippies are all about."

"It's going to be hard to create much of a revolution with a group whose slogan is 'turn on, tune in, drop out,'" Melissa laughed.

"Yes, and there is something shallow, phony, theatric — I don't know, bohemian — something anti-intellectual about the whole movement. I can't quiet put my finger on it. I mean, it seems to me that the counterculture is doomed from the beginning, that it's attempting the impossible. It wants to 'short circuit history,' to propel itself out of the material realm of necessity into an ethereal realm of freedom,[2] to somehow magically just step outside the system. It's like they're only half right. 'Free your mind and the rest will follow,' they say. Well, perhaps freeing one's mind is the first step, but the 'rest' can't be that easy."

They were quiet again.

After a few minutes Eliot said, "Still, it may be that we could use the popularity of the cultural revolution to our political advantage."

"Where would that leave you with the Afro-Americans, the Third World, and your precious workers?" asked Melissa.

"It's a problem," said the young theorist. "You know, when I heard Doctor Marcuse speak in Berlin last year, he said that none of the student opposition was a revolutionary force — that the hippies were not the 'heir to the proletariat.' He believes that all the forces of opposition today are working at 'preparation and only at preparation...for a possible crisis of the system.' This work, he said, involves not only political but also moral opposition. 'The living human negation of the system,' he called it.[3] That's what the hippies are: 'The living human negation of the system.' They're having an impact. I can feel it."

---

1 Walter Benjamin, *One Way Street and Other Writings*, trans. Edmund Jephcott and Kingsley (London: Shorter, NLB, 1979), cited in Buck-Morss, "Walter Benjamin — Revolutionary Writer," *New Left Review*, No. 128, July/August, 1981.

2 Levitt, *Children of Privilege*, 99.

3 Marcuse, "The Problem of Violence and the Radical Opposition" in *Five Lectures*.

CHAPTER EIGHT: FRANKFURT

Rose of memory
Rose of forgetfulness. . .
— T. S. Eliot, "Ash-Wednesday"

The tradition of all the dead generations weighs like a nightmare on the brain of the living.
— Karl Marx, *The 18th Brumaire of Louis Bonaparte*

WEDNESDAY, APRIL 3, 1968

Just after midnight, an enormous blast rocked Schneider's Frankfurt Kaufhaus department store. Seconds later and blocks away, a second bomb ripped through another Schneider store. As the flames began to fill the night sky, a phone rang at the German Press Agency. On the line, one of the bombers, Gudrun Ensslin, was shouting, "This is an act of political revenge." Waiting in the shadows by the phone booth was her boyfriend and accomplice, Andreas Baader.

The bombings marked the beginning of what would later become the notorious Red Army Faction (RAF) and served as a noisy prologue to an almost impossibly bizarre story. The spectacular flames fueled by so many glittering luxury goods etched the first page in the sensationally twisted saga of the left-wing terrorist organization better known as the Baader–Meinhof Gang, a saga in which Andreas Baader and Gudrun Ensslin would be arrested and convicted of arson, would escape from prison with the aid of Elrike Meinhof, and, after being expelled from a terrorist training camp in Jordan, would go on to rob banks and bomb buildings all across Germany until Baader was captured after a lengthy shootout in Frankfurt in 1972. Then in a bizarre twist, in 1977, gang members would try to extort Baader's release by kidnapping a German official and hijacking a Lufthansa airliner. The hijacking would end when German federal police commandos raided the airport in Mogadishu, Somalia; and on that same day Andreas Baader and Gudrun Ensslin would be found dead of gunshot wounds in their respective prison cells. Though all official inquiries on the matter concluded that Baader and his accomplice committed suicide, many in Germany suspected that their deaths had been the result of extrajudicial executions.

On that fiery April evening in Frankfurt, as the two sumptuous emporiums of the German economic miracle were consumed in flame, no one could have foreseen the nine-year epic nightmare of Baader–Meinhof. Nonetheless, it was suddenly quite clear to all, as the flames rose to illuminate the Frankfurt night, that there was more burning on the extreme left than inflammatory rhetoric and fiery student protest. A host of incendiary figures lurked in the shadows beside Andreas Baader that night: anarchy, terror, and the ominous specter of fascism.

TUESDAY, APRIL 9, 1968

Along with the applause of his colleagues, the words of Ralf Dahrendorf, the chairman of the German Sociological Society,[1] rang in Theodor Adorno's ears as he walked to the podium to give the opening address at that organization's much-anticipated Frankfurt Conference commemorating the 150th anniversary of the birth of Karl Marx. In his introduction of Doctor Adorno, Dahrendorf, a former colleague at the Institute of Social Research, had remarked, "Those who had sown the wind might well find themselves unexpectedly reaping the whirlwind."[2] This seemed to Adorno an indictment, a charge that he himself had incited the maelstrom of youthful revolt and terror which only a week earlier had been so vividly illuminated by the department store bombings in Frankfurt. The newspapers overflowed with the radical rhetoric of Baader and his followers as they awaited trail. All over Germany, leaflets filled with the inhumanity of capitalism, exploitation, consumer terrorism, and militancy were being distributed.[3] As he reached the podium, Doctor Adorno felt crestfallen, deeply offended by Dahrendorf's remarks.

They had had such hopes for Dahrendorf at the Institute, but when he had resigned to accept the chair of the sociology department at Saarbrücken, much to the disappointment of Adorno, the little man had sensed conflict. "He hates everything we stand for," Adorno had written to Horkheimer.[4] Now he felt that Dahrendorf was condemning him for inciting the students while at the same time others were charging him with cowardice for not joining them.

Lately, he had come to feel isolated, alone — helpless to combat the overwhelming sadness that each day engulfed him like a shroud. As he approached the podium, he felt the same hollow sadness that he felt when the radical students treated him with disrespect, when Hannah Arendt and others attacked his editorial judgment. It seemed that everyone around him was questioning his integrity, that even his old friends were suddenly suspicious of his motives and skeptical of his conclusions. Yet beneath the anxiety and the sadness he felt little emotion, only a bleak, detached, impotent emptiness. As he began his address on Marxism, his mind drifted back to

---

1 Ralf Dahrendorf succeeded Adorno as chairman of the German Sociological Society in 1967. Dahrendorf had accepted Adorno's appointment to the Institute of Social Research in 1954. Müller-Doohm, *Adorno*, 443, 372-3.

2 Ralf Dahrendorf, *Verhandlungen des 16. Deutschen Soziologentages: Spätkapitalismus oder Industriegesellschaft?: Im Auftrag der Deutschen Gesellschaft für Soziologie*, Theodor Adorno, ed. (Stuttgart, 1969), 4, cited in Müller-Doohm, *Adorno*, 443.

3 Kraushaar, ed., *Frankfurter Schule und Studentenbewegung*, 1:302, cited in Müller-Doohm, *Adorno*, 443.

4 Müller-Doohm, *Adorno*, 443, 372-3.

"Against Barbarism," the lecture he had given in Berlin the previous year. In the summer of 1967, student unrest in Berlin had been growing in the wake of the police shooting of the protesting student Benno Ohnesorg in June of that year. The Berlin Senate had responded by banning demonstrations, and this prohibition had been emphatically condemned by virtually every student group. Earlier in the year, Doctor Adorno had sided with the students by publicly voicing his fears that the democratic spirit in Germany might be "stifled by authoritarian practices."[1] In July, he had been invited by his good friend Peter Szondi to speak at the Free University. His planned lecture for the occasion was "Against Barbarism," which dealt with a theme central to much of his work — namely that capitalist society contained inherent tendencies toward the barbarous evils of fascism, tendencies that he saw manifest in the students' misguided revolt. In the lecture, he took as his theme Goethe's *Iphigenie auf Tauris*, a drama based on the classical myth in which Iphigenie, the beautiful daughter of Agamemnon, is transported to Tauris. There the inhabitants experience unprecedented prosperity and victory over their enemies after suspending their ancient custom of making human sacrifices out of all visitors to the island. For Adorno, the land of Tauris supplied the perfect analogy for modern society with its inherent potential for barbarism. At the same time, Iphigenie symbolized beauty, the ideal of free education, and the possibility to strive successfully against society's barbarous tendencies.

He had begun his address to the students in Berlin: "Every debate about the ideas of education is trivial and inconsequential compared to the single ideal: never again Auschwitz,"[2] when suddenly the doors to the lecture halls had burst open and a group of students had stormed in carrying a huge banner that read, "Berlin's left-wing Fascists Greet Teddy the Classicist." There had been a chorus of boos from the majority of the students in the hall, and a scuffle had ensued in which a number of outraged students seized the banner and tore it to pieces. The troublemakers had then enjoined him to act as a witness in the trail of a well-known student activist in Berlin. The protestors left the hall when he refused to acknowledge the interruption and continued with his lecture.

In reference to the disturbance, he had warned in his Berlin lecture that sometimes the cause of humanity can lead to repression, calling this "the dark secret of revolution and an allegedly enlightened consciousness."[3] At the end of his remarks, an attractive young student in a green mini-skirt had tried to present him with a red teddy bear. Although he had tried to act outwardly unconcerned by the protests, in truth he had found the whole episode exhausting.[4] Nonetheless, he continued to see "Against Barbarism" as the perfect intellectual response to the students' entreaties urging him to join in their protests, for it explained how he could support their cause but not their methods.

"I believe that there is no possibility of using the university as a base from which to change society," he had told the students in Berlin. "On the contrary, isolated attempts to introduce radical change in the university...will only fuel the dominant resentment towards intellectuals and thus pave the way for the reaction." As always,

---

1 Theodor Adorno, *Frankfurter Adorno Blätter*, III, 1994, ed. Rolf Tiedemann (Munich: Theodor Adorno Archive),145, cited in Müller-Doohm, *Adorno*, 452.

2 Adorno, *Critical Models*, 191.

3 Theodor Adorno, "On the Classicism of Goethe's Iphigenie," in *Notes to Literature*, 2 vols., trans. Shierry Weber Nicholsen (New York: Columbia University Press, 1991), 2:161.

4 Theodor Adorno, Letter to Kolisch, July 17, 1967, in *Frankfurter Adorno Blätter*, VI, 2000, ed. Rolf Tiedemann (Munich: Theodor Adorno Archive), 58, cited in Müller-Doohm, *Adorno*, 455.

dark concerns regarding totalitarianism and the specter of fascism had lurked in the shadows of his powerful mind.[1]

Memories of Berlin faded as he was winding up his Marxian address in Frankfurt. He had at least lightly touched on the present student revolt, acknowledging that the students' protest was motivated by "revulsion from the world as swindle." It expressed, he said, the wish for freedom and change.[2] By the time he reached the end of his address, the gathered sociologists were hanging on every word. "The fact that the extended arm of mankind can reach out to remote, empty planets," he said, as Berlin receded from his consciousness, "but is unable to establish eternal peace on its own planet, is a striking proof of the absurd direction in which the social dialectic is moving."[3]

The audience rose to its feet and cheered him as he left the podium, and Theodor Adorno began to feel much better.

TUESDAY, APRIL 23, 1968

Steffi returned to Frankfurt from Paris on the overnight train. She was anxious to talk with Professor Adorno regarding her conversation with Herbert Marcuse and his remarks to the students at Nanterre. She also wanted to discuss Walter Benjamin, his unique vision of history, and her strange revelation at Les Halles. When she arrived at the Institute, Doctor Adorno was not in his office so she left him a note saying that she had met Doctor Marcuse in Paris and that she wanted a minute of his time to pass on his regards, etc. Later that afternoon when she passed his office, the door was open. She stuck her head inside, and he looked up and motioned for her to enter and to be seated. As always, he was lost in his note taking, and he did not speak for several minutes.

Finally, he pushed aside his work, and smiled at her, "So, you have met Herbert?"

"Yes, Herr Professor, I went to the University of Paris X at Nanterre with Karl Wolff and some others. Herr Professor Marcuse spoke to the students there. He sends you his regards, and he asked me to relate to you some of the contents of his remarks."

"Ah, so," said Doctor Adorno.

"I mentioned the pressure you were under from the very students that you have so inspired, and told him you were reluctant to lend them your active support because you feared the politicization of the university. He said to remind you that the university had already been politicized; and, if I may say so, Herr Professor, I think he is right."

"Yes, Fräulein, sadly, he is. We have discussed this in our correspondence. In the West, those in control of industry and society are gaining control of the university. We must not let this happen. If the university is already a compromised political tool, then we must free it, for only in a free state can it work directly toward the de-barbarization and the full democratization of society.[4] The oppressive forces that would

1 Theodore Adorno, "Gespräch mit Peter Scondi über die 'Unruhen Studentenbewegung,'" Kraushaar, ed., *Frankfurter Schule und Studentenbewegung*, 2:304ff, cited in Müller-Doohm, *Adorno:*, 455.

2 Theodor Adorno, "*Späkapitalsimus oder Industriegesellschaft?*" in *Gesammelte Schriften*, 8:368, cited in Müller-Doohm, *Adorno*, 444.

3 Adorno, "*Späkapitalsimus oder Industriegesellschaft?*, in *Gesammelte Schriften*, 8:363, cited in Müller-Doohm, *Adorno*, 445.

4 Adorno, *Critical Models*, 190.

control the university represent an ominous tendency within capitalism toward fascism. They're manifest in a cult of traditionalism and nationalism; an inclination toward militarism, religious fundamentalism, and violence; and an impulse to control the media and the educational system.[1] Only a free university can stand in the way of that, and therefore, although we agree with the students that university reform is necessary, we cannot and will not join in their revolt. No matter how well motivated, their violence runs the extreme risk of becoming part of this fascist tendency that they propose to fight — that is, if it is not part of it already. They're often intolerant of anyone who disagrees with them; they blithely interfere with the rights of others; and they stoop to hoodlumism and strong-arm methods. I fear that Herbert and I will never agree on this."

"Yes, in many ways I agree with you, Herr Professor. It seems to me that they're unable to distinguish between compromise and copping out, between dissent and raw intolerance. Still, Dr. Marcuse told me that you are closer together than you think. He believes that the new student opposition is driven by new needs for peace and beauty."

He was silent in thought for a moment. Steffi was referring to the highly theoretical concept which Marcuse had developed in his now famous book, *The One-Dimensional Man*, the idea that the needs of our current Western society are preconditioned, false needs, imposed by the system — needs to consume and to conform. The fulfillment of such needs may satisfy to a degree, but this also perpetuates toil, misery, and injustice, and insures the continuation of the system itself.

"Perhaps one reason Marcuse defends the hippies' cause is because he sees in their values the evolution of new needs for peace and love and beauty, needs that are not generated within the system," said Steffi after a moment.

"Hmmm, perhaps," said Doctor Adorno finally. "But I am not so sure that he is wise to lump the radical New Left in with the ambivalence of the larger American counterculture of the so-called hippies."

"Yes, Herr Professor, I wondered about that. I also wondered about his justification of the New Left as 'a new break with the repressive continuum of needs.' These new needs seem to flow from somewhere outside of his One-Dimensional society model."

"You sense a contradiction, Fräulein?"

"Yes, Sir."

"Very good, my dear, very good. So do I. However, you must understand that Herbert himself is aware of this. Remember, in *The One-Dimensional Man*, Herbert explicitly renounces any reformism or piecemeal change from within the system. He holds that only 'non-integrated outsiders' can be a truly revolutionary force.[2] He wrote me that he is working to resolve this matter."

"I never quite understood that at the time."

"Herbert is searching. He looks outside the system for his new revolutionary elements. He looks to outcasts, to the exploited and persecuted of other races and other colors, to the unemployed and the unemployable. He believes that opposition from outside the system will not be deflected by the system. It is an elemental force that

---

1 Tyson Lewis, "From Aesthetics to Pedagogy and Back: Rethinking the Works of Theodor Adorno," *InterActions: UCLA Journal of Education and Information Studies*, Vol. 2, Issue 1, Article 5, http://repositories.cdlib.org/geseis/interactions/vol2/iss1/art5.

2 Marcuse, *One Dimensional Man*, 256-7.

violates the rules of the game and, in so doing, reveals that the game is rigged."[1] Doctor Adorno looked at her. "It does seem contradictory, but Herbert is searching for radical politics, and this is how theory grows, my dear."

"The dialectic?"

"Perhaps. Is this the logic of history?"

"I don't know."

"Neither do I, Fräulein. That's the problem. Herbert is struggling with his theory while I suspect that the students are guilty of synthesizing their practice with rigid or even non-existent theory. This evokes horrific memories for me,"[2] he sighed.

There was a pause. Steffi looked at her aging mentor. She suspected he was lost in his own memories of the holocaust. He looked tired, limp. It was clear that all of this was taking its toll. She was suddenly concerned for his health. She wondered if he was getting enough sleep. She knew he suffered from some form of heart disease, but she was unclear as to how serious his condition was. Since the student unrest began a year ago after the police shooting of Benno Ohnesorg in Berlin, Doctor Adorno had tried to work with the students. He had been tireless in his opposition to the *Notstandsgesetze*, the proposed emergency laws, and against what appeared to him to be the government's lack of energy in combating right-wing parties. He had also come down strongly against the banning of demonstrations after the Ohnesorg shooting. In addition, he agreed that the university was in need of reform. Despite his agreement with the students on so many issues, he was reluctant to condemn America on the issue of Vietnam. How could he not feel gratitude to the country that had offered him asylum from the Nazis and later liberated his own country from the grip of oppression? In addition, he felt that the student revolt ran the risk of becoming left-wing fascism. Nonetheless, throughout the last year, Doctor Adorno had made every effort to meet with students and to attempt to define their differences. Adorno himself had broken his own rule banning politics from the classroom, when on June 6, only days after the Ohnesorg incident, he had begun his aesthetics lecture with a call for investigations into the shooting and asked the entire class to stand in memory of "our dead colleague."[3] Still the students hounded him. One leaflet called him an "indispensable theater prop of cultural events, who purveys critical impotence," and concluded that he "preferred to endure in silence the contradictions whose existence he has previously drawn to our attention."[4] All of this had had devastating effects on the sensitive man.

"The students," Steffi thought, as she regarded the weary genius, "have taken a toll."

After a moment she said, "Herr Professor, may I speak to you on a more personal matter?"

"Of course, my dear."

"While I was in Paris, the strangest thing happened. I was walking the back streets near Les Halles when I suddenly had a new insight into the writings of Walter Ben-

---

1 Marcuse, *One Dimensional Man*, 256-7.

2 Theodor Adorno, a letter to Herbert Marcuse, June 1, 1967, *Frankfurter Adorno Blätter*, VI, 2000, ed. Rolf Tiedemann (Munich: Theodor Adorno Archive), 44f, cited in Müller-Doohm, *Adorno*, 456.

3 Theodor Adorno, *Frankfurter Adorno Blätter*, III, 1994, ed. Rolf Tiedemann (Munich: Theodor Adorno Archive), 145, cited in Müller-Doohm, *Adorno*, 452.

4 Kraushaar, ed., *Frankfurter Schule und Studentenbewegung*, 1:264f, cited in Müller-Doohm, *Adorno*, 454.

jamin. I know that he was your friend and that you put great stock in his writing, but his work has always represented something of a mystery to me, Herr Professor. Then in Paris, I suddenly realized that Herr Benjamin's work is not about logical connections, not about cause and effect or temporal sequence. It is as if he explodes history into tiny pieces and then catches them all again, giving things new significance. He seems to rescue and redeem the fragments of history and fill them with new meaning and new connections. With Herr Benjamin, it is not that the past gives meaning to the present or vice versa. It is something completely new, something very radical."

"Very good, Fräulein, you have had a vision of the image of the dialectic wherein the past comes together with the present. It is an insight not given to many."

"I still don't really understand it."

"But you are on the path, my dear," the old man smiled. His soft round eyes seemed to glow. "It is the driving force of history, the positive against the negative, the thesis against the anti-thesis, the mainstream against the 'Other,' the Yin and the Yang."

"Herr Professor?"

"Yes, my dear."

"If I may be so bold as to ask, do you think Walter Benjamin committed suicide?"

Theodor Adorno frowned, looked down, and was silent. Finally he replied, "Yes, I do, but the circumstances of his death are puzzling. During the Spanish Civil War, Portbou, the village in the Pyrenees near the French border where Walter died, was a hot bed of pro-Franco sentiment in the midst of the virtually all-republican province of Catalonia. Certainly, in 1940, there were still close ties in that village to both the Germans and the Russians, and either group might have had reasons to want Walter dead. Still, he was undoubtedly depressed, and his reliance on drugs is well known. What is troubling to me is the note. He gave it to his traveling companion, Frau Gurland, who wrote to me in French supposedly repeating the words of Walter's letter, which she had memorized and destroyed according to his instructions. I have always wondered why a native German speaker would relay a message from another native German speaker to a third native German speaker in French. It's puzzling. Why do you ask?"

"I suddenly find myself haunted by Walter Benjamin," said Steffi. "He really walked across the Pyrenees from France to Spain with a heart condition?"

"Yes, that is the story — only to be turned back by the Spanish border guards at Portbou. He was headed for Lisbon. Dr. Horkheimer and I had obtained a United States visa for him but he had no French exit visa from the Vichy government, so he had to make a clandestine escape from France. He died in a small hotel in that little village — admittedly under mysterious circumstances, a drug overdose perhaps. No one really knows what happened to him or to the manuscript he was carrying. I too have been haunted by Walter's life and death for over 30 years," said Doctor Adorno. "That is why Gretel and I spent so much time editing his works for publication. That I am now accused of 'hoarding' and distorting Walter's work seems incredible to me after all the work I've done to see to the publication of Walter's work, first the two volumes of *Writings* back in the '50s and then the publication of *Letters* the year before last."[1]

---

1 With the assistance of Friedrich Podszus, Theodor and Gretel Adorno edited a two-volume set of Walter Benjamin's *Writings*, which was first published in German by Suhrkamp in 1955. Benjamin, *Gesammelte Schriften (Werkkausgabe)*,1980. Later, Adorno assisted in the editing of Benjamin's *Letters*, which were first published in German by Suhrkamp in 1966. Walter

"No one believes you manipulated Mr. Benjamin's ideas," said his assistant forcefully. "And the majority of the students admire and respect you more than you can possibly know."

"Thank you, Fräulein," said the little man doubtfully. His tone was dismissive as he sadly returned to the papers on his desk.

"Thank you, Herr Professor," said Steffi, rising to leave.

As she turned to go, the old man looked up and pondered her slender shape as she left the room.

"Lovely girl," he thought to himself.

Benjamin, *Gesammelte Briefe*, 6 vols., ed. Theodor Adorno Archive (Frankfurt: Suhrkamp, 1995-2000).

CHAPTER NINE: NEW YORK

The Fire Sermon
— T. S. Eliot, "The Wasteland"

Men make their own history, but they do not make it just as they please; they do
not make it under circumstances chosen by themselves, but under circumstances
directly found, given and transmitted from the past.
— Karl Marx, Attributed

TUESDAY, APRIL 23, 1968

At noon, about 500 demonstrators[1] gathered at the "sundial" in the center of
Columbia University's great quadrangle. A gift to the university from the class of
1885, the octagonal marble base designed by the famous architectural firm of McKim,
Mead, and White had once supported a great green granite orb seven feet in diameter,
the shadow of which had indicated the hour. As the twentieth century progressed,
the enormous stone ball had developed a disturbing crack and it was removed in
1946, leaving only the stump of the marble base. As the angry student demonstrators
massed in protest, only a few among them were aware of the faded inscription that
was still visible on the remains of Sanford White's elegant marble monument. "*Horam
Expecta Veniet*," it read, ironically urging patience. "Await, the Hour Will Come." On
this day, for these students, patience was a virtue unknown.

The crowd was larger than Eliot had expected. Some were jocks, who would
oppose any action; some, on the edges of the crowd, were students who were just
checking out the scene; but in general, most seemed supportive and pretty charged

---

1 Estimates regarding the number of demonstrators at the initial sundial meeting on April 23,
1968, vary from 300 to 1000. This discrepancy is understandable, since the numbers of both
demonstrators and onlookers grew as the demonstration progressed, and because it was at
first impossible to separate serious demonstrators from idle bystanders and from the ranks
of those opposed to the demonstration.

up. There were a few dozen very serious-looking black students concentrated in two large scowling groups and a generous spattering of surprisingly vocal girls from Barnard College just across Broadway from Columbia University.

Mark Rudd stepped atop the sundial pedestal base and used a bullhorn to address the growing crowd. The gathered students punctuated the end of each sentence with rowdy cheers. "We are here for three reasons," Mark barked. "To end the university's participation in the Institute for Defense Analysis and Columbia's service to the American military war machine," the crowd responded with an emphatic cheer. "To stop the construction of the new gym in Morningside Park and to end the university's racist expansion policy," there was another cheer. "And to end the university's unjust, arbitrary, and authoritarian policy and its efforts to suppress our rights to free speech and to protest." This last was followed by an enormous cheer.

Eliot turned to Kurt as the great cheer continued. "It certainly appears that the administration's singling out of the 'IDA Six' for punishment has resonated with the student body as unfair and repressive."

The German youth nodded. "That's because it's a free speech issue at heart. The students feel that in suddenly enforcing that prohibition against indoor demonstrations, the university has revealed its arbitrarily repressive iron fist. Certainly most oppose the war and any racist policies as well, but the disciplinary measures leveled by the administration at Mark and Ted and the four other demonstration leaders hits closer to home in the minds of most students. Mark and the others will broaden the issues soon enough, you watch."

Rudd was in fine form. "The university is now a means of production, producing the mechanism of human oppression," he continued to harangue the crowd. "It has been bought out by the military." There were loud jeers. "Fifty percent of the research done here at Columbia depends on defense money."[1] There were more jeers and shouts.

Robert Weaver joined Kurt and Eliot beside the marble sundial base. "You know that Mark plans to take this demonstration into the Low Library, don't you?" he said.

"Right," said Eliot.

"Well, don't look now, but there's a couple hundred jocks on the steps of Low just waiting."

Eliot and Kurt turned and looked across the great lawn. A tough-looking phalanx of student athletes and members of the ultraconservative Students for a Free Campus occupied the wide stone steps of the great Beaux Arts Library and Administration Building. In front of them stretched a row of uniformed campus security police. It was suddenly very clear where the line was being drawn.

Mark had moved on to the gym issue. "The construction of a high-rise building by a private institution in a public park," he was saying, "without even so much as a token effort to obtain the consent of the adjoining minority neighborhoods smacks of the worst kind of racist arrogance." Mark was about to introduce Cicero Wilson of the SAS.

"This might get really ugly," said Eliot. "I don't mind fighting the administration, campus security, or even the cops, but it won't help our cause to fight with other students. We need the illusion of solidarity here."

---

1 "The Columbia Revolt," a documentary film, Kit Parker Films, 1968.

There was more cheering as the young black student leader climbed atop the marble pedestal. "I don't think a gym nine stories high with facilities for black people in the basement with a back door is something that black people want,"[1] he began sarcastically.

"Maybe we can avoid a clash by changing our plans. I'll try to consult with Mark," said Robert, pushing his way through the crowd toward the SDS chairman, who was listening to Cicero Wilson's address.

"Columbia University lied," Cicero was saying. "University President Grayson Kirk wrote us a letter saying 'We have stopped the gym.' The next day the Board of Trustees states, 'We have stopped the gym temporarily.'"[2] A chorus of boos came in response.

Bill Sales, a doctoral candidate in international affairs, and another SAS leader followed Cicero Wilson. "If you're talking about revolution, if you're talking about identifying with the Vietnamese struggle, you don't need to go to Rockefeller Center, dig? There's one oppressor in the White House, in Low Library, in Albany, New York. You strike a blow at Low Library, you strike a blow for the freedom fighters in Angola, Mozambique, Portuguese Guinea, Zimbabwe, South Africa."[3]

"There it is," said Kurt. "See! It doesn't take much to make local university issues symbolic of a universal struggle. By themselves the local issues are irrelevant, but as 'levers' in a larger revolutionary machine they take on new meaning. The goal here is not the abolition of the IDA or the gym. It's the radicalization of an entire generation."

Eliot knew that Kurt was right. He also knew that he should have found this exciting, but for some reason it suddenly seemed manipulative and depressing. The atmosphere smelled more of anarchy than of the representative democracy they all talked so much about.

After Bill Sales concluded his remarks, Mark Rudd led the group to Low Library where the security officers and the jocks stood their ground despite the fact that they were greatly outnumbered by protestors. The demonstrators were told that the library was locked. At this point, a representative of University Vice President and Provost David Truman delivered a letter addressed to the demonstrators, who now stood massed before the marble steps. In the letter, Truman offered to meet with the demonstrating students immediately in McMillan Theater. After a brief conference, Mark and the other leaders told Truman's emissary that they would meet with the administration only if at that meeting they could form a "popular tribunal" and hold a trial then and there to adjudicate the six students who had been placed on probation for the earlier demonstration in Low Library. Vice President Truman's emissary said he could not agree to those terms without getting authorization from the president. When informed of this, the skeptical crowd shouted down Truman's proposal.

Meanwhile, it was becoming increasingly clear that trying to advance on Low Library constituted a dead end in many ways. Mark led the students back to the sundial, where someone proposed that they take their protest to the gym construction site in Morningside Park. This idea seemed to resonate with the throng, many of whom were feeling a bit impotent after having been turned away so easily by the relatively small contingent guarding the steps of the Low Library. The sagging crowd quickly regained its former frantic zeal as it lumbered down College Walk, across

---

1 "The Columbia Revolt," a documentary film, Kit Parker Films, 1968.
2 "The Columbia Revolt," a documentary film, Kit Parker Films, 1968.
3 Bond, "Morningside Heights."

Amsterdam Avenue, along the short block of 116th Street to Morningside Drive, and down the cascading flights of stone steps that led to the park below.

* * *

Traversing the lush spring glade of Morningside Park, the striking students suddenly found themselves in an unfamiliar world of blossoming green natural beauty. Across the broad avenue lay the flat, cold, colorless tenements of Harlem. At their backs was an un-scalable rock escarpment. High above them, atop craggy cliffs and ancient stone-block retaining walls, they could just see the tops of university buildings and part of the elegant mansion on Morningside Drive that served as the president's residence. The poignant imagery was impossible to ignore. There, impregnable, secured by its medieval ramparts, was the university, a bastion of privilege and a juggernaut of oppression, looking down with uncaring arrogance upon a gray plain of poverty, servitude, and want.

"The Bastille," Eliot shouted to his German friend as they ran, motioning to the great black stone blocks of the walls that formed the boundary between the park and the university above.

"More like the icy walls of Jötenheim," the German shot back. He was excited, and he called up images of the mythological home of the evil frost giants in Norse mythology.

His American friend had no idea what he was talking about.

Since the ground breaking for the new gymnasium in Morningside Park near 113th Street had taken place only two months before, the protestors found the site to be little more than a huge hole in the ground surrounded by a chain link fence. Students began to rattle the flimsy fencing in an effort to gain entrance to the dig. It was not long before a section gave way, and like vandals, they began to roll back the barrier. However, before the opening could be exploited, a surprisingly large number of police appeared, advancing resolutely across the park. They quickly waded headlong into the protestors with nightsticks swinging.

Eliot and Kurt were toward the front of the group that was trying to pass through the opening in the fence when the cops charged. A tall student in front of Eliot suddenly found himself face to face with a young patrolman who was wildly flailing away with his nightstick. As the student raised his arms to protect his head and face, the cop hit him hard in the midriff. There was a dull thud and the student went to his knees gasping for breath, leaving Eliot face to face with the young officer. Eliot held up his hands, palms out, to signal him to stop striking. He felt a glancing blow on his forearm. Just then several other students were pushed into the cop from the side and two more patrolmen came rushing to aid their now-stumbling colleague. Eliot saw his chance, and he and Kurt slipped through the opening created by the students who had been pushed. They began to make their way toward the back of the crowd, which now seemed to be moving slowly backward away from the fence and the line of attacking police.

All around them, students fled or scuffled with the police whose numbers seemed to grow larger magically with each passing second. Physical resistance was clearly a losing cause, and after a few minutes the students had all fallen back, leaving a line of police guarding the breach in the fence. Mark Rudd climbed to the top a large mound of dirt and shouted for everyone to return to the sundial to join about three hundred more protestors who had gathered there since their departure. As the students re-treated up the stone steps to the campus above, they could see the police leading one young protestor away in handcuffs.[1]

The clash had both shamed and angered the mob. They had been weak in the face of the cops' violent defense of the gym site, and they were suddenly determined to redeem their cause. The rebels may have lost another tactical skirmish in this run-ning battle but their numbers were growing, and they knew in their hearts that they would always control the moral high ground. The arrest of one of their own seemed to cast the university's immoral opposition and unjust policy in even starker relief.

Back at the sundial, there was confusion, more speeches, and more shouting.

"Their rage is intensifying," shouted Kurt. Psychologically, even those who earlier had been without political or moral commitment seemed to be moving to the left at near light speed.

Eliot was trying to convince himself that his arm was not broken. "They're be-coming 'radicalized,' alright, but no one is listening," he shouted above the din while continuing to inspect the angry bruise on his forearm.

The German graduate student nodded in thoughtful agreement. It had not oc-curred to him that a massive protest like this one might go unheeded. They were fighting for the ear of those in power, and so far, despite the considerable disruption they had caused, they had been unable to find even one suitable listener. Their cries of protest were echoing harmlessly through the empty halls of power.

As Eliot pondered the situation, he suddenly saw the light. A frustrating sense of powerlessness ironically accompanied the students' apparently unfettered freedom. He suspected that a similar helplessness accompanied by a similar hollow freedom lay at the heart of modern American life. To be free but powerless constituted a con-tradiction. Powerlessness rendered freedom illusory. In that instant, he had an eerie vision of the political impotence that was the true source of the students' anger. For them, change was at once imperative and impossible. Their situation was hopeless, and they knew it. Still, they lashed out at the system anyway.

Meanwhile, Bill Sales was back atop the sundial monument base inciting the largely white crowd. "What are white people going to do? It looks like today you are here to take care of business. Do I need to say more?"[2] The crowd responded loudly.

Mark Rudd and Eliot were on the same wavelength. They both knew that much more extreme action was needed to make their demands heard, but Mark's thoughts were pragmatic, not theoretical. As he took the bullhorn from Bill Sales and stepped up onto the sundial to speak, the crowd seemed to sense that something radical was afoot. "I think there is only one thing we have to do. We'll start by holding a hostage. We're going to hold whoever we can find in return for them letting go of the six people under discipline, letting go of the IDA, and letting go of the damn gym."[3]

That was what they'd been waiting for. The angry throng roared in agreement, chanting the LeRoi Jones line as Mark led the mass across the green and into Hamil-ton Hall, the combined undergraduate administrative center and classroom building on the corner of the quadrangle. Once inside, they took a stand outside the door of the office of Undergraduate Dean Henry Coleman.

---

1 Columbia University Junior, Fred Wilson ('69) was arrested at the construction site and charged with assault, criminal mischief, and resisting arrest. *The New York Times*, April 24, 1968, 30.

2 Fraser, et al., *1968: A Student Generation in Revolt*, 172.

3 Bond, "Morningside Heights."

Columbia University was under siege, and Mark Rudd was making up the plan of battle as he went along.

* * *

Dean Coleman was not in his office when the demonstrators arrived, but within a few minutes he came rushing down the hall and pushed his way through the huge crowd. The angry Dean stood in confrontation with Rudd who, in defiance of the university's recent ban of indoor demonstrations, shouted to the massed protestors, "Is this a demonstration?"

"Yes!" came the collective reply.

"Are we going to stay here until our demands are met?" Rudd bellowed.

"Yes," was the noisy response. And the chant began, "Hell no, we won't go."

Dean Coleman listened for a few moments. Finally he said, "I have no control over the demands you are making — but I have no intention of meeting any demands under a situation such as this."

Someone in the crowd shouted, "Get on the phone."

"I have no intention of calling the president or vice president of the university under conditions such as this," replied Coleman firmly.

The assembled crowd began to sing "We Shall Not Be Moved."

"We're here to stay," said Mark to the Dean. "Food is on the way."

Dean Coleman turned, went into this office, and closed the door behind him. Soon boxes of soft drinks, carrots, bananas, oranges, and cake were being passed around.[1]

* * *

According to SDS ideology, the proper way to guide a revolutionary society is through a participatory democracy, and once inside Hamilton Hall, Rudd and the other SDS leaders set about attempting to construct the political machinery to allow for the operation of such a democracy. This proved somewhat chaotic. Only a few of the student demonstrators had experience with democratic processes and procedures, and although most agreed on the general goals of the protest, the white protestors voiced a wide variety of opinions as to what constituted the appropriate method for obtaining these goals. The black protestors, on the other hand, were well drilled and felt little need for democracy. They let their leaders do the talking and appeared cool, well-organized, disciplined, and clearly fixed on their agenda, By contrast, the white students appeared immature, disorganized, and politically all over the place as they foundered in a sea of rambling speeches, debates, shouting matches, frustrated vacillations, and lingering uncertainties.

In the course of the white protestors' chaotic "democratic discussions," the issues were being blurred. The blacks wanted to barricade Hamilton Hall while the whites feared estranging the majority of white students whom they sought to radicalize. All the while, despite the presence of large numbers of demonstrators, Hamilton Hall was still alive with non-protesting students and administrators going about their normal routines.

As the afternoon progressed, rumors began to circulate on the Columbia campus that some of the protestors in Hamilton were armed or that armed black militants lurked in nearby neighborhoods. As these rumors circulated, all but the most serious demonstrators slowly abandoned Hamilton Hall. In the meantime, demonstration steering committees were elected consisting of five white student leaders representing the SDS, the PL (Progressive Labor Party), the SWP (Socialist Workers Party),

---

1 *The New York Times*, April 24, 1968, 30.

the YAWF (Youth Against War and Fascism), and the other radical groups, and five black student leaders representing the SAS. Once elected, these committees retired to create a list of demands.

Robert Weaver brought the news about the suspected weapons to Kurt and Eliot.

"Well," said Kurt, "I hope it's not true, but either way it will certainly make the administration think twice before calling in the police. This kind of speculation greatly strengthens the SAS's position. It wouldn't surprise me if Wilson and Sales are behind these rumors. If so, it's a shrewd tactic."[1]

* * *

As the evening wore on, the black students of the SAS grew increasingly frustrated with the inefficiency and contention produced by the white students' fumbling efforts at establishing rule by participatory democracy. In the view of the radical blacks, many of the white students were entirely too conservative in their approach, especially when it came to barricading Hamilton, a plan to which the black protestors were unanimously committed.

"The SAS has thought this all through," said Eliot, pulling Kurt aside. It was around 1:00 a.m. The students were seated in small groups on the hallway floors discussing politics, playing guitars, or sleeping wrapped in blankets. Eliot spotted Martin in one of the groups and went over to speak to him. Martin informed Eliot that he had just completed a head count and that their numbers had grown. He estimated that there were over 400 students inside Hamilton, and the percentage of black demonstrators had markedly increased.

From just outside Hamilton came the sound of singing. Martin and Eliot went to a window and soon were joined by Robert Weaver, Kurt Siegel, and Ted Gold. Outside they could see about 50 counter-protestors, most of them jocks, gathered around the statue of Alexander Hamilton singing all the verses to the "Ballad of the Green Berets," a song that had been a hit a year or so before.[2]

"Fighting soldiers from the sky,
Fearless men who jump and die."[3]

The off-key chorus droned insipidly on beneath the statue of the great American statesman.

"Alexander Hamilton," said Eliot. "Perfect!"

Martin looked at him questioningly.

"Hamilton didn't want a democracy," said Eliot. "He was afraid of what he called the tyranny of the masses. He wanted a king."

"Maybe they'll sing in tune after the revolution," said Robert, recalling a line from Dr. Zhivago.

"I think, in Pasternak's novel, it was the revolutionaries who sang out of tune," said Kurt.

---

1 Upon hearing of the occupation of Hamilton Hall, President Kirk had favored calling the police, but citing rumors of possible armed black resistance and concerns for Dean Coleman's safety, Provost Truman persuaded Kirk to embrace a more patient tactic. Bond, "Morningside Heights," 1.

2 *The New York Times*, April 24, 1968, 30.

3 Barry Sadler and Robin Moore, "The Ballad of the Green Beret," 1966; *The New York Times*, April 24, 1968, 30.

Their jokes seemed hollow in the face of the jocks' sophomoric display, so they listened in silence. Both the song and the singers seemed pathetic — blind, bungling, ignorant patriots propelled by a misguided, knee-jerk nationalism.

"I've been talking to Bill Sales," Ted said as they turned away from the window. "I must say the blacks have got it together. They know who they are. They know that they represent the entire black community, and accordingly they see this as a color confrontation. They've invited community leaders into the building — pros from the Harlem chapter of the Congress for Racial Equality, the Harlem Committee for Self-Defense, the United Black Front, and even from SNCC. That's why there are so many more black people in here than there were when we came in. These groups have a long list of grievances against the university, which has been buying up land and buildings in all the adjoining neighborhoods. They charge the administration with callous evictions of black people, with attempting to seize control of their local community, and ignoring their needs. Bill told a *Times* reporter that the university is 'trying to Bogart Harlem.'"[1]

Everyone laughed.

Ted was still serious. "We've got a problem. There are two entirely different political identities at work here. For the Afro-Americans, this is a demonstration, not a preamble to revolution. The whites are filled with revolutionary piss and vinegar, but by contrast they don't have a clue as to who they really are or what the hell it is that they're really doing. The white students are searching for their identity. The black students are in danger of losing theirs through desegregation."

"You're right," agreed Kurt. "Our goal is to radicalize more white students. The black students have no such need, and they have no patience for this kind of democracy. As an abused underclass they're already radicalized, and they have no intension of allowing a bunch of vacillating white middleclass brats to blur their identity, water down their aims, or erode their power. I'm afraid that we are about to lose the link to the true revolutionary class that Mark worked so hard to forge."

WEDNESDAY, APRIL 24, 1968

Despite this friction and the inefficiency of the white students' forums, a list of demands was finally approved and published around 2:00 a.m. It was agreed that the protestors would accept nothing less than the achievement of all of their demands. There was to be no compromise. These demands included amnesty for the IDA Six, an end to the university's ban on indoor demonstrations, the immediate cessation of the gymnasium construction, the creation of a open hearing policy involving both students and faculty for the adjudication of future disciplinary actions against students, the complete disaffiliation of Columbia University with the Institute for Defense Analysis, amnesty for all demonstrators, and assurances that Columbia University use its good offices to obtain dismissal of all charges pending against the demonstrators.

The student demands were presented to Dean Coleman, who after reading them over and discussing them on the phone with Vice-president Truman, told Mark Rudd and the other leaders that Truman was willing to meet in Wolfmann Auditorium right away to discuss their demands. After a brief meeting of the steering committees, the protestors told Coleman that they would not meet without a written guarantee of amnesty to all demonstrators.

Kurt and Eliot were getting tired. At about 3:00 a.m. they found an empty classroom and stretched out on the floor, but sleep would not come. After a time, the

---

1 *The New York Times*, April 24, 1968, 30.

intense young American said, "An awful lot of our demands deal with the issue of amnesty."

"Right," said Kurt, "and it's the one demand they will never grant. We might get them to stop the gym or break ties with the IDA, or even to change the rules a bit, but they will never let all of this go without reprisal. It would mean that they admit they're wrong. As SDS leaders, you and I are as good as expelled right now, no matter what else happens."

Kurt didn't seem to care. Eliot found this deeply troubling.

* * *

At about 4:30 a.m., Robert Weaver came to wake them. "Mark and Ted have come down from the steering committee meeting. They want to see everyone in the lobby."

The main entrance hall to Hamilton was packed. In the center were about 300 white students led by the SDS, and on the stairway, about 100 black members of the SAS and other black community leaders leered down at them. One of the black students held a sign that read, "Malcolm X University." Mark Rudd stood on the steps in front of the black students. He looked very tired.

"The members of the Student Afro-American Society have informed me that they want to make their stand here in Hamilton," Mark began. "After consulting with members of the Harlem community and other civil rights groups in the black community, they think it best that all white protestors leave Hamilton and take other buildings."

There was a crestfallen silence.

Mark continued, "I feel that this is appropriate. It is clear that we have divergent agendas, and that we can best support our brothers here in Hamilton by taking our protest to Low Library where we intended to go in the first place. Talk it over among yourselves. At five, we'll decide what to do."

The white students were clearly dismayed. Many felt the blacks were treating them with the same contempt they displayed toward the white establishment. Still, in all the discussions that followed there was no questioning the reason behind the blacks' ultimatum. Somehow, in the larger sense of things, the white students seemed to feel that they deserved this rebuke.

Eliot saw this immediately, and he addressed the gathered SDS members. "All of us feel that the black students are justified in almost any demand they might want to make of us because they have had to bear injustice from us as members of the white middle class. It is impossible for us not to feel guilty in this, and impossible for them not to feel that our presence dilutes their power in this situation. In fact, it does. These are psychological, social, and political realities. Still, they do not negate our zeal to set society right, to make amends. In this, we're all on the same side. I think we have no alternative but to leave and take another building."

There was a murmur of agreement that slowly grew into rowdy call to advance on their original target, the great domed marble sanctuary of Low Library.

Rudd seized the moment. "Up against the wall,...!" he shouted. The assembled mass picked up the chant, stormed out of Hamilton and ran headlong across the sleeping quadrangle toward Low. Brushing past the security guards, about sixty protestors led by Mark Rudd and Ted Gold charged the Library, smashed open one of the side doors of the sleeping neoclassical Goliath with a park bench and barricaded themselves in President Kirk's sumptuous suite of offices.

CHAPTER TEN: FRANKFURT

> All are twined and tangled together, all are recorded.
> There is no avoiding these things
> And whether in Argos of in England
> There are certain inflexible laws
> Unalterable in the nature of music.
> — T. S. Eliot, "The Family Reunion"

> Art is always and everywhere the secret confession, and at the same time the immortal movement of its time.
> — Karl Marx (attributed)

THURSDAY, APRIL 25, 1968

Details of the Columbia student uprising in New York did not appear in the European press until the Thursday morning following the Tuesday afternoon takeover of Hamilton Hall and the subsequent taking of the Low Library in the wee hours of Wednesday morning. Steffi Siegel noticed the article while scanning the morning paper in her office as she waited for Doctor Adorno to deliver a written reply to a group of striking sociology students with whom he had just met. She read the article twice with concern and then called Karl Wolff at the German SDS to see if he had more details. He did not.

Steffi knew her brother. Given his political leanings and activist nature, she was sure that Kurt had been involved, but she had no idea as to how violent the clash between police and demonstrators had really been. According to the UPI story in the Frankfurt papers there had been only one arrest, and the story made no mention of injuries. Still, Steffi's mind kept going back to the scene in front of the Springer Printing Plant only a few weeks before and to the brutality she had witnessed there. Could the Americans be suppressing or distorting critical facts with regard to the

Columbia riots? She thought not. Nonetheless, she felt a strange and irrational sense of concern for Kurt's safety. Even if the protest had been peaceful so far, there was no guarantee that it would not suddenly turn violent. She had seen that mindless dynamic at work first hand.

As she put down her office phone after speaking with Karl, she returned her attention to the small leaflet on her desk. It was a recent publication of the striking sociology students at the University of Frankfurt who were now conducting the "re-functioning" of university sociology seminars. This so-called "re-functioning" involved turning seminars into discussions of the reform of course studies and the exam system, as well as debates concerning broader political activities. Day and night, ever-changing strike committees occupied the seminar at the Institute for Social Research. In an act of political vandalism, striking students had painted huge rough letters over the main entrance. "Spartacus Seminar," they announced.[1]

Focusing on the leaflet Doctor Adorno had given her, Steffi began to read, "Critical Theory has been organized in such an authoritarian manner," it charged, "that its approach to sociology allows no place for the students to organize their own studies.... We are fed up with letting ourselves be trained in Frankfurt to become dubious members of the political Left who, once their studies are finished, can serve as the integrated alibi of the authoritarian state."[2]

She frowned. Before reading the article about the disturbances at Columbia, the object of her concern had been the pamphlet Doctor Adorno had carried with him when he left the "open discussion" arranged by Frankfurt's own striking students. The meeting had turned out to be anything but open. Student radicals had dominated the event, chanting slogans and interrupting discussions with long leftist political orations. Just before he walked out, there had been roaring cheers when a group of students entered the hall with a large banner inscribed with the slogan, "Smash Science."

At Doctor Adorno's side during this meeting had been his young colleague Doctor Jürgen Habermas, a former student of Horkheimer and Adorno. He had left Frankfurt in 1956 after a disagreement with Horkheimer. Recently, Doctor Habermas had returned to Frankfurt to take over Horkheimer's chair in philosophy and sociology, with the strong support of Doctor Adorno. Sometimes labeled a Neo-Marxist, in his work Habermas focused on an analysis of advanced capitalist industrial society and of democracy and the rule of law in a critical social-evolutionary context. He was particularly concerned with contemporary politics — especially German politics. As the two German intellectuals faced the angry students in April of 1968, few could have guessed that it would be Habermas who would carry the work of the Institute forward by developing a theoretical system devoted to defending the possibility of reason, emancipation, and rational-critical communication, which he insisted was embedded in modern liberal institutions. Long after Adorno and Horkheimer were gone, and in the face of a rising tide of postmodern thought in the closing decades of the twentieth century, it would be Habermas who resolutely defended Critical Theory and its belief in the human capacity to pursue rational interests.

Despite having keen defenses for their position, Doctor Adorno and his colleague had remained calm and generally silent throughout the discussion. In the end, they were called upon to renounce their institutional rights while continuing to carry

---

1 Müller-Doohm, *Adorno*, 464.
2 Theodor Adorno, letter to Herbert Marcuse, December 17, 1968, Kraushaar, ed. *Frankfurter Schule und Studentenbewegung*, II, 499.

out their professional duties. This, according to the striking students, was part of "smashing the bourgeois academic machine." At this, Doctors Adorno and Habermas had left the hall without a word. "'An alibi of the authoritarian state,' indeed!" Doctor Adorno had said as he thrust the pamphlet into Steffi's hand at the doorway to her office. "Wait here, my dear; you can deliver our reply to these young men in writing. I shan't discuss it further today." He seemed calm; Steffi could tell that he was upset, hurt, and frustrated.

Despite Theodor Adorno's frustration and anger, his reply to the students was measured and cool. In the written statement he gave to Steffi, he said that he and Doctor Habermas felt that cooperation with groups that inscribed "Smash Science" on their banners was completely out of the question. Technology, Adorno said, is not to blame, but the real culprit was technology's "entanglement with the social relations that hold it in their grip." Steffi knew that this last was a reference to Adorno's famous theory of the "technological veil" behind which real relations of power and domination are concealed.[1] Nonetheless, Doctor Adorno's message concluded, despite their objections to this kind of harassment, he and the others were still willing to continue a dialogue with the striking students. He said that they would publicly accept demands regarding specific concrete reforms at the university, such as the equal representation of faculty and students and the recognition of working parties as an institutional part of academic activities.[2]

Steffi mimeographed copies of Doctor Adorno's statement, took the copies to the meeting hall, and read the statement aloud to the lingering students. There were jeers and boos as she distributed copies to the striking students, but her mind was far away. She could not get the nagging concern for her brother out of her head, and she was haunted by ghostly memories of the eerie night battle between the mindless student mob and the equally mindless police legions that she had so recently witnessed. Steffi longed for May to arrive so that she and Kurt could be together on the weekend they had planned with their father in Paris.

* * *

Later that afternoon Steffi noticed a small group of students gathered outside the Institute's large conference room. As she drew closer to the locked doors of the great hall, she could hear the lilting strains of a lovely piano melody. She recognized the music immediately.

"What's that?" asked one of the students as she approached.

"The Beethoven C Minor Piano Sonata, Number 32, opus 111," Steffi replied, "his last sonata."

The astute young research assistant had to laugh as she caught the joke. "Some say it represents 'the triumph of order over chaos, of optimism over anguish,'"[3] she added, regaining her composure.

"No, I mean, is it a recording?" said the student, missing the irony entirely. "It sounds live."

"It is Herr Doctor Adorno," Steffi said.

"Get out! He's great."

---

1 Adorno, "*Späatlkaptalsimus oder Industriegesellschaft?*, *Gesammelte Schriften*, 8:363, cited in Müller-Doohm, *Adorno*, 445.

2 This meeting actually took place in December of 1968. Müller-Doohm, *Adorno*, 464.

3 Robert Taub, "Robert Taub on The Beethoven Sonatas" The Vox Music Group, 1998-2005, http://web.archive.org/web/20041014030811/http://www.voxcd.com/taub_beethoven.html.

"He's a world class musician and composer. He's also a noted music critic. He plays the violin and the viola too, and he was part of the classical music scene in Vienna long before he came to Frankfurt and became interested in sociology." Steffi had researched Doctor Adorno's career thoroughly. "He's written a number of famous books and essays on music theory. He even knew Schoenberg, Anton Webern, and Alan Berg in Vienna,[1] and he himself was quite well known. He told me that he still plays for the pleasure of it, to relax, and to ease his mind in times of trouble. I know this piece because he played it completely from memory for us once at an Institute party in his home. It's very demanding, but he played it with such ease. He plays everything with ease. He told us that he played it better when he was twelve. It's amazing."

"I had no idea," said the student who had inquired, shaking his head. "He's great."

"I've never heard him play here at the Institute. I had forgotten that piano was in there," said Steffi, again laughing. "He's a remarkable man."

She knew that Doctor Adorno, too, was enjoying his little joke, even though it was silently passing by somewhere in the ionosphere, many miles above these students' heads.

* * *

On the other side of the door Theodor Adorno was indeed laughing to himself, but the little joke he was making by playing the Beethoven Sonata was far more complex than even his talented assistant could have imagined. In his labyrinthine mind, music contained messages that went far beyond its emotional content, historical messages of dialectic import, messages in a bottle, cryptic texts long ago cast upon the turbulent seas of previous ages.

For years, he had contemplated a book on Beethoven, but the project was repeatedly put aside to make way for more pressing matters, first for *Negative Dialectics* and now for *Aesthetic Theory*.[2] For Adorno, music, like all art, and like thought itself, was molded by the dialectics of a contingent historical process. This meant that there could be no timeless, universally valid, musical method or process of composition. Composers of different eras worked with the evolving "existing stock" of materials of their era, with the historical material that they had at hand. Only composers who vary from what has been handed down historically are able to add something new. Thus, the little man thought, as he expertly made his way through the tangled black and white forest of the Beethoven sonata, "Music, like revolution, rejects the romantic notion of 'spontaneous creation.' Music, like all art, is a rational process of material, disciplined construction."[3]

He had once argued that Mozart had achieved his sublime music by reflecting the society of the imperialist epoch, which in his day was just beginning the process of achieving economic stability. Similarly, the music of Beethoven, he maintained, was both a response to the needs of the new bourgeoisie for luxury goods and an exploita-

---

1 Müller-Doohm, *Adorno*, 88.

2 Müller-Doohm, *Adorno*, 482; Adorno Theodor, *Beethoven: The Philosophy of Music*, trans. Edmund Jephcott (Cambridge: Polity, 1998) from *Nachgelassene Schriften*, ed. Theodor Adorno Archive and Rolf Tiedemann (Frankfurt am Main: Suhrkamp, 1993). This is a fragment from Adorno's posthumous papers, assembled from the various manuscripts and individual pieces of text that Adorno wrote on Beethoven.

3 Theodor Adorno, "*Reaktion und Fortschritt*," in *Gesammelte Schriften*, 17:135, cited in Müller-Doohm, *Adorno*, 112-3.

tion of rising nationalist ideologies achieved by the appropriation of folk melodies.[1] In Beethoven's music, Adorno saw the developing productive energies of bourgeois society with its new-found utopian hopes for a new world, but at the same time, he felt that Beethoven's true genius was that he simultaneously recognized that "the self-reproduction" of the growing enlightened society was false.[2] So it was that, for Theodor Adorno, the music of Beethoven balanced on a razor's edge. Its romantic ostentation is the pre-figuration of a new mass culture that celebrates its own triumphs while it paradoxically also suggests that modern triumphs might represent little more than stagnant illusions.[3] Beethoven, Adorno thought, understood the true nature of change. "He was the master of positive negation," he had written; "Discard that you may acquire."[4] As Adorno played, he knew that almost two hundred years ago Beethoven had breathed in the kind of freedom and fluid open-mindedness that these students were now smothering with their mass hysteria and their well-meaning but ideologically rigid left-wing zeal. That was the real joke.

His mind raced with his fingers. Stirred by Beethoven's musical vision of universal Enlightenment, he was lifted by the composer's harmonious proclamation of "order over chaos," of reason over myth. Science and reason had supplied the systematic intellectual underpinnings for a modern world of material promise, but this progress had come at a numbing price for the individual. Had Beethoven realized this? Surely, this was the dramatic tension in all of Beethoven's music. It was certainly what the Institute's precious Critical Theory was all about. He, Horkheimer, Marcuse, and Habermas labored to produce a critique of the modern scientific world that could save the stumbling project of Western enlightenment, reshape the individual's crumbling identity, and set the world back on the track toward the emancipation of mankind through science and reason. Here was the music of a science triumphant, and yet the heirs to this music now wanted to "smash science." There was something profoundly troubling here, something more complex than just the anarchist's impulse. Such a radical desire pointed to a fundamental shift in the coherent foundations of reason itself.

Sadly, it now seemed to Adorno that the students' call to "smash science" flew in the face of all that he had worked to achieve. It constituted nothing less than a bold-faced rejection of everything he stood for. Had the students lost faith in enlightened reason itself? He knew that something like this had been emanating from intellectual circles in France. Michel Foucault and others were carrying his own ideas to extremes, proclaiming the "death of man" at the hands of advertising, television, consumerism, the capitalist mythology, technocracy, and the domination of society by "things." The student revolts of 1968 seemed to resonate with this new critique of Reason and Authority.[5] Adorno understood this, but he did not believe that a new

---

1 Adorno, "Die Stabilisierte Musik," in Gesammelte Schriften, 18:721ff, cited in Müller-Doohm, Adorno, 113.

2 Rolf Tiedemann, "Vorrede, Editorische Nachbemerkung," in Adorno, Beethoven: The Philosophy of Music, 14, cited in Müller-Doohm, Adorno, 394.

3 Tiedemann, "Vorrede, Editorische Nachbemerkung," in Adorno, Beethoven: The Philosophy of Music, 76f, cited in Müller-Doohm, Adorno, 394.

4 Tiedemann, "Vorrede, Editorische Nachbemerkung," in Adorno, Beethoven: The Philosophy of Music, 39, cited in Müller-Doohm, Adorno, 394.

5 The French Post-structuralists, especially Jacques Derrida, Jean Francois Lyotard and Michel Foucault accepted Structuralism's "rejection of the centrality of the human self and its historical development that had characterized Marxism, existentialism, phenomenology, and psychoanalysis," but they "rejected its scientific pretensions." These men saw "deep

paradigm was emerging; he could never have guessed that in this highly charged political atmosphere a radical intellectual rebellion was taking place and that Postmodernism was about to be born. He knew that postmodern thought, unlike his own ponderings, contained the fundamental assumption that things were chronically amiss, that the world of science and enlightened reason had failed, and that beyond this dying modern world lay something completely new.[1] For Foucault and the other budding postmodernists, the student protests served as an indication that the baby boom generation had grown up with ambiguity and uncertainty as their fundamental experience of society.

In a strange way, these budding postmodern ideas reminded him of some of Walter Benjamin's wild speculations. Upon reflection, he had to admit that even he was a long distance from understanding everything Walter had written, and besides he had not read much of this new French theory at all. It was troubling. Could it be that at the bottom of it all, something else, something more plastic and less rigidly ordered, lay beyond the borders of the single systematic universal order sought by reason? Did the students know something he did not know?

---

philosophical problems with any attempt by human beings to be objective about themselves." The student revolts of 1968 "seemed to resonate with the post-structuralist critique of Reason and Authority." "It was in this highly charged university setting, within an increasingly complex social context, that postmodernism was born." Lawrence Cahoone, "Introduction," in *From Modernism to Postmodernism: An Anthology*, Second Edition, Lawrence Cahoone, ed., (Malden: MA: Blackwell Publishing, 2002), 4-6.

1 The early French postmodernists saw the student protests of the late 1960s as an indication that the baby boom generation had grown up with postmodernism as their fundamental experience of society and that their rebellions represented "incredulity" toward enlightenment, as Lyotard was to later put it. Adorno, Horkheimer and especially Habermas would continue to defend the modern legacy of rationalism, science, and liberal individualism by means of a thoroughgoing critique of Modernity (Critical Theory) and through a non-foundational version of enlightenment thought (Habermas). Jean Francois Lyotard, *The Postmodern Condition: A Report on Knowledge*, trans. Geoff Bennington and Brain Massumi (Minneapolis: University of Minnesota Press, 1984), xxiii-xxv; Jürgen Habermas, "An Alternative Way out of the Philosophy of the Subject: Communications versus Subject Centered Reason," in *Philosophy, Discourse and Modernity*, trans Frederick Lawrence (Cambridge: MA: The MIT Press), 294-326.

CHAPTER ELEVEN: NEW YORK

After the agony in stony places
Prison and palace and reverberation
Of thunder of spring over distant mountains....
— T. S. Eliot, "The Wasteland"

In every revolution there intrude, at the side of its true agents, men of a different stamp; some of them survivors of and devotees to past revolutions, without insight into the present movement, but preserving popular influence by their known honesty and courage, or by the sheer force of tradition; others mere brawlers, who, by dint of repeating year after year the same set of stereotyped declamations against the government of the day, have sneaked into the reputation of revolutionists of the first water. They are an unavoidable evil: with time they are shaken off.
— Karl Marx, "The Civil War in France"

WEDNESDAY, APRIL 24, 1968

At first light on the rainy morning following the occupation of Hamilton and Low Library, Eliot Kincaid looked out from President Kirk's spacious office upon the great lawn of Columbia University's central quadrangle. Considerable student support for the Columbia protesters was clear. Despite the drizzle, huge crowds of supporters milled about outside the two occupied buildings, but opposition groups were also in evidence. Eliot tried to assess the situation. It was unclear where the majority of the students' sympathy lay. Only about sixty or seventy of the white students, mostly SDS hardliners and a few of the more radical girls from Barnard College, had dared the early morning assault on the Low Library. Over in Hamilton, about seventy-five black students had barricaded themselves in, piling desks and chairs against the entrances. The occupants of these two buildings, he reasoned, represented only a small fraction of the original 500 or so demonstrators who had first met at the sundial and only a tiny percentage of the 4,000 or so undergraduates and of the 17,000 that comprised the entire university student population.[1]

The counter-protestors were in fact more numerous than Eliot knew, and they would soon dub themselves the "Majority Coalition." Nonetheless, at the same time, supporters of the demonstration would also claim to represent the majority voice of Columbia University's undergraduate students. In truth it appeared that student opinion was more or less equally split. Many of the students who opposed the methods of the protestors were nevertheless in sympathy with their cause, and it was becoming clear that those who had initially been on the fence were coming over to the side of the demonstrators in large numbers.

"The radicalization of the student population that the SDS has so often discussed may not have been fully accomplished," Eliot mused, "but it is definitely in the air."

* * *

Later that morning Mark Rudd reclined in the president's chair, smoking one of his cigars. All around him was chaos. Demonstrators were roaming the building, coming and going, and climbing in and out of the second story window of the president's office by means of the heavy iron grate that protected the ground floor windows and served as a handy ladder to reach the broad ledge outside the president's window. Some protestors were leaving, a few because they had decided that the occupation of the building was wrong or overly risky, most to recruit more strikers. Other students were riffling through drawers and throwing papers on the floor. One young man was lewdly displaying photos from a *Playboy* magazine he had found in President Kirk's desk.

Despite their growing dedication to activism, both Kurt and Eliot had always feared the mindlessness of the crowd. The irony embodied in this fear was not lost on either of these young revolutionary theorists. In theory, the surging masses were to be the tool of revolution, the oppressed classes or their intellectual vanguard rising up to confront the all-powerful oppressive old order. Out of this conflict was to come a new order; or so the theory went. Yet the crowd always seemed to betray this sacred trust; it seemed anything but the voice of a pent up enlightenment. This was the great contradiction that constantly plagued thoughtful New Left leaders like Eliot and Kurt: the crowd never seemed to represent freedom, progress, or Truth. The mindless mob was tyrannical, repressive. In practice, the active tool of revolution always turned out to be the living embodiment of un-Truth.

Appalled by their fellow demonstrators' behavior, Eliot and Kurt set about trying to organize them. There was work to be done, they told everyone. Meetings had to be conducted to devise strategy democratically. Something had to be done to dispel the atmosphere of chaos. They began to organize groups to go through the president's papers systematically in hope of finding information regarding the university's commitments to the Institute for Defense Analysis and details regarding the construction of the gym. They needed organization, direction, and communication, and to make matters worse the phones in Low were not working.

"So far we haven't had any strategy," Eliot told the group in Kirk's office. "All we have done is react to events as they have unfolded. I mean, we bounced from Low to the gym site, and then kind of wandered into Hamilton and ended up staying the

---

1 In its initial coverage of the Columbia revolt *The New York Times* stated the total 1968 enrollment at Columbia to have been around 12,000 students, while later *Times* articles, *Time* Magazine and many other sources cited the figure to have been 17,000 students.

---

night. Now we find ourselves here. We've been making this up as we go along. We need to make a plan, and then we need to stick to it."

Mark Rudd was in favor of taking more buildings. It had become quite clear to him that the blacks were right, that the taking and holding of buildings was the best way to get the university administration's full attention. Despite the fact that Low Library was still open and people were still freely entering and leaving the building, the demonstrators' presence had put a huge kink in the operation of the university, and with the barricading of Hamilton nearly half of Columbia's undergraduate classes had had to be cancelled. Still, there was considerable opposition to Mark's call to take more buildings. While they were debating the idea, Martin, who had just climbed in through the window, interrupted them, waving his arms above his head to get everyone's attention.

"The pigs are coming!" he panted. "They're massing in the quadrangle. I saw them."

Eliot went to the window. Outside in the drizzle, the number of sympathizers, counter-protestors, and on-lookers was growing. He felt a new tension emanating from the gathering crowds. Then, near the entrance to the quadrangle, Eliot spotted the distinctive light blue uniforms of a group of campus security guards moving along College Walk.

"Security guards," he said, "about ten of them. They'll be here in a minute or two."

Building barricades had been one of the items Eliot had planned to discuss in their strategy meeting, but there was no time for that now. As the guards approached, many protestors left the room to rally those who were out in the hall and elsewhere in the building. As the sound of the guards' hard leather boots against harder marble floors echoed down the halls of Low Library, only about twenty-five of the demonstrations remained in the President's office.

Eliot stood with Kurt, Martin, and the others preparing to confront the security officers. Unconsciously, he gently rubbed the angry red-purple bruise from the nightstick blow on his forearm. There was a deep soreness next to the bone. "At least they sent security guards," Eliot was thinking. "They're a lot more sympathetic than cops."

Ted Gold must have been thinking the same thing, for as the uniformed officers entered the room, he said in a loud voice, "We demand that you respect our right to protest."

"We haven't come for you," came the reply. "Be cool, and there'll be no trouble here."

Ted looked at Eliot, who shrugged his bewilderment.

"What the hell?" said Mark.

"Stand aside, please," said the head guard.

The officers looked serious but kept their eyes down, purposefully avoiding eye contact. While their cohorts stood just inside the door, two of the guards crossed the room, gingerly lifted the enormous painting off the wall behind the president's desk and left the room with it. With that, the rest turned and left, closing the door behind them.

"What the hell?" echoed Martin.

"It's a Rembrandt," said Kurt.[1]

---

1 There are several accounts of this story. *The New York Times* reported that the incident occurred around noon, and that security guards slipped into the Presidents Kirk's office to rescue Rembrandt's "Portrait of a Dutch Admiral" while most of the striking students were out.

"Materialist bastards; what a time to be worrying about a painting," said Mark. "They won't confront us over the university's complicity in a war in which tens of thousands die or over the charge of institutional racism, but they will confront us over a damned painting."

"It's a page right out of Walter Benjamin," said Kurt. "The administration is concerned with the safety of their painting as a commodity. As members of the bourgeoisie, they seek to maintain the painting's value as an exclusive possession, to emphasize the distinct boundary that capitalism creates between the commodity value of a work of art and its aesthetic value. In this way capitalism places formidable barriers between the artist and the people."[1]

"Who the hell is Walter Benjamin?" asked Martin.

"A critic and a Marxist of sorts," said Kurt. "He wrote in German, and not much of his work was been translated into English. Eliot has read him in German."

"Incredibly dense stuff," said Eliot. "*Schwerverständlich.*"[2]

"Easy for you to say," said Martin.

* * *

The "Rembrandt Raid" had a sobering effect on the protestors. They were suddenly aware of just how disorganized and how vulnerable they were. After the security guards left with the painting, running a pantomime gauntlet through the masses of sympathizers and bystanders outside the great marble building, most of the original group of demonstrators returned to the president's office, where Mark and Ted Gold began in earnest the process of democratically planning their strategy.

Mark strongly favored taking more buildings, but this idea met with considerable opposition. Eliot suggested that the group dedicate itself to a systematic search of the president's files in order to obtain more information about the university's "dirty little secrets."

"Hell," the passionate graduate student told them, "a year ago, no one knew that the university was involved with the Institute for Defense Analysis; in fact the administration flatly denied any affiliation. It was our own SDS brother, Bob Feldman, who discovered old de-classified FBI documents in the International Law Library detailing Columbia's institutional affiliation with the IDA.[3] Bob exposed the university's complicity in all kinds of Vietnam research — small arms for counter-guerrilla warfare, tactical nuclear warfare, chemical control of vegetation, the whole nine yards. The faculty and most of the students were outraged, and it's become our cen-

The official Columbia University website's account of the incident relates that at about 8:30 a.m., police entered the president's office to secure the painting and that all but 25 of the students, including Rudd, slipped out through the windows only to return after the police left. In *The Year of the Barricades*, David Caute indicates that Rudd and other SDS members fled at the sight of uniformed authorities and that only 27 remained to confront police. Most investigators side with the *Times* version of the event, although there is still some question as to exactly when the "Rembrandt Raid" took place. *The New York Times*, April 25, 1968, 41; "Columbia Time Line" http://beatl.barnard.columbia.edu/Columbia68/, David Caute, *The Year of the Barricades: A Journey through 1968* (New York, Harper and Row, 1988), 167, 480-81.

1 Walter Benjamin, "The Author as Producer," in *Understanding Brecht*, trans. Anna Bostock, (London: NLB, 1973); Walter Benjamin, "The Work of Art in the Age of Mechanical Reproduction" (1936), in *Illuminations* cited in Buck-Morss, "Walter Benjamin – Revolutionary Writer," *New Left Review*, No. 128, July/August, 1981.

2 "difficult to understand"

3 Wikipedia "Ted Gold," http://en.wikipedia.org/wiki/Ted_Gold, last modified February 5, 2006.

tral issue. I suggest we seize our chance to discover the whole sick story and turn it over to the press. It's the political opportunity of a lifetime. Let's get to it, secure our present position, see to food and other logistics, and table Mark's idea for now. Let's also clean this place up. The press will have a field day with this mess. It makes us look like vandals, not serious protesters with serious demands."

Mark was livid, and when the group voted to table his plan for taking more buildings he immediately resigned as SDS Chairman.[1] Only after counseling with cooler heads like Ted and Kurt was he persuaded to withdraw his resignation and to dedicate himself to the will of the majority.

* * *

After the meetings, things became more orderly. Some protestors began a systematic search of President Kirk's files; others began cleaning up the office, while still others set out to get supplies and to recruit more protestors. A large sign appeared in the window of Grayson Kirk's office. "Liberated Area," it read, "Be Free to Join Us."[2] As the afternoon wore on, several dozen more protestors joined the ranks of those in Low Library, and the demonstrators spread out to occupy more of the building, including the basement offices where the university's administrators normally operated.[3]

By this time, moving in and out of the buildings had become more difficult. In spite of the threatening rain and intermittent drizzle, huge crowds surrounded Low Library, filled its lobby, and wandered its halls. Sympathizers, counter-demonstrators, on-lookers, faculty, press, all combined to create a carnival atmosphere that was at once festive, angry, and surreal. Security guards and university administrative employees brought snacks and "treats" to the demonstrators.[4]

With members of the press seemingly everywhere, there was considerable "mugging" for photographs by the protestors. Groups of students posed with arms raised in salute. The varying convictions of the students were telegraphed by these gestures: the clenched fist of revolt for the ideological radicals and the "V"-fingered peace sign for the less extreme counterculture.

Several students had their pictures taken sitting at President Kirk's desk smoking his cigars. At one point Martin discovered a box of publicity "head shots" of President Kirk in his desk, and he and Ted Gold carefully cut the face out of a number of these photos to fashion masks. Then wearing these identical "Grayson Kirk faces" and clasping pipes borrowed from another of the desk drawers in their teeth, Martin, Ted, and about ten other protestors posed for the outlandish photograph that would later appear in *Life* Magazine: a dozen identical serious-faced pipe-smoking Grayson Kirks sat on the floor of the posh office looking up at the camera.[5] This was considered high satire. Eliot looked on disapprovingly, but he had to admit they did look pretty funny.

Hamilton was the arena for a similar circus-like scene. Although the press was barred, Harlem community activists and civil rights leaders paraded in and out of the barricaded building. At about 3:45 p.m., Dean Coleman was released, and in a brief statement he told the press that he and two other colleagues who had been with him

1 *The New York Times*, April 25, 1968, 41.
2 *The New York Times*, April 25, 1968, 41.
3 "Columbia Time Line: Spring, 1968" http://beatl.barnard.columbia.edu/Columbia68/
4 Frank Da Cruz, "Columbia University 1968," www.columbia.edu/acis/history/1968.html, April 1998-August 2005.
5 *Life* Magazine, May 10, 1968.

all night had been "treated very nicely" by the students. For their part, the students in Hamilton offered no explanation for the Dean's release.[1]

A spokesman for the group holding Hamilton, or Malcolm X University as they were now calling it, addressed the crowd and the press outside the building. Standing in front of posters of Malcolm X and Che Guevara, the young black man read from a prepared statement. "Black university students have barricaded themselves here," he said, "to protest the white racist university that encroaches on the Harlem community." The university has "raped the minds of black people through the IDA," he added.[2] He said morale was high, and then he ominously concluded by saying that "Negro groups" would arrive on campus during the night to augment the militant force in Hamilton.[3]

Not long after his release, Dean Coleman was back in front of Hamilton, attempting to defuse student anger aroused when a group of jocks shouted racial epithets and threatened to physically dislodge the Afro-American occupants from the undergraduate center.

Dean Coleman shouted at the demonstrators, "We're having a faculty meeting to try to solve this thing, but we can't meet if we have to continually come out here and police the situation." The angry jocks were ultimately dispelled less by the Dean's rhetoric than by a timely heavy rain shower.[4]

Meanwhile, in a show of solidarity with the protesting students, seventy graduate students in architecture refused to leave Avery Hall, a block to the south of Hamilton. Although the administration allowed them a "grace period" until 1:00 a.m. to conduct their protest, it was clear that they were not going to vacate Avery, and they began drawing up a resolution demanding that the university cease "overrunning adjacent areas in Harlem, and increase its efforts to recruit black and Hispanic students." As the evening wore on, more students joined the architecture students in Avery. Thus a third building was controlled by the demonstrators.[5]

As a heavy rain washed over Upper Manhattan, university security guards were already preparing to cordon off the occupied buildings and lock all the gates to the campus. "No Classes Tonight," the signs read. This night Columbia University would be placed under a tight lock down. No outside "Negro groups" would be allowed in to "augment" the militant force in Hamilton.

* * *

Despite the padlocks, the security guards, and the great iron gates that secured the embattled university, Columbia was not locked, on this night or on any other night, for the resourceful young Martin Beam. From the crawl space of an air duct in the basement of Hamilton, he had heard the black students preparing their address. Crouching in an old coal service tunnel beneath the security wing of Low Library, he had overheard campus security guards discussing possible police intervention. In fact, he had passed easily from Low all the way to his dorm room almost two blocks away in Hartley without encountering a single soul. He had easily made his way underground beneath Uris Hall and then passed below all of the enormous university buildings that lined Amsterdam Avenue —Schermerhorn, Avery, Fayerweather, Psychology, and Hamilton — all the way to the basement of Hartley.

1 *The New York Times*, April 25, 1968, 41.
2 *The New York Times*, April 25, 1968, 41.
3 *The New York Times*, April 25, 1968, 41.
4 *The New York Times*, April 25, 1968, 41.
5 *The New York Times*, April 25, 1968, 41.

Martin made these and many other clandestine subterranean journeys by means of a complex system of long-ago-closed interlocking underground passageways known as "the tunnels." The oldest of these brick-lined shafts dated back to the mid-nineteenth century, to a time before Columbia University had acquired the Morningside Heights property in Upper Manhattan, back to the days when all of this had been an asylum for the insane.[1]

Virtually every student who has ever attended Columbia knows of "the tunnels." Some of the larger passageways remained in use until the middle of the twentieth century. Recently a few students had been allowed to visit one of the larger underground shafts and had seen the narrow-gauge rails for the little coal car that was used back when all of the huge buildings were heated by coal-fired boilers. Still, most of "the tunnels" had long ago been closed off and bricked up, or so it was said. Despite the university's efforts to block off and bar access to this underground maze, a powerful image still circulated among the students: a vision of a labyrinthine web of coal tunnels and tunnels for steam and huge conduits for electrical service and phones and air shafts and massive storm drains crisscrossing everywhere beneath the campus. It was said that there were many levels of shafts from many eras of construction and countless modifications, a vast multitude of dark passages, some so hot you could not pass through, some flooded, some infested with rodents, some totally forgotten and unexplored even by the small cult of students who, like Martin, diligently sought to discover these ancient mysteries.[2]

* * *

Just after dark, Mark Rudd and the others in Low were eating bologna sandwiches made with the cold cuts, bread, and mayonnaise that Martin had produced as if by magic.

"Where'd you get this stuff?" asked Ted. "How'd you get all of this in here past all those jocks?"

"Through the tunnels," replied Martin, obviously very proud of himself.

Everyone was awestruck. They stared at Martin in silence. With his long hair and brightly-colored flowered shirt, he looked singularly out of place among the drab SD-Sers with their shabby black sweaters and faded corduroy trousers. Everyone knew that the fabled labyrinth of the "Columbia tunnels" was the stuff of local legend, of myth, of magic and fantastic speculation, but few among them had any first-hand knowledge that this mysterious underworld really existed, much less that it was accessible, passable, and comprehensible. They all stared at Martin in wonder.

Just then, an angry shout went up on the lawn. "Get them out!"

A single raw egg came in through the window and broke obscenely against the wall, and a crowd of counter-protestors on the green took up the chant. "Get them out! Get them out!"

Eliot went carefully to the window and peeked out. A large group of jocks and militant members of the newly-formed Majority Coalition stood in a light drizzle

---

1 The oldest part of the Columbia University tunnel system is a passage connecting Buell Hall with St. Johns Chapel. It dates back to when the Bloomingdale Insane Asylum occupied the present site of Columbia's Morningside Heights campus. Charlie Homans, *The Columbia Spectator*, March 27, 2003.

2 The largest of the tunnels emanate from the enormous power plant located below Fairchild Center, but many older smaller tunnels, vents, shafts, and crawl spaces can be accessed below these large passageways. Charlie Homans, The *Columbia Spectator*, March 27, 2003; "The Columbia Tunnels," www.columbiatunnels.org/wiki/

wearing jackets and ties and chanting, "Get Them Out." As they continued to chant, Mark Rudd joined Eliot at the window and loudly informed the crowd that they planned to stay until all of their demands were met. This prompted another barrage of eggs to foul the clean white marble walls of Low.

A group of faculty members could be seen circulating among the counter-protestors. Before long, the rain of eggs ceased, and after some discussion, the anti-demonstration rally broke up.

"Well, it appears that at least the faculty is on our side," said one of the girls from Barnard College, still munching her sandwich. "You didn't happen to bring any mustard, did you, Martin."

"Sorry," laughed Martin, "I'll put it on my list. By the way," he added seriously, "be careful of the faculty. They have their own agenda in all of this. They've been meeting all day in Philosophy Hall on the third floor.[1] They want to act as an intermediary between the administration and us, but they're split on key issues, and not many of them favor amnesty."[2]

"How do you know all this?" said Mark.

"I kind of overheard a little of their endless debating earlier today from the plenum of the air condition return in the central ventilation shaft over in Philosophy. They mostly support us on the gym, but they're split on the IDA. In spite of this, some favor supporting the administration and calling the police, owing to our civil disobedience. They're having trouble justifying our holding of Dean Coleman. Still, the majority oppose calling in the cops. They want to broker a truce and prevent violence. In that regard they'll all stand up to the jocks in our defense, like they just did, but I don't think they'll go for amnesty."

"Well, that's consistent with the proposal we got earlier today from the faculty committee," said Mark. "They offered to halt gym construction while continuing the university's association with the IDA, and to put together a three-part panel made up of students, faculty, and administration members to try student demonstrators.[3] Needless to say, this was totally unacceptable to us, especially on the amnesty issue."

"The amnesty issue is key," said Kurt. "It must be a pre-condition for any negotiations. At its heart, it constitutes an important political statement: that our actions are legitimate and that the actions of the administration and the laws that protect those actions are illegitimate."[4]

"Right," said Eliot. "Only amnesty will send the message that we have rights, and until we get those rights, we have to act in a coercive way.[5] I don't think the faculty really gets it. In many ways, they seem very naïve. They can't seem to see beyond present situation."

"Yeah," said Martin, "and besides, the faculty can't really offer us any deal, I mean, with or without amnesty. What I mean is they know that they can't really speak for the administration. They're trying to sell their solutions to us and to the administration at the same time. They have no real authority in any of this, so be careful."

---

1 Faculty meetings began in 301 Philosophy at 10 a.m. on April 25 and continued throughout the strike. "Columbia Timeline: Spring 1968," http:beatl.barnard.columbia.edu/columbia68/time2.htm.

2 Marvin Harris, "Big Bust in Morningside Heights," *The Nation*, June 10, 1968, 757-763.

3 *The New York Times*, April 25th, 1968, 41.

4 Bond, "Morningside Heights."

5 "The Columbia Revolt," a documentary film, Kit Parker Films, 1968.

"Well, we might do better negotiating with them than with President Kirk and Vice President Truman," said Mark. "Our meeting with Truman today was a total dead end. His attitude is intransigent and their position is completely legalistic. Truman told me that the gym was a matter of principle with Kirk, and that — get this — the university had a legal right to build the gym, and that 'legality alone determines both morality and justice.'"[1]

"I wonder where he studied ethics," said Eliot.

"Lucky for you he wasn't around during your American Revolution," said Kurt.

There was a pause as everyone contemplated this impasse.

"Martin, how did you manage to discover the tunnels, anyway?" asked Ted finally.

"Well, there are a few of us who are interested in this kind of thing, and we all share information. We go over old blueprints of the university's buildings and stuff like that. In fact, information about the tunnels has been compiled by students and handed down for decades. The tunnels are down there all right, and once you're inside they're pretty much open. The trick is knowing where and how to get into the system — a loose ventilation grate here, a pick-able lock or a crawl space there, a manhole, a broken wall panel hidden away in the sub-sub-basement. Then there's the trick of figuring out where you are as you move around down there. It's dark and hot and wet and it can be pretty disorienting. It's easy to get lost. I mean it's really complex and a real mess." The tall self-styled young hippie was getting excited. "One of the tunnels leads to the ground floor of Pupin Hall, which has been locked up since World War II. That's where they split the atom. I mean, for the damn atomic bomb — you know, the Manhattan Project. The old cyclotron is still there. None of that stuff has been touched since the war. It's incredible."[2]

"I'm surprised you don't glow in the dark," said Ted.

"Sometimes, down there, I wish I did," replied Martin.

* * *

Later that night Martin returned from another of his "little subterranean reconnaissance missions," as he called them.

"Big news, both good and bad," he told the group gathered in Kirk's office. "On the good side, there are now about 100 demonstrators holding Avery Hall, and just about an hour ago, small groups of protestors began slipping into Fayerweather. We now control four buildings."

"Now, that's more like it," said Mark smiling broadly.

"What's the bad news?" asked Eliot.

"The university has called in the cops. There're about 40 or so NYPD, both uniforms and plainclothes, in the security wing of Low right now. They're setting up a command center in the security officers' break room. I heard them talking on the police radio to other command posts as well, but I don't know where the other posts are."

---

1 On Wednesday afternoon, April 24, the second day of the strike, University Vice President and Provost David Truman met with Strike Steering Committee member, Edward Hyman. Hyman later reported the substance of that meeting to the press. *The New York Times*, April, 25, 1968, 40.

2 Pupin Hall, on 120th Street at the north end of the Columbia campus, was the site of critical research for the Manhattan Project for the development of the atomic bomb in the 1940s. Until 2003, the research area remained locked and untouched. Charlie Homans, *The Columbia Spectator*, March 27, 2003

"The cops wouldn't have come onto the campus uninvited," said Eliot. "The administration is planning something. We'd better get busy on some barricades."

"I brought this police-band scanner; it might come in handy," said Martin, opening the small duffle bag he carried and producing a strange wooden box with makeshift knobs and wires sticking out all around.

"Martin, you are a piece of work," said Ted. "Where did you get that old thing?"

"It is pretty old, I admit, but it still works. It has twelve crystals. That should cover most of the bands the police generally use."

"We should set up some sort of communication center here," said Mark. "We need to monitor the police frequencies 'round the clock, and we have to get in touch and stay in touch with the demonstrators in Avery and Fayerweather, as well as with the SAS in Hamilton. Martin, do you think you can find some walkie-talkies or citizen's band radios? Is it possible to string commo wire through 'the tunnels'?"

"I'll get on it," said Martin. "By the way, right now there's not much going on outside, and we can pass in and out of this building without any trouble; but that can change at anytime, depending on the mood of the jocks. Still, a squad of messengers might be the best and most reliable form of communication for us now."

"Good. Right now," Mark said, "we need to meet. We have to work out this commo problem, consider barricades, and determine a consistent strategy for everyone to follow if the pigs do try to move us out of here."

Kurt was thinking of one of Doctor Adorno's lectures that he and Eliot had attended in Frankfurt. Still contemplating Columbia's major role in the development of the atom bomb back in the '40s, he was trying to remember what the funny little genius had said about the bomb and revolution.

"First the A-bomb; now the IDA," Kurt thought. Then he remembered Herr Professor Adorno's exact words, and he said aloud to no one in particular: "Doctor Adorno once said, 'The building of barricades is ridiculous against those who administer the bomb. A practice that refuses to acknowledge its own weakness when confronted by real power...is deluded, regressive, or at best constitutes only pseudo-activity.'"[1]

"To hell with Adorno," said Mark Rudd. "Let's go with Marcuse on this one."

---

1 Adorno, "Marginalia to Theory and Praxis," cited in Müller-Doohm, *Adorno*, 463.

CHAPTER TWELVE: PARIS

> Here the impossible union
> Of spheres of existence is actual,
> Here the past and the future
> Are conquered and reconciled.
> — T. S. Eliot, "The Dry Salvages"

> History repeats itself, first as tragedy, then as farce.
> — Karl Marx, *The 18th Brumaire of Louis Bonaparte*

THURSDAY, APRIL 25, 1968

At Nanterre, Danny Cohn-Bendit read the news with great care. Accounts of the Columbia student revolt filled the Paris papers on the Thursday morning following the taking of Hamilton and Low Library. Danny knew that his friend from Frankfurt, Kurt Siegel, Steffi's brother, was at Columbia, and he wished that he could talk with him to get a firsthand report on the situation. The French student movement had drawn considerable energy from the recent student protests that had exploded in West Germany in the wake of the shooting of Rudi Dutschke. Could it derive a similar lift from the American students? Perhaps, but Danny knew that the situation in France was different. Student activists at Nanterre might be bolstered by the radical actions of others but not by any associated pedantic theory or ponderous left-wing ideology. The fiery radical leader knew that deep within *la France profonde* — the irreducible, essential, ineffable heart of the French psyche — there simmered a discontent more radical, more primal, more acute, more quick-to-anger than in any other Western democracy. He knew that French radicalism was visceral, not intellectual.

Danny put down the paper and pondered the situation. Since Herbert Marcuse had spoken at Nanterre, the situation had grown tense. Radical students continued to meet in the hall provided by the university, and lectures were regularly interrupted by demonstrations and rallies. No ideological group was safe from the students' idealistic zeal. On this very morning, Maoists had forcibly prevented a Communist Deputy from speaking at the university,[1] and a week hence, on May 2, Danny's 22nd of March Movement planned to hold a great anti-imperialism "teach-in" and rally at Nanterre. Still, he worried. There were rumors that the feared ultra-conservative and often violent "Occident"[2] would try to intervene and take over the university in order to shut down their leftist plans.

Danny folded the newspaper under his arm and walked down the steps of the administration building where he had been sitting and turned onto the wide allée that ran in front of the university's main buildings, International Relations, Psychology and Education, Social Sciences, English. All around him, the members of the 22nd of March Movement were busy organizing all of the various radical factions of the Left at Nanterre for a building-by-building defense of the university. Their battle plans included detailed maps of the campus and the approaches to the campus, the establishment of sentry posts, the mobilization of "raider groups," and the stockpiling of projectiles for defense. These measures were designed to repel any attempted intervention by the right-wing thugs and French ex-paratroopers of "the Occident" who, according to the information that Danny had received, were bringing in 500 reinforcements from all over the country for the May 2 assault on Nanterre.[3] The image of an army of reactionary ruffians closing in on the University of Paris X at Nanterre under the banner of the Celtic Cross, with its connotations of Christianity and the old Aryan tradition, filled the suburban air east of Paris with the pungent aroma of impending violence.

As he reached the School of English and turned toward the massive *Sciences Juridiques*, Danny waved to one of his Movement's sentries who was posted in the parking lot beside the great modern classroom building. "In all of this," he thought, "there is little room for the theories of Herbert Marcuse." Daniel Cohn-Bendit knew that most of his confederates in the French movement had never read Marcuse and cared little for such ideas. For his part, he took from the great German-American social thinker only what he needed: that the very nature of capitalist society was repressive, that such a society shapes its own type of alienated "one-dimensional man," and that criticism and destruction are a start toward construction.[4]

"The German and American students have been seduced by Herbert Marcuse," Danny thought to himself. At this moment, he didn't give a rat's ass about Marcuse, nor, for that matter, about Marx or Lenin or Trotsky or any of the others. His evolving view of the revolution, of politics, and of society was not tied to any stuffy theory. Except for the color of his hair, "Danny the Red," as the press had dubbed him, may not have been so "red" at all. As the student revolts at Nanterre progressed, the banner Danny waved appeared more like a black flag of anarchy than a red flag of communism.[5] Danny was coming to believe that social upheaval would not be the product of

---

1 The moderate Communist Party Deputy, Pierre Juquin, was barred from speaking at Nanterre on April 25, 1968, by a group of student activists. Labro et al., *This Is Only the Beginning*, 37.

2 The Occident (*l'Occident*) was a militant French right-wing activist group notorious for its heavy-handed treatment of left-wing radicals.

3 From an interview with an anonymous member of the 22nd of March Movement, in Labro et al., *This Is Only the Beginning*, 8.

4 Daniel Cohn-Bendit in a recorded interview by Pierre Hahn for the May issue of *le Magazine Litteraire* taped on or about April 25, 1968, in Labro et al., *This Is Only the Beginning*, 45.

5 *Time* Magazine, May 24, 1968.

the application of set, formal theory. He was becoming convinced that a real revolution must create itself as it goes along.

It was by means of this strange sense of the spontaneous creation of history that Danny Cohn-Bendit had galvanized his Nanterre cadre of "*enragés*" (angry ones), as they called themselves, after the proto-anarchists led by Jacque Roux during the French Revolution. This free-floating, evolving sense of a theory, which had its source only in action, was the glue that held the strange revolutionary bedfellows of the 22nd of March Movement together. As one of the original 142 members of the Movement explained in an interview: "...guys who if they were arguing about Marx would spit in each other's eyes in five minutes and say, 'You're full of bull, you're a counter-revolutionary, you don't understand anything in Marx and Lenin' — all kinds of things — well, these same guys with a specific thing, the occupation of a building — that is, a definite task that doesn't require technical competence but just has to be done: 'do it or don't do it' — they come to an agreement on it.... If you're a revolutionary, you do it. Or else, if you don't do it, you're not a revolutionary; that's the road of revolution, whatever you may think of Marx. To hell with Marx!"[1]

Thus, on their road to revolution, Daniel Cohn-Bendit and the others in the 22nd of March Movement saw a starkly polarized world. Everything was either bourgeois or revolutionary, status quo or action against the status quo. In this harsh light, these radicals had attracted many of the opposing left-wing elements that had been tending toward Communism and united them under the flag of anarchy. The structureless, leaderless union of the 22nd of March Movement functioned well as long as everyone focused on action and forgot about organization and ideology. The red flag and the black flag flew together only in their defiance of the bourgeois state.[2]

The sun was setting as Danny strolled past the enormous School of Economics. In the shadows on the Rue Noel Pons, he spotted another of the Movement's sentries. The young man saluted, and the stout redhead smiled and waved in response.

Danny wondered if the goal of the American students was the same as his: complete, untrammeled individual creativity, out of which political and social solutions would later evolve naturally. The anarchist side of Daniel Cohn-Bendit believed that revolutions are accomplished by the spontaneity of the people, whose instinct is always more accurate than that of their leaders. Revolutions, he thought, are the product of the force of many things germinating for a long time in the depths of the popular consciousness. At some unpredictable time they explode, touched off usually by apparently trivial events.[3] For Danny and the others of the 22nd of March Movement, revolution did not start with ideas, it started with action. It acquired ideas as it went along.

In this regard, despite his dynamic personality, Daniel Cohn-Bendit did not consider himself a leader. He preferred to be seen as a sort of "loudspeaker" for voicing group ideas.[4] In Danny's mind, the 22nd of March Movement, like the revolution they sought to incite, could not be led, for it created its marching orders spontaneously as it moved forward.

---

1 From an interview with an anonymous member of the 22nd of March Movement, in Labro et al., *This Is Only the Beginning*, 84-5.

2 Brown, *Protest in Paris*, 66.

3 Pierre-Joseph Proudhon cited in Brown, *Protest in Paris*, 85.

4 Daniel Cohn-Bendit in a recorded interview by Pierre Hahn for the May issue of *le Magazine Litteraire* taped on or about April 25, 1968, in Labro et al., *This Is Only the Beginning*, 42.

Chapter Thirteen: New York

Treble voices on the lawn
The mowing of hay in summer
The dogs and the old pony
The stumble and the wail of little pain
The chopping of wood in autumn
The singing in the kitchen
The steps at night in the corridor
The moment of sudden loathing
The season of stifled sorrow
The whisper, the transparent deception
The keeping up of appearances
The making the best of a bad job....
All twined and tangled together, all are recorded.
— T. S. Eliot, "The Family Reunion"

The reform of consciousness consists entirely in making the world aware of its own consciousness, in arousing it from its dream of itself, in explaining its own actions to it.
— Karl Marx, letter to Arnold Ruge, 1843

Thursday, April 25, 1968

Despite the leadership of the Columbia SDS with its penchant for pedantic leftist social theory, the Columbia revolt was unfolding in a surprisingly spontaneous manner, just as anarchists like Daniel Cohn-Bendit might have predicted. First, Avery Hall had been occupied by protesting architecture students on the evening of April 25, and then scores had joined the newly declared protestors in Fayerweather Hall in the early hours of April 26. These actions had occurred independently, without leadership from organized radical elements. The occupation of Avery and Fayerweather seemed to materialize magically from the release of the pent-up feelings of repression that many students harbored, the spontaneous expression of deep-seated student notions of powerlessness, alienation, and anger. To the surprise of many, widespread sympathy for the daring of the handful of radical activists, whom the rank and file had often collectively referred to as "pukes" in the past, was leading to the mobilization of hundreds, if not thousands, of undergraduates and graduate students. By the evening of the 26th, six hundred students were inside occupied buildings, and hundreds of sympathizers stood watch outside.[1] Support for the demonstrating students was also beginning to galvanize with scores of faculty members and graduate assistants, especially in the face of the administration's unbending and highly legalistic intransigence.

"There's about fifty holding Avery," said Martin, "and maybe as many as two hundred in Fayerweather."

"Great!" said Mark. "What about commo?"

Mark had sent Martin to reconnoiter and specifically to check on the leadership and the communications setup in the newly occupied buildings. A Strike Coordinating Committee had been set up on the third floor of Ferris Booth Hall, and it was Mark Rudd's plan to restructure the Strike Steering Committee to include representatives from each of the occupied buildings.[2]

"They have all set up communication centers. The phones seem to be working again almost everywhere, but this could change at any time. I managed to get a CB set into Hamilton. All of the occupied buildings now have radios linked to our citizen's band frequency. There's also a set in the Coordinating Committee office in Ferris Booth, and we also have a few walkie-talkies working and a system of runners standing by as a backup.[3] We've have access to a number of mimeograph machines, and we are churning out all kinds of bulletins, lists of demands, and manifestos.[4] As far as I can tell, all the buildings are operating democratically and have elected their own leaders."

"Good! What else?"

"Well, the faculty, now calling itself the Ad Hoc Faculty Group, is meeting again in 301 Philosophy. They're talking about closing off the buildings. Meanwhile, the jocks are meeting down at the gym, debating whether to physically throw us out or barricade us in and starve us out," said Martin. "Coach Rohan is trying to talk them out of interfering."[5]

"We'd better lay in some supplies, just in case," said Mark.

"Oh, by the way," said Martin, changing the subject. "I got us these pins. You know, so we can recognize ourselves. I mean the faculty has taken to wearing those white arm bands and the jocks and the Majority Coalition are wearing their jackets and ties and some of the demonstrators are wearing red armbands and the SDS has

---

1 *The New York Times*, April 27, 1968, 18.

2 *The New York Times*, April 27, 1968, 18; "Columbia Timeline: Spring 1968," http:beatl.barnard.
   columbia.edu/columbia68/time2.htm.

3 "The Columbia Revolt," a documentary film, Kit Parker Films, 1968.

4 *Time*, May 3, 1968. 48.

5 In a meeting at the gym on April 26, Columbia University basketball coach Jack Rohan was
   able to convince angry student athletes not to resort of physical retaliation against the protestors. "Columbia Timeline: Spring 1968," http:beatl.barnard.columbia.edu/columbia68/
   time2.htm.

its same old red and white buttons, you know, the 'Columbia SDS: A Free University, A Free Society' buttons from last year. The police have their uniforms, or at least some of them do, and the security guards have their light blue duds. The fence sitters are taking to wearing light Columbia blue armbands, and there are even a few black armbands being worn over in Fayerweather, so ..... Well, I thought that the strikers and the strike sympathizes could use something consistent. These are a little rough, I know, but then...you know...there's a war on out there."[1]

Martin opened his duffle bag and produced two paper sacks. He turned one of the sacks up and poured its contents onto the table. Out clattered about two hundred round metal pin-on buttons, the kind one wears during a political campaign. The top half of each button featured the top of a white starburst reversed out of a red background and the single word "STRIKE!" in black letters against the white half-starburst. The bottom half of each button was crudely blacked out with magic marker.

"These are 'Strike for Peace' buttons. I got them from the national Student Mobilization Committee to End the War in Vietnam. You know, the day after tomorrow is the nationwide students' 'Strike for Peace' day.[2] I just marked out everything except the word 'strike'; so now all of us 'pukes' can have a button, even those of us who are not in the SDS. What do you think?"

"Cool," said the Barnard coed who had been flirting with Martin the night before. She took a handful of buttons and began passing them around.

"I also got these," said Martin, dumping the second bag onto the table.

A hundred or so very small solid red buttons rattled onto the tabletop. "These are the buttons that the plainclothes cops use to identify each other so they don't bust each other's heads in. I thought they might come in handy."[3]

"Martin, you are a piece of work," said Ted.

* * *

The possibility of a blockade of the buildings posed new problems. So far, demonstrators had been able to come and go pretty much as they pleased. There had been some harassment from the jocks on the green, but with so many sympathizers in the crowd, bold protestors had been able to come and go more or less freely. Bringing in supplies had been a little more difficult, but Martin's knowledge of the tunnels had helped, and so far there had been no shortage of food or other supplies. On the first day, Low Library had been a three-ring circus with the press and on-lookers roaming the halls, but after what many of the strike leaders considered bad editorial coverage on the first day, they barred the press on Thursday morning and restricted access to the building. With the front door blocked, the only way in was to climb the iron grate to the second floor ledge outside President Kirk's office and enter the building through the open window.

At about noon on Thursday, to everyone's great surprise, Tom Hayden climbed in through that window. Mark, Ted, and a few of the leaders who had met Hayden

---

1 Frank Da Cruz, "Columbia University 1968," www.columbia.edu/acis/history/1968.html, April 1998-August 2005.

2 On April 27, 1968, almost a million students, by some estimates, participated in the largest student strike in US history. There were anti-war parades and demonstration all across the country. These mass actions reflected the underlying antiwar sentiment of tens of millions. *International Socialist Review*, Vol. 30, No. 6, November-December 1969, 26-50.

3 Photos and discussion of all the Columbia strike buttons, Frank Da Cruz, "Columbia University 1968," www.columbia.edu/acis/history/1968-buttons.html, April 1998-August 2005.

at SDS events in the past greeted the organization's famous co-founder warmly. The rest stood awe-struck.

Tom Hayden was a real celebrity. He had become involved with the SDS while a student at the University of Michigan in the early 60s, eventually splitting the organization off from the tired, Old Left, socialist faction of the SLID (Student League for Industrial Democracy). Along the way, in 1962, he had penned the now-famous "Port Huron Statement," the original and still operative manifesto of the New Left in America.

With light eyes and a somewhat scarred complexion, Hayden had an easy way, but he somehow also emoted intense passion. The former SDS national president explained to the protestors in President Kirk's office that for the past several years he had been working with inner-city youth in Newark and that when he had heard about their protest, he had been preparing to move to Chicago. "I thought to myself," he laughed, "it would be terrible if the revolution actually started and I was driving across the country."[1]

Most serious SDS members at Columbia had read the "Port Huron Statement." It was a document prepared by an idealistic, articulate, and concerned student who possessed a great deal of faith in the established norms of democratic action within the pluralist political culture of the United States.[2] However, by 1968, its thoughtful rhetoric seemed mild, and Hayden himself, like all active radicals of the era, had become further radicalized by his experiences in the civil rights movement, in the student riots at Berkeley, and in anti-war demonstrations all across the country.

Kurt had just finished reading Hayden's new book about the 1967 Newark race riots. "The tactics of disorder will be defined by the authorities as criminal anarchy. But it may be that disruption will create possibilities of meaningful change," Hayden had written. Still, his central point was rooted in contemporary politics. "Violence can contribute to shattering the status quo but only politics and organization can transform it. We are at the point where democracy — the idea and practice of people controlling their own lives — is a revolutionary issue in the United States."[3]

Tom Hayden was quick to assess the situation at Columbia. In the occupied buildings, he found a miniature of his own formula for radicalization: a community of shared risk. "Danger, Defiance, Democracy," had been his theme.[4] For Hayden, this was what politics was all about, and he was obviously planning to join in, to help with his leadership and vast experience, and to stick it out to the bitter end.

* * *

Facing the possibility of a blockade, Mark had sent a number of those occupying Low out to try to muster more "recruits" and to scrape up supplies. In the event that Low became blocked off while they were gone, they had pre-arranged a meeting place so that Martin could lead them back in through "the tunnels."

Late that afternoon, Martin returned from his listening post in the third-floor air duct. He found Mark and few others in President Kirk's office. "I've been over in Philosophy," he told the abbreviated group. "Things are getting kind of hairy over there.

---

1 James Miller, *Democracy in the Streets: From Port Huron to the Siege of Chicago* (New York: Simon and Schuster, 1987), 291.
2 Christian Erickson, "Up Against the Ivy Wall, Part 2. Columbia University, May–June, 1968," from *Shock Wave: Transnational University Based New Left Revolts: March-October 1968*, http://trc. ucdavis.edu/erickson/mru/sw.htm.
3 Tom Hayden, *Rebellion in Newark* (New York: Random House, 1968).
4 Miller, *Democracy in the Streets*, 291.

Some of the faculty crashed Kirk's press conference early this afternoon, and that pissed off the administration, who, by the way, are talking about canceling classes until Monday."

There were cheers and mutual congratulations all around. After things quieted down, Mark turned to the lanky freshman. "What else, Martin?" he asked.

"Well, after the press conference, Provost Truman came to Philosophy 301 and spoke to the faculty group. He took a really hard stand, and after he left a lot of the faculty sounded off about the administration's mishandling of everything. It got pretty rude; I mean, pretty rude for faculty members. Then they formalized the Ad Hoc Faculty Group, electing a chairman and a steering committee just the way we've done. Finally, they passed some resolutions. They want immediate suspension of the gym construction, the establishment of the three-part disciplinary deal that they proposed before, and then they sort of swore an oath to place themselves between the police and us should the administration call in the heat. While all of this was going on, the Majority Coalition tried to throw some of the demonstrators out of Fayerweather, and the faculty intervened and got them to stop. They met with the jocks in McMillan Theater, and things must have gotten pretty weird because when they got back to Philosophy, there were some who didn't trust the jocks and the Majority Coalition and some who seemed to be taking their side. It was pretty messy. They seem to be split."

The "recruiters" and supply runners were making their way back into Low Library. As food was stored away, Mark called a meeting of the Strike Steering Committee to discuss Martin's "intelligence report." Martin disappeared back into "the tunnels" and the rest of the group in Low began the evening chores, making supper, shaking out blankets for the night, and cleaning the office and restrooms. Most of these students had read about communes, but few had ever been in one. As the hours in the occupied buildings stretched on into days, they all began to realize that they were now living a communal life, and many found a comforting satisfaction in their shared endeavor, their mutual support, and their blossoming group consciousness and sense of mission. A keen sense to group identity and personal closeness grew out of their shared peril, and slowly individuals gave way to the familial will of the collective. For most, this was a new experience and one that strengthened their revolutionary zeal.

FRIDAY, APRIL 26, 1968

After almost three days in Low Library, most of the demonstrators had barely slept at all. A few, like Eliot and Kurt, had tried to keep regular hours, but with all the meetings and comings and goings it was difficult. At about 1:00 a.m. on Thursday morning, Martin shook Eliot awake.

"Eliot," he whispered, "the cops are coming."

"What?"

"I just heard them down in their command post in the security wing. They're sending plainclothesmen first, followed by uniformed cops if needed. The administration has asked them to clear the buildings."

Kurt was also awake now. "How long do we have?"

"I don't know. It sounded like they were on the way."

"OK, I'll talk to Mark. You two get Ted and Robert and get everyone in the building in Kirk's office and in the hallway outside the office. We'll do this thing just the way we discussed."

Martin and Kurt rushed out to find Ted and Robert.

"And get the other buildings on the line. Let them know what's happening," Eliot shouted after them.

One of the most laboriously discussed topics of the protestor's seemingly endless democratic meetings had been what to do when the cops come. Some urged compliance, some resistance. In the end, a strategy of passive resistance won the day. The plan was to sit down, link arms, and force the cops to carry each protestor individually from the building. This might get them a few bumps and bruises, but it would surely avoid any serious injury. "We'll make the pigs carry ten thousand pounds of 'pukes,'" one protestor had vowed.

When Eliot found Mark, he had other things on his mind. "I just got off the phone with Fayerweather. Some of their people and about twenty guys from this building, including Tom Hayden, have just taken Mathematics Hall," he said. "We now control five buildings."

"That's great, but Martin thinks we've got cops on the way here right now," said Eliot. "We'd better execute the sit-in plan. Ted and Robert are getting everyone up to speed."

Even as he spoke Ted Gold came rushing in. "I can't find Hayden and the group in the basement," he said.

"They're taking Mathematics Hall," said Mark. He seemed confused.

"Wow, everything all at once."

* * *

There were about one hundred and fifty protestors in Low Library when the police attack came. About twenty-five tough-looking plainclothesmen approached the main entrance via the hedge-lined central walkway that led across the broad lawn to the south. Above them on the white stone steps, dwarfed by the mass of the great neoclassical Library, a score of faculty members had locked arms. Their white armbands seemed to glow in the dark. All around, students were coming out of the dorms. Word of the attack was spreading, and no one wanted to miss the show. Columbia's great South Lawn was slowly filling up with on-lookers.

As the police approached, about ten of the self-appointed faculty "guards" stood their ground. There was some pushing and shoving. After a brief scuffle, the cops produced nightsticks from beneath their coats and began to swing away. One of the faculty went down, blood streaming from his head.[1] The others rushed to his assistance, leading him off across the green in the direction of President Kirk's mansion on Amsterdam Avenue. The plainclothesmen formed a defensive line at the top of the stairs and a few of them began to fumble with the locked doors of Low.[2]

"It won't be long now," said Eliot, turning away from the window. "We'd better join the others. Everyone be cool."

In President Kirk's office and in the adjoining hallways, everyone sat on the floor with arms locked. The building was strangely quiet. They waited in silence for the echoing sounds of hard soles on cold floors. After what seemed like a very long time, Martin got up and went to the front window overlooking the grand staircase.

Bathed in the soft illumination of the campus streetlights, the great lawn seemed to glow below him. It was almost empty. The gathering mob of students had disappeared, and the police were nowhere to be seen. A few students loitered here and

---

1 A French instructor, Richard Greenman, was struck in the head by police. He was treated at St. Luke's Hospital and released. *The New York Times*, April 27, 1968, 18.
2 *The New York Times*, April 27th, 1968, 18.

there in the shadows and a lonely handful of faculty members once again stood guard at the top of the steps in front of the ornate entrance to Low Library, their armbands appearing phosphorescent in the eerie half-light.

CHAPTER FOURTEEN: FRANKFURT

> Our dried voices, when
> We whisper together
> Are quiet and meaningless
> As wind in dry grass
> Or rats' feet over broken glass
> In our dry cellar.
> — T. S. Eliot, "The Hollow Men"

> ...man is at last compelled to face with sober senses, his real conditions of life, and his
> relations with his kind.
> — Karl Marx and Friedrich Engels, "Manifesto of the Communist Party"

FRIDAY APRIL 26, 1968

Theodor Adorno labored late into the night describing in detail his despair in yet another letter to his trusted friend, Herbert Marcuse. Twice Gretel had called him to bed, and twice he had promised that he needed only "another little moment."

"Dear Gretel," he thought to himself. "What would I do without her?" Yet his eye so often wandered. He pushed away the thought, and returned to more weighty deliberations.

In the weeks following the Springer riots, the interruption of academic life in Frankfurt had not been confined to student disruptions in the university's classes held at the Institute for Social Research. The entire campus had been affected. In the growing momentum of a nationwide March on Bonn, planned for May 11 to protest the proposed repressive Emergency Laws, the belief was spreading among students all across West Germany that a truly revolutionary situation was materializing. Strikes were organized, buildings were blockaded, university administration offices were occupied, and Johann Wolfgang Goethe University was re-christened Karl Marx University.[1]

"Everything is topsy-turvy here at the moment," Professor Adorno wrote to his old friend. "Quite a few of the lecture rooms are occupied. Many seminars cannot take place, including some of the most progressive ones. Valid student claims and dubious actions are all so mixed up together that all productive work, even sensible thought are scarcely possible.[2] I am deeply troubled by this. It seems that everything we have worked for is being crushed beneath the mindless onslaught of student radicalism. We are helpless before its power, for it does not respond to reason. I can no longer eat or sleep. I feel weary, empty, constantly depressed and alone."

Despite increasing student pressure, Theodor Adorno had remained steadfast in his refusal to lend open support to the students' actions, and despite his disagreement with Marcuse, he continued to write regularly to his colleague, laying bare his troubled soul. "The responsibility is great," he wrote to him in Paris, "if you are aware as I am of the contradiction between the students' movement and their actual situation."[3]

Professor Adorno knew that Doctor Marcuse had his own personal problems. Although his Americanized colleague had minimized his difficulties in his correspondence, it was well known that Doctor Marcuse's open support of student protest and revolt had made him extremely unpopular in many circles in the United States. He had even received threats on his life; his faithful students often stood guard at his home in California; and the FBI had finally been called in.[4] Criticism of Marcuse's work had spanned the political spectrum. From California's rightwing gurus, from orthodox Marxist liberals, even from the Pope, a great deluge of censure had rained down on the aging intellectual, characterizing him as a kind of latter-day pied piper corrupting the minds, morals, and manners of the young.[5]

For his part, Marcuse had concluded that the student revolts represented "a new sensibility," a period of "pre-revolutionary radicalism," a radical enlightenment prior to material change, a period in which education would "turn into praxis — social awareness into demonstration, confrontation, and rebellion."[6] In the complex mind of Theodor Adorno, Marcuse's conclusions represented a bold alteration to the character of the Marxist historical revolutionary agent, an unwise manipulation that attempted artificially to prop up the Marxian insistence that, at the moment of revolution, theory and praxis will become one. Doctor Adorno had his own revisionist ideas about Marxism. His growing fear was that, under Marcuse's inadvertent tutelage, the students were becoming increasingly troublesome because they suspected that the revolution was near.

Nonetheless, he knew that despite their disagreements, despite Herbert's support of the student revolt and despite his attempts at intellectual justification for

---

1 The majority of the student strikes and the re-naming of the university actually took place toward the end of May, 1968, after the apparent success of the May 11th March on Bonn. Müller-Doohm, *Adorno*, 460.

2 Theodor Adorno, letter to Herbert Marcuse, December 17, 1968, in Müller-Doohm, *Adorno*, 464.

3 Theodor Adorno, letter to Gabriele Henkle, May 17, 1968, in Müller-Doohm, *Adorno*, 460.

4 Müller-Doohm, *Adorno*, 463.

5 Kellner, *Herbert Marcuse and the Crisis of Marxism*, 1.

6 Herbert Marcuse, *Essay on Liberation* (Boston: Beacon, 1969); 6, 53, in Kellner, *Herbert Marcuse and the Crisis of Marxism*, 287.

their civil disobedience, his friend did not believe that the revolutionary moment was at hand any more than he did. Adorno believed that all the radical events of the decade had simply lifted Herbert Marcuse out of his old Marxist pessimism and inspired him to undertake a revisionist search for new modern revolutionary subjects. Doctor Adorno sensed that his friend was guilty of fashioning theory to fit the facts of the present situation. It seemed to him that Marcuse had been inspired by the depth of the students' resolve, both political and moral. After all, to everyone's surprise, the student protest was not only aimed at Western society's worst imperialist and racist excesses but also at "middle class culture, decaying liberalism, abstract parliamentary democracy, and fetishistic consumerism."[1] They may have contemplated a total rebellion that shook the foundations of society, but Marcuse clearly understood that the students' actions did not constitute a true "revolutionary force," and that the hippies were not the "heir to the proletariat."[2]

At the bottom of it all, Theodor Adorno and Herbert Marcuse agreed that the old Marxism no longer fit the facts in the post-industrial world and that modifications in Marxist theory were needed to put Socialist dreams of a better world back on track. However, neither man believed the revolutionary moment had arrived. Their primary disagreement concerned the significance of the current upheaval.[3] Indeed, each of them was convinced that their differences were not fundamentally theoretical and did not, at heart, involve a disagreement over how to conceptualize the relationship between theory and practice. Both men knew that in the present communist world, the celebrated unity of theory and practice implied by Marxian theory had degenerated into a kind of blind dogma whose sole function was to eliminate theoretical thinking altogether.[4] Both men realized that despite what Marx had said, practice could transform theory into irrationalism. In the final analysis, their dialogue boiled down simply to their differing assessments of the current political situation. Herbert Marcuse had unabashedly affirmed the counterculture as a manifestation of his "new sensibility," which put forward liberating new values. Theodor Adorno believed that his friend greatly exaggerated the emancipatory potential of the student revolts.[5] "You believe," Professor Adorno wrote, "that practice in an emphatic sense is not prohibited today; I see the matter differently."[6]

The little man sighed, and signed his letter "Teddy." Why can't they see? He had tried to make it clear. The moment was not near. The power of the capitalist, industrial, consumer society was ascendant. It had ensnared the entire population of the West in a web of consumerism, celebrity, and false values. The true revolutionary element has been assimilated, seduced into a hollow culture of things and images. Here was the central point of his *Negative Dialectics*, a book in which he had labored to show the present incompatibility of theory and praxis. Of this, he was certain: theory and praxis cannot come together until there is a correct interpretation of contemporary

---

1 Kellner, *Herbert Marcuse and the Crisis of Marxism*, 288.

2 Marcuse, *Essay on Liberation*, 93, cited in Kellner, *Herbert Marcuse and the Crisis of Marxism*, 288.

3 Kellner, *Herbert Marcuse and the Crisis of Marxism*, 277-90.

4 Theodor Adorno, *Problems of Moral Philosophy*, ed. Thomas Schröder, trans. by Rodney Livingstone (Stanford, CA: Stanford University Press, 2001), 3.

5 Kellner, *Herbert Marcuse and the Crisis of Marxism* 285.

6 Theodor Adorno, letter to Herbert Marcuse, June 19, 1969, cited in Müller-Doohm, *Adorno*, 462.

experience, and that interpretation is still awaited.[1] This is what Critical Theory is all about.

* * *

Not too many blocks away, in a quiet neighborhood near the university, Steffi Siegel also lay awake late into the Frankfurt night. She was still deeply concerned for the safety of her brother in New York. She had checked with people she knew at the West German Department of State, with journalists she knew, with Karl Wolff, and even with her father in Paris. Everyone had confirmed that the press reports appeared to be accurate, that the student rebels were still barricaded inside five university buildings, that police were on the scene, that no action had been taken yet to confront the protestors, and that no serious injuries had occurred. Everything indicated that Kurt was safe for the moment, but still her heart felt strangely heavy. Her mind raced ahead to the long weekend in early May when she and Kurt planned to be with their father in Paris; but thinking of Paris reminded her of Charles, and that also tore at her heart. They had to work something out. His wife, the distance between them, her fears that his view of the world differed fundamentally from her own, all of this could not go on. She feared that their affair was hopeless, and yet any attempt to elude their attraction seemed equally hopeless.

---

1 O'Connor, Brian, ed, *The Adorno Reader* (Oxford: Blackwell Publishers Ltd, 2000), 54; Theodor Adorno, *Negative Dialectics*, trans. E.B. Ashton. (London: Routledge, 1973).

Chapter Fifteen: New York

Words strain,
Crack and sometimes break, under the burden,
Under the tension, slip, slide, perish,
Decay with imprecision, will not stay in place.
Will not stay still.
— T. S. Eliot, "Burnt Norton"

One of the most difficult tasks confronting philosophers is to descend from the world of thought to the actual world. Language is the immediate actuality of thought. Just as philosophers have given thought an independent existence, so they were bound to make language into an independent realm.
— Karl Marx and Friedrich Engels, *German Ideology*

Friday, April 26, 1968

"They're gone," Martin shouted to the others. "It's as quiet as a graveyard out there. The cops are gone! Everybody's gone!"

Mark and Ted went to the window in disbelief. The platoon of tough plain-clothesmen were nowhere in sight; the curious crowds were gone from the lawn, and a frail squad of faculty members were back in their place at the top of the steps.

"What the hell happened?" said Ted. "Martin, see if you can get a line on what's up. Kurt, get the other buildings on the line. See what's happening over there. We'll post some lookouts in case they come back. Everyone else may as well try to get some sleep."

Martin made his way down to the very bottom of an obscure Low Library stair-well, and, by means of a loose ventilation grate, he entered one of his secret accesses to the service tunnels that circled the building three stories below ground. He carefully replaced the grate behind him as he entered a small ventilator shaft. He crawled down the narrow opening for about ten feet to a larger vent, which opened unobstructed into the main hall of the tunnel. Half way around the circular service passage, he climbed a small flight of steps and very carefully and quietly opened the door to the corridor above. He placed tape over the latch so that the door would not lock and then carefully closed it behind him and made his way along the hallway. He could hear loud voices in the distance, and he didn't have to get too close to hear what he had come to hear. He listened breathlessly around the corner from the police command post in the security guard's old break room.

There was a great deal of cursing. Apparently the administration had asked the police to clear the buildings, beginning with Low Library, but after the faculty had presented President Kirk and Vice President Truman with their bloodied colleague, they had lost their nerve and called off the attack.

Goddamn college brats," shouted one of the patrolmen in frustration. "We ought'a just line 'em all up and shoot 'em. If my kid ever gets to go to college, I mean if he gets a scholarship or something like that, I guarantee he'll never act like these ungrateful little Westchester assholes."

The lanky freshman shook his head. This was not exactly the unified voice of the noble international proletariat bravely manning the barricades.

* * *

The next morning, a dark blue line of uniformed police about twenty strong stretched across the broad marble steps leading to the Low Library. Later in the day, throngs of jocks and members of the Majority Coalition, now sporting new "Stop the SDS" campaign buttons on their ubiquitous jackets and ties, ringed the occupied buildings just outside of the ring of uniformed police. Outside of this ring of counter-protestors there soon developed a third ring of student sympathizers or "pukes" (as everyone, including the sympathizers themselves, had now taken to calling the strikers and the supporters of the strike). Still later, members of the Ad Hoc Faculty Committee wearing white armbands would attempt to form a fourth "buffer" ring between the jocks and the "puke" sympathizers. They saw themselves as a kind of special constabulary whose mission it was to keep apart "the hysterical, the vindictive, and the authoritarian."[1]

The Ad Hoc Faculty Group was also serious about its self-cast role as mediator. Faculty members voted to allow food and the protestors' messengers, identified by their red armbands, to pass freely in and out of all of the occupied buildings. They also voted to let anyone pass out of the buildings, but only upon the surrender of that person's identification card. Only students with ID cards were to be allowed back in, thus effectively sealing the protestors inside the occupied buildings. Although this was the theory, as it turned out the faculty had no more control over the situation than anyone else did. Some food was passed in across the emerging battle lines, and a few red-banded messengers came and went, but these passages proved increasingly contentious and by late Friday, the fourth day of the strike, the demonstrators inside Low Library were in large part cut off from their source of supply and were besieged.

Martin and a few others began a project of underground supply through the tunnels, but their efforts were limited by the fact that, once on the outside, they had to be very careful not to draw attention to themselves and thereby reveal the secret of the underground access to all of the buildings. So it was that the primary method of

---

1 Spender, *Year of the Young Rebel*, 16.

supplying sustenance to the barricaded demonstrators became "food throwing." This somewhat comical scheme was fraught with problems. First, owing to the system of rings, the sympathizing "pukes" outside who purchased and threw the food were denied close access to the buildings by the inner rings of faculty, jocks, and cops. Thus, food had to be thrown into second story windows from at least twenty yards away. This took a pretty good arm. Adding to the difficulty was the fact that most food just doesn't "throw well." The sad fact was that the weight, shape, and aerodynamics of most packaged food renders it a very poor projectile. At first, most of the provisions thrown by sympathizers missed the mark and fell to the ground to be conspicuously gobbled up in a show of ravenous delight by the jocks. After some experimentation it was determined that apples, oranges, small cans, and packets of luncheon meat were best for throwing.[1]

* * *

Late in the afternoon, Martin returned to Low to pass on to Mark and the other SDS leaders the results of another of his "little subterranean reconnaissance missions."

"Well," he began sitting comfortably on the windowsill, "Tom Hayden has been elected chairman of the group in Mathematics Hall. Overall, that's a pretty radical crowd over there with a lot of weirdo hangers-on. They're flying a red flag from the rooftop. It's pretty dramatic. Oh, and they're building some really far-out barricades. Meanwhile, the faculty is still meeting and meeting and meeting. They're interviewing jocks, pukes — everybody — and they're talking to the administration. I even overheard your interview, Mark. Despite your insistence on total amnesty, they still think some sort of committee should oversee all disciplinary measures. It seems President Kirk is encouraging their efforts to continue to sell to us the three-part disciplinary committee, even though he has not officially endorsed the idea."

"I told them that the three-part deal wouldn't fly," said Mark. "Why can't they move on?"

"They're still badly split on many issues, and even the three-part committee idea seems too soft for some," replied Martin. "Meanwhile, the Trustees have issued a public statement backing Kirk and Truman's authority to the hilt. Nobody is talking about amnesty, and there is some talk that the guys over in Fayerweather are thinking about accepting the three-part tribunal idea."

"Get Fayerweather on the radio," said Mark. "We can't let them break solidarity. It would be disastrous. Get Hayden on the line too. Maybe he can go over there and speak to them. What else, Martin?"

"Well, the campus is still supposedly closed to everyone except students and employees of the university. There are cops on all the gates and a few faculty members as well. In fact, there are cops everywhere.[2] Still, sometime just after noon, about 250 black high school students from the surrounding neighborhoods stormed the Amsterdam Avenue gate and pushed past the police and onto the campus. They tried to get into Hamilton, but the SAS wouldn't let them in, so they sat around on the

---

1 Frank Da Cruz, "Columbia University 1968," www.columbia.edu/acis/history/1968.html, April 1998-August 2005.

2 After the aborted attempt to clear Low Library, police were called in to guard all university buildings. By 3 a.m. on Friday morning, *The Times* reported that there were 100 police on the Columbia campus. Later in the day a larger force arrived. Estimates vary as to the size of the police presence on campus in the following days. Some sources place the number as high as 600. *The New York Times*, April 26 1968, 1.

grass outside chanting 'black power' and 'we shall overcome' and stuff like that. They were getting pretty worked up and shouting about taking another building on their own. Then one of the SAS guys came out and told them not to do it. He told them to sit down and shut up, which is what they did. While this was going on, Charles 37X Kenyatta, you know, the head of Harlem's Mau Mau sect, led a group on a 'sympathy march' right through the middle of the campus.[1] In the meantime, Stockley Carmichael and H. Rapp Brown also got through one of the gates with their own crowd of followers. They met with the SAS in Hamilton, and then Brown came out and told the press that the black community 'was preparing to come and deal with Columbia University at some point.' He said that if they built the gym, they would 'blow it up.'[2] The crowd outside Hamilton is enormous.[3] Everyone is really freaking out over the possibility of a race riot. There is a very real concern that the university might be overrun or even burned down."[4]

As the others pondered this explosive situation, Martin glanced out the window at the crowd gathered on the lawn. "Oh my God!" he exclaimed. "It's him. He's here. This is great! You gotta see this."

"What? Who? What's going on?" came the confused response.

"It's 'The Chicken Thrower,'" said Martin as they all gathered at the window. "This guy is amazing. I saw him over in Avery earlier today. Watch this."

Martin pointed to a tall thin young man with waist-length blond hair carrying a large shopping bag. The lanky youth approached Low from College Walk along the walkway that flanked the South Lawn to the east. He descended the steps to the courtyard in front of the great library, stationing himself near the outer ring of strike sympathizers about 25 yards from the building. He placed the bag on the ground, carefully removed his jacket, folded it neatly, and placed it beside the bag. A large group of student on-lookers gathered around him, cheering as he stretched his arms with fingers intertwined above and behind his head. Then he bent at the waist and touched his toes with his fingertips a few times, flexing and shrugging his shoulders to them loosen up. Taking a small packet from the bag at his feet, he turned to the side, and then like a youthful Sandy Koufax, he gave a high leg-kick and hurled a fried-chicken-filled packet high in the air. There was a breathless silence as the packet arched over the crowd, crossing high above the rings of students, faculty, and police. It disappeared into the second story window of President Kirk's office. A great cheer went up from the growing crowd below. Again and again, the young man methodically came set and threw. Each parabolic flight found the bull's-eye of the open window. Inside the protestors scurried about gathering up the bags of chicken. The crowd at first cheered with each direct hit and then began a chorus of counts, "four, five, six...twelve, thirteen." Fifteen packets were thrown, fifteen direct hits.

"What an arm!" Ted exclaimed.

It was astonishing, a peerless display of accuracy — such a long throw and such a small target. After the last packet of chicken found its mark, the young man folded the shopping bag, put his jacket back on, and left the way he had come, ambling up the walk with the folded bag under his arm, turning left onto College Walk, and

1 *Time*, May 3, 1968, 49.
2 *The New York Times*, April 27, 1968, 18.
3 The *Times* estimated the crowd outside Hamilton on the after noon of April 26th to be over one thousand individuals. University Sociology Professor Immanuel Wallenstein pleaded with the mob, "Please restrain your emotions." *The New York Times*, April 27, 1968, 18.
4 Trilling, "On the Steps of the Low Library," *Commentary*, November 1968.

passing out of sight between the tall buildings that faced 116th Street. No one had any idea who he was, where he came from, or who had prepared the chicken.[1]

"Jesus, this is great!" said Eliot, biting into a drumstick. It was, without a doubt, the best fried chicken he had ever tasted.

* * *

As the day wore on, it was clear that each of the five occupied buildings was developing its own unique character and style. The SDS strike leadership and their political support group occupied Low, while the most radical SDS members had migrated to Math, which had also attracted a number of off-campus "crazies" including a notorious group best described as "quasi-intellectual street-gang antichrists." Led by the mysterious leather-jacketed switchblade-carrying Ben Morea, they were theatrical and highly politicized. The group once piled heaps of stinking garbage from the East Village onto the steps of Lincoln Center, claiming that the act represented a cultural exchange — "garbage for garbage." They rallied in support of Vallerie Solanas, the tormented feminist who shot Andy Warhol, and a year later they would cut the fences at Woodstock, famously helping to turn it into a free concert for thousands. Math was a bastion of militancy steeped in a communal culture of total resistance to society, which advocated the taking of every building on campus. Out of Mathematics would come some of the future members of the ultra radical Weathermen, the section of the SDS soon to dedicate itself to clandestine armed struggle.[2] Avery was the haven for the Trotskyites, and the anarcho-syndicalists populated Fayerweather along with mixed bag of counterculture types, graduate liberals, and some heavy student politicos.[3] Fayerweather offered personal and social liberation, films, concerts, and endless political discussions.[4] Meanwhile the blacks of the SAS, of course, held Hamilton and conducted their own negotiations almost completely independently, maintaining little contact with the white protestors in the other buildings.

SATURDAY, APRIL 27, 1968

The next day, Mark Rudd met for the second time with the Ad Hoc Faculty Committee in Philosophy. This time he made sure to make the demonstrators' position regarding the amnesty issue crystal clear. "Any mediation effort by the committee that does not contain complete amnesty for all of the protesting students is bull," he told them flatly.

When he returned to Low wearing his red armband, he was escorted safely through the battle lines of the "rings" by a white-banded faculty associate professor of anthropology. Back inside Low, the news was that Fayerweather was still waffling

---

1 In June of 2001, Frank Da Cruz's research into the matter of the mysterious "Chicken Thrower" finally paid off when an informer told him that the anonymous hurler with the major league arm was John Taylor, the son of Nuremberg prosecutor and Columbia Law Professor Telford Taylor. The senior Taylor had declined to lend his name to a statement, signed by most of the other Law School faculty, which said the student protests had exceeded the "allowable limits" of civil disobedience. According to Cruz, the chicken was cooked by Mrs. Gloria Sánchez of the Bronx. Frank Da Cruz, "Columbia University 1968," www.columbia.edu/acis/history/1968.html, April 1998-August 2005; *The New York Times*, May 24, 1998.

2 Fraser, et al., *1968: A Student Generation in Revolt*, 173.

3 Frank Da Cruz, "Columbia University 1968," www.columbia.edu/acis/history/1968.html, April 1998-August 2005; Erickson, "Up Against the Ivy Wall, Part 2. Columbia University, May – June, 1968," from *Shock Wave: Transnational University Based New Left Revolts: March-October 1968*, http://trc.ucdavis.edu/erickson/mru/sw.htm

4 Fraser, et al., *1968: A Student Generation in Revolt*, 173.

regarding their acceptance of the faculty's three-part deal regarding amnesty. Having just confronted the faculty with a hard-line position on amnesty, this seemed to chip away the SDS's leadership and credibility. Mark was apprehensive. By 3:00 p.m., however, Fayerweather was again back in the fold and re-embracing a hard line on amnesty.

Despite Fayerweather's faltering, student opinion seemed to be galvanizing and becoming increasingly radicalized. Martin reported in his daily reconnaissance that a large group of Barnard College girls had held a candlelight vigil the previous night in sympathy with the protest, and that ten student leaders, six members of the student council and four members of the President's Committee on Student Affairs, had come out in support of the demonstrators' cause.

As Martin spoke, Mark smiled broadly. Right before their eyes, he and the other demonstrators inside Low Library were at last witnessing the radicalization that they had so often discussed. Moderate students in the center were beginning to get the uncomfortable feeling that those to the left of them held the more correct position. Student opinion was consolidating. A new political force was emerging and spreading like a contagion, even to those who, by normal conviction and temper, had been most unlikely to identify with the cause of the fanatical few. Mark knew that at the bottom of it all, radicalization had begun with wanting to stop the construction of the gym, and that it would end with the idea of destroying the entire university. A mysterious connection had been made. In the minds of many students, the demonstrations were suddenly taking on "the stature of a revolution — a power seizure effected within a single institution which they regarded as a microcosm of the whole of society."[1]

The resourceful flower child also reminded them that this was the day of the long-awaited demonstrations that were part of the national student "Strike for Peace" that had been organized by the Mobilization Committee to End the War in Vietnam, an all-encompassing antiwar organization known to everyone as "the Mobe." He reported that the cops were busy trying to police Mobe-sponsored antiwar activities all over the city. "Early reports claim that on Friday over a million kids cut school in protest," he said. "And today, it sounds like demonstrators are marching from everywhere in the city and converging on Central Park. I hear there are tens of thousands in Sheep Meadow right now. The same thing is going on in every major city in the country."[2]

Later, outside the police command post in the security wing of Low, Martin would learn that the cops' concern was that some of the "Mobe" parades would lead more demonstrators straight to the university. Gate security was being tightened, and the police were nervous.[3]

---

1 F. W. Dupree, "The Uprising at Columbia," *New York Review of Books*, September 29, 1968, quoted in Spender, *Year of the Young Rebels*, 9.

2 Over 200,000 people in New York City took part in demonstrations during the Ten Days of Protest organized by the Student Mobilization Committee to the End the War in Vietnam. The centerpiece of this event was an international student "Strike for Peace" and a huge rally held in Sheep Meadow in Central Park that attracted an estimated 87,000 demonstrators on April 27, 1968. Similar demonstrations were held in scores of U.S. cities, and it was estimated that over one million high school students skipped school on Friday April 26 as a protest against the war. *The New York Times*, April 29, 1968, 1-2.

3 About 1000 demonstrators from Sheep Meadow did make a march from Central Park to Columbia University late on the afternoon of April 27, 1968. They were contained in a designated protest area outside the gates of the university and eventually they disbanded.

Secretly Mark Rudd and his followers hoped that the success of the Mobilization Committee's carefully planned "Ten Days of Protest" would direct a great ground-swell of popular opinion in the direction of their cause and help to legitimize their bold act of civil disobedience in the public eye. The authorities, on the other hand, knew that the legions of demonstrations and the successful student "Strike for Peace" were the results of months of careful planning and hard-fought negotiations on the part of the Mobilization Committee and of countless other antiwar groups that were participating in worldwide demonstrations and the boycotts. Everyone knew that the origins of this national and international outpouring of protest had little to do directly with the student revolt at Columbia. Still, on that troubled Saturday, deep in their hearts, the police, the faculty, the university administration, and the Board of Trustees secretly feared that, as the day wore on, things might change, that the local revolt at Columbia might spontaneously become the national center of serious American social unrest. Could it possibly be that the prelude to revolution would be written on ivy-covered walls? The idea seemed preposterous.

SUNDAY, APRIL 28, 1968

As the weekend wore on things seemed to settle into a kind of routine. The carni-val atmosphere faded and tensions seemed to diminish. Still, the rings remained, and police, faculty, jocks, and onlookers at various times and in varying degrees of agita-tion remained on guard outside Low. By Sunday afternoon, the Majority Coalition's blockade of the Low Memorial Library was in full effect and maintained around the clock, and anti-demonstration groups were occupying two other university build-ings in order to preempt their being taken over by demonstrators. However, the counter-protestors lacked the manpower to blockade other buildings, and so Avery, Fayerweather, and Math remained relatively open. Inside the occupied buildings, the seemingly endless meetings lumbered on, and fatigue was beginning to take its toll on the protestors. Throughout the weekend, the entire Columbia University campus remained closed.

Later on Sunday afternoon, Dean Coleman came onto the green outside Low and talked to some of the members of the Majority Coalition who were on guard there.

"He acts like a goddamned general reviewing the troops," said Eliot.

"Yeah, something must be up," said Kurt.

* * *

On Sunday evening, Martin reported to the SDS leadership in Low.

"Well, the guys over in Hamilton have rejected the new Ad Hoc Faculty Commit-tee proposal regarding amnesty and discipline, just the way we did," he began.

"Good!" said Mark, "I told them that anything short of complete amnesty was 'bull.' They just don't get it."

"Well, the word is," said Martin, "that the administration and the majority of the faculty representing those who are not part of the Ad Hoc Faculty Committee have rejected the proposal anyway. Of course, the Ad Hoc Committee is not telling us that. I heard that Vice President Truman said that he would resign if that proposal was ratified by the administration."

All weekend the Ad Hoc Faculty Committee had been busy hammering out a new, softer version of its tripartite plan. The new plan called for a single uniform punishment to apply to all protest participants without regard for the degree of their participation. This punishment was to be decided upon by a three-part committee made up of students, administration leaders, and faculty. The theory was that the university could not severely deal with all seven hundred or a thousand students, and thus the plan was designed to hold out the expectation of little more than a simple slap on the wrist for everyone involved. For the SDS leadership, and indeed for most of the strikers, the severity of the punishment was not the issue; it was the idea of punishment itself. In principle, only complete amnesty could send the message that the students' actions had been justified. They sought absolution, legitimation, not leniency.

"Oh, and President Kirk has just announced that the campus will remain closed on Monday," Martin added.

"Well," said Eliot, "That's a fairly certain indication that no police attack will come tonight, anyway."

All weekend, the feeling had been that a police attack was imminent. Signs of this concern were everywhere in the occupied buildings: larger barricades, taped windows to prevent glass from shattering, stocks of Vaseline to protect skin from the burn of Mace, soaped stairways to impede the police.[1]

Everyone knew that something had to give.

---

1 *The New York Times*, April 29, 1968, 28.

Chapter Sixteen: Paris

Or say that the end precedes the beginning,
And the end and the beginning were always there,
Before the beginning and after the end.
— T. S. Eliot "Burnt Norton"

The architect raises his structure in imagination before he erects it in reality.
— Karl Marx, *Capital*

Monday, April 29, 1968

Each day the walls at Nanterre cried out with the graphic shrieks of slogans, graffiti, and photographic montage. There were wall posters in the Chinese style and huge tracts of tightly written text. All of this colorful art and utterance was methodically removed every night by the university's custodial staff only to reappear in tangled new arrays of radical impertinence every morning. "Over time, the result of this, along with the 22nd of March Movement's radical efforts to create a working model of the 'free university' — not in place of but alongside the existing university — had the effect of mobilizing student attention, reflection, participation."[1] When it all began, Daniel Cohn-Bendit and the 22nd of March Movement had inspired only a small fraction of the student population, but their sway grew daily. Student participation did not grow "organically out of dissatisfaction with a general condition," but revealed its contradictions and became politicized "through words and deeds."[2] This was not an attack on the university so much as it was an invention, the release of something new in addition to the university. During the entire month of April, classes had barely been disrupted. An auditorium was made available to student political groups, and the dean left it up to the department heads to determine whether or not to put other

---

1 Touraine, *The May Movement*, 146.
2 Touraine, *The May Movement*, 144.

lecture halls at the disposal of the radical student workgroups. Those in charge of philosophy, psychology, and sociology had agreed to do so. By the end of April, the vast majority of the students at Nanterre were, in one way or another, part of the movement, and junior faculty members were becoming sympathetic to the students' cause in large numbers.

Danny's role in all of this was catalytic, and he knew it. He was a man of revolt, not of alliances and strategy. He wanted to break down structures, denounce trickery, expose flimsy schemes and hollow revolutionary words, to do away with conformist action. With the 22nd of March Movement he had effectively silenced all of the diverse "little groups" of the extreme Left by creating a unity of action out of a confusion of radical ideas. He knew that his friend from Frankfurt, Kurt Siegel, would be critical of his reliance on disruptive action as a vehicle to create radical unity. He was certain that Kurt favored radical action only if it was motivated and confirmed by carefully worked out political and social theory. Because the 22nd of March Movement had no doctrine, no organization, no program, Danny knew from the very beginning that it was bound to quickly exhaust itself. No, Kurt would not have approved; neither did his lovely sister Steffi. The shrewd redhead had seen the signs of her mistrust, watched her fawning over Doctor Marcuse, and observed her knitted brow when he talked of the spontaneity of true revolutionary action.

So it was that Danny read his friend's letter with great care, even though it was over a week old when he received it. He wanted to know the situation in America, it was true, but he was more interested in Kurt's assessment of the fabric of the American revolt. Did it represent a groundswell of spontaneous revolutionary zeal, a reflection of real dissatisfaction with modern society, or was it merely a mirror of the growing popularity of the Left, which had been currently declared in vogue by growing and fashionable concerns over the injustices of the Vietnam War and American racial discrimination?

April 21, 1968

Columbia University

Dear Danny,

There is a crude but graphic saying they use here in America when something awful is about to be spattered about uncontrollably, and that appears to be exactly what is about to happen here. Our SDS organization here at Columbia has recently made an alliance of sorts with the radical black student organization, and a big demonstration has been planned for the 23rd, the day after tomorrow. Some sort of indoor sit-in is contemplated, and this will surely result in a strong reaction by the university. Things could get messy. Our own chairman has verbally assaulted the administration in a way calculated to cause a deep and irreparable breach in relations.

Although it is hoped that our action will have effects well beyond the confines of the university, there is no effort to bring the workers into any of this. Here, they have definitely been completely sated by capitalism's alluring materialism. In fact, the question is unclear as to whether there is in America a potential revolutionary subject. Doctor Marcuse seems to want to focus on the candidates at hand: students, intellectuals, blacks, culturally and economically estranged groups, the unemployed, etc. — all groups on the fringes of the system, not elements embedded within it. Professor Marcuse also seems to be searching for a cultural element to drive the revolution, something that affects the system from without, something aesthetic — a need for beauty, peace, and happiness. The significance of the hippies and the American counterculture is unclear in this regard. I won't try to explain this enigmatic movement to you. Again, I can only say there is nothing quite like it in Europe. As to this counterculture group's potential as a revolutionary force, I have my doubts. In fact, Marx would say that culture and aesthetics will be shaped by revolution and not the other way around. To be precise, Marx said that the social agents of revolution are formed only in the process of transformation itself. Certainly, this is something that you can strongly relate to. Even Marcuse believes that it is wrong today to try fully and categorically to identify in advance the revolutionary subject as any particular social class, group, or tendency.[1]

Anyway, in my mind, for these and many other reasons, this is not the revolutionary moment. In the United States there are many social and political struggles now, each with its own limited issue-driven agenda. None of them constitutes the emergence of an explicitly anti-capitalist and pro-socialist strategy defining capitalism as the source of political and societal problems and heralding socialism as the cure.[2] Perhaps today we are not revolutionaries, but only beginning "the long march through institutions."[3]

I plan to be in Paris on May 4 to visit with Stef and my father. I hope to see you then.

With my warmest regards,

Kurt

Danny folded Kurt's letter carefully and put it in his pocket. He savored the words: "The social agents of revolution are formed only in the process of transformation itself."

Even traditional Marxists like Kurt and high-minded New Leftists like Herbert Marcuse were suddenly coming around to his own interpretations of Marx. The long march through institutions was a crock. Capitalist institutions would inexorably absorb and assimilate any sustained efforts at gradual subversion. The assault had to be quick, decisive, complete. Marx knew it, and he also knew that when push came to shove, when it came right down to blood in the streets, theory and praxis would become one. In the oddest kind of way, Daniel Cohn-Bendit and Theodor Adorno agreed on this point. For Danny, it was just another way of saying that theory was baloney. For Doctor Adorno, it meant that practice would always usurp the power to manipulate theory.

Danny smiled. "They will all see soon enough," he thought. "Blood has to come first. Then...well, then, things will at least be free to work themselves out...or not."

---

1 Kellner, *Herbert Marcuse and the Crisis of Marxism*, 316-7.

2 Kellner, *Herbert Marcuse and the Crisis of Marxism*, 317.

3 Antonio Gramsci, an Italian Marxist theorist who ran afoul of the fascists in the 1930s, spoke of the gradual achievement of social reform through radical action from within, for which he coined the now well-worn phrase, "the long march through institutions."

CHAPTER SEVENTEEN: NEW YORK

> Would it have been worth while,
> To have bitten off the matter with a smile,
> To have squeezed the universe into a ball
> To roll it toward some overwhelming question,
> — T. S. Eliot, "The Love Song of J. Alfred Prufrock"

> Force is the midwife of every old society pregnant with a new one.
> — Karl Marx

MONDAY, APRIL 29, 1968

On Monday afternoon, Eliot and Kurt were sunning themselves on the wide ledge outside the window of President Kirk's office. Below, police and faculty stood guard, and scores of students milled about. The well-defined rings of opposition, sympathy, and defense seemed to disintegrate in times like this when tensions were relaxed, only to resume their rigid, concentric order in periods of stress or activity. Mark and the other SDS leaders had just rejected another of the Ad Hoc Faculty Committee's proposals, and the standoff appeared destined to continue indefinitely with both sides blindly entrenched in its own brand of unbending intransigence.

"I hear President Kirk said that if he failed to take disciplinary action, it would 'destroy the whole fabric of the university community,'" said Eliot. "That's bull. The word is that Kirk is telling the faculty that he agrees with the 'essential spirit' of their three-part uniform disciplinary committee plan, but he will not agree to be bound by the committee's decisions.[1] He wants it both ways. We can't trust him."

"No," said Kurt, "at the bottom of it all, he hasn't really given an inch, despite all of the faculty's efforts. Still, we haven't had a chance to negotiate directly with President Kirk and Herr Truman. The faculty has placed themselves in the middle.

---

1 *Time* Magazine, May 10, 1968, 49; May 10, 1968, 77.

They mean well, but they don't get it. The liberalism they are so proud of is weak and meaningless in the face of the real political struggle. The faculty with all of their meetings and proposals has only muddied the waters. Besides, we haven't given an inch either. To many, I'm sure it appears that we are far more interested in a bloody confrontation than in meaningful negotiations. Perhaps we are. We've reached *eine Sachgasse*. What would you say, a dead end?"

"More like a deadlock, an impasse," said Eliot.

"Yes, that's it, a deadlock," replied the trim young German. "This won't go on much longer."

"Good," said his American friend, "I'm ready to move on."

"Me too. I'm supposed to fly to Paris later this week to visit my father and my sister. Why don't you come along? You won't be welcome around here for a while. I promise you that. *Komme mit mir, mein Freund.*"

"*Vielen danke,*" said Eliot. "I just might do that, by God, I just might."

* * *

A little later Eliot spotted a large group of youths carrying shopping bags and cardboard boxes. As they approached the center of the green along College Walk, they began chanting, "Food, food, food."

The chant was picked up by throngs of sympathetic students on the lawn outside of Low Library.

"This looks like trouble," said Kurt.

As this ragtag supply corps approached, a great cheer went up from the protestors in Low as they rushed to the open windows. Just below Kurt and Eliot's perch, 200 or so jocks began tightening up their ranks as the self-appointed providers of sustenance circled the huge building three times and massed for a charge. Again the chant went up, "Food, food, food," growing louder as they paused to gather their nerve. Then, with a sudden surge, they charged the ring of jocks, which held firm. There was considerable violent pushing and shoving, but the jocks stood their ground.

"Hold that line! Hold that line!" shouted the gleeful onlookers who supported the Majority Coalition.

"Food, food, food!" came the reply from the equally enthusiastic strike sympathizers.

While the police passively watched, the shoving escalated into a mêlée. After about ten or fifteen minutes, most of the brawlers had worn themselves out, and a few faculty members had managed to get in between the remaining combatants and keep them apart. There were split lips and bloody noses, and a number of students were led away with blood on their shirts. The rest milled about and attempted to throw grapefruits, oranges, bread, and canned goods over the line of jocks and into the second story windows. Some of these missiles made it; most bounced off the walls to be ceremoniously consumed by the jocks below.[1]

"Well," said Eliot, "that's the first time Columbia ever held the line."

The young German looked at him quizzically. He knew nothing about American football, and he had no clue that the Columbia Lions had won only ten of their last ninety NCAA Division II football games.

* * *

Around 6:00 p.m. another confrontation between the jocks and the strike sympathizes seemed to be brewing on the South Lawn. About forty police were moved into

---

1 *The New York Times*, April 30, 1968, 36.

position on the west side of Low and the demonstrators in the great library filled the windows to see what would happen. Suddenly Martin burst in. Breathlessly he told them that something was up over in Hamilton.

"The SAS has been meeting with arbitrators, negotiators, I don't know, administration representatives or 'hired gun' outsiders including the famous black psychologist Dr. Kenneth Clark," he told Mark Rudd and the other leaders.[1] "I think they're trying to convince the blacks to give up without a fight so they can then bust our asses good without the fear of inciting a goddamned race riot. I couldn't get close enough to hear what they were talking about, but I got the feeling that they made some kind of deal. If so, our ass is grass. I did a little eavesdropping at the pigs' command center in the security wing, and they're all talking like the blacks have given up. They're undoubtedly getting ready to move in on us — talking about warrants, trying on helmets, and that kind of thing."

"They're just waiting for Harlem to go to sleep," said Eliot.

TUESDAY, APRIL 30, 1968

Just after midnight, the phones began ringing in all the occupied buildings. Sympathizers all over campus were calling to report that the police were massing in front of the 100th Street police station in full riot gear. Around one-thirty, someone had reported that paddy wagons were lined up along Broadway all the way from 110th to 118th Street,[2] and another caller estimated uniformed police manpower to be in the thousands.[3] There were also reports of burly plainclothesmen and mounted police as well.

Outraged by the police presence, a large crowd of students sympathetic to the demonstrators gathered at the sundial where passionate speakers condemned the university administration and urged everyone to join members of the Ad Hoc Faculty Committee in repelling the police if they tried to enter the buildings.

At about 2:00 a.m., the phones in Low went dead.[4]

Eliot and Kurt and fifty or so demonstrators sat on the floor in the president's office, and about one hundred and fifty more sat in the second-floor hallway outside. Although the great lawn was filled with on-lookers, jocks, sympathizers, and faculty, the campus was strangely quiet. In the distance, eerie sitar music could be heard coming from one of the dorms.

"Here they come," said Ted, who was acting as a lookout at the window.

"Well, I'm out of here," said Martin, "See ya."

"Chickening out, Martin?" said Ted.

"Well, you can call it that, if you like," said the lanky youth, "but I think I've proved my courage. It's not that I'm chicken; it's that I am a man of peace. Although I agree with much of what you say, I'm not like you. I made a promise to myself that when the time came, I would not be a part of any violence. Peace and love, brothers." He

---

1 At 1:45 p.m. on Monday, April 29, 1968, Dr. Kenneth Clark and Theodore W. Kheel, a well-know labor negotiator, met with demonstrators in Hamilton and later with President Kirk. *The New York Times*, April 30, 1968, 36.

2 Harris, "Big Bust on Morningside Heights, 757-63.

3 Approximately 1,000 handpicked New York City policemen took part in the Columbia University "Big Bust" of April 30, 1968. *The New York Times*, April 30, 1968, 1.

4 The police cut the phone and water lines to all occupied buildings at 2 a.m. *The New York Times*, April 30, 1968, 36.

smiled broadly, flipped them the two-fingered "V" of the peace sign, and disappeared around the corner, heading for his mysterious tunnels.

"So much for the hippies and the counterculture as a part of the revolutionary vanguard," Eliot mused.

Martin planned to make his way underground to the sub-basement of his dormitory, Hartley Hall, using the main tunnels beneath the buildings along Amsterdam Avenue, but as he entered the large tunnel leading from Low to Uris, he notice that the lights were on. He was pondering this mystery when he heard a loud noise and the sound of footsteps coming on fast. He ducked behind a row of old steam pipes just as a phalanx of about twenty cops came charging past in full riot gear. They were led by two university maintenance staffers who serviced that tunnel, which, although closed, was still in operation. One of the maintenance workers held a large ring of keys in his hand. Martin doubled back, taking the old asylum tunnel known to "tunnel rats" as the "Buell Crawlspace." It took him beneath Buell Hall to Philosophy Hall, and there, finding the building open, he slipped out the front door and blended into the crowds on Amsterdam Avenue.

* * *

Back in Low Library, things were tense. Eliot went to the window. About 200 helmeted police were advancing in formation across the lawn. The scene was eerie, a foggy, half-lit, slow motion Fascist nightmare. As the police mounted the great marble steps, a few faculty members and a handful of students tried to block their way. They were no match for the riot police, and they were easily brushed aside. The few who attempted any real defense were "subdued" and led away to the waiting vans that now moved up onto College Walk to form a neat row of blinking red lights. Washed in the strange, pulsing red glow, the crowd on the lawn was growing — becoming active, taunting, angry, threatening. Police on the edges of the formation began swinging their nightsticks at any bystanders who ventured too near.

At the top of the stairs, the police paused.

"There're ten or twenty cops in the lobby," cried one of the lookouts in the hallway. "They must have come in through the tunnels. They're pushing aside our barricades."

Eliot again took his place on the floor with the others. It was quiet once more.

After what seemed like a long time, the tension was cut by the edgy sound of a bullhorn. "This is Police Commander Howard Leary of the New York City Police Department. We want you to come out and come out now. We are authorized by the trustees of the university. This is it. Come out now. You have made your point. Come out now."[1]

The crowd on the lawn replied with a chorus of "boos," which slowly evolved into a rhythmic chant, "Pigs must go! Pigs must go!" There was the explosive sound of shattering glass as the cops axed the front doors of the great library.

The protesters in Low began to sing "We Shall Not Be Moved," softly at first, and then with increasing vigor until it became an emotional Wagnerian anthem. The girl next to Eliot was crying. In the spaces between the choruses, they could hear terrifying sounds: shouts, cursing, and screams of anger, frustration, outrage, and pain. Chants of "Pigs must go" were mingled with the chants of the counter-demonstrators, "More police! More police!" Somewhere out on the green a student with a bullhorn was delivering breaking news to the crowd like some kind of latter-day town crier.[2]

---

1 *The New York Times*, April 30, 1968, 1, 36; and May 1, 1968, 36.
2 *The New York Times*, April 30, 1968, 36.

The police took about forty minutes to clear the protesters from the hallway out-side President Kirk's office. One by one, they were offered the choice: stand and leave, or to be dragged out and arrested. Eliot heard the cops grumbling among themselves, shouting orders to the seated students, and laughing as they dragged the catatonical-ly passive protesters down the hard marble stairs. The students sang, shouted insults and slogans, cried out their outrage, yelped their pain.

When it finally came Eliot's turn to be carried out, a young cop told him to stand and walk out. The passionate young protestor refused, and the cop hit him hard on the shoulder with his flashlight. "I'm getting tired of lugging you spoiled punks down those steps," the patrolman said raising his club to strike again. Eliot put out his hand in acquiescence and tried to stand. As he did, the cop hit him again, this time in the back, a painful kind of "kidney punch." Eliot went to his knees. Two other cops grabbed his ankles from behind and began to drag him across the floor toward the stairs, face down.

"OK, I'll walk!" cried Eliot, "Please, officers, I'll walk."

"That's more like it," said the young cop lifting him by the collar of his jacket.

As he was led from the building, he saw others who were not so lucky being dragged down the steps in front of Low. Some were being pulled by their feet, their heads bouncing down the stone steps behind. The cops had set up a kind of gauntlet, and as each protester was dragged past, each cop took a swing at him with his stick.[1] Eliot looked away. The steps of Low were spattered with blood.

As Eliot was led across the lawn toward the dark line of paddy wagons on Col-lege Walk, the "town crier" with the bullhorn blared out more news. "Hamilton and Avery have surrendered peacefully. There are more police vans massing outside Fay-erweather. There's a hell of a battle shaping up over in Math."

On College Walk, outside the police van, Eliot stood next to a young girl who was being held firmly by the arm by a heavy-set cop. "Go home and wash, you little tramp," shouted someone in the crowd.

"Wash your dirty mind," the girl shrieked back as she was lifted into the waiting van.

In the distance came the rising voice of a huge crowd chanting, "Kirk must go! Kirk must go!" Inside the waiting vehicle, Eliot spotted Kurt seated in the corner. There was blood on his face and shirt.

"This boy has been injured. He needs help," a woman cried, pleading with police to let her pass so she could render aid to the wounded student.

Eliot looked up to see a blinking, red-tinted crowd closing in around the van.

"They'll be OK," said one of the cops holding back the crowd, "We'll take care of them. Just go on home now. Just go on home."

"Are you all right?" Eliot asked Kurt stupidly.

"I guess I bumped my head," said Kurt with a kind of half smile

The doors of the police van swung shut with a secure-sounding bang, and they were in the dark. The van lurched and moved slowly along College Walk past the sundial with its poignant inscription still unseen and un-translated.

"*Horam Expecta Veniet*," "Await, the hour will come."

The van turned right onto Amsterdam Avenue and sped away, its familiar siren-scream unheard in the Harlem night.

* * *

1 Frank Da Cruz, "Columbia University 1968," www.columbia.edu/acis/history/1968.html, April 1998-August 2005.

"He's in the bedroom," said Melissa. "A little the worse for wear and totally exhausted, but at least he's here. Go on in."

"Thanks," said Martin, handing her a twenty-pound bag of ice. "Here's the ice you asked for."

"Eliot, Martin's here," she said going over to the bed and retrieving the ice pack from beneath Eliot's back.

"Hey!" said Eliot smiling, "What's the news from the front?"

"It's wild. Everyone is outraged. Over 700 students were arrested, 130 injured, probably a lot more, since many students didn't go to the hospital for fear of being arrested.[1] They're coming over to our side by the thousands — everyone, students, faculty, staff. It's wild. It was that last big charge that did it."

"What charge?"

"You don't know? Of course you don't. Well, after the police cleared the buildings, in fact while they were cleaning up at Fayerweather and Math, where our guys put up one hell of a fight, the crowd on the lawn got pretty angry. I mean they saw a lot of bloody heads, some faculty that were beat up, kids dragged around by the hair, you know. Anyway, that sparked some pretty nasty reactions from the crowd. Even some of the jocks were starting to get pretty upset with the police. Well, after the buildings were cleared, the crowd was still pissed, milling around and shouting insults, so the police tried to clear the lawn. They made a big charge with helmeted cops behind mounted police, and things got really nasty. A lot of heads got bopped, and a lot of innocent by-standers got roughed up. Injured people were lying around in the grass unattended, moaning. I even saw a cop beating up some newsmen.[2] It's hard to describe. I mean, later I was walking down Broadway when I saw a group of students running down the middle of the street being chased by cops on horseback. It was really wild."[3]

"Incredible," said Eliot.

"What's incredible is the support we're getting now, I mean from everyone. It's like the entire campus has been magically radicalized, as you guys like to say. Mark is out there negotiating with the police right now, setting the ground rules for a really big demonstration this evening."[4]

The graduate student could only shake his head in wonder.

After a moment Martin said, "So, enough about that. What the hell happened to you?"

"Well, there's not a lot to tell. We were stuffed into a paddy wagon, bused downtown to some precinct house on the Lower Eastside, where we sat for a few hours. Some of the guys from Math and Fayerweather were also brought over, so we knew that it had been pretty rough there. Still, we had no idea about the big charge and the clearing of the campus and all that. We were pretty bummed out, and the cops were being really rude. It was clear that they saw us as spoiled, un-American, rich kids enjoying college deferments while members of their families had been drafted and are in the mud in Vietnam fighting for our freedom or whatever. It would never occur to them that the war is wrong or that we are the patriots. Anyway, after a few hours,

---

1 *Time* Magazine, May 10, 1968, 77.

2 A *Life* Magazine photographer and the newsman Walter Winchell were attacked by police. *Time* Magazine, May 10, 1968. 36.

3 *The New York Times*, May 1, 1968, 35; *Time* Magazine, May 10, 1968, 77; Harris, "Big Bust on Morningside Heights," 757-63.

4 *The New York Times*, May 1, 1968. 35.

they took us to central booking, you know, 'The Tombs' over on Centre Street. We were charged, booked, fingerprinted, photographed, and all that stuff, and then put in a cell. This morning we were arraigned and set free. No bail. My court date is in late June. It's funny when they charged us, it was totally arbitrary, some were charged with criminal trespass, some with resisting arrest, some with criminal mischief, and some other charges. I don't remember. I was charged with all three, Kurt was charged with criminal trespass only. There was no system to it, no facts established to back up any of the charges, really. It was totally arbitrary. It makes you wonder."[1]

"Eliot's going to Paris, Martin. How about that?" said Melissa suddenly.

"Really?"

"Yes, Melissa and I've talked it over. It's only for a week or so. Kurt invited me. His father is there with the West German foreign service."

"You're going to Europe with a guy who talks to Karl Marx?"

"Come on! He's been a good friend to me, and he knows virtually everyone in the movement in Germany and in France. This might prove useful. Anyway, this semester is shot for sure. I'll certainly be suspended, if not expelled. Besides, I'm done with most of my course work and I've begun work on my thesis, so nothing much is lost. Whether or not they'll take me back, and whether or not I even want to come back, are questions that will work themselves out in the future. There's nothing to do about it now. So I might as well grasp the ring of opportunity now."

"Wow, Paris! Far out!" said Martin.

FRIDAY, MAY 3, 1968

Taking off toward the west from Kennedy, Paris-bound Air France Flight 102 made a sweeping turn to the north. Eliot and Kurt had a fine view of lower Manhattan. They could even make out the irregular ring of tall buildings surrounding the grassy quadrangle that was Columbia University. The mass of the Low Memorial Library was barely visible, an alabaster dot in the center of a tiny green lawn. The miniature dark-green ribbon that was Morningside Park stretched out along the university's eastern border.

"The gym in that park will never be built," Eliot was thinking, "and certainly the days of the university's affiliation with the Institute for Defense Analysis are numbered. Even President Kirk is probably done at Columbia."[2] After the police raid, almost the entire student body and a good part of the faculty had come down on their side.

Still, the events following the police action were oddly troubling. "Did we really win?" Eliot wondered.

On Wednesday, the day after the "Big Bust" the campus had teemed with demonstrations — with the electricity of protest, with bold words and demands for change, with radical activism. Twenty-five hundred had joined in an assembly on 116th Street between Amsterdam Avenue and Morningside Drive. That night thirteen hundred people, all vigorously anti-administration and ready to follow radical leadership, had attended an open meeting of the strike steering committee, and an enlarged committee had been elected. A debate had raged over the requirements for sitting on the committee. The radicals had favored some kind of revolutionary political coher-

---

1 Interview with Mr. Frank Da Cruz, former Columbia University protester arrested on the morning of April 30, 1968.

2 Plans for a gymnasium in Morningside Park were scrapped, Columbia University severed all ties with the IDA, and Grayson Kirk resigned in 1969.

ence while the liberals, gathering around the graduate students, junior faculty, and student-council types, had favored the broadest political base possible. The liberals had won the day, and a new strike committee of seventy members from all across the leftist political spectrum had been elected. Discussions had quickly turned to "the restructuring of the university." Despite the ambitious proposals for reform, as the proceedings progressed it was clear to Eliot, Mark Rudd, Ted Gold, and the other SDS leaders that the sharpness and militancy that had defined their struggle had vanished — gone forever.[1]

At one point during the meeting, Mark had turned to Eliot and said, "The organization, I mean, the committee, has been the weakest link in this whole thing all along. We spend all our time meeting and ignoring the real base, the real power, which is with the people. The question is, how does a mass radical movement involve greater and greater numbers in decision making? How does it maintain its radical politics when faced with the demands for coalition?"[2]

Eliot, intense as ever, pondered all of this as the plane turned to the northeast and Manhattan passed from his view. "Liberty can be made into a powerful instrument of domination,"[3] Doctor Marcuse had cryptically written. Now Eliot was beginning to understand what the great man had meant. When a system allows for dissent and opposition, the system appears free, and it is generally assumed that change will come "in the normal course of the open marketplace of ideas." However, when powers within that system are unequal, the wholesale manipulation of ideas occurs. With control of the media and of ideas, the system can not only marginalize or assimilate any opposition, it can also increase its own power by making the opposition appear unreasonable or threatening.

Such had been the case at Columbia. After the revolt they had still been free to demonstrate, deliberate, and discuss, to speak and to assemble, but they were rendered helpless and harmless when they tried to embrace politically an all-encompassing new liberal majority, which, as always, in all of its diverse constituencies, unwittingly manipulated against radical change.[4] As usual, the new liberal majority at Columbia missed the point. They sought to "restructure" the university. Everyone failed to understand that such a restructuring was meaningless as long as the university remained a tool of an oppressive society.[5]

Eliot knew that Tom Hayden understood this well enough. Earlier that day, he had been reading Hayden's article written in the wake of "the big bust." "The goal written on the university walls," Hayden wrote, "was 'Create two, three, many Columbias,'...expand the strike so that the U.S. has to either change or send its troops to occupy American campuses. American educators are fond of telling their students that the barricades are part of our romantic past, that social change today can only come about through the process of negotiation. But the students at Columbia discovered that the barricades are only the beginning of what they call bringing the war home."[6]

---

1 Mark Rudd, "Columbia," in *Movement*, March 1969.

2 Rudd, "Columbia."

3 Marcuse, *One-Dimensional Man*.

4 Marcuse, "Repressive Intolerance," in Wolff, Moore, Jr., and Marcuse, *A Critique of Pure Tolerance*, 95-135.

5 Mark Rudd, "Columbia," in *Movement*, March 1969.

6 Tom Hayden, "Two, Three, Many Columbians," in *Ramparts* Magazine, June 15, 1968.

Like Hayden, Eliot knew that the "restructuring" of the university was a red herring which only served to justify the students' capitulation to an empty rhetorical liberal reformism. The heartfelt spontaneous revolutionary zeal would be sucked out of them, first sated and then absorbed by a vast, ingrained, liberal rationality, until they were once again prisoners of a misguided Enlightenment.

The real struggle had been lost.

PART TWO: MAY, 1968

After the torchlight red of sweaty faces
After the frosty silence in the gardens
After the agony in stony places
The shouting and the crying
Prison and palace and reverberation
Of thunder of spring over distant mountains
He who was living is now dead
We who are living are now dying
With little patience.
— T. S. Eliot "The Wasteland"

Those on the barricades have no ideals to realize but to set free the elements of the new society with which the old collapsing bourgeois society itself is pregnant.
— Karl Marx, "The Civil War in France"

Chapter Eighteen: Paris

What the Thunder Said...
— T. S. Eliot, "The Wasteland"

"The proletarians...have nothing of their own to secure and fortify; their mission is to destroy all previous securities for, and assurances of, private property."
— Karl Marx and Friedrich Engels, "Manifesto of the Communist Party"

Friday, May 3, 1968

As the waiter carefully placed the two glasses on the tiny round table between Charles and Steffi, the late afternoon Parisian sunlight seemed to ignite the pale liquid inside, and the wine appeared to glow with an iridescent energy all its own. Deep in conversation and suddenly transfixed by this magical new source of light, the couple was oblivious to the gathering crowds outside the little café on the Boulevard Saint-Michel near the Sorbonne.

They had spent the better part of the day in Charles's apartment, talking. That they were in love was clear, but despite their undeniable attraction and determined devotion, they had very real problems to discuss. Steffi had told Charles that she felt that only by directly addressing these problems and openly expressing their individual hopes and fears related to these problems could they reach a comfortable understanding as to how to proceed. She knew that if they did not agree, or agree to disagree, and if they did not learn to respect one another's position in any disagreement, the affair would be doomed no matter how much they loved one another.

Steffi smiled at Charles and held his dark eyes with a comfortable but penetrating gaze. She remembered how they had met, at a party she had attended with her father at the West German Embassy in Paris. The tall, dark Frenchman spoke good German and perfect English, and his conversation had been charming and quite engaging in all three languages. Steffi was immediately drawn to his powerful intellect, and yet at first she had ignored his romantic attraction, owing to the fact that he had openly referred to his wife and child who, he told her, lived north of Paris near Beauvais in Oise. A few months later, Steffi had accompanied Doctor Adorno to the French capital on a speaking tour, and she had bumped into Charles at the Sorbonne. Charles later admitted that this meeting was not accidental, that he had known of Adorno's lecture, had known that she would accompany him, and had "laid in ambush for her," as he put it. On that occasion, the tall Frenchman had asked her to join a group of his friends for lunch, and he and Steffi had remained at the restaurant long after the rest of the luncheon party returned to the university.

They had talked for hours — her work with Doctor Adorno, his students at the Sorbonne, her father's diplomatic work in Paris, his thesis and his subsequent interest in the works of Charles Baudelaire. In this connection, Charles had mentioned Walter Benjamin and his pioneer modern criticism of Baudelaire centering on the great poet's fascination with the street life of nineteenth-century Paris. Steffi responded enthusiastically. She had described for Charles her difficulties in coming to grips with Benjamin's world of collage and incoherence, of impossibly complex interaction, of disjoined history. Despite the somewhat vague nature of her still-evolving understanding of Benjamin's vision of the modern dilemma, Charles seemed to understand her concerns completely, and he had carefully traced for her the source of Walter Benjamin's images all the way back to Baudelaire's sad but beautiful poems. Steffi had been amazed.

After the restaurant they had walked along the Seine, and the afternoon wore on, Charles had confided that he and his wife were living apart, and that there had been talk of beginning divorce proceedings as soon as his daughter began attending a girl's preparatory school on the Côte d'Albâtre in the fall. On the way back to the university, Charles had showed her where he lived and had asked her up for a drink, but she had declined, not so much out of any feeling that it was "too soon" for that kind of thing — she was not coy — but rather because he was married, and she had felt uncomfortable visiting the apartment of a married man.

A few days later, back in Frankfurt, she had received a lovely note from him, telling her that he could not get her out of his thoughts, that he had that very day begun divorce proceedings, and asking if he could see her the next time she was in Paris. When Steffi read the note she laughed aloud, for the day before it arrived she had decided to go back to Paris and to see him. Their mutual attraction was overpowering, and she had not been inclined to suppress such an emotion despite her principles regarding his marital status. She never regretted that decision, but over the past year difficulties had begun to multiply until she knew the time had come to clear the air.

As she fixed her lover with her mesmerizing gaze, she felt as though she were falling in love with him all over again. All afternoon they had talked about the difference in their ages, about the distance separating them, and about their unflinching loyalties to their work, he to his assistant professorship at the Sorbonne in Paris and she to Doctor Adorno and the work of the Institute for Social Research in Frankfurt. They had discussed his wife, his separation, and his prospects for a divorce. In the end, Steffi felt much better. Perhaps this could be worked out after all. She had new respect for his aspirations, his passion for his field of study, for nineteenth-century French poetry, for Baudelaire, and for the immediate value of the two books that Charles had written on the great poet's life and work. In the end, she had realized that his work had more relevance in the present than she had originally thought and that, indeed, his critique of nineteenth-century literature was timely and remarkably poignant. In addition, she felt that he now had a better understanding of the practical nature of her work at the Institute and the importance of Critical Theory. She sensed that he had come to realize that her dedication to building a better society and a freer, more equal world was not just an intellectual dreamer's naïveté but a realization that modern society could no longer grasp its own functioning, and that societal transformation must begin with a critical examination of our foundering society. In the end, they had come away with a new respect for one another, and they re-embraced the possibility of building a life together despite the obstacles that they faced. Now only her activism and their differences regarding revolution remained to be confronted — the age-old question of theory versus praxis.

As the afternoon wore on, Charles had suggested that they pursue this last issue over a glass of wine, so they headed for a little café they liked on the Boulevard Saint-Michel just around the corner from his flat. They began to discuss the current political crisis and the ongoing student revolts, and it quickly became clear that each of them was conflicted. They both had opinions on the subject, to be sure, but both had serious doubts, both harbored nagging sympathies for the position of the other side. At the bottom of it all, they both questioned the students' methods. Charles felt them wrong-minded, and Steffi feared activism's seemingly inevitable abuses, despite the fact that she believed in the necessity for extra-parliamentary action.

It deeply troubled Steffi that, in the back of her mind, she continually questioned Charles's politics. Had she been blaming her lover for her own vacillating concerns regarding the methods of the radical Left, or was her fear much deeper — did she suspect that Charles lacked the passion, the goodness, the moral certitude necessary to support liberal causes and social justice? She could never live with such a flaw. On the other hand, perhaps Charles's rational powers were simply greater than her own. Perhaps he was simply able to curb his passions because he knew them to be presently counterproductive, even suicidal. Her mind told her that, if this were the case, then he was right, that he might even be a better liberal, a more effective reformer than she currently was. On the other hand, her heart feared that he, like herself, might be weak, only in a different and somehow less noble way. Whatever the case, Steffi reflected, they both feared the irrational crowd.

"They have no real program," Charles was saying of the student radicals as the waiter placed the luminous glasses before them. "They refuse to examine the issues, and they ignore possible parliamentary solutions. Instead, they rush to the streets in order to attempt to force or intimidate the authorities to do things that those in power can neither believe in, nor rationalize, nor find support for in their electoral mandate. Worst of all, they fail to realize the mind-boggling complexity of the issues involved. Never has there been an era when the problems of public policy approached the complexity we face today. Everything is changing so fast. I mean with technology and the explosion of knowledge, gaining understanding of the ambiguities involved, much less formulating solutions, takes years. Yet these students, who have not studied the issues in any depth, possess such a cock-sure certainty as to the correct course to be followed."[1]

"Politically and socially you are right," said the beautiful young German, "and you know full well that, with my work at the Institute, I have carefully studied the complexities of these issues. Still, for me, that is not the real point. At the bottom of it all, it does not always turn on a political or a social issue. It turns on a moral issue. Take opposition to the war, for example."

---

1 George F. Kennan, *Democracy and the Student Left* (Boston: Little Brown, 1968) quoted in Spender, *Year of the Young Rebels*, 121.

"My point, exactly," said Charles. "Moral issues always reduce the complex to the simple."

"You can't have it both ways, my darling," said Steffi. "No matter how complex the reasons for the war may be, war itself is the classic example of reducing the complex to the simple. Napalm bombs iron out all the complexities of politics. I'm not saying that there are not times when war is justified. I am only saying that there are many times when it is not, and this is one of them. There are times, perhaps most times, when war is morally wrong. All of the complexities in the world do not invalidate the position of a person who thinks a war is morally wrong. The person who objects on moral grounds is not answered by saying that he knows too little about it. All of the laws in the world, all of the governments in the world have no right to reach into the domain of the individual soul. In the end, every individual is responsible to a higher authority, and whether it be religious or merely personal, within certain limits, personal moral judgments are sacrosanct."[1]

"I can't argue with that," smiled Charles. "Within limits one's morals must be one's own. Still, if our government is so wicked that the young are justified in disregarding the established process and refusing to obey the law, then democracy will surely degenerate into revolution, anarchy, and probably dictatorship."

"That's what I am afraid of," said Steffi. "Nonetheless, if the reasons for war are so complex as to be unexplainable to the average man in the street, much less to the students, then our democracy is already in a world of trouble."

Charles thought about this for a long while. Finally, he raised his glass and smiled, inviting her to a toast. "Touché," he said.

As their glasses touched, they became aware for the first time that the broad boulevard outside had become engulfed by a surging mob of angry students.

* * *

Only hours before, a rare rogue's gallery of radical leaders had gathered in the *cour d'honneur*, the central courtyard of the Sorbonne in Paris. All week students at Nanterre, directed by the 22nd of March Movement, had been preparing to defend their suburban university complex against an attack threatened by the reactionary forces of "the Occident." The prospect of such extreme violence had forced the administration to close the Nanterre campus on Thursday, May 2, and with that closing, activist leaders of all stripes had gravitated toward the Sorbonne the next day. There, they were joined by their urban counterparts on the Left Bank.

Everyone knew that in three days the disciplinary committee of the university would meet to decide the fate of the eight student leaders from Nanterre who had been charged in connection with the disturbance at the American embassy. The pending sanctions against Danny Cohen-Bendit and the others had become a rallying point for the radicalization of students at Nanterre, and now it was spreading to Paris where 150,000 students attended the enormous University of Paris I-V complex. Tensions were high as several hundred radical leaders gathered in the shadow of the historic *Eglise de la Sorbonne* in the heart of the Parisian Latin Quarter, so called because long ago the Latin spoken in the classrooms by professors and students had often spilled over into the streets.

Only a few blocks away, the well-drilled quasi-military rightwing forces of "the Occident" marched in opposition to the student Left, distributing leaflets that read: "...we have decided to bring to an end the Bolshevik agitation in the schools of the

---

1 Spender, *Year of the Young Rebels*, 120-5.

university by all means. We shall show on Friday the 3rd that we are able to oppose Red terror and to re-establish order with the means required."[1] To add to the tension, the night before a fire had been set in the offices of the student association at the Sorbonne. The arsonists had left their mark: a Celtic cross, the unmistakable sign of the reactionary forces of "the Occident." In response to these provocations, some of the leftist student leaders who met in the Sorbonne's great internal courtyard wore helmets and carried sticks.

On his way to the Sorbonne, Daniel Cohn-Bendit had seen the Celtic crosses worn on the sleeves of the helmeted rightwing army of "the Occident" as it paraded along the Boulevard de Saint-Michel toward the Sorbonne. Farther along, he had passed squads of riot police with Plexiglas masks, armored sleeves, and white clubs waiting to disperse the on-coming reactionary army.[2] When Danny entered the *cour d'honneur*, the meeting was already underway. Plans were being laid for a mass demonstration on Monday, May 6, to protest the sanctions that were sure to be leveled against the eight student leaders that morning. Looking around the courtyard, Danny recognized the heads of many different radical factions. Members of his own 22nd of March Movement were there as well as other groups with stronger ties at the Sorbonne: two brands of Trotskyites, the Maoists, the left-wing socialists, and a few communists. It was a "who's who" of the Parisian radical Left; only the Marxists-Leninists were not there.

"This is not their kind of affair," Danny thought to himself. "They don't like cocktail parties. Beside, they're probably off somewhere licking their wounds. They have taken quite a beating lately."[3] The fact was that Danny himself found these "strategy" meetings tedious. Such gatherings often degenerated into forums for ideological rhetoric with which he had no patience.

The meeting was orderly enough. The 400 or so student leaders occupied only a corner of the enormous courtyard. Around and above them loomed the ornate Second Empire style walls of the late nineteenth-century architecture that was so typical in Paris. High arched first-floor arcades supported elegant neoclassical fenestration on the second and third floors topped with steep gray slate mansard roofs bedecked with elaborate dormers and flamboyant rondelles. At one end of the great courtyard stood the *Eglise de la Sorbonne*, begun in 1635. Inside lay the remains of Cardinal Richelieu. Outside, larger-than-life statues of Louis Pasteur and Victor Hugo stood guard. There was some irony in that. Richelieu's Sorbonne had stood as an unassailable bulwark defending the Catholic Church against the corrupting forces of the Enlightenment. Now two great marble symbols of enlightenment, Pasteur and Hugo, the scientific and artistic voices of a well-established Age of Reason, watched over the resting place of the great defender of superstition and myth. Danny recalled Victor Hugo's famous image: the author in his garret looking out upon the distant towers of Notre Dame and holding his pen aloft to declare, "This will kill that." So it had been. And now, he egotistically mused, "We are on the edge of another revolutionary era; another chapter in the great dialectic of history is about to be written."

* * *

1 Singer, *Prelude to Revolution*, 119.

2 From an interview with an anonymous member of the 22nd of March Movement, in Labro et al., *This Is Only the Beginning*, 92.

3 From an interview with an anonymous member of the 22nd of March Movement, in Labro et al., *This Is Only the Beginning*, 92.

Around 4:00 in the afternoon, the meeting was cut short by the news that the police had completely surrounded the Sorbonne. In the ensuing confusion, a spokesman
for the left-wing socialists addressed all those who suddenly found themselves prisoners in the *cour d'honneur*. "The police have no right to be on these grounds without
the express permission of the university administration. Obviously, the administration has betrayed us. This is unprecedented. The Sorbonne is student territory, and
the authorities now dare to infringe on the university's traditional independence, on
freedom of expression and critical thinking.[1] Today we see the repressive face of the
Gaullist university system as it commits an oppressive crime right in the symbolic
heart of French academic freedom."

There was considerable discussion as to how to respond. It was reported that the
police force outside, fresh from dispersing the Occident crowd, was massive, number-
ing perhaps in the thousands, and that the notorious CRS[2] (*Compagnies Républicaines de
Sécurité*, or National Security Guards) riot squad stood poised, helmeted, truncheons
in hand, tear gas grenades at the ready. It was clear that physical resistance would
be suicidal. After some discussion, they wisely decided not to fight. Then, following
more talk and a short negotiation with representatives of the police, an agreement
was reached. If the students would disperse, leaving the courtyard in small groups of
twenty-five, women first, they would be allowed to pass through the police lines and
would not be arrested.

By 4:15, the women were filing out of the courtyard past the army of police outside.
At about 4:30, as the men were preparing to leave, a tough squad of CRS commandos
suddenly burst into the yard, formed a line, and forced the remaining students out of
the enclosure through the narrow passageway into Rue de la Sorbonne, where they
were methodically herded into the black paddy wagons that the French call *"paniers à
salade,"* "salad bowls." It was an ignominious double-cross.[3]

Danny struggled and shouted insults at the policeman, who threw him into a
waiting van. All around, vans filled with cursing students were pulling out into Rue
de la Sorbonne and turning left into Rue des Écoles, heading for the Boulevard Saint-
Michel. On the wide boulevard, the scene was chaotic. Angry crowds lined the street.
Farther on, the vans slowed to a stop as huge throngs of angry students filled the
roadway. With fanatical abandon, an enormous mob blocked the way, closing in on
the police motorcade and chanting *"Libérez nos camarades."* Helpless inside one of the
vans, Danny and his fellow arrestees could only look on in wonder. Who were these
people? Where had they come from?

"Are these your people?" one of them asked Danny.

"No. Are they yours?" the redhead replied. "This is incredible."

The swarming mob began to rock the van. Sirens blared. More police waded into
the crowd, nightsticks swinging. This only served to further enrage the surging students who responded with a hail of cobblestones, bottles, ashtrays, and even mustard
pots from nearby cafes. Students ripped up huge iron grates and lay them in the path
of the vans. Others ignited pyres of papers to prevent the motorcycle police from
getting through.[4]

---

1 Fraser, et al., *1968: A Student Generation in Revolt*, 178.
2 The *Compagnies Républicaines de Sécurité* was organized after World War II as a notional security
 force aimed at neutralizing the threat that the regular police might oppose the government
 in a civil war.
3 Singer, *Prelude to Revolution*, 178.
4 Fraser, et al., *1968: A Student Generation in Revolt*, 178-9.

"This is incredible," repeated Danny, laughing wildly.

The revolution had begun unpredictably — just as he had predicted. It was clear that there were no leaders, for all the leaders were inside the besieged vans. The actions of the crowd were completely spontaneous. The surging multitude had become a living thing. Each individual had unwittingly surrendered his or her personal autonomy to the single unthinking collective rage of the crowd. All of their passions had become one flesh.

SATURDAY, MAY 4, 1968

At 8:00 a.m., Eliot and Kurt claimed their bags at Orly and as they emerged from customs Steffi rushed to greet them. Embracing Kurt warmly, she greeted Eliot over her brother's shoulder. "Welcome to Paris, Eliot. So good to see you again," she said in English.

"Happy to be here," said Eliot, "but let's speak German. I need the practice."

"*D'accord, où Français, peut-être?*" she said, smiling.

"No, no, please," said the young American. "I'm afraid my French is non-existent, *Nicht sein, komdisch.*"

"Very well," said Steffi, releasing her younger brother from her grasp, "German it is." She continued in that language, "Come, Papa has sent the Embassy car for you."

"Really!" said Kurt. "What's with all the pomp and circumstance?"

"There's been some trouble on the Left Bank. The papers are playing it down, but he seems to think it's serious, and so do I. Come on, I can tell you all about it on the way. I'm so glad we're in Paris again, just like when we were kids. I can't wait."

The black Mercedes deftly negotiated the tangled web of interchanges surrounding the airport and headed north toward the city along the Avenue d'Italie.

"I don't know how anyone ever finds the way out of this airport, Stefan," said Kurt to the driver.

"I come here nearly every day, Sir," came the reply.

"So what's up on the Left Bank, Stef," said Kurt settling back into the plush leather.

"Well, I haven't pieced it all together at this point, but I know what I read, what I was told, and what I saw on the Boulevard Saint-Michel last night. It's pretty frightening. Thousands of students and police in the streets, fierce fighting, even barricades. Over 600 arrested, 100 injured, including many police, according to the papers. The real figure is probably much higher."

"What was it all about?" asked Kurt.

"That's the mystery; it's really hard to say. I don't think anyone has a really good grip on what's going on, not the authorities, not the police, and not even the students. It was certainly not planned, and as far as I can tell the intensity of the violence surprised everyone involved."

Her handsome younger brother closed his eyes and shook his head slowly from side to side, "Good God, here we go again. Incredible." Then turning to Eliot he said, "You Americans have a phrase for this kind of thing. You know, jumping from the cooking pot or something like that."

"Yeah," said Eliot grimacing, "We've jumped out of the frying pan and into the fire," he replied in English.

"That's very good," said Steffi in English, "and very apt, because I don't think this is over, not by a long shot, as you Americans say."

"How did it start?" asked Eliot, reverting to German.

"Well, I can tell you what little I know along with a lot of what I suspect. You know, of course, that it has been an edgy spring here, I mean, the Paris Peace Talks will be starting up and that's fired a lot of antiwar and pro-North Vietnam demonstrations here.[1] The talks have provided the student Left with a visible forum for protest. Add to that the violence in Caen in January and the nationwide students' free-speech demonstrations in February,[2] as well as all the protests that erupted in the wake of Rudi's assassination attempt in April, and you can get a feel for the kind powder keg that exists on French campuses today. There's been a deep dissatisfaction for years, a sense that the French university system is hopelessly over-crowded and outdated. There is also the truly radical situation at Nanterre. I was there in April; I wrote you about that."

Kurt nodded. "Yes, I've been corresponding with Danny too. He told me about your visit and the situation there."

"Well, it was pretty extreme, and it's gotten a lot worse. Last week "the Occident" was threatening to march on Nanterre, and, fearing an all-out street war, the administration closed the entire campus there on Thursday. In the meantime, there is a strong feeling among the students both in Paris and in Nanterre that Danny and seven other leaders from Nanterre are being unfairly singled out for disciplinary action. They're scheduled to go before the disciplinary committee at the Sorbonne on Monday, the 6th, the day after tomorrow. Everyone is up in arms about that."

"Sound familiar?" Kurt looked at Eliot.

"Vaguely," said Eliot.

"Anyway, the best I can tell, yesterday, Friday, radical leaders from the Sorbonne and from Nanterre held a meeting in the *cour d'honneur* at the Sorbonne to discuss demonstrations to be held on Monday in support of Danny and the others. Again, *l'Occident* threatened to intervene, but the CRS broke up their march. This is only speculation on my part, but I think that the Dean then called in the police to arrest the leftist leaders (some 400 altogether) while they were all confined in one place and while the rest of the student body was at home cramming for exams. He must have run this idea by government authorities higher up, who must have also seen it as a golden opportunity to strike a deathblow to the radical Left once and for all without the rest of the student population being able to interfere. As it turned out, this was a colossal miscalculation."

"The arrogance of power backfired," said Eliot.

"More like it set off a powerful explosive chain reaction that no one was prepared for. Around 4:00 yesterday afternoon, I was having a glass of wine with Charles in a little café around the corner from the university when all hell suddenly broke loose. It was wild. Students swarmed out of the classrooms, out of the libraries, out of the cafés and into the streets, filling the Boulevard Saint-Michel, shouting for the release of their comrades. Rumors of police treachery spread like wildfire throughout the

---

1 On March 31, 1968, in the same speech when President Johnson announced that he would not seek re-election, he also announced that peace talks had been scheduled to begin in Paris on May 10. Preparations for these meetings provided anti-war activists in France a rallying point. These public talks resulted in stalemate, and they were suspended in 1969. Secret talks continued in Paris until the Paris Peace Accord calling for a U.S. withdrawal from Vietnam was reached in 1973.

2 On January 26, 1968, there were violent exchanges between police and student demonstrators backing the striking workers in Caen. On February 14, 1968, there were incidents at universities throughout France in connection with a national student protest demanding freedom of speech and movement within the university.

Latin Quarter, and the student's reaction was beyond anyone's imagination. Word of police treachery and the sight of heavily-armed CRS and special police units in the Sorbonne sparked a fierce anger in even the most mild-mannered of students. Even the girls fought with abandon."

"For their part, the police were caught completely off guard, and in the course of the mêlée a lot of innocent by-standers got clobbered. We saw helmeted police venting their rage on passers-by and even patrons in the café. This further enraged almost everyone. Before long, it was truncheons and grenades against sticks and stones, but the more the police clubbed and the more tear gas they used, the larger, angrier, and more daring the student mob became. Hundreds quickly became thousands. They didn't give ground. They attacked the police, who had apparently never encountered this kind of tenacity before. In the end, the CRS and other police groups fell back and set up defensive positions around the Sorbonne."

"At that point Charles walked me across to the Right Bank and I caught a cab to Papa's flat. On the way, across the Île de la Cité and crossing the Pont d'Arcole to the Quay de Gesvres, we passed hundreds of young people running toward the Latin Quarter. Farther west, on the Pont au Change, we could see a line of police vans also heading that way. Charles said that, by the time he got back to his place off Rue Saint-Jacques near the university, it had become a territorial war, the police defending the Sorbonne, and the students staking out their turf along the Boulevards Saint-Germain, Saint-Michel, Rue Gay-Lussac and to the south and west toward Montparnasse. He said they had even built a small barricade in Saint-Michel. This morning students were still pouring into the Latin Quarter. We saw them crossing the Seine from the Right Bank on Rue de la Cité as we passed along the river on our way to the airport."

"So it's still going on, now?" asked Kurt.

"Yes, I think there's a kind of stalemate now, but the students' numbers are growing. We even saw high school kids heading that way this morning. At this point, no one knows how many are in the streets of the Latin Quarter. By now they must certainly number in the tens of thousands."

They were silent for a while. The car entered the Place d'Italie and turned right into the Boulevard Vincent Auriol. At last, Kurt's beautiful sister broke the silence. "It was like a dream," she said. "I mean, it couldn't have happened so quickly, so seamlessly, so spontaneously, so violently. It wasn't possible. It couldn't have been real." She spoke these last words to no one, but rather she rhythmically and methodically mouthed them like a familiar litany, as if reciting some kind of mantra with the power to create a new version history in which the whole thing had never happened.

* * *

That night Kurt and Steffi's father treated them to a lovely supper in a little restaurant in Rue Jean Goujon, not far from his apartment. All the talk was of the events on the Left Bank. Herr Siegel told them that the intelligence received today at the West German Embassy indicated broad support for the student revolt all across France. The morning papers had been full of reports of police brutality against innocent bystanders, and the nation was outraged.

"Right now, I suspect that public support is with the students, who, despite their leftist rhetoric, don't frighten good people the way the unions and the communists do," he told them. "The occupation of the Sorbonne, the arrests, the oppressive police violence are seen by the nation as scandals." What is more, recently General De Gaulle has shown a lofty disdain for public opinion. Our diplomatic intelligence tells us that the French people resent this kind of paternalism, that they feel impotent, powerless, cut off from the free flow of their own politics. I fear that the violence last night and the apparent righteousness of the student cause will beget a great deal more violence in the coming days. Most of the student leaders who were arrested in the courtyard yesterday have been freed, and they're now organizing a huge demonstration to take place outside the Sorbonne for Monday, the sixth. Their immediate cause is to free the Sorbonne and obtain the release of those arrested in the fighting last night and still being held by authorities. The university teachers' union and a good portion of the faculty support the student rebels."

As a father, Herr Siegel's inclination was to tell them to stay away from the Left Bank, but he knew that they were no longer children, so he let it go with a simple warning. "You have to understand that the CRS is not like any other police you may have encountered. They're a national police force specially trained to stifle dissent. They're notoriously brutal. In my opinion, they're part of the problem, so be very careful. I'm afraid this whole affair is fraught with serious danger for France and for everyone who participates in this attempted emancipation."

Wolfgang Siegel the diplomat was a well-informed, charming, and gracious host, and the food was superb. Eliot knew that he was very high up in the West German government, and very well connected. Kurt had once told Eliot that his father was close friends with both Theodor Adorno and Herbert Marcuse. Nonetheless, after his trans-Atlantic flight, the American was having trouble keeping his eyes open. As soon as they returned to Herr Siegel's apartment, he made his excuses and retired. Herr Siegel shuffled off to his study, leaving Steffi and Kurt alone on the small balcony overlooking the pleasant tree-lined street. It was difficult to imagine that, not far away, students and police were engaged in a battle for the streets of the Latin Quarter.

Kurt related the details of the Columbia revolt, his misgivings about the American Left, and the seeming futility of any efforts to dislodge the American public from their velvet prison of material comfort, conformity, and the growing seductions of modern capitalist consumerism. Steffi listened carefully and declared that Europe was certainly moving quickly in the same direction. They discussed her work at the Institute in this regard and Herr Doctor Adorno's increasing melancholy in the face of the audacity of the revolting students.

After a short silence, Steffi turned to her brother. "I've been having...well, visions," she began. "It's very troubling. Perhaps I'm going a little over the edge."

Her brother looked at her quizzically. His first impulse was to laugh, but for some reason he did not. "Tell me about these 'visions,'" he said.

"Well, do you know what Charles Baudelaire looked like?" she said after a moment.

Every French schoolchild had encountered late nineteenth-century photographs of the great poet. With dark haunting disillusioned eyes, Charles Baudelaire stared out, malnourished and forlorn, from the pages of virtually every French literature textbook published in the twentieth century.

"Sure, I guess so," he mused. "Gaunt, debauched, thin, deep-set eyes, thinning hair, like the brilliant, sad, syphilitic drug addict that he was."

"Well, I've seen him here in Paris," said Steffi, "or his ghost — twice now."

Kurt didn't know quite what to say.

"I caught a glimpse of him on the Metro platform at Les Halles a few weeks ago. I thought it was just some kind of daydream, but last night I saw him up close. He was real. I mean, he seemed real — not ten feet from me on the edge of a crowd of students gathered beside one of the old bookseller's stands on the quay by the Petit Pont on the Left Bank. He was staring at me. Then he was gone."

Her brother nodded for her to continue.

"I've been reading Walter Benjamin's. 'Charles Baudelaire, A Lyric Poet in the Era of High Capitalism.' Charles gave it to me. You know, Charles is considered an expert. He says that Baudelaire was, in many ways, the inspiration for Benjamin's masterwork, *The Arcades Project*. Benjamin was inspired because he grasped the contradiction in Baudelaire's poetry — that the modern hero is both immersed completely in modern capitalism and simultaneously engaged in a struggle against it."

"Yes, I've read some of that. Walter Benjamin is difficult," said Kurt.

"Yes, so I read Charles's book too. He says that Benjamin understood that Baudelaire articulated the paradoxes and illusions of modernity even while he participated in it. Charles says that, central to all of this, is the figure of the *Flaneur*, the city wanderer, the passionate urban spectator. According to him, for Walter Benjamin this figure gleaned from Baudelaire gave voice to both 'the shock and the intoxication of modernity.' I'm beginning to believe that this contradiction is the key to Walter Benjamin. As he himself put it, 'We are unable to respond to the new technical possibilities with a comparably new social order.'[1] The result is a contradiction most clearly manifest in the commodity, a contradiction that determines all forms of expression and makes them appear displaced as in a dream. That's why, for Benjamin, all cultural expressions are merely dream images, phantasmagoria, since the old and the new elements appear in them all mixed up together."[2]

"*Mais je poursuis en vain le Dieu qui se retire; L'irrésistible Nuit établit son empire, Noire, humide, funeste et pleine de frissons*,[3] Kurt muttered thoughtfully, reciting something he had been made to memorize in high school. "The end of God, the beginning of a cold, harsh modern age, images of fear and death."

"Yes. Charles says, 'Baudelaire is the heir to the failed revolutions of the spirit, and to the successful revolutions of matter, commerce, industry,'[4] meaning he is 'the first real poet of the Modern Age.' The title of his masterwork says it all: *Les Fleurs du Mal, The Flowers of Evil*, the ambiguous tension of the modern world."

"Right, good. Listen to me. It's OK. Don't fight this, Stef," said Kurt. "Embrace these visions, they're only that, visions, and like all dreams, sleeping or waking, they are simply figments of your fertile brain. Clearly, they involve your feelings for Charles. But that's not all. Can't you see, they're also related to your work, to the revolution, to your striving for a better society, a better world? Recognize this vision for what it is: just another critique of modern society. So what if you happen to receive your critical revelations in visions of Charles Baudelaire? Hell, I talk to Karl Marx, and half the time I really almost believe we're conversing. It's OK. Remember what you just

---

1 Benjamin, *Gesammelte Schriften*, 1257, quoted in Bernd Witte, *Walter Benjamin: An Intellectual Biography*, trans. James Roilleston (Detroit: Wayne State University Press, 1991), 177.

2 Witte, *Walter Benjamin*, 177.

3 But it's in vain I chase my God receding.
Night irresistible, damp, black, unheeding
Establishes her empire, full of fear.
—Charles Baudelaire, "*Le Coucher du Soleil Romantique*" ("The Setting of the Sun of Romanticism"), in *Fleurs du Mal (Flowers of Evil)*, trans. Roy Campbell, *Poems of Baudelaire* (New York: Pantheon Books, 1952).

4 A. S. Kline, "Voyage to Modernity: The Poetry of Charles Baudelaire," pttp://www.tonvkline. co.uk/PITBR/Frecnh/VoyageToModernitypage.htm.

told me, the modern world is 'a contradiction that determines all forms of expression and makes them appear displaced as in a dream.' Like Benjamin and Baudelaire, you are participating in the dream world we're fighting. We're all seduced by dreams. We just have to recognize these modern dreams for the hollow falsehoods that they represent. That's what Benjamin and Baudelaire are trying to tell you."

"You know, I've always thought that they were love poems," said Steffi after a minute, "very sad love poems."

"They are," said Kurt.

Chapter Nineteen: Frankfurt

Would it have been worth while
If one, settling a pillow or throwing off a shawl,
And turning toward the window, should say,
"That's not it at all,
That is not what I meant at all."
— T. S. Eliot, "The Love Song of J. Alfred Prudrock"

The road to Hell is paved with good intentions.
— Karl Marx (attributed)

Monday, May 6, 1968

Theodor Adorno was depressed, overwhelmed by a debilitating sadness. Everything seemed to be in shambles. The student strike at the University of Frankfurt had escalated into a siege, complete with marching pickets, a blockade of the main entrance, the violent occupation of the rector's office, and the renaming as "Karl Marx University." Relentlessly the students pressured him. As the leading representative of Critical Theory and its compelling critique of capitalist society, he was under constant pressure to endorse their cause and openly share solidarity with their radical goals. However, in a steadfast effort to preserve his independence as a theoretician, he refused. As always, on the threshold of practice, he retreated into theory.

Today the striking students were complaining about his refusal to join in the great National March on Bonn planned for May 11 — a mass demonstration organized to protest the government's proposed "Emergency Laws." Adorno tried to defuse this criticism with self-deprecating humor. "I do not know if elderly gentlemen with a paunch are the right people to take part in demonstrations,"[1] he said. But the students were in no mood for humor. He tried a rational approach, declaring that

---

1 Adorno, Theodor, "*Diskussionsbeitrag am 23 September 1968*," *Frankfurter Adorno Blätter*, 4:77, in Müller-Doohm, *Adorno*, 461.

---

his "natural aversion to practical politics" and the "objective futility of practical action" coincided at this particular moment in history. He tried a frontal attack on the students' behavior, charging that their approach was "narrow-minded" and that their strategies were degenerating into "abominable irrationalism."[1]

Despite all his efforts to keep theory and practice separate, the students viewed his failure to back their cause as a contradiction. "Herr Professor Adorno is ready at all times to certify that the Federal Republic has a latent tendency towards inhumanity," one student leaflet charged. "Confronted with the inhumanity...he declines to make a statement. He prefers to endure in silence the contradictions whose existence he has previously drawn to our attention."[2] Such charges were deeply hurtful. After all his years as a teacher, how could he be so misunderstood? Every day, his feelings of helplessness and isolation were becoming more intense.

He wrote to his friend Marcuse that he no longer felt that he had his feet on the ground, "a state of mind that occurs with normal people only under the influence of drugs. I am only thankful that I have no need of them."[3] The thought of drugs reminded him of Walter Benjamin, and he tried to imagine the state of mind of his long lost friend in the last days before his suicide. These dark imaginings drew him even deeper into depression.

Adding to his melancholy was the ongoing criticism stirred by the remarks of Hannah Arendt upon the publication of *Illuminations*, her edited English translations of Walter Benjamin's best work. As the primary editor of Walter's original writings in German, Doctor Adorno had been charged by Arendt with censoring Walter's manuscripts and distorting his old friend's intent. The charge had resulted in something of an intellectual witch-hunt. He could not avoid taking these charges personally; after all, one old friend had accused him of betraying another, and he found that devastating. "She would really like to turn us into murders, even though it was we who kept him above water for seven years,"[4] he wrote to Marcuse. In the same letter, he told his Americanized friend that he thought that people were attacking him because they had lost faith in him as a theoretician when he refused to involve himself in practical politics.[5]

His doubts and anxieties were clear between the lines of this correspondence. Irrationalism was on the increase; the university of the future was in danger of losing the freedom without which speculative thought was impossible; his friends were suddenly attacking him. In the hope that Marcuse, with his newfound celebrity among the young, could reason with the students, he tried to persuade his old friend to come to Frankfurt.[6] He also altered his summer vacation plans, booking his customary month in the Alps at the Hotel d'Etrier in Crans-sur-Sierre in the Valais instead of his customary haunt in Sils Maria at the Waldhaus Hotel, in part because he knew Marcuse would be in nearby Zermatt, and he hoped that they might meet to work out their differences.

---

1 Theodor Adorno, letter to Günter Grass, November 4, 1968," *Frankfurter Adorno Blätter*, 4:78, in Müller-Doohm, *Adorno*, 461.

2 Kraushaar, *Frankfurter Schule und Studentenbewegung*, 2:161, quoted in Müller-Doohm, *Adorno*, 454.

3 Theodor Adorno, letter to Peter Szondi, June 14, 1968, Theodor W. Adorno Archive, Frankfurt am Main.

4 Theodor Adorno, "*Zur Onterpertaion Benjamins*" quoted in Rolf Tiedemann, "Notes," in Theodor Adorno, *Über Walter Benjamin*, Revised Edition (Frankfurt am Main, 1990), 99.

5 Theodor Adorno, letter to Gabriele Henkel, May 17, 1968, Theodor Adorno Archive, Frankfurt am Main.

6 Müller-Doohm, *Adorno*, 464-5.

CHAPTER TWENTY: PARIS

Looking into the Heart of Light...
— T. S. Eliot, "The Wasteland"

The commodity appears at first sight an extremely obvious, trivial thing. But its analysis brings out that it is a very strange thing, abounding in metaphysical subtleties and theological niceties.
— Karl Marx, *Capital*

MONDAY, MAY 6, 1968 (BLOODY MONDAY)

In Kurt's fertile mind, his sister's visions of Baudelaire served to reinforce the validity of his own odd habit of discussing revolutionary theory with Karl Marx, and he was quick to return to the subject at breakfast the next morning. As soon as Herr Siegel left for the embassy, he explained his sister's apparitions to Eliot, who found them vaguely troubling even though Kurt and Steffi seemed to accept her paranormal visitations as if they were quite usual. Both siblings seemed to know that these manifestations were not real, and yet, at the same time, they appeared to regard them as a natural source of intellectual insight. Somewhere in all of this was a contradiction that Eliot could not resolve. Nonetheless, it all seemed so normal, so matter-of-fact, to his two companions that he was compelled, if not to accept the sources of his friends' insights, then at least to move beyond them and surrender himself to the natural flow of the conversation.

Steffi was trying to explain Walter Benjamin's Marxist fascination with the great poet and his Parisian wanderings. After a little discussion, she excused herself and returned with the English translation of Charles' book, "For Walter Benjamin," she read aloud, "the passage through the bourgeois world acts as a critique of a world in which the new worship of commodities and the spectacle of their display functions like the old religion, as an opiate of the people. It is a world of image and illusion. He found the historical roots of this world in the Paris Arcades and in the poems of Charles Baudelaire. This is the world of the character that Benjamin called 'the *flaneur*,' the urban wanderer. Baudelaire himself was such a wanderer. To these historical notions, Walter Benjamin added a modern Marxist twist: the illusory capitalist display and the crowds that are drawn to it illuminate the ambiguity that characterizes our era. The crowds are immersed in both fantastic illusions and utopian wishes, a montage of realities and fantasies that both attract and repel the them. In this ambiguity, we find the potential to both pacify and to incite a kind of anarchy. The true revolutionary element can only be released by dispelling the illusions, exposing the mass marketing of dreams for what it is: the creation of a false demand dependent on fashion not on utility, the numbing sedation of the collective consciousness, and the illusion of individualism. 'The illusion of novelty,' Benjamin writes, 'is reflected, like one mirror in another, in the illusion of infinite sameness.' In the end, it all goes back to Marx."[1]

"That's deep stuff," said Eliot, continuing in English.

Looking up, Steffi's shining blue eyes fixed him, and for an instant he was reminded of Melissa. Melissa did not possess the classic beauty that Steffi wore so comfortably. She was tall, thin, her face angular and unadorned by eye shadow or even lipstick, yet there was something in the eyes. Melissa had an odd way of catching a fleeting glace and holding it the way Steffi now held his gaze. For an instant, he thought of Melissa's lean body against his. For that instant, he missed her terribly.

Steffi smiled at him and looked away. In that instant his lust was gone, and he blushed, wondering if she had been reading his mind.

"Let's be *flaneurs* today," said Kurt suddenly. "Let's take a new look at Paris, lose ourselves in the crowds, allow ourselves to be drawn to fashion and illusion, discover the ambiguity of Baudelaire's *Flowers of Evil*."

"That's what we've always done," said Steffi. "We've been *flaneurs* all along. We just didn't know it."

* * *

Just before 9:00 a.m., Daniel Cohn-Bendit and the seven other radical student leaders from Nanterre, who had been summoned to stand before the Disciplinary Committee at the Sorbonne, made their way to judgment through streets already teeming with angry students. Approaching the great university, they encountered an occupied fortress in hostile territory. Seemingly thousands of police surrounded the venerable institution: the regular police; the *gendarmes mobiles*, who were part of the army; and the CRS or *Compagnies Républicaines de Sécurité*, a special national riot police force well known for callous brutality.[2] As they entered the Sorbonne single file through a vast cordon of heavily armed police, the eight accused students began resolutely singing *The Internationale*, the traditional anthem of socialist worker solidarity. At the sound of their raised voices, the students gathered across the street cheered loudly, and as the chorus began, the crowd joined in and sang along in lusty defiance.

"*C'est la lutte finale*
Groupons-nous, et demain
L'Internationale
Sera le genre humain."[3]

---

1 Buck-Morss, "Walter Benjamin—Revolutionary Writer," *New Left Review*, No. 128, July/August, 1981.
2 Singer, *Prelude to Revolution*, 125.
3 The original French words were written in 1870 by Eugene Porrier (1816–1887), (later a member of the Paris Commune) and were originally intended to be sung to the tune of "La

---

The farcical absurdity of the impending proceeding was not lost on the protestors outside the Sorbonne any more than it was on the robed inquisitors inside. Outside the world was crumbling. Pitched battles raged nightly. Hundreds had been injured. Tens of thousands openly defied police in the streets, and the nation seemed to be teetering on the edge of insurrection if not outright revolution. Nonetheless, inside the empty university, impotent and alone, a formal panel of academic dignitaries tediously heard testimony from eight students charged with the laughably trivial offense of having "held meetings without permission" and "disturbed the peace."[1] Danny and the others went through the motions, knowing that no one's heart was in the judicial charade. In the end, they were told that a verdict would be rendered on Friday, but it was clear to everyone that this was not going to happen. The administration's unswerving determination to sit in judgment of these students, regardless of the surrounding circumstances, provided a poignant illustration of just how far the French university system had drifted from reality.

* * *

After the meeting of the Disciplinary Committee, Danny and the others joined the growing crowd outside the police lines that surrounded the Sorbonne. There was confused discussion as to what to do — storm the Sorbonne or move into working class neighborhoods to try to muster support. There was impassioned rhetoric regarding the importance of soliciting the workers to join the ranks of the protest. Others thought that autonomous student action would itself naturally draw the workers into the fray. Daniel Cohn-Bendit had no patience for such debates; they only fostered disunity. Using a bullhorn, he urged the crowd to disregard the theoretical debates and to act. "The time for debate is ended," he declared. "Only in action is there unity."

Since his release from police custody on Saturday morning, Danny had been attempting to foil the schemes of the various left-wing groups to take control of the situation. The Maoists wanted to leave the Latin Quarter and concentrate on propaganda through action committees in working class neighborhoods. The Trotskyites wanted the powerful student union to induce labor to take to the streets and join in the protest. The communists in the government and the labor unions were critical of the student rebellion, calling it "an irresponsible political adventure," "pseudo-revolutionary," and detrimental to the cause of the workers. "Stalinist creeps," Danny spat as he read the stilted accounts of Friday night's Left Bank battle in the communist newspaper, *L'Humanité*. Through it all, Daniel Cohn-Bendit and the 22nd of March Movement had opposed all attempts to manipulate the moment and to mold the stu-

---

Marseillaise." Pierre Degeyter (1848–1932) set the poem to music in 1888 and his melody became widely used soon after.

Literal translation:
It is the final struggle
Let us gather, and tomorrow
The Internationale
Will be mankind!

The most common English versions are not direct translations. For example:
" So comrades, come rally
The last fight let us face
The Internationale
Unites the human race.

1 Touraine, *The May Movement*, 166.

dents' sudden revolutionary zeal to fit any of the myriad theoretical and ideological images of what a revolution should be like, or what it should strive to achieve.

The crowd outside the Sorbonne was unsure, and as it began to move forward it encountered the massive police barrier. Deflected and not yet ready to fight, the throng moved northward and crossed the Seine, marching toward the center of Paris and shouting, "Sorbonne for the Students," "CRS — SS," and "Down with Police Repression." As they marched, their numbers grew. Students streamed out of the side streets to join the masses in the boulevards, singing *The Internationale*, waving red and black flags, and chanting, "Free the Sorbonne." Danny noticed that some of those joining the march were high school students. "The last two years' efforts to politicize the high schools are paying off," he thought. "The creation of the CAL (*Comités d'Action Lycéens*) is bearing fruit."

Spectators lined the streets. Even in the finest of neighborhoods and in the business districts there were cheers of support. To Danny's surprise, there were no boos. After a few hours of marching through the city, he could feel the pressure to return to the Left Bank beginning to build. Now several thousand strong,[1] this great moving mass of anger and protest needed no leaders. Born of both the fiery spontaneity of Friday night's bloody clashes with the police and the smoldering frustrations of a lifetime, the will of the crowd was above any leadership, beyond the control of any man or group — free, impulsive, arbitrary, fearless, and bent on retaking the Sorbonne.

* * *

Kurt, Steffi, and Eliot were sitting in a sidewalk café in Avenue Victoria across from the Place du Châtelet when the students surged into the streets surrounding the great square that was considered by many to be the historical center of Paris. The animated mass of shouting marchers came boldly down the Boulevard de Sébastopol, shouting "*Libérez nos camarades!*" (Free Our Comrades)! Blocking traffic, they circled the plaza and headed south toward the Pont au Change and the Left Bank.

"I read that the French authorities held special courts over the weekend and sentenced some of the demonstrators from Friday night's fighting to jail terms," said Eliot.

"Yes," said Kurt, "they have released most of the 600 or so that were arrested, but four were sentenced to prison terms. Very foolish. It works to justify the students' cause and creates public sympathy for them. The feeling is that those who were jailed were only trying to free the university that had been taken from them by the police."

"There's Danny," exclaimed Steffi, pointing to a dense mob of students passing by the famous Napoleonic column that stood in the center of the plaza. Sure enough, following her gesture, Kurt could make out the stout elfish figure of his friend at the front of one of the surging student bands.

"He's the little red-headed guy in front. There!" said, Kurt pointing out his fiery friend for Eliot's benefit.

"Should we join them?" said Steffi halfheartedly.

"No!" said her gray-eyed brother. "Not today. We're on vacation."

* * *

---

1 Estimates of the crowd size on Monday, May 6th, vary. The most conservative accounts place the size of early morning crowd at the Sorbonne as about 200 and estimate that it grew to as many as 10,000 by night fall. Other estimates are considerably higher placing the number of morning protestors at the Sorbonne at 2000 and estimating that as many as 20,000 participated by that evening.

At about 3:00 p.m., Danny moved to the head of the crowd of angry students as it paralleled the Left Bank moving slowly along the Boulevard Saint-Germain. It was hard to gauge the size of the teeming mob that he led, but it appeared to be close to 5000.[1] Danny knew that beyond a certain point numbers were not important. "The streets behind the Sorbonne are narrow, and only those marchers at the front will be engaged in the fight," he mused. "The rest will only push them forward. The important thing is that they be ready to fight."

After a few hours of parading around the Right Bank gathering strength, Danny knew these "soldiers" were indeed ready. He also knew that they could not be led — only marginally directed and then unleashed.

Expertly Danny and few others directed the crowd past the Boulevard Saint-Michel, which led to the main entrance of the great university at the Place de Sorbonne. That plaza, he knew, was teeming with riot police. A few blocks away, he could see the police coaches parked across the broad thoroughfare where three rows of helmeted CRS menacingly stood their ground. Attempting a kind of flanking movement, he and the others coaxed the throng up Rue Saint-Jacques, which led to the rear of the main university complex. A few blocks ahead, he could see a black line of police silhouetted against the elegant white marble of the Sorbonne, their steel helmets gleaming. Goggled, and armed with nightsticks and shields, a booted army of shock troops loomed impregnable before France's most cherished symbol of free and enlightened education.

Approaching the police line, the student mob slowed to an unsure halt. Then, quite unexpectedly, the police charged, catching the students completely off guard. With their cruel clubs flailing, the police waded into the first ranks of the demonstrators, who turned to run, but they were met head-on by thousands of their own colleagues who were still pouring into Rue Saint-Jacque and pressing forward.

Within seconds, a handful of students lay wounded in the street. For a moment there was chaos, and then suddenly the entire mob was in full retreat, passing back down Rue Saint-Jacques and spilling into the Boulevard Saint-Germain. As they fled, they fought, overturning cars and even buses in the path of the advancing police and raining a thick barrage of cobblestones on the crack riot troops. Danny followed the arc of one of the stones as it looped over the makeshift barricade and glanced off the shoulder of a young cop, who went down in a heap. A tear gas grenade exploded nearby, choking Danny with its noxious yellow smoke. Torrents of mucus flowed from his nose. Temporarily blinded, he coughed his way down the boulevard, guided by his fellows.

Despite the hail of cobbles, the police continued to advance, forcing the students eastward along Saint-Germain toward the Place Maubert, the ancient site of protestant executions in the religious struggles of a previous age. There in the broad open square beside the picturesque fountain, the students dug in their heels. Recovered from the effects of the tear gas, Danny and a few others tried to direct the defense of the square, but the angry crowd was beyond the control of anyone. Nonetheless, even without leaders, the mob miraculously managed to transform itself into an effective fighting force. Everyone seemed to find something to do. Steel spikes pried at the cobbles. Hand lines formed as those in the rear methodically passed the hefty stones forward to the throwers. Whistles and calls sounded quickly-learned codes to relay police positions, movements, and weaknesses.

---

1 *The New York Times* estimated the size of the crowd on the Left Bank at 3pm on May 6th to have been about 5000. *The New York Times*, May 7, 1968, 32.

Clearly baffled by the tenacity and effectiveness of the resistance, the police fell back and called for reinforcements. What followed was a war without bullets, a real battle with charges and counterattacks, advances and retreats, cobblestones and Molotov cocktails against truncheons and grenades. Tear gas engulfed the plaza, but the students seemed magically unaffected by its sting, while passengers on the subways passing below coughed and cried. Finally, after about an hour of fighting, the CRS managed to clear the square, but the students maintained the advantage. They were infinitely more mobile, instinctively quicker, and they knew every inch of the terrain. As the police at last surged in to secure the Place Maubert and make their arrests, the students melted away into the side streets and alleyways of the ancient neighborhood that they knew so well.[1] One moment they had been there fighting; the next moment the square was empty, and there was no one there to arrest.

"6:30 p.m.! Denfert-Rochereau!" Word of the meeting place spread throughout the city. The battle had only begun.

* * *

Danny felt good. Surveying the spectacle at Denfert-Rochereau, he liked what he saw. The size of the crowd was difficult to gauge — ten thousand? twenty? — it was impossible to guess.[2] University students were in the majority, but there were also young workers, high school students, and faculty. "Certainly it is several times over the size of the mob that fought so well in the Place Maubert a few hours ago," he thought. "Clearly word of the valor of the students and the brutality of the police is spreading. We were stronger today at Maubert because of the violence on Friday night," the Danny mused, "and we are stronger now at Denfert because of the violence at Maubert earlier today. The police are playing right into our hands."

The great square at the Place Denfert-Rochereau in the heart of Montparnasse was an ideal rallying place. Large, easily accessed from the Latin Quarter, and complex enough to afford myriad escape routes, it lay at the confluence of the Avenue Denfert-Rochereau, the Boulevard Saint-Jacques, Boulevard Arago, and Boulevard Raspail, as well as many other lesser streets and passageways. Once called *Place d'Enfer* (Hells' Square), the huge plaza radiated outward from an enormous black marble lion known as the Lion of Belfort, a copy of a monument in eastern France commemorating French valor in the siege of Belfort during the Franco-Prussian War.

As Danny looked on, various leaders were attempting to get the crowd's attention. Perched atop the statue-base, they shouted their directions with the aid of bullhorns. The teeming throngs paid them no heed. Danny passed easily through the crowd toward the famous monument. "Even the lion is perfect," he mused. A symbol of French resistance to tyranny in the previous century, the great marble lion smiled impassively down on the chaotic masses.

Emboldened by their swelling numbers, the crowd was not to be distracted or diverted, and soon the entire mass, as if of a single mind, set out for *Saint-Germain-des-Prés* and the Sorbonne. This time the students had their own clubs and helmets. But the police were ready for them — or at least they thought they were ready.

---

1 The above account of the events of the afternoon of May 6, 1968, comes primarily from Fraser, et al., *1968: A Student Generation in Revolt*, 180; Singer, *Prelude to Revolution*, 125-8; *The New York Times*, May 7, 1968, 1,32.

2 Accounts of the size of the crowd at Denfert-Rochereau on May 6th vary. Fraser estimates between ten and thirty thousand. *The New York Times* estimates that as fighting broke out later that evening the were more than ten thousand rioters in the Boulevard Saint Germain alone. Fraser, et al., *1968: A Student Generation in Revolt*, 180; *The New York Times*, May 7, 1968, 32.

By 9:00 p.m., there were 10,000 protestors in the Boulevard Saint-Germain, and students were assaulting police positions in five of the major intersections surrounding the Sorbonne.[1] After a few violent head-on clashes, it was clear that the students could not be dispersed by the usual CRS strategy of unified frontal assault. Unaccustomed to this kind of bold resistance, the police changed their tactics. They began to launch concussion grenades and tear gas from afar and then attempt to "mop up" by marching forward in great phalanxes once the gassed and bombarded masses of students began to show signs of disorganization. All the while, a torrent of debris rained down on police from the rooftops.

In response to these strong-arm tactics and superior weaponry, the students took advantage of their mobility. They quickly devised a system of reconnaissance and communication that allowed them mysteriously to disappear from areas where the police were strongest only to suddenly reappear in areas where the police presence was small. Throughout the Latin Quarter students on motorcycles sped here and there gathering information about police movements. Whistles and calls relaying this information could be heard above the fighting everywhere. The brutal mêlée went on until 10:00 p.m., when most of the students finally melted away into the back alleys and byways, and the police temporarily took control of the streets. Still, until after midnight, mobile bands of student protestors employed "hit and run" tactics to harass police. It had become clear that the police could defend the Sorbonne but that the streets would ultimately belong to the students.

Throughout the evening, the unexpected tenacity and resilience of the student mobs had brought out the worst in the CRS who rained heavy beatings on those who were unlucky enough to fall into their hands. Even the local police exacted their pound of flesh.

In the course of the heaviest fighting, street barricades had been erected by the students to help defend against the concussion grenades and the mass police charges that followed their use. Several of these redoubts were quite impressive and withstood numerous police assaults, including a few massive attacks staged behind truck-mounted high-pressure water cannon. Constructed of overturned cars and even buses and covered with paving stones and any other materials the students could lay their hands on, the barricades were more than defensive barriers. In the European mind, they symbolized popular resistance against oppression. For almost every Frenchman, barricades evoked a strange national reverence for the Parisian workers' defense of Paris in 1871 and for the idealistic but ill-fated French commune. For Frenchmen everywhere barricades recalled pitched street battles fought in the name of *liberté* against the forces of *tyrannie*.

Perhaps no one was more familiar with this romantic symbolism than Daniel Cohn-Bendit. The son of German Jews fleeing Hitler, Danny had been born in France, and he had spent his childhood there. Although his parents had returned to Germany when he was a teenager, Danny saw himself as every bit as much a Frenchman as a German, and as a native Frenchman he understood the lure of the barricades. Sitting behind one of these make-shift defensive barriers in the Boulevard Saint-Germain, he was stirred by the glorious French Revolutionary tradition, and he knew that the events of this night — the barricades, the police brutality, the calls for reform and freedom from the oppression of the de Gaulle machine — would soon capture the

---

1 *The New York Times*, May 7, 1968, 32.

hearts and minds of the French nation. He knew General Charles de Gaulle's days were numbered. He could feel it in his bones.

Danny picked up a paving stone that was lying nearby. It fit neatly in his hand. He tossed it to the other hand and felt its substantial heft. "*Le pavé,*" the French called it. He rolled its smooth form about in his hand, and closely examined its rounded shape.

"Here is the true symbol of revolution," he thought. "Here is our weapon and the brick for our defenses. Here is the end of all theory and the beginning of all action. This is what Marx had in mind when he said that theory and praxis would become one. Right now this heavy little stone is all that matters."

Inspired by these musings, Danny stood up, gave the cobble a heave, and watched as it slowly arched above the barricade, above the open square, above the first of the on-rushing rows of steel-helmeted, goggled, black-shirted police, and finally disappeared into a platoon of black uniformed storm troopers who were pressing forward in support of their attacking comrades about thirty meters beyond the barrier.

TUESDAY, MAY 7, 1968 (THE LONG MARCH)

The next morning at breakfast Kurt translated the headlines from the French papers into English for Eliot. "Police reported 487 injuries and 422 arrests,"[1] he read.

"That's just the police casualties," said Steffi, in English. She had already devoured all the papers. "There's no guessing as to the number of students injured. They're afraid of reprisals from the authorities, and so they won't seek treatment in public hospitals or treatment centers. Even the most conservative, pro-establishment papers are reporting terrible police brutality — students beaten senseless, broken arms and legs, broken ribs. It's horrible"

"That should swing public opinion in the students' direction," said Kurt.

"Yes, especially here in France," said Steffi. "Normally it is relatively easy for Western governments to paint a frightening picture of those who take to the streets in violent protest. Those who defy law and order are usually denounced by the authorities as threats to democracy. However, things are different here. For years, the French government has used violence to maintain 'democratic' order. In France, the brutality of the CRS is well known, and the de Gaulle regime that the CRS supports is the object of widespread public resentment. In the minds of most Frenchmen, the police on the Left Bank right now don't represent the forces of order; they appear more like some kind of occupation army, surrounded by hostility, showered with insults, attacked with stones. The occupation of the Latin Quarter by the police is viewed as a scandal, an insult; their presence in the Sorbonne symbolically desecrates the sacred heart of the free French university. The students are breaking the ice, speaking the unspeakable, and expressing what many have felt for years."[2]

"Indeed, our diplomatic intelligence tells us that this is the case," said Herr Siegel. Eliot was startled by his perfect English. Up until now, he had only heard Kurt and Steffi's father speak German.

"The students have captured more than just the spirit of resentment here," Herr Siegel continued. "Many think that they are now actually capable of mobilizing a

---

1 Again, accounts vary, for example, Singer reports 345 police injuries while *The New York Times* reported over 700 injured with 434 arrests. Singer, *Prelude to Revolution,* 128; *The New York Times,* May 8, 1968, 1.

2 Fraser, et al., *1968: A Student Generation in Revolt,* 181. Touraine, *The May Movement,* 162-3.

large segment of the population. I spoke with Herbert Marcuse about this only yesterday. By the way, did you know that he is still in Paris?"

"Yes," said Kurt, "Steffi spoke with him at Nanterre a couple of weeks ago."

Herr Siegel looked at his daughter.

"Yes, Papa, I forgot to tell you, Herr Professor Marcuse sends you his best."

"He mentioned that he had met you," said Herr Siegel. "Anyway, Herbert seems to think that there is a possibility here for significant change, that is, if the unions can be persuaded to support the students' broader political cause and put forward their own agenda. Our people believe that the workers could actually come into this. It is even happening to a very limited degree in Germany. Did you know that this week, the students marched again in Berlin? They said they were trying to 'awaken the public consciousness of the oppressive situation' in our country. A surprisingly large number of workers joined in that march. There were over thirty thousand in the streets of Berlin on May 1. Here in Paris, the situation is much more volatile. Our observers at the embassy are of the mind that this might not be the beginning of a simple revolt or insurrection but the genesis of a significant new social movement. At least that is the speculation from our analysts. Call it what you will."

"*Eine Revolution?*" said Eliot.

"*Nicht ohne die Kugelen* — Not without bullets," said Herr Siegel.

"No!" said Steffi firmly. "This is no revolution. Not yet. We've examined this kind of situation at the Institute in Frankfurt. In this case, the student movement is neither conscious nor organized. They have no real political agenda, at least not one that they can agree on. To be sure, this is an attack on the prevailing society and the present regime, but its specific objectives are vague. This makes their cause all the more attractive to the average Frenchman, who would ordinarily be put off by the radical politics of the Left. The immediate student cause is simply the liberation of the Sorbonne, a universal image of freedom that everyone can identify with. The students are not attacking the centers of power: government buildings, arms depots, prisons, or courts.[1] They're only asking that those who were arrested be freed, that the police leave the Sorbonne, and that the Sorbonne and Nanterre be reopened. These politically benign demands attract broad popular support. The more the police bar the students from the university and attempt to limit protest movements on the Left Bank, the more repressive they appear. However, if the workers come in, as Papa's intelligence suggests, then we will surely see specific left-wing socialist political objectives come to the fore. Then, if the violence escalates, the situation may develop a revolutionary component, but then a large part of public support will dissolve owing to the radical nature of the workers' politics."

Herr Siegel nodded his agreement. He was proud of his daughter's intellect and of her position at the Institute.

For their part, Kurt and Eliot were not so sure. This certainly looked revolutionary enough to them — tens of thousands in the streets, hundreds arrested, barricades, tear gas, cobblestones. It had all the earmarks of a major social upheaval. Besides, if this did not qualify as revolution, or at least slightly revolutionary, what should one call their recent little sit-in at Columbia? A week ago, their actions had seemed so radical, so bold. Now, by contrast, they appeared childish and insignificant.

* * *

---

1 Touraine, *The May Movement*, 164-5.

Again, the great Place Denfert-Rochereau overflowed with protestors: students, high school kids, faculty, young workers, intellectuals, and sympathizers of all spots and colors.

"Twice the size of last night's crowd," said Danny, excitedly climbing high up on the stone base of the great Lion of Belfort at the center of the square.

"Thirty thousand? Forty?" he calculated as he contemplated the vast army of would-be revolutionaries below. "It's incredible."

Red and black flags were everywhere, along with the flags of North Vietnam and Cuba; and there were banners, "De Gaulle — Assassin!" they read, and "Free the Sorbonne!"and "*Libérez nos camarades*" (free our comrades).

Around the perimeter, Danny could see the communist "marshals" at work. "The French communists are hopelessly tied to in the establishment," he thought. "Their attempts to defuse the revolt are stupid and self-serving. They're afraid that the violence will harm their political cause by placing them in the same category as anarchists in the public eye. At the same time, they would use the power that the riots have produced to further their own political ends inside the parliamentary political process."

He shook his head as he watched thousands of communist marshals, specially trained to control such demonstrations, at work trying to keep the crowd from moving toward the Latin Quarter — trying to prevent more violence. "Communist finks!" he spat. The violence worked in favor of the rebel cause, not against it. The papers that very morning had been filled with accounts of unprovoked police attacks against students, innocent bystanders, and even foreign tourists, who were badly brutalized owing to the fact that, unlike the students, they didn't fight back.[1] The brutal police response to the students' bold refusal to knuckle under was building public support for the student cause daily. How could the communists and the communist student union be so stupid as to ignore this? This was no time to negotiate petty reforms, no time to compromise. The repressive nature of the enemy they fought was being made clear to all, and the rebels were getting stronger every day.

As it turned out, the crowd at Denfert-Rochereau did not need communist marshals to keep them out of the Latin Quarter. The police would see to that. Oblivious to the efforts of the marshals, the throngs began to move southward toward the Sorbonne, but before long, they encountered a massive police blockade. For reasons that Danny could not understand, this night the huge crowd was in no mood for a fight. "Last night they would have charged the police head-on," he mused. "Tonight, despite their superior numbers, they back-track."

The marshals rushed to gain control, but before they could catch up, the crowd, as if guided by some unseen beacon, began to move west along the Boulevard de Montparnasse toward the heart of Paris. Shouting and singing as they approached the Seine, they filled the great lawn in front of Les Invalides, where they came face to face with more police barricades, this time blocking the entrance to the broad Pont Alexander III that led across the river to the Right Bank.

In mystical possession of a logic all its own, the great crowd did not hesitate. Bypassing the police roadblock, it surged eastward, paralleling the river along the Quay d'Orsay. Passing in front of the National Assembly without so much as a pause, it turned left onto Pont de la Concorde and crossed unobstructed over the Seine, filling the Place de la Concorde opposite the National Assembly. From there, where another

---

1 Harry Braverman, "Six Days in Paris" *The Nation*, June 3, 1968.

crowd had witnessed the decapitation Louis XVI almost two hundred years before, their way was now clear along the full mile-and-a-half length of the grand Champs Élysées all the way to the Arc de Triomphe, the symbolic heart of commercial Paris.

* * *

Again, guests of Herr Siegel, Steffi, Kurt, and Eliot eat another fine supper in another elegant little brasserie. This one in Rue de Berri not too far from the West German Embassy. At about 9:30 p.m., they were strolling along the Champs Élysées heading back to Herr Siegel's apartment in Rue Jean Goujon when they heard distant chanting.

"The power is in the street," came the repeated refrain, eerie and faint at first, and then louder and more insistent as the throng of marchers approached. "The power is in the street!"

People began to line the curbs to get a view of the masses of students and young workers as they passed. The man next to Steffi turned to her as the procession drew near and said, "They passed in front of the National Assembly without even a sideways glance? I don't understand these students. What kind of revolution are they waging that ignores the seat of government?"

"*Écoutez là, Monsieur*," said the beautiful young German, "Listen to that, sir. For these youngsters, it is just as they say: 'the power is in the street.' They have no use for that impotent body. In their minds, the elected government long ago ceased to represent real political power in France."

"Ah, *bien!*" said the man smiling. "*Vive la révolution*," he shouted and waved his handkerchief. At that moment, several students paraded past carrying short, stubby red flags. Upon inspection, it was clear that they had simply taken the French tricolor and torn off the white and blue fields, and reattached only the red field to the staff.[1]

"Defacing the national flag," said the man next to Steffi, pointing toward the stout banners. Then he turned toward her, his eyes twinkling. "Treason!" he said with delight, and laughed aloud.[2]

It was a stirring sight. On they came, forty abreast, chanting, singing, waving flags, urging onlookers to join them. The great dark flood of students surged past, moving westward toward the Arc de Triomphe, filling the broad avenue of the Champs Élysées, and stretching back eastward toward Concorde as far as the eye could see.

Overcome by the moment, Kurt took Steffi and Eliot by the hand. "The power is in the street," he shouted in perfect French as he rushed to join the marchers, pulling his companions along with him.

"*Vive la révolution*," shouted Eliot, and Steffi laughed at his American accent as they ran.

"Be careful. Stay away from the Left Bank," shouted Herr Siegel in German. He shook his head as if to admonish the imprudence of the young, but in his heart he wanted to join them.

As the marchers approached the great rotunda that was the site of the enormous Arc de Triomphe, they began to sing. It was a moving moment.

Il n'est pas de sauveurs suprêmes

Ni Dieu, ni César, ni tribun

Producteurs, sauvons-nous nous-mêmes

Décrétons le salut commun

1 Touraine, *The May Movement*, 164

2 Braverman, "Six Days in Paris" *The Nation*, June 3, 1968.

Pour que le voleur rende gorge

Pour tirer l'esprit du cachot

Soufflons nous-mêmes notre forge

Battons le fer quand il est chaud

C'est la lutte finale

Groupons-nous, et demain

L'Internationale

Sera le genre humain [1]

As the singing students surrounded the great arch, wave after wave of marchers continued to flow into the great roundabout known to all Parisians as *l'étoile*, the star, the vast open space where twelve major Parisian boulevards converged.

"Clearly, this is a spontaneous event," thought Eliot. And yet there was some evidence of planning. Students circulated among the marchers, handing out sheets containing the lyrics to *The Internationale*. There were six verses, and few among them knew all the words.

The intense young American tried to gather in all the shades of meaning, all the subtle overtones that were so uniquely French, so strangely contradictory, so emotionally compelling, so unlike the cold, hard, calculatingly American confrontations at Columbia. Here on this May evening, in the center of France's most famous square, in the shadow of France's most sacred patriotic architectural symbol, a 15-story celebration of Napoleon's victory at Austerlitz and the resting place of the nation's Unknown Soldier, forty thousand students sang the anthem of international socialist revolt. Here, where tradition demanded only the singing of *The Marseilles*, these rebels defiantly echoed a song that should have fallen on the French patriotic ear like a discordant blasphemy. It did not. It was then that Eliot realized that, for most Frenchmen, the spirit of revolution in the name of *liberté* aroused a more fundamental patriotism than any devotion born of mere nationalist zeal, regardless of its political or social overtones. It was as if the entire nation had all imbibed a radical penchant for revolt along with their mother's milk.

The passionate young man wished he could say the same for the patriotism of most of his countrymen. Could it be that the spirit of a revolution accomplished fades slowly from memory and is eventually taken for granted, while the idealism of a revolution failed forever lingers unrequited in the national soul?

---

1 Eugene Porrier and Pierre Degeyter, "*L'Internationale*." Literal translation:
    There are no supreme saviors,
    Neither God, nor Caesar, nor tribune.
    Workers, let's save ourselves!
    Together let's enact a common decree
    To force the thief to return his loot,
    So that the mind is set free from the prison cell!
    Let us blow upon our furnace ourselves,
    Strike the iron while it is hot!
    It is the final struggle
    Let us gather, and tomorrow
    The Internationale
    Will be mankind!

CHAPTER TWENTY-ONE: FRANKFURT

And I have known the arms already, known them all —
Arms that are bracelet and white and bare
[But in the lamplight, downed with light brown hair!]
Is it the perfume from a dress
That makes me so digress?
Arms that lie along a table, or wrap about a shawl.
— T. S. Eliot, "The Love Song of J. Alfred Prufrock"

Anyone who knows anything about history knows that great social changes are impossible without feminine upheaval.
— Karl Marx

MONDAY, MAY 6, 1968

The students were up to something. Professor Adorno could feel it in his bones. After forty years of teaching, he could sense these things. But what? More banners, leaflets, another abusive outburst? Only last week one of the students had proclaimed, "If Adorno is left in peace, capitalism will never cease,"[1] and another had written "Adorno as an institution is dead."[2] He could not recall a single lecture in the past few months that had passed without some kind of interruption.

In an effort to restructure his lectures along the lines of the participatory democratic reforms the students were clamoring for, he had invited them to put questions to him at any time during the lecture. This radical departure from past practice, he hoped, would create a forum of more open discussion. Sadly, it was doomed from the

---

1 Müller-Doohm, *Adorno*, 475.

2 Hans Jürgen Krahl, "Adorno as an Institution is Dead: How the Consciousness Changer was Driven Our of the Lecture Hall," *Frankfurter Rundschau*, April 24, 1969, cited in Müller-Doohm, *Adorno*, 611.

start, and the students shamelessly took it as license to disrupt the proceedings even further.[1]

This morning he was sure that some sort of demonstration was imminent as he began lecturing a large class concerning the dialectics of subject and object. Sure enough, no sooner had he begun than three young women climbed up on the podium and began scattering rose petals over him as he spoke. As he was about to ask them to return to their seats, they suddenly bared their breasts and began to move seductively toward him in a kind of erotic pantomime. Doctor Adorno's discomfort was clear to all. As the girls approached, he quickly grabbed his hat and coat and made his escape into the hallway, waving his briefcase at the young women in self-defense.[2]

He felt singled out and deeply wronged by this incident. Later he wrote to Marcuse regarding his feelings. "To have picked on me of all people, I who have spoken out against every type of erotic repression and sexual taboo! To ridicule me and set these three girls dressed up as hippies against me in this way! I found that repulsive. The laughter that was aimed at me was basically the reaction of the philistine who giggles when he sees girls with naked breasts. Needless to say, this idiocy was planned."[3]

Still Doctor Adorno was careful not to publicly denounce this childishness for fear that such criticism would further widen the already substantial gap between himself and his students. He also knew that reactionary factions would seize on such criticism as an opportunity to smear the students' anti-authoritarian movement. Privately he told Marcuse in his correspondence that he was well aware that this kind of "idiotic brutality of the left-wing fascists" would trigger the "malicious joy of all reactionaries."[4]

TUESDAY, MAY 7, 1968

Professor Adorno was nearing the end of his rope. He had done everything in his power to mediate between the striking students and the university's administration, and still the students denounced him for not joining their demonstrations. The pressure mounted as protests at the University of Frankfurt escalated in the shadow of the upheaval in France. Moreover, with the impending national March on Bonn planned for Saturday, May 11, Doctor Adorno was coming under increased pressure from the radical students to participate in the long-awaited demonstration in the West German capital that aimed at stopping the passage of the so-called *Notstandsgesetze* (Emergency Laws). Although he opposed this potentially repressive legislation with all his heart and mind, Theodor Adorno refused to associate himself with any extra-parliamentary actions organized by the students for fear of losing his independence and that of the Institute. Like the students, he sought reform, but he refused to join with those whose stated aim was to "smash the bourgeois academic machine." For their part, the students saw Professor Adorno's refusal to participate as a clear sign that he did not support their quest for reform.

---

1 Müller-Doohm, *Adorno*, 475.

2 This incident, which was widely known in Germany as "the breast incident," occurred on April 22, 1969. Müller-Doohm, *Adorno*, 475.

3 Theodor Adorno, "*Keine Angst von dem Elfenbeintrum*," in *Gesammelte Schriften*, 1: 406, cited in Müller-Doohm, *Adorno*, 476.

4 Theodor Adorno, letter to Eduard Grosse, May 5, 1969, *Frankfurter Adorno Blätter*, 4:42, cited in Müller-Doohm, *Adorno*, 476.

On the morning after the so-called "breast incident," word reached the Institute of Social Research that a group of students had threatened to strip some of the university seminar rooms of their furnishings — or as they termed it, "remove the means of production." This had forced the professors in charge of those seminars to summon the police and close the facilities. The presence of the police inside the university worried Doctor Adorno, but no sooner had he received the news than a group of students paraded into the Institute and took over several of the seminar rooms there. After some back and forth, it was clear that the students intended to occupy the building, and Doctor Adorno and the other directors of the Institute felt they had no choice but to consider the students' intrusion an act of trespass. They reluctantly called in the police to clear the building. Several students were arrested in the process.

Adorno knew that summoning the police spelled an end to any rapport he may have thus far managed to maintain with the striking students. He knew that, in the student mind, this act would forever brand him as an enemy, a part of the repressive capitalist establishment that they fought — but they had forced his hand. His only solace came in the knowledge that the students' irrational tendency to see the world in black and white was every bit as repugnant as the repression they sought to end. He knew that all oppression, whether it came from the Left or from the Right, was a product of a polarized point of view and an unbending mindset.

Later that day he again wrote to Marcuse, once more inviting him to come to Frankfurt and proposing that they personally meet soon in the Alps. The term was almost over. "I am in a phase of extreme depression,"[1] he told his friend. Then, before signing his letter, "a badly battered Teddy,"[2] he added, "God knows what will happen in the coming term."[3]

He concluded his correspondence and sat for a long while at his desk staring out the window toward the university. "Adorno as an institution is dead." He could not get these words out of his mind. After a few minutes, the dark, empty sadness that had become his constant companion engulfed his thoughts, and he began to cry softly but uncontrollably.

---

1 Müller-Doohm, *Adorno*, 477.

2 Theodor Adorno, letter to Herbert Marcuse, July 25, 1969, cited in Müller-Doohm, *Adorno*, 478.

3 Theodor Adorno, letter to Hans Heinz Stuckenschmidt, February 25, 1969, *"Aktennotiz,"* *Frankfurter Adorno Blätter*, 4:42, cited in Müller-Doohm, *Adorno*, 96.

CHAPTER TWENTY-TWO: PARIS

A Game of Chess
—T. S. Eliot, "The Wasteland"

Democracy is the road to socialism.
— Karl Marx

WEDNESDAY, MAY 8, 1968

As a light rain fell on the Left Bank, thousands filled the courtyard of the new Faculty of Science which had recently been erected on the site of the ancient Halle aux Vins on the embankment that formed the northern edge of the Latin Quarter. Despite yesterday's triumphant march through the heart of Paris, the students' mood was no longer buoyant. Leaders of the student union and several other communist student factions seemed to be waffling, attempting to reduce the broader movement to a series of petty reformist negotiations. Behind the scenes, these leaders appeared to be trying to take the dispute out of the streets and place it back inside the parliamentary system. Union leaders and faculty members announced that they were in touch with the Minster of Education. There were rumors that the Sorbonne and Nanterre would be re-opened. For those who aspired to broad social and political change, it appeared that some of their leaders were caving in at the very moment of triumph.

Danny could sense deals being made behind closed doors. "These communist clowns are about to accept some meaningless university reform in exchange for defusing a revolt that could have toppled the government," he thought. "This is madness. How can they be so blind?" The gathered students sensed it too. Their revolt appeared to be about to fizzle, and so Wednesday's planned march through the Latin Quarter began in uncertainty.[1]

---

1 Singer, *Prelude to Revolution*, 131-2.

As the marchers set out down the broad rain-swept boulevard, the communist marshals kept them in check, channeling their flow. Danny wondered if he should cancel his scheduled interview with the BBC and go with them. Just then, the communist leaders tried to take a place at the head of the march, and the moving throng shouted them down. A platoon of helmeted student fighters rushed to take the lead, and the procession surged northwestward along Rue Jessieu. As Danny turned to keep his appointment with the press, the marchers began to chant and disappeared into the rain.

After almost a week of violence, Daniel Cohn-Bendit had emerged as the central media figure in the Parisian student revolt. "Danny the Red" everyone called him. A forceful vocal reflection of the radical activism of the 22nd of March Movement at Nanterre, Danny had been at the center of the initial revolt on May 3. He had publicly addressed the student masses outside the Sorbonne on the sixth, and in prelude to the fighting of that "Bloody Monday" he had spoken to the gathered throngs at Denfert later that same evening. Then again on the seventh, atop the Lion at Denfert, he had harangued the protestors just before the triumphant "Long March" on the Right Bank. His message was always the same: pure democracy and unfettered freedom. He expressed a simple faith in the wisdom of the autonomous and leaderless crowd in confronting the violence of the police and in overcoming the tyranny of the de Gaulle regime. The media adored him. He was radical, uninhibited, articulate, reasonable, and wildly enthusiastic. Relentlessly pursued and ceaselessly interviewed, he appeared regularly on French TV and radio, and his quotes found their way into almost every newspaper article. He insisted that the immediate issues — the re-opening of the Sorbonne, the reform of the university system, and the freeing of the jailed student protestors — were only symbols for a much larger battle aimed at ending the oppressive reign of the government of Charles de Gaulle in France. Through it all, Danny remained focused on his cause and steadfast in his insistence that he was neither a leader nor even a spokesman. In his mind, the purely spontaneous French student movement functioned perfectly well without leaders and intuitively created its own causes as it went along.

* * *

After his interview with the BBC, Danny went in search of the marchers. He found the streets of the Latin Quarter almost deserted. The police were still in place blocking the approaches to the Sorbonne, but the students were nowhere to be found. Danny asked a passer-by who informed him that the march had ended at the Luxembourg Gardens. Heading in that direction he encountered groups of disoriented students wandering back toward the river in disarray. Some of them were crying.[1]

"Tear gas," he thought, but he soon found that these were tears of frustration.

When Danny reached the Luxembourg Gardens, he found large groups of students still lingering, forlorn and let down. With the help of additional marshals from the trade unions, the communists had forced the marchers along a predetermined route and then insisted that they disband upon reaching this prearranged destination. It was clear they were making a peace offering to the authorities. Surely, the communists had made some kind of deal behind the students' backs.[2] There was nothing the students could do. Their numbers reduced by the rain and by the fact that few had trusted the communists enough to attend their meeting at the Halle aux Vins in the first place, they had not been numerous enough to resist.

---

1 Fraser, et al., *1968: A Student Generation in Revolt*, 182.
2 Singer, *Prelude to Revolution*, 132.

Daniel Cohn-Bendit wasted no time. He knew what to do. He had to assemble the 22nd of March members, reinvigorate the students, and fight for the autonomy of the revolt.[1]

This was the critical moment.

THURSDAY, MAY 9, 1968

Again, the breakfast conversation at Herr Siegel's flat revolved around the situation on the Left Bank. Steffi had risen early, gone out, and returned with an armful of newspapers: French, German, the London *Times*, and *The New York Times*. Over coffee, she, Kurt, and Eliot devoured them all. It was clear that after Monday night's bloody fighting in the Latin Quarter and Tuesday's triumphant march through the center of Paris, public opinion was turning even more in favor of the student cause.

"According to this," said Steffi, reading from *Le Monde*, "Four fifths of the population of Paris is siding with the students and against the government."

"It's not limited to Paris," said her brother. "This article says that there were large demonstrations in Marseilles and Toulouse in the south, Lille in the north, and Strasbourg and Rennes in the east, as well as strong shows of student solidarity virtually everywhere in France — Grenoble, Nancy, Aix-en-Provence, Clermont-Ferrand, Nice. Fifteen were injured in battles with police in Lyon."[2]

"Everyone is shocked by the police brutality," said Eliot looking up from the London paper. "*The Times* reports that the police threw grenades into a café on Tuesday night during fighting in the Latin Quarter after the march. There was a fire. Innocent people were trapped inside. It was a close call.[3] What's more, in the face of the ruthless tactics used by the police, student resistance is being seen by the public as courageous. The police are turning law-breakers into national heroes. It's a nightmare for the authorities."

"Wow! Danny is all over the news. He's making quite a name for himself," said Kurt.

Steffi picked up a copy of *L'Humanité*, the French communist newspaper. "The communists and the workers unions have changed their tune as well," she said. "Two days ago, the communists were charging that the students had no business giving revolutionary lessons to the working class, and calling them 'bourgeois papa's boys.' Now the communist attacks are aimed at the de Gaulle government. Two days ago, the unions and the communists were attempting to defuse the situation and divert whatever advantage may have been gained back into normal political channels. However, yesterday they were suddenly urging communist faculty and students to attend the meeting of the student union at the Faculty of Science on the embankment.

"I don't know," said Kurt. "It looks to me like the communists are still trying to defuse the situation and cut some kind of reformist deal with the government." He held up a four-page student-produced tabloid called *Action*. "It says here that the students were not happy with the decision to disband the demonstration last night after they reached the Luxembourg Gardens. They say Danny was livid. The rumor is that the march through the Latin Quarter last night was not challenged by the police because it followed a route prearranged by the communists and the government. Now the government has been making vague noises about reopening the Sorbonne. Sounds like a sell out to me."

1 Fraser, et al., *1968: A Student Generation in Revolt*, 182.
2 *The New York Times*, May 8, 1968, 13.
3 Singer, *Prelude to Revolution*, 130.

"Yesterday the Minister of Education all but promised the students that the Sorbonne and Nanterre would be reopened today," said Eliot. "There was also the sense that the government was going to make some concession regarding the freeing of the arrested students. Now, according to this, the authorities are saying that they will reopen the Sorbonne only under heavy police guard, and they're making no promises concerning those who were arrested. The students are beside themselves. They feel betrayed by the communists, the unions, and the government. There's a feeling in some quarters that the revolt has burned itself out, but others say this last double-cross will surely re-ignite it."

The phone rang. Steffi went to answer it, and after few minutes she returned.

"That was Charles. He wants us to join him for lunch," she said. "Kurt, I so want you to meet him. You too, Eliot. We know a great little restaurant in Rue Saint-Jacques near his flat. He wants us to meet him there. Please do come. It can be our little farewell party. I'm going to stay tonight with Charles before I go back to Germany tomorrow. Do come."

"Isn't that near the Sorbonne?" asked Kurt.

"Charles says it's perfectly fine during the day. It's only at night that you have to be careful. Of course, we don't need to be afraid of the students anyway, and the police keep behind their barricades unless the students are active in the streets. Charles says that every day the whole Latin Quarter is overrun with tourists vicariously reliving the fighting. It's fine, really.

* * *

As they crossed the Petit Pont from the Île de la Cité to the Left Bank, Steffi paused. "This is where I saw Baudelaire," she said.

They stopped to survey the scene. The sidewalk by the bookseller's stalls was crowded with browsers, and life on the Left Bank seemed normal enough. The cafés were full. The streets teemed with tourists. Baudelaire was nowhere in sight, and neither were the rioting students nor the armies of police. Kurt's gray eyes scanned the Boulevard Saint-Michel in the direction of the Sorbonne, expecting to catch a glimpse of the police blockades. Instead, he saw that the broad boulevard was filled with students, some standing, some seated in the street, gathered into hundreds of small groups.

"*Qu'est que c'est que ça?*" he asked a passing young man who was handing out leaflets.

"They're calling it a 'teach out,'" said the young man, thrusting one of the leaflets into Kurt's hand. "It's kind of like a sit-in, but it's outside. The students refuse to enter the Sorbonne as long as the police are there. It was Danny the Red's idea. They won't confront the police. Instead, they're just sitting around deciding what to do, discussing politics, revolutionary strategy, you know, how to react to the lies of the government and how to counter the communists' efforts to control the situation. Danny calls it 'direct democracy.' He's declared the street our lecture hall."

"Is Danny there?" asked Kurt.

"Oh, yes. I saw him just a few minutes ago speaking to some students in the Place de la Sorbonne."

With the size of the crowds and the chaotic nature of recent events, it had not occurred to Steffi and Kurt that they would have a chance get together with their old their friend from high school days in Frankfurt. No one knew where the now notorious "Danny the Red" was staying. He seemed to be the man of the hour, sought after by the media, wanted by the police, adored by the students. Steffi had, of course, seen

Danny briefly at Nanterre the month before, and Danny and Kurt had corresponded, but it had been some time since they had had a change to have a relaxed personal exchange. Suddenly the prospects for such a meeting seem very good, indeed.

"Let's go find him," said Kurt.

As they walked up the Boulevard Saint-Michel toward the Sorbonne, Kurt roughly translated the leaflet for Eliot's benefit.

"The Closing of Nanterre and the Sorbonne: Repression in the Latin Quarter," the headline read.

By way of answer: More and more numerous demonstrations. Tuesday evening 50,000 students and workers marched as far as the Arc de Triomphe.

Yet, on Wednesday evening, another traditional meeting was inflicted on those who answered the call of the UNEF (French National Student Union). Loud-speakers for the "officials," "jawboning" that opened up no perspectives, and to end with, a long walk that finished without explanation with a call to disperse in spite of the obvious discontent of most of the demonstrators, and at the risk of breaking up the movement.

During all of this time the press, with nuance and varied tactics, misrepresented the facts, lied about the movement's objectives, and, as in Berlin and Rome ..., tried to pit the workers against the students.

To avoid the recurrence of a dangerous mistake like that of Wednesday evening at Luxembourg.

To avoid all other maneuvers.

To expand our movement.

To deepen and define our objectives.

1. Liberation of university premises and surrounding areas.

2. Liberation of all our comrades still in prison, and annulment of penalties.

3. Annulment of *faculté* lockouts.

4. Resignation of those responsible for police intrusion onto the Sorbonne courtyard.

5. Complete freedom of political expression in the *facultés.*

In order to popularize our struggle among workers,

We Must Organize: Create Action Committees.

Everyone at Denfert-Rochereau, Friday Evening at 6:30 p.m.[1]

"It's signed '*Les Comités d'action du 3 mai, 1968*,'" said the young German. "They're trying to rekindle their revolution."

"I'll bet Danny has a hand in this," said Steffi.

The scene in the streets surrounding the Sorbonne was crowded but orderly. Student groups were gathered everywhere, earnestly debating strategy. The police looked on with contemptuous detachment from behind their barricades.

It didn't take long to find Danny. He was standing in front of a group of students, waving his arms in broad gestures as he spoke. "The issues must be decided by the demonstration," he was saying, "not by some party demagogue. The people are clearly sympathetic, the National Assembly is divided, and we now have a chance to prove

---

1 *Comité d'Action du 3 mai, 1968*, leaflet, in Schnapp and Vadal-Naquet, *The French Student Uprising*, 180-1.

that the power of General de Gaulle will collapse like a house of cards if we go about this the right way."[1]

When Danny looked up and saw Kurt and Steffi standing nearby, he let out a shout. "*Mon Dieu!*" He rushed to greet his friends. "What are you doing in France?" he said switching to German. "You should be at the great march on Bonn tomorrow."

"Yes," Kurt added laughing, "but we thought you could use some help. Quite a mess you've stirred up here."

"Yes, isn't it?" said Danny smiling and eyeing Eliot.

"Oh, sorry," said Kurt. "Danny Cohn-Bendit, this is Eliot Kincaid, an American friend of mine from Columbia. Eliot and I were students of Doctor Adorno at Frankfurt."

The redhead offered his hand, and they shook with the brief single formal downward movement that was the European custom. "It is nice to meet you," said Danny in heavily accented English.

The young American replied in German. He said the pleasure was his for he had heard a great deal about Danny from Kurt and Steffi. "And now you are all over the news," Eliot added.

"Yes," said Danny continuing in German. "Reporters are everywhere. I don't trust them."

Then, eyeing the leaflet still in Kurt's hand, he said. "So you got one of those, eh? It was a last minute effort to right the ship. The communist unions tried to do us in last night, but I think we've put things right. The leaders of the student union and the teachers' union came to me last night, crying that they had been tricked by the authorities. They said they were promised that the Sorbonne would be cleared of police if the violence stopped. Then they found out at 2:00 a.m. that the government was not clearing the university but reinforcing it. We spent all night working on that leaflet. Then this morning I had to lie and say I had already printed 10,000, in order to get the union to print 100,000 more. My little bluff worked, and *voila*"[2] He gestured toward the single sheet of paper in Kurt's hand.

"Danny, you're shameless," said Steffi.

"*C'est la guerre, Mademoiselle*," said Danny, smiling that strange smile in which his flexible face beamed in a half-lunatic grin while his eyes remained steel-hard. Then, quite suddenly, he began to preach in French, the way he had when Steffi visited him at Nanterre back in April. "None of the lies told by the communists and the unions can detract from our achievements," he boasted as a crowd of students gathered around. "Last night everyone was afraid that the power of the revolt had been seized by parties, unions, organizations and was being bartered away in some sort of shady deal. But today, even in a society that seeks to crush the individual, forcing him to swallow the same lies, a deep feeling of collective strength has again surged up and people refuse to be browbeaten. We have to get rid of these 'leaders' who decide things behind our backs. We have to let people decide what they want to do. And if they feel like clashing head-on with the police, then so be it. We are no longer thousands of little atoms squashed together but a solid mass of determined individuals. The rashness of our youth does not spring from despair nor from the cynicism of

---

1 Cohn-Bendit and Cohn-Bendit, *Obsolete Communism*, 62.
2 Fraser, et al., *1968: A Student Generation in Revolt*, 180-1.

impotence; it springs from the discovery of our collective strength. We are here to help the movement express its collective will and then to side with that will."[1]

The gathered crowd cheered and closed in around Danny, who continued to harangue them. Kurt, Steffi, and Eliot were brushed aside by the swarm of eager students. Steffi waved goodbye as he drifted away with the crowd. Catching her wave from the corner of his eye, Danny smiled his strange smile again and raised his clinched fist in the universal salute of solidarity.

Three blocks away, the scene was placid. Sidewalk tables were set with white linen. Waiters dressed in black and wore ankle-length white aprons. Charles was waiting. Wine was poured. Life was good. Eliot wished that Melissa were there. At moments like this he missed her. He wanted to share his pleasures with her. He looked across the table at Steffi. She seemed lost in thought. For the first time since he had arrived in Paris, the beautiful Steffi Siegel seemed unfocused, unaware of his gaze.

Steffi found the sudden contrast between the angry students and the pleasant restaurant un-nerving. It was as if there were two Parises. She felt displaced, as in a dream. Suddenly, somewhere in that displacement, somewhere in the contrast between the enraged student mob in front of the Sorbonne and the placid crowds passing in front of this charming little restaurant only a few blocks away, she thought she glimpsed the gaunt figure of Baudelaire. However, when she tried to remember exactly in which crowd and where in that crowd she had seen him, he was gone. The great poet had again disappeared into the ambiguity of a modern world that simultaneously appalled and sustained them all.

FRIDAY, MAY 10, 1968 (THE NIGHT OF THE BARRICADES, BLOODY FRIDAY)

By 5:30 p.m., the square at Denfert-Rochereau was beginning to fill. The early arrivals were largely high school kids who had somehow managed unilaterally to declare May 10 a strike day and had been roaming the streets of Paris for most of the afternoon. By 6:30, thousands of university students and young workers had joined them, and the pavement around the great Lion of Belfort again teemed with demonstrators.

Danny was getting good at estimating crowd size. "Twenty thousand, at least," he calculated. "Not so large as the crowd Tuesday night before the 'Long March' but easily more than half that size." Certainly, the movement was far from the dying ember so many had feared it might become, and at last the big labor unions were coming around. They had called for nationwide demonstrations on Tuesday to show support for the students. Looking out on the masses, Danny smiled his wild smile.

As student leaders began to address the throngs from the top of the statue base, it soon became clear that there was no consensus as to what should be done. No one wanted to take on the police at the Sorbonne again. Some clamored for an assault on La Santé, the nearby central prison where the arrested students were being held. Others wanted to attack the town hall as had been done in the days of the Commune of Paris, back in the 1871. Still others declared all these schemes "suicidal." One group wanted to make for the TV station, which was also heavily guarded. Several leaders vehemently opposed this idea. "Who will speak for the entire movement?" they asked the gathered mob, and no one could answer. As always, Danny favored a direct demo-

---

1 Cohn-Bendit and Cohn-Bendit, *Obsolete Communism*, 63; Singer, *Prelude to Revolution*, 130; Fraser, et al., *1968: A Student Generation in Revolt*, 182.

cratic approach. The marchers should decide for themselves. However, faced with the wild mob at Denfert-Rochereau, even he had to admit that perfect democracy had its limits.[1]

As the leaders went back and forth proposing various schemes and then in turn declaring them unworkable, the crowd began to move in the direction of La Santé. They found no riot police guarding the prison, and the demonstrators cheered as inmates waved handkerchiefs from the barred windows. As they passed, the marchers chanted "*Libérez nos camarades*" (free our comrades) and struck up *The Internationale*, which by now almost everyone knew by heart. As the demonstration moved on, communist marshals attempted to direct the route.[2]

Danny was angry. The communist leadership had promised him that there would be no marshals. He went to the head of the march, climbed up on a bench, and lifting his bullhorn to his lips, he began to harangue the multitude as it passed by. "There are no marshals, no leaders today!" he declared. "Nobody is responsible for you! You are responsible for yourselves; each row of you is responsible for itself! You are the marshals!" Danny soon realized that his efforts were unnecessary. As in the early marches, this crowd seemed to have a mind of its own. They circled around the Sorbonne, but the police had the streets blockaded. The bridges leading to the Île de la Cité were also blocked. In fact, the government had made sure that all of the bridges across the Seine were blocked this night. The delegates to the Paris Peace Talks had arrived in town. The American and the North Vietnamese delegations were in their hotels on the Right Bank, and French officials were making sure that none of the nation's dirty laundry would be visible to these guests or to the army of international press that attended them. Soon it became clear that these blockades were arranged in such a manner that only the roads leading back to Denfert remained open. This would not do. At a square in front of the Luxembourg Gardens, the marchers halted, unsure as to how to proceed. Their leaders gathered on the pavement in the center and tried to work out some kind of strategy. All around them, students were shouting suggestions. It was difficult to communicate, impossible to think.[3]

Then Danny had an idea. "We must occupy the whole of the Latin Quarter," he shouted, picking up his bullhorn. "We must break up into small groups, and stay the whole night if need be — stay until all of our demands are met. We will not enter this whore of a Sorbonne so long as our comrades have not been freed. Don't stay crowded here together; occupy the Latin Quarter from Rue Gay-Lussac to Rue Mouffetard. Form groups of twenty, fifty, a hundred, for discussion and action."

The students cheered, and Danny leapt up onto the hood of a nearby parked car. "Comrades!" he shouted. "We are here to occupy the Latin Quarter, not to fight the police![4] Do not attack, but if attacked, retaliate!"[5]

"How shall we retaliate if attacked?" one student yelled.

"*Avec les pavés!*" replied Danny. "With cobblestones!"[6]

A great cheer went up, "*Les pavés!*"

Almost immediately, the students scattered. Filling every street and alleyway in the Latin Quarter, they began to pile up cobblestones, prying them free from the

1 Fraser, et al., *1968: A Student Generation in Revolt*, 184.
2 Fraser, et al., *1968: A Student Generation in Revolt*, 184.
3 Fraser, et al., *1968: A Student Generation in Revolt*, 185.
4 *The New York Times*, May 11, 1968, 14.
5 Fraser, et al., *1968: A Student Generation in Revolt*, 185: Touraine, *The May Movement*, 174.
6 Fraser, et al., *1968: A Student Generation in Revolt*, 185.

broad boulevards and passing them forward hand-to-hand in long lines to form large piles. As the piles became larger, they became barricades. The communists tried to stop the building of these fortifications, insisting that they constituted a provocation, but there was no stopping their feverish exertions.[1] Militarily speaking, the barricades of May 10, 1968, would have little effect on the outcome of the battle that was to come, but politically and psychologically, they made all the difference. They symbolized the struggles of poor and the downtrodden workers against the oppressive reactionary armies of tyrannical rulers. These modern barricades were bulwarks of the spirit; they fortified minds, not streets.

Barricades sprang up everywhere in a kind of building frenzy. Facing in all directions, they reflected no central plan. Ten stood, one behind the other, in Rue Gay-Lussac alone. Some were large, almost ten feet tall, with overturned autos and even buses at their core; others were merely low piles of rubble covered over with paving stones. One group of students felled the ancient chestnut trees that lined the Boulevard Saint-Michel to reinforce their defensive positions.

As the barricades rose, they took on new meaning for the students. They became walls of separation, physically dividing the forces of repression from a new society in the process of being born. The Sorbonne now belonged to the police and to the leaders of the oppressive society that hid behind the police, but with the erection of the barricades, the rest of the Latin Quarter belonged to the students and to the people.[2]

After a few hours, a young student brought Danny a map of the Latin Quarter, detailing the position of all of the barricades. He had located over fifty in all. Danny studied the map carefully. "Go back," he said to the boy. "Tell them to leave room for retreat. If the first barricade is taken, let's make sure the second does not impede the defenders' escape."[3]

The mood was buoyant. The students building the barricades felt the power of their cooperative efforts, the strength of their solidarity. The local residents were at their windows, cheering, offering food and drink. In the beginning there were nearly as many on-lookers offering support as there were protestors. Reporters were everywhere broadcasting live coverage of the event. Everyone tuned their transistor radios to Radio Luxembourg, the station whose news was known to be the least colored by Gaullist governmental pressure, and residents placed speakers in their windows to broadcast the breaking news into the streets below.

The live radio coverage created an odd loop of psychological feedback. Every action was being verbally documented at the very moment it happened. One could be doing something and hearing the news of it at the same time. Only radio could disseminate a record of history so immediate as to affect the history being recorded. Newspapers were far too slow, and television in France had long ago been discredited, a well-known and transparently regulated pawn of the Gaullist regime. As the evening wore on, the students on the individual barricades became more isolated and would have been totally out of touch had it not been for the up-to-the-minute news coverage coming from the radio. Not only did it aid them in their tactical decisions — where to reinforce, when to retreat — it also buttressed their sense of mission and meaning. The radio assured the students that their efforts were known to the French public, and that the inflexibility and ineptitude of the repressive government that they opposed and the dogged brutality of its police were widely understood. Radio

---

1 Fraser, et al., *1968: A Student Generation in Revolt*, 185.
2 Touraine, *The May Movement*, 175.
3 Fraser, et al., *1968: A Student Generation in Revolt*, 185.

reports of the tensions that were rising in the Latin Quarter brought thousands of young people from all over Paris to the Left Bank to reinforce those already on the barricades. The radio legitimated their cause and their actions, made their rage credible, and supplied them with an ongoing, dynamic, and reinforcing sense that, on this night, they were a part of history.

Danny felt good as he toured the prospective battlefield. A well-known figure by now, the students all cheered him. The atmosphere was fantastic, even festive. Immersed in the work of building their symbolic fortifications, the defenders of the Latin Quarter were drinking in an unfamiliar vintage. They were tasting, perhaps for the first time, the product of the potent grapes of community, of collective effort, of mutual respect and support, and of unified commitment. They were drinking the wine of freedom.

"We've got them where we want them," said Danny, as he huddled around a transistor radio with the defenders of a large barricade in Rue Gay-Lussac. "The government can't shoot us. They can't make us go away without publicly playing the role of the oppressor, and they can't give in for fear of encouraging more of this kind of action." They listened as the presidents of the student union and the teachers' union negotiated with the Vice-Chancellor of the Sorbonne in a conference set up by one of the radio stations and broadcast live throughout the nation. "This will reveal to all of France the true character of the government," Danny said, and sure enough, when the student leaders repeated the demand, "*Libérez nos camarades*," that had so loudly echoed earlier in the square at Denfert-Rochereau and at La Santé, the university official waffled, saying that this was not within his authority. He said he would contact the Interior Minister and call back in ten minutes.

Almost an hour went by, and finally the call came. The Vice-Chancellor said that he could make no change in his original position. "I am only empowered to say that the rector is willing to negotiate. But we can't talk this way over the air waves," he said.[1] Danny nodded and smiled. He knew how blind and unbending the French authorities could be, but thanks to the radio, now the entire nation knew it as well. All along, the government had been publicly insisting that the students had continually "refused dialogue."[2] The radio now exposed this lie to the entire nation. It was clear that the government was still treating the situation as just another illegal domestic disturbance, that they would not, or could not, accept the reality that what they faced was the beginning of some kind of deep-seated social upheaval that demanded radical change. It was also now clear that the de Gaulle government was so bureaucratically constricted that it could make no concession that ran counter to its original official objectives. "Order must be restored," the aging general had declared at the outset, leaving no room for negotiation. This regime knew only one way to accomplish their orders. It would once again employ the tactics of legalized violence. It would again confront the French nation with its most effective public face: that of the police.

With the authorities' refusal to release the arrested students, the leader of the teachers' union then used this grand electronic forum to deliver a skillful political thrust that echoed across the country like a unifying battle cry. "We have put forward our positions publicly in front of the people who are listening," he said. "If the

---

1 *The New York Times*, May 11, 1968, 14.
2 Singer, *Prelude to Revolution*, 138-9.

government is not prepared to assume its responsibility in this matter, then it is the people who will have to do so.[1] We stand behind our barricades."[2]

Throughout the Latin Quarter, a great cheer went up. "I couldn't have said it better, myself," said Danny, smiling his maniacal smile.

Not long after the radio broadcast of the "negotiations" between the Sorbonne Vice Chancellor and student leaders, one of Danny's sociology professors from Nanterre sought him out and asked if Danny would accompany him to meet with the Chancellor of the Sorbonne. He readily agreed. As they passed through the police lines and into the Sorbonne courtyard, Danny could clearly see the fear and hatred on the faces of the police. He was led up a marble stairway and down a long empty hall. Suddenly he found himself face to face with the Chancellor, who had not been apprised of Danny's identity.

"What do you want me to do?" asked the old man, looking away.

"It's very simple," said the redhead. "Get the police out. Re-open the Sorbonne. I'll find three or four bands, spread the word, and that will be that. A festival — nothing else will happen. People will dance and drink and be happy."

Suddenly the phone rang in the next room. The Chancellor went to answer it, and when he returned, he asked, "Are you Cohn-Bendit?"

"Yes," said Danny.

"I am sorry, there is nothing I can do," said the old man, and he left the room.[3]

Danny then knew that there was someone higher up who did not want to negotiate with the un-elected power of the street. There were those who refused to grant recognition to the unfettered voice of the people.

SATURDAY, MAY 11, 1968

As midnight came and went and night began to stretch itself into the wee hours of morning, the confrontation that everyone thought inevitable failed to materialize. The police stood their ground guarding the Sorbonne, and the student multitude began to thin. By 1:00 a.m., everyone seemed to sense that the events of this night were over, and all of the onlookers and a great many of the students went home, leaving only a few thousand of the original thirty thousand or so who had gathered at Denfert-Rochereau to man the now elaborate barricades. Those who remained began settling in for the night, trying to make themselves as comfortable as possible.

* * *

Steffi and Charles had enjoyed a relaxed evening in his flat despite the fact that all around them the students had been busy transforming the Latin Quarter into a battlefield. Just below Charles's window, motorcycles scurried about, and gangs of students sang and chanted as they labored to erect their fortifications. Four floors above this activity, Charles and Steffi cooked a little veal scaloppini and some pasta, ate a little salad, drank a nice bottle of red, and made love. Although they had not intended to go out on this night, when they heard the clock at the Eglise de la Sorbonne strike two and no fighting had yet erupted, they decided to dress and go down to sample for themselves the mood in the now quiet the street below.

They were only a few blocks from the Sorbonne in Rue de L'Abbé de l'Épée, a small passage-way, only one block long, that ran diagonally between Rue Saint-

---

1 SNE-SUP secretary general, Alain Geismar, quoted in Fraser, et al., *1968: A Student Generation in Revolt*, 186.

2 *The New York Times*, May 11, 1968, 14

3 Fraser, et al., *1968: A Student Generation in Revolt*, 187.

Jacques and the broad avenue of Rue Gay-Lussac. As they stepped onto the side-walk, they immediately saw that all of the cobblestones in the narrow street had been removed, leaving the sandy raw earth exposed below. Steffi thought of a graphic student poster she had seen at Nanterre. "Beneath the cobblestones the beach," the artist had declared.

Not far down the block, they could see the outline of a high barricade silhouetted against the streetlights. As they approached, they studied its construction. At its base were three overturned cars lying on their sides. Between the cars, the students had piled all manner of junk, benches, fencing from a nearby construction site, the heavy iron grates that encircle the base of street-side trees, street signs, boxes, garbage cans, and the like. Then the entire structure had then been covered over with cobbles to a height of about seven feet. Three large piles of cobbles lay behind the barricade.

"Ammunition," one the defenders volunteered. He was obviously proud of his work. "We have left the sides near the sidewalk low so that any of our comrades retreating from Rue Guy-Lussac can pass through. If the police try to pass there, they will have to negotiate a very narrow passage between the barricade and the wall of the adjacent building, and we can clobber them," said the young man hefting a cobblestone in his gloved hand.

Farther down, Rue Gay-Lussac looked like a war zone. There were overturned cars and buses scattered about in such a way as to block the passage of any large ve-hicle. Gasoline ran in the street, filling the air with the distinct aroma of danger. Then there were the barricades. Larger and more formidable than the one they had seen on Rue de L'Abbé de l'Épée, they stretched from the Boulevard Saint-Michel all the way back across the Boulevard Saint-Jacques and then out of sight, northeastward along Rue Gay-Lussac There were ten barricades in Rue Gay-Lussac alone, and sixty altogether in the Latin Quarter.[1]

The atmosphere was electric. The students were obviously pleased with their handiwork. The residents shouted encouragement and offered hot coffee and choco-late. Radios blared news from every windowsill. Wine bottles moved hand to hand, each student taking a swig and passing it on. Songs and chants seemed to begin and end instinctively under the unseen direction of some omniscient invisible maestro.

Still, despite the buoyant mood, there was something foreboding about the scene. Charles frowned. He felt uncomfortable — conflicted. As a junior member of the faculty, he supported the students' campaign for university reform. He even sympa-thized with their quest for governmental reform, and yet, there had to be a better way. This lawless brutality went against everything he believed in.

"I support these students' zeal for reform," he said to Steffi. "And with a mood like this, I could even support a little civil disobedience. But this!" He indicated the devastation all around them. "This smells of war, of revolution...."

"Of death?" Steffi interrupted. Her support of the student revolt was fundamental. Despite the fact that she had worked hard to understand Charles's conservative — even reactionary — uncertainties, and although at times she could not help but view his waffling as a sign of fearful weakness, in this case, she shared his reservations. Despite her devotion to reform and her understanding that it would take extreme measures to achieve meaningful change, when it came down to the moment of revolt itself, it always seemed to her to involve violence for its own sake. It was always manifest in crass thoughtless action with no apparent intellectual underpinning at

---

1 *The New York Times*, May 11, 1968. 1.

all. She could see that, in an odd way, Danny was right. Action like this could not be led. It had a mind of its own. It made up its strategy, its goals, and even its ideology as it went along. How could that be right? Where now was all the glorious theory she had spent her life studying?

She thought of Danton and the horror that was the French Revolution. "*L'audace, et encore de l'audace, et toujours l'audace!*"[1]

Steffi took Charles's hand, and as they turned back toward his flat, they suddenly heard a distant cheer. It came from the direction of the Sorbonne and was followed by screams, shouting, the faint plop of tear gas canisters, and deep dull thud of concussion grenades. The police were storming the first barricades on the Boulevard Saint-Michel in front of the Luxembourg Gardens. It had begun.

* * *

It had been prearranged that, if fighting were to begin in the Latin Quarter this night, Daniel Cohn-Bendit would not be among the active participants. Everyone agreed it was far too dangerous. Given Danny's high visibility and radical approach, it was clear that if captured — that is, arrested by the police — he would surely be in for a hard time. Accordingly, when the police charged the first barricades facing the Luxembourg Gardens, a small escort sought Danny out and led him to a safe house — the apartment of a friend near Rue Saint-Jacques.[2]

The escort found him behind the first barricade in Rue Gay-Lussac, a strategic point. The first barricade would be the most difficult for the police to take because it was easily reinforced by students from behind, and a fresh supply of student defenders could be quickly shuttled in to repel charges and replace those overcome by tear gas. Once the first barricade fell, the others would quickly follow. Danny was still shouting encouragement to the defenders as he was led away.

After a block or so, they heard canisters of tear gas behind them, and they turned to look back. A blinding cloud of smoke and gas rose from the first barricade. The police were lobbing in tear gas and the defenders had set a number of cars on fire to impede their advance. Behind the barricade, dim silhouettes of the student fighters danced and swayed amid the dense smoke. Pressing damp handkerchiefs over their faces against the sting of the gas, with ant-like organization they were passing hefty paving stones forward to unseen throwers at the front.

The wind shifted and the cloud of gas suddenly cleared, allowing the students to catch their breath, and with a hail of well-aimed cobblestones they repelled the on-rushing police who fell back and re-grouped for another charge. A few minutes later, Danny was listening to the radio reports from a safe hideout.

A well-known soccer personality was reporting on the fighting in Rue Gay-Lussac. "Now the CRS are charging; they're storming the barricade. Oh, my God! There's a battle raging. The students are counter-attacking; you can hear the noise. The CRS are retreating. Now they're re-grouping. Getting ready to charge again. The locals are throwing things from their windows at the CRS. Oh! The police are retaliating, shooting grenades into the windows of the apartments...."

The voice of another commentator cut in. "This can't be true. The CRS wouldn't do things like that."

---

1 Georges-Jacques Danton, "Audacity, more audacity, always audacity, and France is saved."
2 Fraser, et al., *1968*, 188.

"I'm telling you what I'm seeing," said the ex-soccer star on the scene. The live feed went dead. They had cut him off, and the voice of a studio reporter quickly picked up the story as if nothing had happened.[1]

* * *

Steffi awoke from a troubled sleep. Her eyes were burning. The noise from the street was terrifying — vicious shouts of the riot police, whistles, screams, the exploding gas tanks of overturned cars, the dull thud of grenades. In the distance, she could hear a cacophony of sirens and somewhere a large crowd was singing the Marseilles.

She went to the window and closed it. Below in the tiny Rue de L'Abbé de l'Épée, the students sat patiently, bravely on the single barricade. The police were now close by, occupying the larger boulevards that lay both ahead and behind them. Steffi could clearly see the thin mist of tear gas that was filling the neat canyon formed by the buildings that lined the narrow street.

"We'd better get out of here," said Charles who now stood beside her. Tears flowed from his eyes, but he dared not rub them. "Let's go up on the roof," he said, throwing on his clothes.

As the young blonde donned her blouse and pulled on her jeans, she glanced at Charles and noticed that his nose was running freely, irritated by the gas. She went to the sink, moistened two washrags, handed one to him, and placed the other over her face.

They ascended a narrow dimly lit passage at the end of the hall and opened the door at the top of the stair. A gentle breeze was blowing, and the rooftop air was clean and sweet. They spent a few minutes just breathing deeply. Across the rooftops in the direction of Rue Gay-Lussac, they could see a large crowd backlit against the glow from the street. Everyone was looking down into the street below, transfixed.

Stepping carefully from building to building, Steffi and Charles made their way over to join their neighbors. Engulfed in smoke, the students below were waving their red flags atop an expansive barricade and taunting a stationary line of police about forty yards away. The police were lobbing rifle-mounted tear gas grenades across the open space between them. A grenade looped above the street, landed behind the barricade, and detonated. After a second, it began to emit the dense yellow smoke of the gas. The students wore wet kerchiefs across their noses, giving them the odd look of the outlaws in a B grade Western movie from the 1950s. This "old movie" effect was further enhanced by the yellow smoke, which gave the entire scene a sepia cast. Residents on the lower floors of the adjacent buildings were pouring buckets of water on the students in an effort to neutralize the gas. Some students ran about heroically picking up the fuming grenades and throwing them back. The police too began to choke.

A little breeze swept away the gas for a moment, and Steffi could see that injured students littered the street behind the police line and the adjacent barricade which the police had just cleared. A few were being attended to by first-aid workers who had managed to get past the police line, while others were being roughly forced to their feet by police. Most were just lying there motionless. Beyond the injured students, a sea of barricades and overturned autos held up ambulances and more aid workers. No one could get through, and the aid workers who had managed to reach

---

1 Fraser, et al., *1968: A Student Generation in Revolt*, 187-8.

the injured had braved both the students' barrage of cobbles and the police's ubiquitous tear gas.[1]

Back down Rue Gay-Lussac toward the stalled ambulances, Steffi counted five
overrun and abandoned barricades. Oil soaked and burning, they issued plumes of
black smoke. The students had also set fire to many of the parked cars that lined the
street, adding to the inferno in their wake. Below Steffi and Charles watched as student defenders led away their companions who had been overcome by the gas, while
more student reinforcements flowed in from the rear.

Suddenly the police charged with a great shout. The students waited until their
assailants were a dozen or so paces away and then let fly with a barrage of cobblestones. There was an odd pause. The police seemed wobbly for an instant, but recovered their momentum, and then, with a second yell, they began to resolutely advance
again, this time more slowly. The student defenders let fly another volley of cobbles
and then took to their heels and ran, sprinting down the wide boulevard to the safety
of the next barricade, which received them with a loud "hurrah."

The police bludgeoned the unlucky stragglers with clubs and rifle butts, leaving
them lying in the street, and then quickly moved on, stopping about forty yards from
the next barricade and launching another round of rifle-mounted tear gas grenades.
It continued that way until 5:30 a.m., when Danny Cohn-Bendit called a radio station
and broadcast an appeal for his colleagues to break off their resistance.[2] At the end of
his appeal, Danny suggested that the time had come for the unions to read the handwriting on the wall. If the trade union movement did not call a general strike now, he
said, it meant that they were "no longer on the people's side."[3]

By 6:00 a.m., the last of the barricades had been abandoned. With the first light
of morning came the realization that the students had disappeared, retreated up tiny
alleys, fled along passageways, and faded into the ancient cityscape like so many
ephemeral spirits. The police again controlled the streets. They had again won all the
battles, but this time it was clear to the entire nation that they had lost the war.

* * *

The next morning, Steffi and Charles encountered an odd scene in Rue Gay-Lussac. By 9:30 a.m., thousands of tourists had already accomplished a second conquest
of the Latin Quarter. They rushed about madly taking pictures and posing on the
smoking barricades. The police were escorting lines of arrested students with fingers
laced behind their heads, marching them single file along the sidewalks and roughly
herding them into waiting "Black Marias." The students looked grim, haggard; their
eyes still red, their clothing wet. The police prodded their unlucky captives along
using rifle butts and batons. Some had dried blood on their faces and clothing.

Police brutality had been widely reported, and France was outraged. To add
to the national horror, it was also widely reported that, in the wake of the fighting, armed police had conducted forced searches of private apartments all across the
Latin Quarter in an attempt to root out student protestors who they suspected were
harboring within.

In the Boulevard Saint-Michel, the carcasses of automobiles and buses still
smoldered, and the abandoned barricades gave off the thin residual black smoke of
burning gasoline. Here and there neatly dressed students who had not participated
in the riots were seen scurrying toward the various university buildings that had

---

1 *The New York Times*, May 11, 1968, 1.
2 Singer, *Prelude to Revolution*, 142.
3 Fraser, et al., *1968: A Student Generation in Revolt*, 188.

not been affected by the closing of the Sorbonne. The police stood about in clusters, heavily armed, helmeted, and seemingly uninterested in anything that was going on around them. Everywhere there were broken store windows, and yet there was no sign of looting. On the streets where traffic still ran, there was gridlock, but the police seemed oblivious. Except for the devastation and the extraordinary numbers of police, it was as if nothing had happened. Everything seemed normal, routine. All of the tension was gone.

Street crews were already on the scene, removing the barricades, repairing the ravaged streets, sweeping, clearing, and hauling off the debris. Bulldozers and dump trucks droned loudly. As Steffi passed a group of workmen, she heard one of them say, "Maybe they are *fils de papa*, but you have to hand it to them. They showed real courage."[1] The workers' charge that the rioting students represented little more than "*Fils de Papa*" always made the seriously radical protestors bristle. It implied that these sons of well-to-do bourgeois families were little more than spoiled playboys who have had it easy.

"Perhaps the unions, the workers — the real communist political might in France — are finally being swayed by the students' resolve," Steffi said. "Maybe now they'll do more than shout, 'Spoiled brat, go to work!' "

Charles didn't want to talk politics. Steffi's train back to Frankfurt would depart in less than twenty-four hours, and he wanted this last day to be filled with tenderness and love. "The unions and communists will not stand for this kind of violence," he said dismissively. "They'll take this revolt in an entirely different direction, in the direction of parliamentary reform, not revolutionary chaos. If the unions come into this, they may score a few concessions from the government, but they will not take on the authorities the way the students have. They may not accomplish any meaningful change, but they will put an end of this madness."

Steffi knew he was right, but she could not decide whether this was good or bad. She wanted an end to the senseless violence, but she knew that the French communists and the workers' unions had no stomach for the kind of resistance it would take to accomplish any real revolutionary change.

MONDAY, MAY 13, 1968

On Monday, the day after he and Kurt had seen Steffi off at the Gare de l'Est, Eliot returned to New York. As his plane took off, Eliot knew that hundreds of thousands of Frenchmen were massing in front of that same grand depot from which Steffi had departed. He knew that great crowds were gathering everywhere in France, that the unions were promoting a great triumphal march through the streets of Paris, the largest in France's long history of marches. Over a million would march in Paris alone, or so some said, but no one dared predict the exact numbers. All across France, they would march — in Lyon, Marseilles, Toulouse, Bordeaux, Nancy, Nimes, Caen, Rouen, and Strasbourg. The massive national trade union, the CGT (*Confédération Générale du Travail*, General Confederation of Labor) had called for demonstrations and for a national strike; the communists had uneasily included the radical students in the enormous march. The government was capitulating, opening the Sorbonne, and freeing the imprisoned students. One million Frenchmen were demanding reform in the streets of Paris.

They had won. Or had they?

---

1 *The New York Times*, May 12, 1968, 3.

As the plane banked in its turn to the west, Paris lay below. Eliot could see the loops of the Seine, the Île de la Cité, and crowds filling the Place de la République. He sensed that this was the day of transition between two distinct phases of the ongoing French crisis. From here on, the students would no longer constitute the catalytic force behind the Paris May. The struggle would now be led by the workers, the communists, the big unions. It had been the students' object all along to bring the workers into the struggle, but the young American theorist feared that the French proletariat had long ago sold out to the lures of image, comfort, and commodity, just as they had in America. He thought of Baudelaire, the modern *flaneur*, and of the aim-less window shoppers in Walter Benjamin's Paris Arcades. Like the workers, all of them were captives, both drawn to the glitter of the modern world and at the same time repelled by it. The proletariat, Marx's heroic revolutionary agent, was just an-other willing captive in the most tender of traps, hopelessly ensnared in the self-per-petuating logic of late capitalism, an invisible, culturally ingrained logic so smooth, so adaptable, so all encompassing, that it had easily become one with any adversary seeking real social justice and equality, assimilating it, digesting it, and seamlessly moving on unchanged.

Something had changed. Eliot felt conflicted, disillusioned, lost. Returning to New York after the tumultuous Paris May, he saw the Columbia riots of the month before in a new light. Not only did they now appear trivial, insignificant, and inconse-quential, they also appeared wrong-minded. Mark Rudd and the others in the SDS's so-called Action Faction were wrong. Without the proper grassroots intellectual groundwork, violent action was futile. Until a large portion of the population under-stood the nature of the glittering prison in which they were confined, any efforts to bring about a popular uprising were doomed, and all of the splinted factions of the New Left would simply be absorbed into the system it sought to over throw. Doctor Adorno was right. The revolutionary moment was not at hand.

CHAPTER TWENTY-THREE: FRANKFURT

What is the city over the mountains
Cracks and reforms and bursts in violent air
Falling towers
Jerusalem Athens Alexandria
Vienna London
Unreal.
— T. S. Eliot, "The Wasteland"

The bourgeoisie of the world, which looks complacently upon the wholesale massacre after the battle, is convulsed by horror at the desecration of brick and mortar.
— Karl Marx, "The Civil War in France"

SUNDAY, MAY 12, 1968

Steffi arrived back in Frankfurt to find the University and the Institute closed. Student unrest in the days leading up to the long-awaited demonstrations in Bonn had forced the Chancellor to close the entire university complex for a week. She read the papers and called Karl Wolff at the SDS office in the hope of getting an update on the situation. She felt a little guilty about missing yesterday's much-touted Bonn rallies, but worse than that, she felt terribly out of touch.

"It was a disaster," said Karl, "more like a festival than a demonstration. The papers say 70,000 in the streets of Bonn, but I know there were nowhere near that many.[1] The workers didn't show. They stabbed us in the back at the last minute and called for their own demonstrations in Dortmund. The police had the entire Federal

---

[1] Estimates of the size of the May 11th Bonn demonstrations vary greatly. The *Times* puts the size of the crowd at 30,000, most German papers said 70,000 and some Leftist publications reported numbers as high as 100,000. *The New York Times*, May 12, 1968, 3; Fraser, et al., *1968: A Student Generation in Revolt*, 234.

District sealed off. It was a six-mile march, and by the time we got to the end at the Royal Gardens adjacent the university and the Bundestag, everyone was so tired that they just lay down in the grass."

"The unions didn't support the Bonn march, after all we've been through?" said Steffi incredulously.

"We had asked the unions to declare a strike, but they refused. Then they failed to turn up in Bonn. The SDS and the student movement in Germany in general is now being driven back, not by the repressive forces of the bourgeois government, but by the refusal of the trade unions to break their post-war consensus with the state. I am very much afraid that we are losing all the momentum that we gained after Rudi got shot."

"What will you do?" asked Steffi.

"The only thing we can do is to strengthen our struggle within the university in hopes of drawing in new recruits. We are not ready to go back to the streets, and we can't do much until the university re-opens of Wednesday. We have to act. The SDS all over Germany is fragmenting, falling apart. There is no ideological consensus. Our only unity is in the unity of direct action."

There was a pause. Steffi had never heard Karl Wolff so down, so desperate. She didn't know what to say. Further disruption in the university seemed like a strategy of panic. In many ways, the university was the students' ally in their larger battles against the reactionary government and against the repressive nature of modern society in general. She was anxious to discuss this with Professor Adorno. She remembered that he had recently told her that he considered the student disruptions at the Institute to be acts of desperation. The student movement was losing steam, he had said, and so it panicked and began attacking everything, even those who supported it intellectually. "Like the French Revolution," her diminutive mentor had told her, clearly referring to himself, "it is eating its own children."

"Perhaps you would consider speaking at one of our rallies," said Karl suddenly. "Maybe something about the New Marxism, the kind that Rudi preached, the kind Doctor Marcuse champions. You know, the return to the pure doctrine of Marx but with rearranged modern players — intellectual players who carry the banner not of class struggle but of the struggle against the forces of neo-capitalism and the consumer society. It might help take the sting out of the workers' refusal to support our efforts."

"I can do that," said Steffi, "but only if you agree to leave Herr Doctor Adorno completely out of it. That is, you are not to mention my connections to him or to the Institute. The students have given him enough trouble without me adding to his woes."

"I can respect that," said the SDS leader. "It will be Wednesday, probably. I'll call you."

"I'll speak with Professor Adorno tomorrow and make sure he has no objection," said Steffi.

"Great!" said Karl, "Sometimes a little shot of theory can re-invigorate action."

"Theory is not just about inspiring people to do the right thing," she said. "It is about inspiring people to do the right thing for the right reasons."

MONDAY, MAY 13, 1968

The next day when Steffi arrived at the Institute, everyone was speculating about Friday night's violence in Paris and the subsequent massive demonstrations all across France. What effect would all of this have on the student unrest in Frankfurt?

Everyone agreed that the events in the French capital along with the Bonn march protesting the proposed Emergency Laws had created a highly volatile situation at the university. The Institute, like the university, would remain closed to students until Wednesday, and many classes had been canceled altogether.

Doctor Adorno was nowhere to be found, but he had left Steffi a long list of research projects the way he always did before he went on holiday. Steffi wondered. Since the Institute was closed and his lectures had been canceled for the rest of the term, perhaps he had already left. When she inquired, Doctor Adorno's personal secretary told her that he planned to leave tomorrow for Zermatt, at the foot of the Matterhorn, but that he would call in to check for any messages, and that she would inform him that Steffi wanted to talk to him.

When Dr. Adorno checked in the call was transferred to Steffi, who told him that Karl Wolff had asked her to address the striking students, possibly on Wednesday. She explained their agreement to keep the Institute out of this, and she told him that she felt that this was an opportunity to place before the radical students a more realistic and moderate approach to their protests. Dr. Adorno suggested that she drop by his home around five.

* * *

Doctor Adorno came to the door himself. He looked thin, exhausted, lifeless. There were dark circles under his eyes. He showed Steffi to his comfortable study, and when they were seated, he said, "I am glad you came by, Fräulein. I said my goodbyes on Friday, but of course, you were in Paris. Tell me about that."

"It was brutal, Herr Professor. Brutal beyond words," said Steffi, not wanting to go into detail.

"Yes, and it now it appears that the French government has shot itself in the foot with their continued reliance on the police in the face of popular protest."

Steffi wondered if he was alluding to his own earlier use of the police to clear the Institute. "Do you think the French government will topple?" she asked.

"No. There may be some give and take. De Gaulle may even have to step down, but in the end, it will be more or less business as usual. At the bottom of it all, this is not a political or an economic issue. It is a cultural issue. The culture of modern Western capitalism is too deeply ingrained to allow any truly revolutionary movement even the slightest chance of success."

"So, all of this is for nothing?"

"Well, there will be some progress. Despite my opposition to the nature of the student movement here in Germany, I will be the first to admit that changes within the university are in the works, changes that never would have occurred without the student revolts. Nonetheless, this is very different from the radical societal upheaval the students are hoping for. Once again, widespread blindness to the repressive nature of late capitalism is far too deeply ingrained in our present culture. At this point in history, the system is unshakable. They're proving that right now in Bonn."

"You mean the Emergency Laws will pass?"

"Yes, sadly. They will expand the totalitarian power of the present government. The people are blind to this danger. They feel that it is more important for the government to protect their material progress than to maintain their freedom as individuals. The Emergency Laws will put totalitarian power only a pen stroke away: conscription, the use of military force to replace the police, military leaders in positions of governmental power, wiretaps, and other privacy abuses. Yet, in a way, I fear the radical opposition just as much. It seems to me that authoritarian attitudes are bound to prevail within these militant groups. Already here at the university, the word 'professor' is used to dismiss people, to 'demolish' them as the students say, just the way the Nazis used the word 'Jew.' I told Herbert in a letter just this morning that I take the risk that the student movement may turn to fascism much more seriously than he does."[1]

There was a pause. Steffi sensed a profound sadness in her mentor, a deep and lingering melancholy.

She loved him deeply; he represented everything that was good and right and rational in the world. She knew that, in his own odd kind of way, he loved her too. To be sure, her beauty was part of it. She knew that she was beautiful, and that Doctor Adorno had an appreciative eye for feminine charms. Still, she was not vain, and she rarely let her good looks get in the way of what she saw to be her higher calling. In any event, she knew that at the bottom of it all, it was for her mind, not her beauty that he had selected her to work at his side. Accordingly, Steffi bore the old man no ill will for the occasional lustful glance, for she knew his love and respect, like everything else he had to give, grew from his powerful intellect. Thus it was that, in a most perfect way, she loved him, and he her, and they would never speak of it.

"Herr Professor, I would like to accept Karl Wolff's invitation to address the SDS. I have his word that they will not bring the Institute into this, and I think that I can define for them an alternative course that is still radical but more reliant on thought than action. I want to tell them that their mission is not to occupy buildings and to fight the police, but to awaken a new consciousness, a consciousness of the fact that people in Germany today are not really free, a consciousness that reveals that all of us are being manipulated by consumerism and the false needs generated by neo-capitalism."

"You have my blessing, my dear," said the old man.

"Thank you, Herr Professor," said Steffi.

"But don't set your hopes too high, Fräulein. The next day they will be back smashing in the doors of the university," said Doctor Adorno.

It was an uncharacteristically cynical remark. "I hope not, Herr Professor," she replied.

WEDNESDAY, MAY 15, 1968

The day the university reopened, fifteen thousand marched in the streets of Frankfurt.[2] Steffi was awed by the size of the crowd and surprised by the large numbers of workers who joined the student protest. Despite their differences, the SDS had convinced the unions to call a half-day strike.[3] They had also apparently managed to radicalize the majority of the university students in Frankfurt. To be sure, this radicalization had come not only from their continued pressure for university reform but from the immediacy of the constitutional crisis that surrounded the impending passage of the Emergency Laws and also from some sense of solidarity with

---

1 Theodor Adorno, letter to Herbert Marcuse, June 19, 1969 *Frankfurter Adorno Blätter*, 8, 4:112, in Müller-Doohm, *Adorno*, 478.

2 Accounts of the size of the demonstrations in Frankfurt on the day the university reopened vary. Fraser reports 15,000 marchers, while the *Times* estimated only five thousand. Fraser, et al., *1968: A Student Generation in Revolt*, 235; *The New York Times*, May 16, 1968, 3.

3 Fraser, et al., *1968: A Student Generation in Revolt*, 235.

the French students and the increasingly revolutionary pageant that was being enacted in the French capital.

Steffi was among the speakers to address the huge crowd at a SDS rally planned by Karl Wolff at the Paulskirche, the site of the first German parliament in 1848. Most speeches lamented the inability of the Left to divert the parliamentary locomotive that propelled the Emergency Laws inexorably toward passage. To the cheers of the gathered throngs beneath the spires of the historic Frankfurt landmark, the radical leader, Hans-Jürgen Krahl, declared, "Democracy was at an end in Germany." Steffi knew that Krahl was one of the radicals who had led the attacks on Doctor Adorno.

When Steffi's turn came, the exuberant crowd was quiet, not knowing what to expect. Despite her considerable experience speaking in public, the young scholar was nervous. She stepped to the podium, adjusted the microphone, and stared out into a sea of blank faces.

"The current German government is a giant conspiracy to let sleeping dogs lie,"[1] she began.

The crowd responded with a deafening cheer. She had won them over with a single sentence.

"It is a conspiracy fabricated by those who have benefited from *Der Wirtschaftswunder*, the German 'economic miracle,' a conspiracy to hang on to what they've gained. The public, including many of the more prosperous workers, does not want to be disturbed. They have a bad conscience, having been bought off.[2] They resent any reminder of this sell-out and refuse to face the ghosts of the past. To this public, the student protest is repugnant. The government exploits this perception and tries to paint a hysterical picture of student unrest, to characterize the students as enemies of the people. Sadly, with some of our violent actions, we play right into the government's hand."

The crowd had grown quiet again, but they were listening intently.

"The goal of our demonstrations, our publications, all of our action and rhetoric must be to unveil the manipulations of the government. Our goal is to awaken the consciousness of the German nation to their situation. We must persuade our countrymen that they're not really free, and make them see that modern capitalism is still a society of war, hunger, and the exploitation of the Third World."

There was a thunderous cheer. Steffi smiled. Now she could give them a little theory without boring them to death.

"Marx's thesis of class struggle has to be converted into a new vision," she began. The crowd was silent again, but they were still listening.

* * *

After the speeches at the Paulskirche, the demonstrators marched through the streets of Frankfurt toward the university. There they set up a blockade and vowed to bar entrance to the institution for at least two days. There were several clashes with other student groups. Finally, the students smashed in the front door to the administration building and occupied the Chancellor's office.[3]

At this point, the workers deserted. They saw the occupation of the university as an overt seizure of a real seat of power, and they wanted no part of it. The union leaders were unmoved by the students' arguments that this was merely a symbolic act.

---

1 Spender, *Year of the Young Rebels*, xx.
2 Spender, *Year of the Young Rebels*, xx.
3 Fraser, et al., *1968: A Student Generation in Revolt*, 235.

Doctor Adorno had again been right. Steffi went home in disgust.

Chapter Twenty-four: New York

Time present and time Past
Are both perhaps present in time future,
And time future contained in the past.
If all time is eternally present
All time is unredeemable.
— T. S. Eliot, "Burnt Norton"

Every act and event is the inevitable result of prior acts and events and is independent
of human will.
— Karl Marx, Attributed

Monday, May 13, 1968

When Eliot arrived back in New York, Melissa handed him a letter from the university informing him that his disciplinary hearing was to be held in early June. According to the letter, the hearing would be conducted along guidelines set up by the new student–faculty–administration committee. Failure to respond, it warned, would result in suspension.

About 500 such letters had been sent to those involved in the occupation of the buildings at Columbia. "It is generally believed that a one-semester suspension will be enforced in most of these cases," she said. "Both students and faculty voiced considerable objection to the new disciplinary guidelines on the grounds that they in no way resembled due process."

"Undoubtedly those arguments are still lost on the university administration," said Eliot sarcastically. "What will they do about exams, grades, missed course work, graduation?"

"Some exams have been postponed," she told him, "and many students have been given the choice of attending informal classes for the rest of the year or of taking an 'incomplete' and making up work the following year. There will be no grades for undergraduates this term, but graduation will be held on schedule. Since you are a graduate student with most of your course work completed, this will have little effect on your situation."

After speaking with his faculty advisor, Eliot found that he could easily pick up his research where he left off, after sitting out his suspension. He decided to simply reapply to the University of Frankfurt for the fall semester and pick up his studies there. Then, next year, he could return to Columbia and finish his degree on schedule in the spring.

Eliot was glad to see Melissa. He had missed her terribly, and he told her so. They spent the afternoon and evening hanging around her apartment, making love, reading, and cooking. After supper, Melissa tried to catch Eliot up on the situation at Columbia.

"The university is trying to sort out the pieces," she began. "They're enacting modest reforms, and trying to move on. Members of the Strike Steering Committee were even allowed to meet with the Board of Trustees, but the campus is still in turmoil.[1] A general student strike is still going on, and there has been more violence. Last week, radical students led by Mark Rudd occupied a university-owned apartment building on 114th Street and were later ejected by the police. It's still a big mess, with lots of ill-will and angry rhetoric. There are demonstrations and disruptions almost daily."

FRIDAY, MAY 24, 1968

Eliot had not seen much of Martin since his return, and he was glad when Melissa announced that she had invited her brother to supper. Despite all of his hippie affectations, Eliot had come to really like the lanky young man. "He's a one of a kind," he told Melissa.

As they sat down to eat, all the talk was about the new eruptions of protest and violence on the Columbia campus. On Wednesday, almost a month to the day after the original occupation of Hamilton Hall, occupying students had returned to Hamilton. Police were again called in, and again there had been considerable brutality: 70 injured including many innocent bystanders, 170 arrested, and 80 suspended —including Mark Rudd.[2] Neither Martin nor Eliot had participated in the demonstrations or in the re-occupation of Hamilton.

After some more talk of the university's seemingly reckless penchant for relying on the police to settle policy issues, Martin asked Eliot what he thought of the progress of the student revolts and the current state of the SDS.

"Well, I must say I am a bit confused," he replied. "After my experiences in Paris, I find myself conflicted in new ways, and I haven't participated in any functions since I got back."

After the monumental upheavals in Paris, Eliot found everything at Columbia trivial, petty, insignificant. He had turned down an invitation from the new SDS president to address some of the organization's new members regarding the relevance of Marxist theory to the current situation. Even his convictions regarding the current relevance of Marxist theory suddenly seemed to be in flux.

"Yeah, I'm having second thoughts too," replied Martin. "Not about Marx, of course. I don't care about all that stuff. It's just that things are so uptight, so angry.

---

1 *The New York Times*, May 24, 1968, 33.
2 *The New York Times*, May 24, 1968, 33.

This mess is a long way from peace and love," said Martin, trying to tie his long flowing hair into a ponytail.

"You're right," said Eliot. "When I step away from the controversy, I can easily see the inflexible battle lines that are now being so deeply etched here at Columbia. On one side, the moderate students favor reform and non-violence. On the other side, there are the radical activists. There is no dialogue between these camps, and the stereotypical prejudices by which each side characterizes the mentality of the other are extreme. When the radicals refer to all moderates as 'jocks,' they imply Neanderthal ignorance, and when the moderates refer to all radicals as 'pukes,' they are implying repugnant juvenile hooliganism. In all of this, the SDS is fragmenting, breaking into pieces and factions. The first and most serious split came back in April, right after the police cleared Low, Hamilton, Avery, Fayerweather, and Math, when the group calling itself the Students for a Reconstructed University split off from the restructured Strike Coordinating Committee. This weakened the solidarity of campus radicals and created serious friction within the Left."

"So where do you stand?" asked Martin.

"My commitment is still with the more radical activist Left, but I'm afraid the SDS is splintering, losing influence. I see the power of the system clearly at work. It is proving that radical movements do not constitute opposition from outside the system the way Professor Marcuse suggests. They really act more as Doctor Adorno postulates. They're part and parcel of the system itself — movements not to be evaluated and considered, but simply to be experienced, appropriately reacted to, and then broken down, demolished, and re-absorbed."

"You mean the SDS is part of the system?" Martin was clearly struggling with this idea.

"Yes, the system allows us the illusion of resistance. It gives us our little victories to placate us. Look at it this way. In a local sense, we have won. I mean, classified war research has been halted, the gym project has been canceled, ROTC has left the campus, and military and CIA recruiting at Columbia has been stopped."

"But that's not what it was really about," said Melissa.

"Exactly. These issues were symbolic of larger political and societal issues. That's the trouble. We might successfully address specific issues through active protest, but when it comes to the rotten core of Western consumer society, the system protects itself first by allowing our issue-directed protests and then by slowly, invisibly assimilating them into its flexible culture of false consciousness. Real reform can only come from the fabrication of a new critique of society, new patterns of thought and self-realization that are alternatives to the ingrained reflexive logic of the present cultural system. According to Doctor Adorno, when it comes to real change, we are at a point in history where we must advance through theory. In order to advance, we must first create a new political, social, and economic consciousness that reveals our true condition — that exposes the lies. Without this new consciousness, this cultural shift, this revolution is impossible. Critical Theory insists that the self-perpetuating forces of late-capitalist culture in the West are currently far too strong, too adaptable, too entrenched to allow even a possibility of revolutionary change. This seems clear enough to me here in the U.S., but in France it first appeared that Doctor Adorno was wrong, that a truly revolutionary situation was emerging there. Now, I'm not so sure. Even though the violence continues, and many factories are now occupied by radical workers, even though ten million are out on strike,[1] labor negotiations have begun. The workers will surely be offered huge concessions: wage increases, better hours, benefits.[2] The system will try to buy them off and re-assimilate them. If Dr. Adorno is right, the French unions will cave in, and the French people will soon demand an end to the chaos. I'm afraid that they're just like us: slaves to materialism, oblivious prisoners of the cultural logic of a system they fail to recognize as repressive."

"That's exactly it," said Martin. "I don't think fighting the system the way we did accomplished a damn thing, except maybe to reinforce the mindset of all those who oppose us. You're right! The deck is stacked against that kind of protest. However, I don't think sitting around thinking about some radical 'new consciousness' will do any good, either. The system is too strong for that too. As you say, it is so ingrained, it can't conceive of any alternative, not to mention understand one. We say we want socialism. If we do, we first have to have some picture of what socialism might really look like, what a socialist system might really be. People aren't able to do this, not even in communist countries, I mean, people who are living in so-called socialist societies. We may have personally gotten some idea of this kind of community when we were all holed-up in the Low Library last month, I don't know, but most people can't imagine what it would be like to be a truly socialist, truly democratic society. First, you have to be able to imagine something before you can achieve it. We can't imagine any kind of change, not really."

"What do you recommend we do?" asked Melissa.

"We have to move outside of the system," said Martin. "We have to 'drop out,' as they say. Once we're on the outside, we have to live our radical dreams. We'll never find them in this culture. In order to create a world of peace and love, we have to live lives of peace and love, and we can't do that within this system."

"That sounds like you believe in Doctor Marcuse's new aesthetic needs that come from somewhere outside the one-dimensional world of the system," said Eliot. "Your youth counterculture is trying to reject the false needs of a corrupt materialist society. Hell, the hippies reject damn near everything. It's hopeless utopian idealism. Marx would not approve."

"It's the truth," said Martin.

"Dropping out won't be easy," said Melissa.

"I know. I don't think you can do it intellectually. It's a commitment to a life of community and communal respect. You can't just think it, dream it, or rationalize it. You have to live it. I may go to California or out in the country somewhere. I don't know. All I know is that I have to try. All of the rest is bull."

---

1 Following the great demonstration in Paris of May 13, a number of French factories were occupied by workers. More factory occupations and worker revolts followed, and strikes spread throughout the nation, leading to the declaration of a general strike on May 17. Within a week the unions claimed that ten million workers were on strike. Later studies placed this figure closer to six million. Although some essential services including electricity remained in operation, the national economy for all practical purposes ground to a halt. Brown, *Protest in Paris*, 13-4.

2 On Saturday, May 25, 1968, leaders of all the major French trade unions met with French Prime Minister Georges Pompidou and other government officials to attempt to end the strikes. These negotiations resulted in the so-called Grenelle Agreement, so named because the negotiations were held in the Hôtel du Châlet, a small Louis XV style palace in Rue de Grenelle. The generous settlement was announced on Monday, May 27. It included general wage increases, reduction of the workweek, increased family allowances, and payment for half the time lost in the strike. Brown, *Protest in Paris*, 20-1.

* * *

Eliot didn't press the matter at the time, but later that evening, when they were alone, he told Melissa that he considered her brother's counterculture hippie dreams to be hopelessly unrealistic. "I'm afraid Martin will find that there is no place outside the system," he said. "I think Paris helped me to understand. As Kurt put it, 'It all goes back to Marx. It all comes together in Marx' — Walter Benjamin's self-reflecting view of history, Doctor Adorno's penetrating critical theories of society, and even Danny the Red's antichrist belief that revolution creates its own ideology as it goes along. It's the dialectic. Not only is opposition to the system contained within the system, so is the outcome. Marx teaches us that socialism is not some new ideal to be found only in a distant ideological Utopia but that it is already contained within the present system — that it is already coming into being within capitalism. Don't you see? Karl Marx saw the future as contained in the present, the present as contained in the past. For Marx there is no stepping outside of the present reality. That's what he meant when he said, we 'have no ideals to realize but to set free the elements of the new society with which the old collapsing bourgeois society itself is pregnant.'[1] Contrary to most people's understanding of Marxism, it is all about freedom. 'Freedom' Marx said, 'is converting the state from an organ superimposed upon society to one completely subordinate to it.'[2] We'll never do that by dropping out."

"And you won't do it by revolt," added Melissa. "So what's left?"

"Theory — critique," said Eliot. "We must achieve a new consciousness before we can move on."

---

1 Karl Marx, "The Civil War in France," in *The Collected Works of Karl Marx and Friedrich Engels*, 50 vols. (New York: International Publishers, 1975-2004), 2:504.
2 Karl Marx, "Critique of the Gotha Programme," 1890, in Karl Marx and Friedrich Engels, Selected Works, 3 vols., (Moscow: Progress Publishers, 1973), 3:13-30.

CHAPTER TWENTY-FIVE: PARIS

> Journey to no end,
> Conclusion of all that
> Is inconclusible
> — T. S. Eliot, "Ash-Wednesday"

> The modern bourgeois society that has sprouted from the ruins of feudal society
> has not done away with class antagonisms. It has but established new classes, new
> conditions of oppression, new forms of struggle in place of the old ones.
> — Karl Marx and Friedrich Engels, "Manifesto of the Communist Party

MONDAY, MAY 20, 1968

Crossing over to the Left Bank, Kurt felt as though he were entering a foreign
republic during Carnival. The police were gone, withdrawn discreetly to the perimeter of the district, and the students had taken over. On the Boulevard Saint-Michel,
the mood was buoyant. Students directed traffic at all the intersections. Everywhere
the trim young German looked, he saw purveyors of radical literature and posters,
the shopkeepers of a wild, outdoor ideological emporium of the Left. Inside the Sorbonne's central courtyard, where it had all begun only a little over two weeks ago, the
great stone figures of Louis Pasteur and Victor Hugo now silently clutched billowing
red flags. A grand piano had been dragged out into the plaza and a jazz band played
something like Dixieland. There were more stands with more books and leaflets, and
the walls were covered with posters and graffiti. Larger than life likeness of Ché,
Lenin, Marx, Trotsky, and Mao stared sternly down on the gala proceedings in the
cour d'honneur. Students gathered in clumps, smoking and hotly debating left-wing
strategy, theory, and protocol. All the official signs proclaiming "Smoking is Forbidden" had been crossed out and overwritten with the words "Forbidden is Forbidden."
Everywhere Kurt found the unruly evidence of free expression. Lectures, tirades, and

debates raged, while the endless writing on the walls exuded passions, imparted random thoughts, babbled obscenities, quotations, poems, gibberish.[1]

Kurt hoped he might get a line on Danny's whereabouts, but everyone he asked looked at him suspiciously and feigned ignorance. Finally, one girl said she had seen him earlier over at the Odéon.

The nearby national theater, known as the Odéon, had been taken over by the students and employed as a forum for self-expression. Symbolically, the extension of the insurrection from the Sorbonne to the national theater was intended to represent a shift from the goal of an autonomous university to that of a full-fledged revolution. The Odéon would now function as a permanent forum for discussion between students and workers, a center for "creative revolution."[2]

The place was packed. Some sort of open debate was in progress, but Kurt couldn't hear the speakers well enough to glean what it was about. Finally, he spotted Danny in a hallway in the middle of a large group of students, waving his arms as he spoke. As Kurt drew near, his friend saw him, immediately broke off his discourse, and rushed over.

"Isn't this fantastic?" he shouted above the roar. "It's like living on a constant high. I mean, what more could one ask. Life is beautiful, the weather is lovely, the men are handsome, and the women superb. Everything we do belongs to history. Where are your sister and your American friend?"

"Steffi's gone back to Frankfurt, and Eliot went back to New York a week ago. I decided to stay on since you insist on making things so exciting here."

Danny laughed and shrugged.

"Let's go outside." Kurt motioned to his ear, indicating that he was having difficulty hearing.

Out on the street, Danny went on with his euphoric account of life in the new university but Kurt noticed that he look tired.

"You look shot," he said.

"I'm exhausted," said Danny, "but we must go on. I was on TV last week. Did you see me? I'm going to Berlin tomorrow to speak there. There's so much to be done. I'm glad you are here. It'll be good to talk things over with someone who doesn't have an agenda. It's exhausting, all the bickering. Now that we've won back the Sorbonne and achieved the release of the arrested students, now that most of the fighting has stopped, all of the old differences within the Left are resurfacing. The reformists are going at it toe to toe with the radicals. We must structure a university program that is acceptable to both, one that will remain as a base for resistance should the system remain in power, and one that can act as a revolutionary juggernaut should the system fall."

"That's a tall order," said Kurt.

"Yes, but we have more immediate problems." Danny's mind was racing as usual. "The government and the communists are trying to isolate us. We have to fight this by linking with workers who have now taken the lead. I mean, everyone thought that the unions were done after the big march last week, but, boy, did they ever come through."

On Tuesday, May 14, workers at the Sud Aviation factory in Nantes had locked their managers in their offices, taken over the plant, and gone out on strike behind

---

1 Singer, *Prelude to Revolution*, 166.
2 Brown, *Protest in Paris*, 17.

the back of the union. There were only a few hundred strikers at first, but it had spread like wildfire.

"It was great," said Danny. "The next day, two million were out on strike all across France. The communists and the unions tried to stop it, but they couldn't. It was spontaneous. In another three days, there were nine million strikers. No one called a general strike, but suddenly there was the largest strike in French history, a spontaneous movement spreading across the country with incredible speed. Factories and offices, oil refineries and shipyards, transport and post offices, banks, department stores, administrative buildings, high schools — everything ground to a halt. All over France people were refusing to live and work under the authoritarian conditions of the de Gaulle regime."[1]

"I thought the CGT called a general strike on the 17th," said Kurt.

"Sure, but it was a done deal by then. They had to. The bulk of the workers were already striking, or getting ready to strike, and the factories had been occupied — the Renault factories in Cléon, then in Billancourt, Flins, and Lemans, then the trains, then the chemical industry. It was already happening before the CGT responded."[2]

Kurt nodded, "So the workers are finally in it? Just when everyone though they had been bought off."

"Yes, and we've got to become one with the workers if we are to advance the revolution. Otherwise we're finished," said Danny. "We've got to get to the grassroots, the rank and file, because at the top, the communist leaders of the unions are against the students. They're locking us out of the striking factories. They're knifing us in the back, going to the government and the bourgeois establishment and charging that we're lawbreakers and foreign agents. I mean, the communists are defaming internationalism. That's a twist. They're accusing me of being a puppet of evil foreign powers because I'm a German Jew. The Communists are trying to take over the movement and keep it in check. They're ruthless."

"Really? I've heard some pretty radical rhetoric coming from some of the unions," said Kurt, "something about 'radical anti-capitalist transformations,' and 'socialist domestic policy and anti-imperialist foreign policy.'"[3]

"Yeah, the PSU and the teachers' unions are more radical than the big workers' unions. But it's the big union leaders that have the power; and I think, at the bottom of it all, they don't really want change. They want to negotiate for more money, more trinkets. So, it's like we've always known. The revolution must come from below. We're trying to maintain the grassroots revolutionary spontaneity of the students, the workers, and the French people. It's hard to do, now that the police have backed down."

"The government knows what it's doing," said Kurt. "They're letting things ripen, giving you leeway, allowing you your successes in the hopes that they'll turn into excesses, waiting for public opinion to turn.[4] The garbage is piling up in the streets,

---

1 Fraser, et al., *1968: A Student Generation in Revolt*, 190-1.

2 Singer, *Prelude to Revolution*, 156-7.

3 The PSU (*Parti Socialiste Unifié*) declared, "Those who would try to deflect the movement toward purely quantitative demands, without questioning the preset power structures, would bear a very heavy responsibility." Alian Geismar of the UNEF (*Union Nationale des Étudiants de France*) stated, "Together with the reform of the university, we consider that radical anti-capitalist transformations are indispensable to get the confidence and the support of the popular masses for any new regime, which implies a socialist domestic policy and a resolutely anti-imperialist foreign policy. Singer, *Prelude to Revolution*:, 171.

4 Brown, *Protest in Paris*, 17.

there's no gas at the pumps, there are shortages, the trains aren't running. The strikes may appear to be a revolutionary success, but if things remain at a standstill for too long, they may become a liability."

"You're right. We have to force the issue," said Danny. "We need organization, programs, strategy. We are not good at these things...." The sentence trailed off, unfinished.

"And the communist and the government are," Kurt concluded it for him.

"Yeah, pigs and Stalinist scoundrels," said the fiery redhead, smiling his disarming wild smile. His lips grinned broadly, revealing a mouthful of oversized white teeth, but his riveting blue eyes remained cold, steely.

"Why did you stay in Paris, Kurt?" asked Danny, suddenly becoming serious and fixing his friend with a penetrating gaze.

"I don't know really," said the grey-eyed German. "I hate the violence, and yet at the same time, I find myself drawn to it. The student mobs here seem to me completely mindless. Their only aim seems to be to level everything that stands before them. Can this be revolution? It seems more like anarchy to me. They seem to be driven by some kind of blind faith, some kind of vague notion that if they could totally destroy the present system, then something better will rise up to take its place, but they don't seem to know or much care what that something might be. For some, there may be a dreamy sense that all of this will lead to some kind of utopian egalitarian socialism, but everyone seems to have different ideas as to how this new system might work. Can this be the dialectic? Do the opposing forces that drive history flail away at each other blindly and brutally without concrete principles, without set goals or designed strategy, without sound theory to guide them? I guess I'm troubled by these questions, and so here I am."

"The hell with theory," said Danny, again smiling his unnerving smile.

FRIDAY, MAY 24, 1968 (THE NIGHT OF THE *BOURSE*)

"We are all German Jews!" the crowd outside the Gare de Lyon chanted. It was the initial theme of a protest march Kurt felt obliged to support. The events of the past two days had brought Kurt back into ranks of the protesting students. Two days before, the French government had declared Daniel Cohn-Bendit an "undesirable alien" and had refused to let him back into France after his trip to Berlin and Holland.[1] In Paris, sporadic rioting had followed the news of Danny's rejection at the frontier, and in the Latin Quarter angry students once again clashed with police in all-out battles.[2] The nightly fighting between police and students on the Left Bank had by this time evolved into something of a ritualistic pantomime. The students would build up the barricades, the police would launch tear gas and charge, and the students would throw a few cobbles and run away. Now with the barring of their symbolic spokesman, serious student resistance re-erupted and clashes with police were characterized by a new and brutal vigor.

Still, through all of this, Kurt had known that the radical leaders were waiting for the large demonstration planned to begin at the Gare de Lyon on the night of the Friday, the 24th. Up until this point, Kurt had steered clear of the fighting, but his fascination with the chaotic course of the French upheaval had compelled him stay on in Paris; and in this case, he felt obliged to participate out of loyalty to his friend.

1 Singer, *Prelude to Revolution*, 175.
2 Over 200 were injured in the fighting in Paris on the nights of Wednesday, May 22, and Thursday, May 23, 1968. Brown, *Protest in Paris*, 18.

He would attend the demonstration, and if fighting broke out — well, he would just have to decide what to do when the time came. He knew that this was just the kind of mindless, non-logical behavior that Danny loved. It went against everything that the young German believed in, but somehow, in this case, it seemed the only way to proceed. Trapped in the maddening paradox of his generation, Kurt Siegel saw action against the system as both imperative and futile at the same time.

When Kurt arrived at the Gare de Lyon, it was clear that the large crowd assembled before the great nineteenth-century rail terminal was being reinforced by its own enormity. "We are twenty-five thousand strong," student leaders assured the surging masses. "Danny would be proud."

"The government has expelled him because he is a German Jew," another leader added, in an effort to harangue the students with a charge of governmental anti-Semitism.

The crowd began to chant, "We don't give a damn about borders. We are all aliens. We are all German Jews!"[1]

"We are all German Jews!" shouted a black student next to Kurt.

Kurt looked at him quizzically.

"I can shout that, but no one will believe me,"[2] he said, laughing.

Kurt laughed too, and the man went on in good French, but with some kind of Caribbean accent. "This is incredible," he said. "When I came here tonight, I brought with me an old red flag from my student days. I was walking down the street with the flag over my shoulder, and people began to follow me. Before long they fell into step with me, and by the time, I got here, I was leading a thousand people. Incredible!"[3]

Everyone was elated by the large turnout, especially since the communists and the leaders of the large trade unions had tried to divert attention and support from students' efforts on this night by calling for demonstrations of their own to be held elsewhere.

At about 8:00 p.m. Charles de Gaulle addressed the nation. The crowd went silent. Transistor radios appeared everywhere. Everyone listened intently, showing surprising respect. The speech was stiff, predictable. The aging general spoke of preserving order and of reform "involving a more extended participation." A referendum was proposed. In it, the French people would give the state a "mandate for revolution." If they failed to do so, he would resign, de Gaulle promised.[4] They had heard it all before. It all had a hollow ring. The students knew it; every elected French official knew it; the nation knew it. Even Charles de Gaulle knew it.

"Vive la France!" de Gaulle said weakly, in closing, and one of the students in the great open space before the grand façade of the Gare de Lyon shouted, "Adieu, de Gaulle, adieu!"

The chant went up, "Adieu, de Gaulle, adieu!" Thousands of white handkerchiefs waved a symbolic, "goodbye," above the crowd, "Adieu, de Gaulle, adieu!"

The march began. Twenty abreast they followed a famous Revolutionary route: up Rue de Lyon to the Bastille, then westward on Rue Saint-Antoine and Rue de Rivoli to the Hôtel de Ville, the traditional place for proclaiming new governments in France. Here the police attempted to break up the demonstration.

---

1 Singer, *Prelude to Revolution*, 403.

2 These were actually the words of Aimé Césaire, the French Negro poet and progressive deputy from Martinique. Singer, *Prelude to Revolution*, 178.

3 Fraser, et al., *1968: A Student Generation in Revolt*, 197-8.

4 Singer, *Prelude to Revolution*, 178.

To combat the unified police charge, the student leaders ordered the marchers to split up. One group splintered northward, marching up Rue de Richelieu toward the Bourse. Another skirted the police lines and moved northwestward toward the Opera, and still another returned to the Place de la Bastille to build barricades in that historic square.[1]

In the midst of the group on Rue de l'Opera, Kurt felt confined, helpless. He was surprised to see the police attempting to intervene on the Right Bank. Up until now, all the violence had played out in the Latin Quarter. Now the students were not only dangerously near the Hôtel de Ville and the famous Paris Opera, but they would also soon be only a stone's throw from the Place Vendôme, the site of the French Ministry of Justice and Ministry of Finance. The police were off balance. They had come prepared to take on a huge mob. Now they were unclear as to how they should counter the mobility, speed, and flexibility of so many smaller marauding groups.

For a brief moment, it looked like this might be the beginning of a new chapter in the gathering saga of the current insurrection and indeed in the evolving tome of French history, but it was not to be. As the students split into smaller and smaller groups, fragmented by the police charges, word circulated that the CRS was trying to take over the Latin Quarter. All the diverse student groups scattered about the Right Bank now suddenly became one in intent and resolve. Everyone made for the Left Bank to support their colleagues there. An expeditionary army in a foreign land, they had just received word that their homeland had been overrun, and they broke off their attack just as victory seemed assured.[2] As the throngs turned southward toward the river, word circulated that some of the students had set fire to the Bourse, the famous Paris Stock Exchange, the very heart of French capitalism.[3]

Kurt felt troubled, unsure. Something about all this did not set right. The students, too, seemed suddenly grim. He could not explain it, but in a single breath the wonder had gone out of the thing. Approaching the Seine, he hesitated. For reasons that were not exactly clear to him, Kurt suddenly had no stomach for barricades and cobblestones. It was not for lack of courage that he wavered. Something was wrong. This was not like the triumphal march of a million along the Champs Élysées, the one he, Eliot, and Steffi had so joyfully joined weeks before. Although it had begun joyfully enough, this time all of the joy had been sucked out of them. The event had been somehow stripped of that intoxicating, vicarious elation derived from defending a just cause, of that proud confidence that flows from boldly confronting the perennial oppressor. Gone was idealistic conviction, and even youthful folly was losing its grip on these students' resolve. In a sudden change of the prevailing winds, the cheering crowds of well-wishing onlookers had disappeared. Gone were the shouts of support. The windows above the now-silent streets remained closed and latched. Kurt could feel it in his very soul. Fear had set in. Support for the student cause was suddenly waning.

They crossed over Rue de Rivoli and surged past the Tuileries, heading for the Seine. The bridge was open — strangely unguarded. Had the police planned it all? Had they been tricked, lured away from the vulnerable centers of government and

---

1 *Time* Magazine, May 31, 1968, 20.

2 Singer, *Prelude to Revolution*, 179.

3 On the night of May 24, 1968, a small group of radical protestors briefly took over the French Bourse, setting token fires in several phone booths. The taking of the undefended Bourse was hailed as a symbolic assault of the temple of French capitalism. Singer, *Prelude to Revolution*, 178.

back to the Left Bank again to fight it out in the burned out streets of Saint-Germain-des-Prés, again to hunker down behind makeshift barricades amid the rubble that was the Latin Quarter?

Kurt left the march and walked alone back to his father's flat.

SATURDAY, MAY 25, 1968

The next morning when Kurt came down to breakfast, he found his father reading the paper.

"I heard you come in last night," his father said casually, trying not to sound concerned. "You were early. I'm glad you had sense enough not to go over to the Left Bank. Things got pretty messy over there — 500 hundred injured, 600 arrested.[1] It was another 'Bloody Friday.' That makes three now."

His son nodded, unsurprised.

"This time it wasn't limited to Paris," his father continued. "A policeman was killed in Lyon, and a student demonstrator here in Paris was knifed to death.[2] A number of cities all across the country are not under government control this morning."

Kurt looked at the headlines. "I think we are losing," he said, absently. "Something went wrong. I can't explain it."

"You may be right," said Herr Siegel. "Our people at the embassy say that French public opinion is clearly beginning to shift. People are tired of so many pitched battles and barricades, tired of gas lines and garbage. They want to be able to find a taxi and buy meat and watch TV and ride the Metro. They're afraid the electricity will be cut off."

"The materialist addictions of their self-constructed capitalist prison," said Kurt, duly mouthing the leftist dogma that he was sure his father expected to hear.

"Last night may have turned the tide." Herr Siegel continued his political analysis unscathed by his son's knee-jerk doctrinaire rhetoric. "The public is behind the students as long as they're kept in the Latin Quarter and as long as they're not aligned with the unions. In the French mind, the students are *supposed* to protest. That is what students do. But when the violence spreads to the Right Bank, and when the workers begin to occupy the factories, things are different." He paused and looked at his son, who nodded his agreement. "And when the lights go out...," Herr Siegel rolled his eyes skyward.

"It's ironic," said the youth. "The unions are fighting us every step of the way; they try to control the students; and when they fail, they try to distance themselves and discredit the students. They can't even control their own workers, and yet the public fears revolution from them. They're the ones who are trying to compromise, trying to gain concessions, to negotiate."

"There are negotiations going on right now. Both the CGT and the CFDT[3] are meeting with the government in Rue Grenelle.[4] Something is in the wind," said Herr

---

1 Brown, *Protest in Paris*, 19. According to *Time*, 130 police and 447 civilian were injured, and 795 rioters were arrested in the fighting in at least 30 separate street battles in Paris on the night of May 24. *Time* Magazine, May 31, 1968, 20.

2 Singer, *Prelude to Revolution*, 180.

3 CGT (*Confédération Général du Travail*, General Confederation of Labor) and CFDT (*Confédération Française Démocratique du Travail*, French Democratic Workers Confederation).

4 On Saturday, May 25, 1968, leaders of all the major French trade unions met with French Prime Minister George Pompidou and other government officials to attempt to end the strikes. These negotiations resulted in the so-called Grenelle Agreement, so-called because it met in the Hôtel du Châlet, a small Louis XV style palace in Rue de Grenelle. The gener-

Siegel. "De Gaulle is no fool. When he senses that the time is right politically, he'll stop talking about referendums, dissolve the Assembly, and call for national elections. If your revolution hasn't happened by then, it is over. Once he calls for elections — well, how can one argue with that? Anyway, I suspect it is already over — 'all over but the shouting,' as the American like to say."

He said this last phrase in English, and Kurt replied in English. "I think the police offered a provocation in the Latin Quarter last night. They deliberately started a fight to get us to cross over and defend the Left Bank. The bridge was open, unguarded."

"I don't really think the government is trying to start fights," said the German diplomat, returning to his native tongue, "but they will try to put their own spin on the fighting if they can. They know the public is getting tired of the student violence and burning cars and tear gas and all of the revolutionary rhetoric that seems to lead only to more violence. The Latin Quarter is a mess. At this point, more fighting there only strengthens their position." Herr Siegel sipped his coffee. "People are sick of it," he said again.

"We had a choice last night," said Kurt. "What if we had seized the seats of government and ignored the Latin Quarter?"

"People are afraid of that too. You know all too well that the students aren't prepared for that. They have no agenda moving forward, and although the public will, now and again, support or at least tolerate a little revolutionary song and dance from the students, the public is in no way ready for the real thing. You were damned no matter what you did. Only the workers can make a revolution now, and if they did, it would be a blood bath and everybody knows it. That's why their leaders are already at the bargaining table. There may be some revolutionary wildcat cells among the rank and file here and there, but they're quickly becoming as isolated as the students."

"Doctor Adorno is right, then," said Kurt. "This is not the revolutionary moment. The forces of capitalism are too strong, too ingrained, too much a part of modern life. I mean, if it can't be done here, then where in the industrial world? Nowhere!" he answered his own question.

"Yes, Doctor Adorno is right," smiled Herr Siegel, returning to his paper.

The trim youth looked at his father. "And Doctor Marcuse?"

"I'm having dinner with him on Thursday," his father said in an offhand manner, without looking up. "If you'd like to join us, you can ask him yourself."

This was typical of the diplomat's habit of snaring an unwary prey. He had a natural gift for delivering an unsuspected blow with the most nonchalant of gestures. Despite Herr Siegel's opaque dispassionate predilections, Kurt was suddenly and unexpectedly overcome with love for his father; but not in a thousand years would he dare to tell him so.

THURSDAY, MAY 30, 1968

At 4:30 p.m., De Gaulle again addressed the nation. Kurt sat in a café on the Left Bank and marveled at the wily old French general's resolve. How did this embattled veteran see the present political situation? "He should be near giving up," Kurt reasoned, "but he's attacking. Can't he see the handwriting on the wall?"

The young German went over the events of the last few days in his mind. On Monday, the union's rank and file had rejected the negotiated Grenelle Agreement.

---

ous settlement was announced on Monday, May 27th. It included general wage increases, reduction of the workweek, increased family allowances, and payment for half the time lost in the strike. Brown, *Protest in Paris*, 20-1.

Daniel Cohn-Bendit had managed to sneak back into the country, and in dramatic disguise, at midnight on Tuesday, he had addressed and inspired a large gathering of students at the Sorbonne. Then yesterday, Wednesday, the unions had again demonstrated *en masse*, and the streets of Paris had again echoed with anti-Gaullist slogans. There had been fears that the workers would march on the presidential palace and take it, but then it was learned that de Gaulle had disappeared.[1] No one seemed to know where he was, not even his Prime Minister Georges Pompidou. It was a day of speculation, uncertainly, panic, hope, illusion.[2]

"It is a new and reinvigorated de Gaulle who has resurfaced," Kurt thought, as he heard the confident strength of the aging leader's voice on the radio.

"*Eh, bien, non! Je ne retirai pas,*"[3] said de Gaulle.

Then the general barked out orders in a voice that only thinly veiled his threats of retaliation against any who stood in his way. He would dissolve parliament, call for general elections, mobilize the armed forces. His voice was like thunder. Elections would be held right away, he said — unless there were attempts to "gag the French people" through "intimidation, intoxication, and tyranny" exercised by groups under the control of some "totalitarian party." Then he called on the French people to join him in his fight against the "subversion," of "totalitarian Communism." "The Republic will not abdicate," the general concluded.[4]

He spoke for only three or four minutes. When it was over, the Left Bank café where Kurt sat was abuzz with speculation as to what this new hard line meant. De Gaulle had clearly answered the challenge that had been put to his government, and in so doing, he had radically upped the political stakes. How would the nation react? Everyone seemed suddenly unsure.

Kurt Siegel felt no such uncertainty. He knew that it was over.

* * *

"It's not like Kurt to be late," said Herr Siegel, looking up at his old friend across the elegant table setting.

Doctor Marcus smiled patiently as the waiter carefully poured the aperitifs. "He's probably caught in the crush of the demonstrations. There are hundreds of thousands of jubilant pro-de Gaulle marchers on the Champs Élysées tonight — some say millions.[5] It seems the General's speech this afternoon has turned the tide. Not surprising, I suppose."

"Yes, since the unions came into this, the situation appears more conventionally political and less radically revolutionary, despite the workers' continued violence and occupation of so many factories."

Doctor Marcuse nodded.

"The students captured a spirit in their countrymen," Herr Siegel continued. "The workers, it seems, have not. Still, despite their idealism and their public appeal, everyone knew that the students were harmless, really — a bit like a dog chasing a car."

"How so?" asked Herbert Marcuse, smiling at his friend's strange metaphor.

---

1 Without a word to anyone in his cabinet, Charles de Gaulle slipped out of Paris and held secret meetings with the French military on May 28, 1968.

2 Singer, *Prelude to Revolution*, 186-95.

3 "No, I shall not stand down!" Fraser, et al., *1968: A Student Generation in Revolt*, 200.

4 Singer, *Prelude to Revolution*, 201.

5 Singer, *Prelude to Revolution*, 201. *Time* estimated 600,000 to 1,000,000. *Time* Magazine, May 31, 1968, 32.

"A dog may chase cars, but he never considers what he might do with one if he were to catch it."

Professor Marcuse smiled.

"Ah, here is Kurt now," said Herr Siegel, rising to greet his son.

Doctor Marcuse also rose. "Kurt, so good to see you again. It's been a long time."

"Yes, Herr Doctor, since your lectures in Berlin last year. Thank you for sending me Herr Doctor Adorno's book. That was very thoughtful of you."

"Ah, Berlin, yes; we spoke of Utopia then, did we not?" said Marcuse, motioning for everyone to sit.

"Yes, Herr Professor," said Kurt as they all sat down. "But I must say there is no Utopia in Paris tonight. I am so sorry to be late. The streets are jammed. It's impossible to move out there."

"I saw your sister a few weeks ago at Nanterre."

"Yes, she told me that you were in Paris for the celebration of the 150th anniversary of the birth of Karl Marx."

The silver-haired philosopher explained that he had come to Paris to speak at the UNESCO Symposium, and that since the disturbances began he had been involved in numerous debates and speaking engagements all over — in bookstores, at the Sorbonne, the École des Beaux Arts. He said that he even had an opportunity to meet with Nguyen Than Le, the chief negotiator for the North Vietnamese at the peace talks.[1]

"And I have been to Berlin," Doctor Marcuse concluded, "where I spoke at the Free University and visited your friend Rudi Dutschke in the hospital."[2]

"Really! I heard he had another operation. How is he?"

"He's doing remarkably well. The operation, they say, was successful, and Rudi is recovering his memory at a remarkable rate. However, it's difficult to tell how much is really his memory returning and how much is a function of his considerable efforts to re-learn everything about his life. Even he does not know. It must be unnerving not to know if you really remember something, or if you have simply been told what was in your past. It appears that this kind of thing is never black and white. He is told about his past, and that seems to trigger partial vague memories that are hard for him to assimilate. Then he is told more, and he begins to get the picture though a combination of re-learning and the stimulation of actual memory. In the end, it is impossible for him to tell where one begins and the other leaves off. Still, when you think about it, I suppose all of our memories operate a little like that. Indeed, all of history is an odd combination of what actually happened and what we have been told happened. In the end, we accept it all as truth. It reminded me of something Teddy Adorno once showed me that Walter Benjamin wrote. 'Indeed, the historical facts become something that has just happened to us,' Walter wrote, 'to establish them is the task of memory.'"[3]

"And awakening is the exemplary form of remembering," Kurt added, recalling Doctor Adorno's lectures on the illusions of modern history.

"Bravo, my boy!" said Doctor Marcuse, "Are you a student of Walter Benjamin?"

"No, Herr Doctor, I too was Doctor Adorno's student. He taught me that."

"Well, you must be in a state of wakening, for your memory is very good indeed,"

1 Katz, *Herbert Marcuse and the Art of Liberation*, 185-6.

2 Herbert Marcuse visited Rudi Dutschke in the hospital in Berlin on June 14, 1968. *The New York Times*, June 15, 1968, 2.

3 Benjamin, *Gesammelte Schriften*, 5: 1057.

"Thank you, Herr Professor," said the graduate student. "I'm glad to get news of Rudi. I wrote to him a few weeks ago. I heard he was working a little."

"Yes, he is writing. And most interestingly, he is carrying on a correspondence with his assailant who is now in a mental institution.[1] They have become quite close in an odd way."

"Really!"

"Rudi believes that Josef Beckmann, the man who shot him, did not act alone," said Doctor Marcuse. "He is certain that he was put up to it by reactionary elements in West Germany. He hopes to get to the bottom of the plot and expose the conspiracy. In the meantime, I think he has developed a kind of affection for this man, who is clearly deranged."

The waiter poured Kurt an aperitif and handed everyone a menu.

"I highly recommend the *fois de veau, avec sauce framboise*," said Herr Siegel.

They were quiet for a short time while they considered the ordering of the meal.

Kurt found it hard not to be distracted. Just a block away, the Champs Élysées was filled with a million wild de Gaulle supporters. The students were doubtless on the barricades in the Latin Quarter, and in factories all across France armed workers had barricaded themselves in and were ready to fight. He felt disoriented. Inside this posh restaurant, he and his father were sipping aperitifs with Herbert Marcuse, while outside all hell was breaking loose.

After they had ordered, Herr Siegel attempted to rekindle their previous conversation.

"Herbert and I were just discussing the upcoming elections, Kurt. Our analysts at the embassy think that de Gaulle will win in a landslide of backlash and that the workers are done and will soon go back to work."

"That's probably true," said Kurt. "But don't write this all off too casually. The French workers did a great deal more than just shake up French bourgeois society; their valiant struggle cast a shadow on the new Left's notion of the obsolescence of the working class as the revolutionary agent. Perhaps they have not been 'bought off' after all. Remember, in order to strike, to occupy factories, to rebel, the rank-and-file workers broke not only with the authorities but also with their own traditional leadership, which seems to be in bed with the authorities. Their rejection of the concessions offered by the government and the unions frightened a lot of people."

"Are you still talking to Karl Marx?" Doctor Marcuse smiled at Kurt. "Your father told me about that."

Kurt felt a sudden flash of anger, "Yes, Herr Professor. Are you?"

Herr Siegel frowned. His son was on the edge of impertinence, but Doctor Marcuse didn't seem to mind at all. He just nodded.

"Yes, yes, Kurt, don't underestimate my Marxism. I know Marx a great deal better than you, I dare say. When I talk to Marx, he tells me to look to history. History will reveal exactly how revolutionary the French workers have been, are, and will be. I suspect that they're not so revolutionary as the vanguard element of the French students, for all of their misguided zeal. The time for revolution has not come, but the time for rethinking the nature of our society is now at hand. I believe history is revealing the obsolescence of the traditional Marxian model of a centralized, mass-based revolutionary movement. I don't like it and you don't like it, but it's the truth."[2]

1 Rudi Dutschke, *Jeder Hat Sein Leben Ganz Zu Leben: Die Tagebücher 1963-1979* (Cologne: Kiepenhuaer and Wistch, 2003), 189.

2 Herbert Marcuse quoted in Katz, *Herbert Marcuse and the Art of Liberation*, 186.

"That sounds like Herr Doctor Adorno, Herr Professor," said Kurt. He had calmed down, and he was counting himself lucky not to have forced a heated debate regarding the nature of Neo-Marxism with one of the preeminent Marxist scholars of the era. Besides, he knew in his heart that Doctor Adorno was right, that the time for revolution was not at hand.

"Yes, Teddy and I are closer than you might think. We both feel it is not the time for revolution, that the power of the system that engulfs us is far too strong. The difference is that Teddy feels that the path to the kind of informed consciousness that will lead to radical change must lie solely in critique and in theory. I agree, but for my part, I don't mind a little action in the process. Teddy fears that such action will lead to fascism. I admit it is a risk, but I think it a necessary one. Action builds hope and awareness. However, we must be very careful. The risks are high, and the system we oppose is ruthless and very powerful. Action has its dangers. Still, I fear that theory alone is not enough. The system has enormous capacity to neutralize the theoretical and critical opposition and to integrate the values of intellectual and aesthetic culture into the established life-forms of industrialized society."[1]

"Excuse me, Doctor Marcuse?" the waiter interrupted.

"Yes."

"I am sorry to interrupt, but there is an urgent call for you. If you will please follow me."

Professor Marcuse look puzzled. He rose and excused himself.

Herr Siegel looked at his son. "You were impertinent, son. Doctor Marcuse deserves your respect. He is a great man."

"Yes, I'm sorry. I don't know what came over me. Of course, I know my place in this. I will apologize," said Kurt.

"I don't think that's necessary, but in the future, when you sit at my table, you will engage your brain, and your manners, before your mouth."

"Yes, sir. I apologize to you."

"Accepted," said Herr Siegel, looking across the room to see Doctor Marcuse returning.

They both rose. Herbert Marcuse looked pale, old, weary. The aura of vitality that had surrounded him only moments before had disappeared.

"Theodor Adorno is dead," he said without preamble, and sat down heavily.

"What? When? How?" babbled Kurt.

"In Switzerland, on holiday, of a heart attack, they say."[2]

"What a tragedy," said Herr Siegel. "I know what a dear friend he was to you, Herbert. I am so sorry."

Doctor Marcuse did not reply. He only squinted oddly into space as if he were trying to focus on something far away, something faint, difficult to decipher.

After a moment, he turned to Herr Siegel. "The students killed him," he said angrily. "The SDS killed Theodor Adorno."

"You can't mean he committed suicide," said Herr Siegel.

"His doctors warned him. His heart was weak. He was not to exert himself — no strenuous exercise. And yesterday he climbed a 3000-meter mountain. Madness! I know that peak. There is a cable lift all the way to the top. He could have taken that.

---

1 Herbert Marcuse quoted in Katz, *Herbert Marcuse and the Art of Liberation*, 191.
2 On August 5, 1969, while on holiday in Switzerland, Theodor Adorno scaled a 3000-foot peak. The next day he died of a heart attack. *The New York Times*, August 7, 1969, 2. Müller-Doohm, *Adorno*, 478-9.

He must have known what he was doing. He was depressed — more than you can know. He begged me to come to Frankfurt. However, I felt that the Institute had changed, that he had been overlooking the political content that used to be such a natural part of Critical Theory. And I told him so. It must have hurt him greatly, but he refused to embrace any active role. He felt that I was wrong to assume that the current student protest had 'even the slightest chance of having any impact on society.'[1] Because the students attacked him, humiliating him in such a shamefully disrespectful and slanderous way, he was doubly sure that their militant movement had fascist tendencies. "

There was another silence. Again, Herbert Marcuse stared out into space, looking for distant answers.

"They might as well have taken a gun and shot him," he said finally. "I am sorry, Wolfgang, Kurt. I have to go now."

"Of course, Herr Professor. If there is anything we can do."

"I'll call you," said the white haired philosopher as he rose and turned to go.

* * *

It took Kurt and his father almost an hour to walk the six blocks back to the flat in Rue Jean Goujon. The Champs Élysées was Bedlam. Businessmen, old ladies, shopkeepers, aging veterans in tattered uniforms bedecked with medals all linked arms and sang the Marseilles. "Down with Anarchy" and "Liberate the Sorbonne," the marchers chanted. Kurt winced at the irony. What a reversal!

Back at Herr Siegel's flat. They sat quietly, contemplating Doctor Adorno's death.

After a long while, Kurt rose and went out on the balcony. The pleasant tree-lined street stretched out below, empty but for a solitary couple strolling arm in arm.

"Herr Doctor Adorno was right, Karl," the trim young German said softly, but with conviction. "It's just like his book said. This is all wrong. We've all been wrong. Everyone will now go back to work, and there will be no further outcry when the police bash heads to clear the Sorbonne and the occupied factories. It's so depressing, Karl. Everyone knew all along that this was not a real revolution, that it was merely a pantomime revolution, a ritual performance acted out by students and workers demonstrating against vague and incomplete notions of oppression that they don't really understand, oppression that they can't really feel any more. A revolution without goals. Revolutionaries with no real expectation of change. Actors in a cheap charade. De Gaulle and Grayson Kirk always win. There may be reforms, but nothing really changes. Everyone knew it from the beginning. Doctor Adorno was right. 'Praxis must be a response to a correct and indeed contemporary interpretation of experience.'[2] He kept telling us that such an interpretation is yet to be found, but we wouldn't listen. Like Lazarus come back from the dead, we would tell them all. 'Up against the wall!' we told them. '*Toujours l'audace*,'[3] we said. And our voices echoed unheard in the corridors of power."

---

1 Müller-Doohm, *Adorno*, 478.

2 Theodor Adorno, *The Positive Dispute in German Sociology*, in O'Connor, ed., *The Adorno Reader*, 174.

3 Georges-Jacques Danton, "Audacity, more audacity, always audacity, and France is saved."

Chapter Twenty-Six: Frankfurt

And would it have been worthwhile, after all,
After the cups and the marmalade, the tea,
Among the porcelain, among some talk of you and me,
Would it have been worth while,
To have bitten off the matter with a smile,
To have squeezed the universe into a ball
To roll it toward some overwhelming question,
To say: "I am Lazarus come from the dead,
Come back to tell you all, I shall tell you all" —
If one, settling a pillow by her head,
Should say: "That's not what I meant at all.
That's not it, at all."
— T. S. Eliot, "The Love Song of J. Alfred Prufrock"

All that is solid melts into air.
— Karl Marx and Friedrich Engels, "Manifesto of the Communist Party"

Monday, September 3, 1968

Eliot looked up from his unpacking when he heard the footsteps on the stair. He was glad to be back in Frankfurt and away from New York. It seemed like a fresh start. In New York, he had been distracted by the protests, and he had neglected his work. Now he was looking forward to renewing his studies. Here he would re-dedicate himself, although he knew that without Doctor Adorno's sociology lectures things would not be quite the same as it had been last year.

"Danny's back in Frankfurt," said Kurt as he entered the small apartment that Steffi had found for them on Falkstrasse, near the university. "I'm on my way to meet him now. Steffi's coming too. Want to join us?"

"Sure. Great! I'd like to hear what he has to say. He's had one hell of a ride."

"So have we all," said Kurt.

They descended the four flights of dark narrow stairs and burst into the sunlight on the street, turning eastward toward the university. After two blocks, they saw Danny and Steffi sitting at a shady sidewalk table outside a little café, drinking beer.

They shook hands all around in the European style. "Steffi was just telling me about her work at the Institute," said Danny as they sat down.

"Yes, I've been fortunate," said Steffi. "After Herr Professor Adorno's death, things really began to fall apart. Herr Doctor Habermas left, and work on Critical Theory looked as though it would grind to a halt.[1] Fortunately for me, they have begun the Theodor Adorno Archive. Gretel Adorno and Rolf Tiedemann are trying to finish *Aesthetic Theory* and organize Doctor Adorno's material on Beethoven.[2] An edited edition of his work is in the offing, and organizing and cataloguing the rest of the material in the archive itself will take years. I've been offered a position as assistant to Doctor Tiedemann. It's a wonderful opportunity for me."

"Congratulations" said Eliot.

"Thank you," Steffi smiled faintly. "The best part is that, in a way, I will remain close to dear Doctor Adorno and his work. You know, I can't quite get his death out of my mind. I've been thinking about Walter Benjamin's death after climbing the Pyrenees during his escape from France in 1940. Benjamin too had a heart condition. I've read accounts that his companions had to literally drag him up the last part of the ascent. It must have been horrible.[3] I wonder if Herr Doctor Adorno was thinking about his friend when he was climbing that mountain in Switzerland — some kind of penance or vicarious déja vu."

"But Walter Benjamin killed himself with a drug overdose," said Kurt.

"Maybe," said Steffi. "There are all kinds of theories. No one really knows how he died. The death certificate is questionable. It states that Walter Benjamin died of natural causes, but in a Catholic country, virtually no death certificate ever lists suicide as the cause of death regardless of the circumstances — and there were other possibilities. Portbou, the Catalan town where he died, had been one of the last strongholds of resistance against Franco's rioting troops. After that, it was the scene to terrible reprisals, corruption, horrible secrets — a town of secrets, clandestine crossings, deportations, contraband networks. Some say the Nazis killed him. Some say the Russians. Other think it was his heart, you know, the climb. There's a lot of speculation. We'll probably never understand the depths of the tragic ends of two of the greatest minds of the century. "[4]

There was an awkward silence.

"I'm sorry," said Steffi. "I didn't mean to rain on our little reunion. Danny, tell them what you have been doing."

"Yes. What about you, Danny?" Kurt asked.

"Well, I'm staying here with my parents for now, and I'm involved in the creation of the Karl Marx Buchhandlung. When the bookstore is up and running, I plan to

---

1 Jürgen Habermas left the Institute for Social Research in 1971 to become director of the Max Planck Institute in Starnberg. He returned as director of the Institute for Social Research in 1983. Wikipedia, "Jürgen Habermas," http://en.wikipedia.org/.

2 Müller-Doohm, *Adorno*, 485.

3 Lisa Fittko, "Old Benjamin: Flight over the Pyrenees," in Benjamin, *Arcades Project*, 929-54.

4 David Mauas, *Who Killed Walter Benjamin*, documentary film (Barcelona: Malagros Productions, 2003).

work there. In addition, I just wrote a book, *Obsolete Communism*.[1] A big publisher paid my brother and me a lot of money to write it, so why not? In the meantime, we are also organizing an autonomous group, *Revolutionärer Kampf*. It's an exciting time for me.[2]

"My God, not another left-wing group!" said Kurt. "The entire movement seems to be exploding into a thousand pieces. It is impossible to find the center of the thing anymore. The radical students are even more isolated, more divided now. People resent them here. Germany still has a very bad conscience, and the violent student protests remind everyone of the all-too-recent past. Our marches must remind people of torchlight and violence and horrible coercion. I'm sure that's what Herr Doctor Adorno saw. To the older generation we must look like ghosts 'risen from hastily covered graves.'[3] Whatever the case, just at the peak of its visibility, the German SDS is disintegrating. It is nearly gone already, vaporized into unconnected atoms, supporting countless causes, ricocheting off in so many directions."

"It's the same in the States," said Eliot. "When we went to the Democratic Convention in Chicago last month, the SDS had already changed its leadership and declared itself totally "revolutionary." The organization refused to take part in any of the organized protests in Chicago. It was a mess. I mean no one could agree on what the protest was about — the war, civil rights, women's rights, poverty, the environment. No one knew how to protest. Was it to be marches like at the Pentagon, nonviolent sit-ins like the civil rights movement, violent resistance like the barricades in Paris, terrorism like the Weather Underground was producing? No one had a clue. There were scores of causes, scores of strategies, no organization, no communication. At the very moment of its most visible protest, the American Left is a shambles."[4]

"I think the same thing has happened in France since the May uprising," said Steffi. "The students have gone back to their diverse 'grouplets,' Trotskyites, Maoists, Marxists, Situationists, anarchists, and so on. The unifying call to action is, for now, silent. The leaderless spontaneity is gone. Now, the disputes as to whether to have leaders at all, whether to organize or not, has become a divisive factor in itself. Most students are convinced that the only path to substantial social change is through unity with the workers, but the workers want no part of the students' elitist intellectual revolutionary ideas, and they're divided themselves— some of the rank-and-file members have autonomous revolutionary notions while the unions and the leadership are reformist appendages of the system itself. The French time bomb has been expertly defused. The system has won."

---

1 *Obsolete Communism* was completed in five weeks following the May revolts in Paris. Daniel Cohn-Bendit and Gabriel Cohn-Bendit, *Obsolete Communism: The Left Wing Alternative*, trans. Arnold Pomerans (New York: McGraw Hill Book Company, 1968).

2 Daniel Cohn-Bendit returned to his family home in Frankfurt after the Paris May. There he taught kindergarten for a while and was one of the founders of the Karl Marx Buchhandlung. In the late 1970s, he became the editor of *Pflasterstrand*, the alternative magazine of the anarchist-oriented Sponti-Szene in Frankfurt. In 1984 he joined the Green Party and in 1989 he became deputy mayor of Frankfurt, in charge of multicultural affairs. In 1994, he was elected to the European Parliament. He is currently the co-president of the group European Greens – European Free Alliance in the European Parliament. Wikipedia, "Daniel Cohn-Bendit," http://en.wikipedia.org/.

3 Spender, *Year of the Young Rebels*, 95.

4 In August of 1968, the National Convention of the American Democratic Party in Chicago was the site of a week of often-violent protest by left-wing radical groups. The Chicago police's reaction to the demonstrations and protest was particularly brutal.

"It has won everywhere, just as Doctor Adorno said it would," said Kurt. "All this talk about a search for the new revolutionary agent, a new vanguard, is a bunch of baloney. I tried to tell Herr Doctor Marcuse that to his face in Paris. The students are frustrated. They represent no noble vanguard. They're grasping at straws. They've been rejected by the workers and are unable to form alliances with the Third World. Local efforts by the young to mount resistance is scoffed at by the proletariat, feared by the public, and easily crushed by the police. The tragedy of our generation is that it now sees radical social change as both mandatory and impossible. Words are no longer enough, and we don't know how to act. So, we suffer maddening frustration. In reaction, our leaders create fantastic realms of theory until we are completely unable to come to grips with reality, much less mediate it."

"You're right," said Danny. "I don't think many can see what is really going on. Most are blind to the fact that it was action, not theory, that held us together, that propelled us along, that led to our accomplishments."

"What accomplishments?" asked Kurt.

"Good God, man, are you really that blind?!" roared Danny. "We accomplished a lot. There will be reforms in the university and in society. People are more aware now of the government's repressive and violent nature, of ecological issues, of racial and sexual repression. The current movement may have fragmented and collapsed, but it left behind a host of smaller single-issue movements to address issues like war, race, women, homosexuality, ecological responsibility. There was no absolute victory, to be sure. There are no absolute victories, but there were steps taken. It's all about steps. We might not make the revolution, but we've prepared the way."

"I suppose," said Kurt.

"Anyway, that's not really the most important thing," said Danny, again smiling crazily. "The most important thing is that in France we proved that the workers are not an obsolete revolutionary force. Only their leadership has been proved obsolete. This is always the way. It's always the leadership that becomes corrupted. Once something is gained, then it must be organized, led, bureaucratized, controlled. Once freedom is won, the vehicle of freedom then becomes the new oppressor; the revolution ossifies and becomes counter-revolutionary and again enslaves us. The synthesis becomes a new thesis, and a new antithesis arises to oppose it. Only on the barricades do we have the feeling that we can change the world. Of course, that spirit of ecstatic freedom cannot last. It's impossible to sustain. And yet, we must keep on. Even if capitalism has discovered lasting materialist and nationalist responses to the universal challenge of socialism, we have to remember that we are all aliens, for whom the only answer is continuing revolution — perpetual, spontaneous, leaderless revolution. Therein lies our only freedom. Everything else melts into air."

Epilogue

On May 30, 1968, the *Notstandsgesetze* (Emergency Laws) were approved by the West German parliament.

On June 23 and June 30, 1968, the government of Charles de Gaulle received an overwhelming vote of confidence in the French general elections.

On November 5, 1968, Richard Nixon was elected president of the United States of America.

Selected English Bibliography

Adorno, Theodor. *The Adorno Reader*. Edited by Brian O'Connor. Oxford: Blackwell Publishers Ltd, 2000.

—— *Beethoven: The Philosophy of Music*. Translated by Edmund Jephcott. Cambridge: Polity, 1998.

—— *Critical Models: Interventions and Catchwords*. New York: Columbia University Press, 1998.

—— "The Culture Industry: Enlightenment as Mass Deception." In Horkheimer and Adorno, *Dialectic of Enlightenment*, 1944.

—— *The Culture Industry: Selected Essays on Mass Culture*. Edited by J. M. Bernstein. London: Routledge, 1991.

—— *The Dialectic of Enlightenment* (with Max Horkheimer). Translated by John Cumming. 1944. New York: Continuum, 1973.

—— "Marginalia of Theory and Practice." In Adorno, *Critical Models*, 1998.

—— *Negative Dialectics*, Translated by E.B. Ashton. London: Routledge, 1973.

—— *Problems of Moral Philosophy*. Edited by Thomas Schröder. Translated by Rodney Livingstone. Stanford, CA: Stanford University Press, 2001.

Aronson, Ronald. "Herbert Marcuse: A Heritage to Build On. In *Moving On*," Fall, 1968.

Benjamin, Walter. *The Arcades Project*. Translated by Howard Eiland and Kevin McLaughlin. Cambridge, MA: Harvard University Press, 1999.

—— "The Author as Producer." In Benjamin, *Understanding Brech*, 1973.

—— "Goethe's Elective Affinities." In Benjamin, *Selected Writings*, 1996.

—— *Illuminations, Walter Benjamin, Essays and Reflections*. Edited by Hannah Arendt. Translated by Harry Zorn. New York: Schocken Books, 1969.

—— *Notes to Literature*, 2 vols. Translated by Shierry Weber Nicholsen. New York: Columbia University Press, 1991.

—— *One Way Street and Other Writings*. Translated by Edmund Jephcott and Kingsley Shorter. London: NLB, 1979.

—— "On the Classicism of Goethe's Iphigenie." In Benjamin, *Notes to Literature*, 1991.

—— *Selected Writings*. 4 vols. Edited by Marcus Bullock and Michael W. Jennings. Cambridge: Harvard University Press, 1996.

—— *Understanding Brecht*. Translated by Anna Bostock. London: NLB, 1973.

—— "The Work of Art in the Age of Mechanical Reproduction" (1936). In Benjamin, *Illuminations*, 1968.

—— "Thesis on the Philosophy of History," in Benjamin, *Illuminations*, 1968.

Bond, Lawrence. "Morningside Heights: The Causes and the Protest of 1968," student paper, http://ww2.Lafayette.edu/-histclub/lawrencebond.html.

Braverman, Harry. "Six Days in Paris." In *The Nation*, June 3, 1968.

Brown, Bernard E. *Protest in Paris: Anatomy of a Revolt*. Morristown, NJ: General Learning Press, 1974.

Buck-Morss, Susan Buck. "*Walter Benjamin – Revolutionary Writer*." In New Left Review, No. 128, July/August, 1981.

Cahoone, Lawrence, ed. *From Modernism to Postmodernism: An Anthology*, Second Edition, ed. Malden: MA: Blackwell Publishing, 2002.

Caute, David. *The Year of the Barricades: A Journey through 1968*. New York, Harper and Row, 1988.

Cohn-Bendit, Daniel and Gabriel Cohn-Bendit. *Obsolete Communism: The Left Wing Alternative*. Translated by Arnold Pomerans. New York: McGraw Hill Book Company, 1968.

Cooper, David, ed. The *Dialectics of Liberation*. London: Harmondsworth, 1968.

DeBord, Guy. *The Society of the Spectacle*. Translated by Donald Nicholson-Smith. Brooklyn: Zone Books, 1995.

Fittko, Lisa. "The Story of Old Benjamin." In Benjamin, *Arcades Project*, 1999, 929-54.

Fraser, Ronald et al. *1968: A Student Generation in Revolt*. London: Chatto and Windus, 1988.

Harris, Marvin. "Big Bust in Morningside Heights." In *The Nation*, June 10, 1968.

Horkheimer, Max and Theodor Adorno. The Dialectic of Enlightenment. Translated by John Cumming. 1944. New York: Continuum, 1973.

Isenberg, Noah. "On Walter Benjamin's Passages." In *Partisan Review*, LXVIII, No. 2, 2002.

Jay, Martin. The *Dialectical Imagination: A History of the Frankfurt School and the Institute of Social Research*. London, 1973.

Katz, Barry. *Herbert Marcuse and the Art of Liberation*. London: Verso, 1982.

Kellner, Douglas. *Herbert Marcuse and the Crisis of Marxism*. Berkeley and Los Angeles: University of California Press, 1984.

von Keunnelt-Leddihn, Erik. *Leftism: from de Sade and Marx to Hitler and Marcuse*. New Rochelle, NY: Arlington House, 1974.

Labro, Phillip et al. *This Is Only the Beginning*. Translated by Charles Lam Markmann. New York: Funk and Wagnalls, 1969.

Levitt, Cyril. *Children of Privilege: Student Revolt in the Sixties: A Study of Student Movements in Canada, the United States, and West Germany.* Toronto: University of Toronto Press, 1984.

Marcuse, Herbert. *A Critique of Pure Tolerance,* (with Robert Paul Wolff and Barrington Moore, Jr.). 1965. Boston: Beacon Press, 1969.

—— "The End of Utopia." In Marcuse, *Five Lectures,* 1970.

—— *Essay on Liberation.* Boston: Beacon, 1969.

—— *Five Lectures: Psychoanalysis, Politics, and Utopia.* Translated by Jeremy J. Shapiro and Shierry M. Weber. Boston, Beacon Press, 1970.

—— "Liberation from the Affluent Society," in Cooper, *The Dialectics of Liberation,* 1968.

—— *The One-Dimensional Man.* Boston: Beacon, 1964.

—— "The Problem of Violence and the Radical Opposition." In Marcuse, *Five Lectures,* 1970.

—— "Repressive Tolerance." In Marcuse et al., Critique of Pure Tolerance, 1969.

Marx, Karl and Frederick Engels. *The Collected Works of Karl Marx and Fredrick Engels,* 50 vols. New York: International Publishers, 1975-2004.

Miller, James. *Democracy in the Streets: From Port Huron to the Siege of Chicago.* New York: Simon and Schuster, 1987.

Müller-Doohm, Stefan. *Adorno: A Biography.* Translated by Rodney Livingstone. Cambridge: Polity Press, 2005.

Rudd, Mark. "Columbia." In *The Movement.* March 1969.

Schnapp, Alain and Pierre Vadal-Naquet. *The French Student Uprising: November 1967 – May 1968:* An Analytical Documentary. Translated by Maria Jolas. Boston: Beacon Press, 1969.

Singer, Daniel. *Prelude to Revolution: France in May 1968.* New York: Hill and Wang, 1970.

Spender, Stephen. *The Year of the Young Rebels.* New York: Random House, 1968.

Trilling, Diana. "On the Steps of the Low Library." In *Commentary,* November 1968.

Touraine, Alain. *The May Movement: Revolt and Reform: May 1968— the Student Rebellion and Workers' Strikes— the Birth of a Social Movement.* Translated by Leonard F. X. Mayhew. New York: Random House, 1971.

Witte, Brend. *Walter Benjamin: An Intellectual Biography.* 1985. Translated by James Rolleston. Detroit: Wayne State University Press, 1991.

Wolff, Robert Paul, Barrington Moore, Jr., and Herbert Marcuse. *A Critique of Pure Tolerance,* 1965. Boston: Beacon Press, 1969.